T0367255

THE CURSE OF THE
BLACK PIPER

THE CURSE OF THE
BLACK PIPER

ESCAPE FROM ENSENADA

HARRIS T. VINCENT

authorHOUSE®

AuthorHouse™
1663 Liberty Drive
Bloomington, IN 47403
www.authorhouse.com
Phone: 1 (800) 839-8640

© *2015 Harris T. Vincent. All rights reserved.*

No part of this book may be reproduced, stored in
a retrieval system, or transmitted by any means
without the written permission of the author.

Published by AuthorHouse 01/19/2015

ISBN: 978-1-4969-6401-4 (sc)
ISBN: 978-1-4969-6402-1 (e)

Library of Congress Control Number: 2015900446

Any people depicted in stock imagery provided by Thinkstock are models,
and such images are being used for illustrative purposes only.
Certain stock imagery © Thinkstock.

This book is printed on acid-free paper.

Because of the dynamic nature of the Internet, any web addresses or
links contained in this book may have changed since publication and
may no longer be valid. The views expressed in this work are solely those
of the author and do not necessarily reflect the views of the publisher,
and the publisher hereby disclaims any responsibility for them.

This book is dedicated to Lynne, Brian, Ava and Wyatt

Thanks to Tom, Ernie, Emmet and all my friends at the SBAC and the "Tree" who inspired this work and made it possible.

This book is a work of fiction. People, places, events and situations are the product of the author's imagination. Any resemblance to actual persons, living or dead, or historical events is purely coincidental.

Harris T. Vincent has been a sailor for most of his life. He has sailed in regattas in Santa Barbara, Bermuda and Hawaii and most recently sailed a sloop down through the Grenadine Islands in the Caribbean

Table of Contents

The Squash Buds

Tom stood frozen to the helm. His iced fingers held the wheel like a vice as the fifteen foot swells crashed and sprayed over the decks. Crashing through a behemoth wave, he could see that off to the starboard side, one of the Mexican HSB gunboats was on course to either board the Swan or ram her.

Flying over the crest of a swell, the Mexican HSB came around broadside to the Swan's starboard side and the Mexican sailors readied their grappling hooks and began to swing them in the air to hook the Swan and bring her within boarding distance.

"Damnit" thought Tom. "Just when I thought we were in the clear. Now we're dead! How in the heck did I ever get into this to begin with? This is the last time I ever listen to that son of a gun Ernie again!"

He had only moments to think of a way out before he and the crew were to become either inmates of a Mexican prison or residents of Davy Jones' locker.

~

Tom, Ernie and Emmet had become fast and inseparable friends after meeting at the bar overlooking the squash courts at the Santa Barbara

Athletic Club. And after innumerable Stella Artois' shared there, had several times conjured up the idea of a quick trip to Rio where Ernie's antics had more than once almost landed them all in a Brazilian jail.

Ernie, the lacrosse captain at San Diego State and an ex-Navy SEAL, loved the ocean and especially body contact. He was also the son of a cop. As engaging as he could be, if you crossed him he could snap you like a twig. He had served two tours in Iraq honorably but was notorious for fighting and causing trouble. His CO had finally sent him back stateside during the second tour after he had been caught breaking into the officer's mess and attempting to steal a case of Jack Daniels for his annual "Luau by the Tigris" party. A live pig was found in the stolen Iraqi army jeep he had sequestered. A devout atheist, he was not one to tolerate anyone's religious convictions and was quick to debate any related moral issues.

But Tom had him under control at least most of the time. As the brains behind this notorious trio, he had graduated from Stanford Law School but hated his profession and had been thinking about changing careers. However, he did take pride in defending underdogs in the legal system against overzealous and clueless prosecutors while managing to keep the respect and confidence of the judges in his jurisdiction.

And being suave and charming, his low fees were compensated in other ways by his clients. They greatly appreciated not only his legal sagacity but also his sensitivity and wit.

He was also more than a little mischievous. One of his favorite pranks was to duct tape a coffee cup to the roof of his car. You wouldn't believe the chaos it could cause. People in other vehicles would wave and point to it as if it were an 800 lb. alligator or something. And of course, gluing quarters to the sidewalk at the homeless mission was another favorite dalliance of his. He considered the highlight of his career the time when he tied a dead raccoon to the rear bumper of a rival attorney's 500 SE. It normally would have been just thought odd but in this particular instance the attorney was on his way to the Four Seasons to attend a benefit for the SPCA. It was on the front page of the News Press the next day.

But in spite of all his mischief, Tom had one secret phobia. He was scared to death of storms and feared that if he ever found himself in one on the ocean he would crack and not have the courage to ride it out. This phobia was the result of being caught in a small thunderstorm while sailing on a skiff on a lake where he grew up. Strong winds had capsized the craft and he found himself trapped underwater when the main sail traveler line wrapped around his leg and prevented him from surfacing. He had managed to escape only because he had a Swiss army knife in his pocket and managed to cut the line. He had been deathly afraid of storms ever since.

Then there was Emmet. Emmet was born a natural promoter and salesman. Slick as deer guts on a doorknob, he had become a multimillionaire many times over by taking a mundane idea and turning it into a goldmine. As the creator of websites such as Antennaballs.com and as the creator of companies such as Lucky Wishbone, he was set for life. His activities were now mainly golf and sailing. But as successful an entrepreneur as he was, he had an attitude. Humility was not his thing and sometimes he acted as if his presence on earth was some sort of a gift to mankind.

Each of these people individually was harmless. But place the three of them together in one of their many escapades and you have a volatile prescription for madness, lunacy and the bizarre.

As Tom stood there in horror at the helm with his icy fingers locked to the wheel as the gun boat grew closer portending his doom, he thought this was one prescription he wished the pharmacist had lost.

~

Santa Barbara, the Gloved
One and the Mobster

Santa Barbara is usually beautiful in January, cold at night but warm and clear during the day. As the sun peeked through the east window and the alarm kicked on to *MPR*, Tom awoke with a start and a parched thirst. Ernie had done it again.

After three sets of squash and two pitchers of Stella Artois at the Athletic Club the previous evening, Ernie had coerced Tom once again into Chopin shots and more Stellas at Brophy Brothers.

"Damn that Ernie… he 'effin' does this to me every time! I think my head is going to explode" he grumbled as he dragged himself out of bed. "I have to get ready and be in court by 8:30. Why today of all days did I let him do this to me?"

Not only did Tom have to be in court but also the trio was scheduled to rendezvous at Emmet's scenic Alta Vista mansion the following day at 6 pm to drive the Range Rover to Ensenada to take delivery of the Swan and sail it back to Santa B.

"This headache is a bad omen," Tom thought. And he was right.

~

The Rover was ready to roll. Everything that was needed for the Swan was packed. Cases of Stella and Chopin Vodka, French bread, fresh Brie and Chardonnay were provisioned in case any south of the border 'chiquitas' were to find their way to the Swan's anchorage.

The group's spirits were high. Although Tom's previous two day's events had proved highly unusual and quite bizarre, he hadn't shared them with Ernie the previous evening because of client confidentiality and besides, he didn't have the energy to share them right now. There would be plenty of time later on the sail back from Ensenada.

But all were anxious to be sailing soon. Emmet hopped into the driver's seat and gunned the 4.6 SE as Ernie cracked a Stella and lit a Marlboro.

"Warp five engage" Ernie snapped to Emmet as Tom reclined the rear seat and started to doze.

"Aye, aye Captain" quipped Emmet in his best *Scottie* imitation as he slammed the Rover into gear and roared down the hill toward the awaiting adventure.

Adventure was to be an understatement.

~

Tom's dozing was restless. Besides the fact that Ernie had the Stones cranked on the Rover's sound system, the two previous day's events had been quite out of the ordinary. His arrival at the courthouse was marked by a series of events he would define as strange to say the least.

As he pulled the CLK into the parking garage that morning he noticed a myriad of reporters and paparazzi mulling about in and around the courthouse gardens. He was already late for court and he knew Judge Atkins did not tolerate tardiness.

Screeching to a halt in the closest available spot, Tom grabbed his briefcase and file materials and ran for the Santa Barbara street light, hoping to make the green one in time. Just as his feet hit the crosswalk, it changed to yellow.

Normally Santa Barbara traffic isn't congested but its drivers are well known for running yellow and red lights. Being already late, it was a risk he had to take.

What exactly happened then he couldn't tell. But when he regained consciousness, he saw that his brief case and files were strewn all over the crosswalk and intersection. He felt a slight pain on the back of his head. Mobs of people were gathered about him and when he began to focus his eyes again, he noticed something quite peculiar. Four or five men who looked like professional wrestlers were making their way through the crowd toward him and they didn't look very happy. From his view on the pavement he noticed a splash of rainbow like colors moving quickly between them.

Pushing the mob out of the way, they formed a circle of protection around Tom and their colorful follower. A strange looking individual in sun glasses, a tie-dyed shirt and a huge black hat knelt over him and spoke in a melodious and soft tone. "Are you alright, sir? We almost hit you!"

There was something extremely familiar about this man's voice and as his eyes began to focus and his head began to clear, he realized who was speaking to him. It was none other than the *Gloved One* himself.

~

Chief Warrant Officer Anthony D'Amato sat on the bridge of the frigate *USS Simpson* anchored in Mission Bay Harbor near the Coronado Naval Base in San Diego. After having spent the last three decades assigned to various U.S. Embassies in the middle east as a liaison, he had requested transfer to Coronado Naval Base for reasons only he knew about and had received clearance two months later from the Vice Admiral of the Pacific Fleet.

A rather short, ugly and ill-tempered man, he had grown up the spoiled son of a well- known mob boss and even after thirty-two years in the Navy, he still went by the nickname Tony *the bull* D'Amato. After Sam Giavanni was whacked and the feds started infiltrating the mob in the sixties and early seventies, he decided the best place to hide was the U.S. Navy. He had entered the Navy after being expelled from NYU for breaking and entering a professor's office to steal tests.

He had pretty much run the college campus the same way his father had run the rackets in New Jersey. The thugs that worked for him were not college students but rather *made* guys assigned to his territory by his father.

Among other nefarious activities, he operated a loan shark business for students who had lost their tuition money from their wealthy parents gambling or who needed drug money. His rackets included extorting the campus businesses run by students and he had his goons rough up anyone who refused to cooperate. When kids couldn't pay up, he told them they had forty-eight hours and then suggested they make a clandestine night time visit to either their parent's homes or one of the many beach homes in the Hamptons.

He would accept fine art and object d'art in lieu of cash. He even provided them with burglary tools, maps and a list of homes with significant art collections which his goons had cased on the Sotheby's Real Estate online tours. In the process, he had become quite an art expert. He loved art but not for art's sake. He loved the money it brought him.

~

The Slip and the Altercation

"Are you alright, sir? You slipped on the pavement. We almost ran you over!"

As his head cleared and his eyes began to focus, Tom realized what had happened. That morning, in a fog, he had put on the new Cole Haan loafers he had bought on sale at Nordstrom the week before. Soft and comfortable, they had one drawback; the leather soles were flat with no grip. He had gone backward onto his head when the slippery sole of his right foot hit the newly paved asphalt.

"Sir, we'll have to take you to a doctor."

"No need" said Tom as he got up and dusted off. "Just slipped that's all. I'm also due in court" he said as he began to gather his strewn papers.

"So also am I" said the *Gloved One*. "But please let me to take you to my doctor afterwards. You may have injured your head."

"Really, I'm alright. It's not necessary."

"I don't think you heard him correctly, sir" said one of the gorillas. "You will be seeing his doctor! And I'm coming with you to see that you will do exactly that!"

As Tom looked over this band of steroid induced muscle heads, he began to calculate his odds of escape and he could see that they weren't good.

"Looks like I don't have much choice, do I? Where's the doctor?"

One of the bodyguards stepped forward and moving his face within six inches of Tom's, he asked with a smile, "have you ever heard of *Tierra Bella?*"

~

E rnie was glad to be on the road. His on and off again romance with Debbie had plunged to new depths this past week when she had seen his cell phone bill and redialed some of the phone numbers only to find that they were mostly numbers belonging to other women.

Ernie loved women and as an alpha male, took advantage of the fact that many women loved his bad boy aura. He didn't cheat much but every once in a while, being a man, he couldn't say no when the opportunity presented itself. Now he'd been busted big time and after a horrendous fight with Debbie, she had thrown him out again for the fiftieth time.

He loved her but just wasn't ready to commit, probably never would be. Marriage didn't make much sense to him. For some people it seemed to work for a while but then inevitably, sooner or later, it would self-destruct. It was a dilemma but one he could forget about as soon as he was sailing again on the high seas.

"Dude, this is so sweet being on the road again" said Ernie.

"Right on, brother…soon we'll be back on the high seas sailin' our boat back to Santa Barbara" said Emmet.

"Yeh, well there's that part, definitely. But mostly because now the heat's off."

"Heats off…how's that, dude?"

"Let's just say I got busted."

"Busted…by whom…?"

"Debbie…she kicked me out again."

"That's about the fifth time, isn't it?"

"Yep, something like that…she got the cell phone bill and called some of the numbers. Unfortunately they were to some lady friends of mine."

"Real swift move there, Nesto."

"How was I to know she'd do that? Oh well, its history now."

"Ancient history, dude… no worries though…the sailing gods will save you."

"There are no gods, Emmet. There is no good and there is no evil. We are nothing but cosmic detritus dwelling on a speck of rock traveling through a meaningless and random universe at warp speed. Disaster and chaos is our legacy in this life. If you think there is some sort of omniscient deity watching over us, then you are living in a fairy tale. Grow up and face the music, boys. This is a lonely road we travel and we travel it to the final ugly end where nothing awaits us but oblivion."

"Whoa dude, that's deep."

"Yes, deep and self- centered" interjected Tom. You'll never win the Nobel Prize. That's for certain".

'Well, well…look who woke up" replied Ernie. "Good timing…as I was saying, add the fact that most of mankind is in a deep sleep and totally unaware of this condition."

"You really think so, dude? No wonder I can never get out of bed in the morning."

"You are hopeless, Emmet. It's a good thing you're rich."

"Rich and handsome, dude…hey, we're almost to Del Mar. Let's grab some chow" suggested Emmet as the Rover hit Del Mar. He remembered a little dive called *Turtle's* which he had frequented on his weekend leaves while at Camp Pendleton in the Marine Corp in the late seventies. In spite of the fact that it was an enlisted Marine and Navy man's hangout, it had always been known for great tap beers and incredible seafood.

"Sounds good" retorted Tom from the rear. "Ernie?"

"You're on, dude! I could use some Patron and some tacos."

Emmet pulled the Rover into the parking lot amidst what seemed to be a proliferation of '70s Cameros, TransAms and navy vehicles. Being an SUV, the Rover just barely squeezed into one of the marked spots. It was tight but there was just enough room for the three to open the doors and slide out. Exiting the Rover, Emmet hit the remote lock and the trio started walking toward the restaurant entrance. Then out of nowhere, what appeared to be a squad of sailors suddenly blocked their way as they approached the neon sign over the entrance door.

"Hey dickhead" yelled one of the gang. "How am I supposed to get in my vehicle with your girly Range Rover blocking my access? I suggest you move that piece of shit immediately!"

"Hey sailor, we're not looking for trouble" said Emmet as the gang of drunken sailors closed in on the three.

"Then you best fricking better move it now, scumbag" screamed the leader of the pack.

"And suppose we don't?" asked Ernie.

"Then you are in big ass trouble!" yelled the leader. And as the seaman reached for Ernie's throat, the ex-SEAL grabbed the thumb of the out stretched hand and in one second snapped it back with a click. The man howled in pain. And in the next instant Ernie had swung around in a 360 degree circle and using one of his old lacrosse tricks, had smacked his forearm across the nose of the man next to the first, knocking him off his feet. .

"What the hell is going on here...break it up!" yelled a voice from the rear of the pack. "Make way!"

A short smarmy naval officer with enough dangling chains to tie up all the elephants in Africa pushed his way to the front of the fray. "What is happening here? These are my boys, what are you doing to my boys?" Two of his *boys* were on the ground bleeding and writhing in agony.

"We didn't start this" said Tom. He figured if this was going to be some sort of negotiation, that was his forte as much as kicking ass was Ernie's.

"I don't give a flying shit" said the head sailor. "You just took out two of my best boys. If I ever see you three scumbags again you're gonna' be dead meat! Pick 'em up and let's get the hell out of here" he yelled at the remaining seamen still standing.

"And remember, pukes...if I ever see you're sorry asses again you will regret it!"

The trio watched as the sailors picked up their pals, piled them into the navy van and roared off in a cloud of exhaust and dust.

"Nice moves Ernie" said Tom. "You learn them in ballet class?"

"I guess having played lacrosse comes in handy sometimes. Now let's get some food and some shots. Hopefully we'll never see the likes of them again. That last guy looked like a miniature Al Capone. What a character."

The trio had just had their first encounter with Chief Warrant Officer Anthony D'Amato. It wouldn't be the last.

~

The Marketer and the Paparazzi

Linda Squires couldn't sleep. "What the heck am I going to do now", she asked herself while staring at the ceiling. Having worked at the Santa Barbara Art and Film Institute as its Marketing Director for the last three years, she had finally reached the end of her rope.

Working sometimes up to sixteen hours a day, six and sometimes even seven days a week, she was weary to say the least. Not only had the politics of the position become untenable but also the reality of having to deal with huge egos and unbelievable prima donnas had finally burned her out. She couldn't go on like that any longer. She had quit the position before they had a chance to fire her for refusing to be a part of the Institute's new questionable agenda. Now she was ready for a change. What it was to be she didn't have a clue.

She had been the wife of a cosmetic surgeon and after being married to him for seventeen years and bearing him two beautiful daughters who were now grown, he had dumped her for a bimbo half his age whom he had met at an appointment in his office. She wanted breast implants. He gave her two 36 DD's.

But she did have a few trump cards to play in her job search. She did have an MBA degree in marketing and although she was in her forties, she was intelligent and still attractive. She knew she liked boats and dreamed of sailing in the Rolex Regattas off the coast of Sardinia. But going to Europe was not realistic for her right now. She had just sold a house with a thirty day escrow and now had to make some fast decisions.

She needed a place to live and something to provide her with some sort of income. The divorce settlement had provided her with a dependable monthly stipend but the ex was constantly dragging her back into court in an attempt to have the alimony readjusted. He usually won.

She got up to make some coffee. It was early but too late to try to get back to sleep. As the sun rose over the magenta bougainvillea surrounding her front door, she stepped outside to retrieve the morning newspaper.

Pouring herself a cup of coffee, she opened the paper to the classified want ads. As she turned the pages gingerly to the marketing and sales categories, she noticed a small ad that caught her attention. It read:

Individual with marketing experience needed to work with art auction houses and bidders in the sale of extensive art collection. Applicant must have experience working with high profile and frequently difficult people. Art history degree a plus but not necessary. Please send resume to P.O. Box 63266, Santa Ynez, California 93165.

She had the cover letter and resume printed and placed in a stamped envelope and was on her way to the Summerland post office within twenty minutes.

~

Tom gathered up his papers and notes and shoved them into his brief case. He had regained some composure.

"Well then, you'll excuse me while I attend court. Thank you for your concern, but really I'm perfectly okay."

"Your head hit the pavement quite hard, sir! I'm sorry but you have to let my physician examine you," the *Gloved One* said.

"Okay, so what's going on here?" Tom thought to himself. "Is he afraid I'll sue him? His vehicle didn't touch me so why is he so insistent upon my seeing his doctor?"

Then it hit him. The paparazzi had probably taken a thousand photos of the incident by now. By this time tomorrow, photos of the near accident would be plastered all over the tabloids. The headlines would read *Jeremy Princeton Nearly Kills Man on Way to Legal Arraignment*. The negative publicity would just add more kindling to the fire over which JP was being burned at the stake. He had to take this man under his care to show the world he was not the evil demon they thought he was. Perhaps he was shrewder than the public and the media gave him credit.

"Please let me help you! We'll have you back by tomorrow morning, I promise!"

Tom was never one to say no to an adventure, and as he thought about it more, he concluded this might be the adventure of a lifetime.

"Well alright then…by the way my name is Tom."

"I'm Jeremy, and thank you."

~

The Hangover, the Limo and the Ride

Tony *the bull* awoke with a killer hangover. It was 0530 hours and he had to be at an officer's briefing at 0700 hours. The Naval Air Station's Officer's Quarters lights flashed on like lightening in a mid-western thunderstorm.

"Shit, where is my damn Excedrin?" he asked himself as he pulled himself out of the bunk. Probing blindly into his foot locker, he found some Excedrin and some Alka Seltzer. He proceeded into the officer's head and threw back four Excedrins and plopped a couple of Alka Seltzer tablets into a glass of water. And as a coup de grace to his hangover, he pulled a flask from his robe and poured a couple of shots of Stoly into the mixture.

"Ah yes…the working officer's breakfast" he thought to himself as he downed the concoction in one swig. "I should be sharp as a tack by 0700."

It worked. By 0700 Tony *the bull* was ready to brief the Admirals on the illegal immigration problems with policing the coastal waters between the United States and Mexican borders. Forget the land borders of California, Texas and Arizona. An equal if not greater number of illegal aliens were crossing the border daily by water on anything from rafts to high powered cigarette speed boats.

The Department of Defense satellites could verify these movements and there were even satellite photographs showing that the Mexican Navy was clandestinely involved in transporting illegal aliens. Although much of the graft and corruption of the Mexican government had become much less obvious under President Pero, the same could not be said for the Mexican Navy. That branch of the Mexican military was virtually a rogue state. They operated within the parameters of their own jurisdiction. Once a Mexican vessel was out at sea, it was virtually nothing less than a pirate vessel.

The number of American Coast Guard and Naval ships assigned to patrol the area between Ensenada and San Diego amounted to a hill of beans compared to the myriad of ships dodging them in the open seas. The cutters and frigates assigned to protect this stretch of coast were less than fifty, even though the tallies of illegal vessels entering U.S. coastal waters verified by satellite cameras were close to two hundred or more daily.

They were simply outnumbered. This fact and the decision to give geographic areas like Omaha, Nebraska more pork barrel funds than this prolific area of illegal immigrant smuggling was a decision only the U.S. Congress could make. Like many governmental decisions, it made absolutely no sense.

Tony *the bull* knew these facts well. But he wasn't about to make them apparent to anyone in the admiralty high command. He was grateful for the situation being what it was. It made his goals much more achievable if these facts were to remain unknown. He had plans to take advantage of this situation and make himself enough money to retire for a hundred lifetimes.

~

The twenty-five year old airline flight attendant had been booked on an assaulting an officer charge. Tom had presented to Judge Atkins a long list of community involvements which the young lady had been involved with in her youth and had portrayed her case as a rarely occurring state of inebriation brought about by another flight attendant's birthday celebration.

Judge Atkins gave her a lecture on the virtues of abstaining from the evils of alcohol and dismissed the case upon her word she would be more careful. Tom had saved another damsel in distress from the consequences of her own wicked activities. She was of course overjoyed at the outcome and after hugging and kissing Tom, suggested that she be able to repay him that very evening with wine and dinner at her apartment.

"Please, Tom, come over tonight so I can cook dinner for you!" she pleaded.

Tom was ready to concur to the sentiment but upon glancing toward the back of the courtroom and seeing the *Gloved One's* body guard who was eagerly awaiting his return, he knew he had to postpone the date.

And judging from the look on his face, the bodyguard was not going to leave without him.

"I'll have to take a rain check, Jennifer" he said and started his journey toward the courtroom doors.

"Call me soon" she yelled as he reached the passageway where he was promptly escorted to the black stretch limo waiting curbside near the courthouse atrium.

The muscle head gripped Tom's arm like a vice as he walked him to the awaiting limo. There was something foreboding about this scenario and when the goon opened the rear door, Tom felt a flash of electricity shoot up his spine.

"Please, get in" said Jeremy.

"This should be interesting indeed," Tom thought to himself as he sat down in back and the door of the limousine slammed shut, sealing his destiny.

~

"Nice ride, Mr. Princeton" Tom remarked.

"Please call me Jeremy. And thank you again for being my guest. How are you feeling? Did your court date go well?"

"I'm fine really. And yes my court appearance went well enough, thank you".

"I wish I could say the same" declared the Prince of Pop. "For the third time in ten years I have been blackmailed and this time the prosecutor has decided to run with it. No one believes me but I mean no one any harm, please believe me."

"I'm sorry about that" said Tom.

As the stretch limo exited the Mission Street off ramp and unto the 101 freeway a cell phone rang. It was Jeremy's.

"I'm so sorry, please excuse me. I have to take this."

"No problem."

"Well then, please just relax and enjoy the ride. Would you care for something to drink?"

"No thanks, I'm good" answered Tom.

"Very well then, excuse me" Jeremy said as he turned away.

Although most of the ensuing conversation was unintelligible, Tom could make out some of what was said.

"Yes Peter…no…we have to move it…yes anyone… yes the *Piper, now*! Call anyone…call Liz….Gates… Ranier…..Princess Jasmine…just do it …I'll be there shortly."

JP hung up. "My apologies, we are having a small problem with some art I have collected lately. Tell me, what do you know about art?"

"I took some art history classes in college. That's about it."

"I would like to tell you a story but you must swear to keep it confidential."

"Okay, I swear."

"I would also like to hire you as one of my attorneys regarding my dilemma. Do you accept?"

"Accept for client confidentiality?"

"Exactly" said Jeremy.

"Great. But on second thought, I think I will have that drink."

Jeremy pushed a button and the inlayed walnut paneled bar suddenly appeared in front of them.

"What would you like to drink, Tom?"

"A beer would be fine, thank you."

JP opened the refrigerator and after opening the beer with what appeared to be a diamond studded bottle opener, he handed it to Tom. He then poured himself a snifter of Drambuie on the rocks.

They both leaned back into the plush Corinthian leathered seats.

"Now then, let me ask you a question. Have you ever heard of the *Black Piper*?"

~

The Response, the Mission and the Black Piper

Linda got the phone call three days later.

"Ms. Squires" inquired the voice in a very refined English accent.

"Yes, this is she."

"My name is Peter Harrison. I received your resume in the mail regarding the art curator position. Would it be possible for you to pay us a visit so we could chat a bit?"

"Well absolutely. Thank you for calling. I'm available anytime really."

"Jolly good! Where do you live and I'll send a driver to pick you up."

"Thank you but that's not necessary. I do have a car I can use."

"Yes, of course you do. Unfortunately, for security reasons I am obliged to send a car. Do you mind terribly?"

"Well no, I guess not."

"Excellent then, can you give me your address and I'll send a car for you straightaway!"

"Ah...okay but can you give me an hour?"

"Certainly, take two. I shall see you when you get here then!"

"That's perfect! And thank you for calling."

"My pleasure and have a pleasant journey. Goodbye" the gentlemen said as he hung up.

The stretch Limo arrived that afternoon right on time! Linda was ready. The driver had rung her doorbell and greeted her with a very polite "Good afternoon, Ms. Squires. My name is Ferdinand and I will be your driver this afternoon."

"Wow-cool", Linda thought to herself as he opened the door of the white stretch. "I could get used to this!"

"White is for our lady guests," Ferdinand remarked.

"Thank you, one of the fleet?"

"Actually, yes ma'am. Now, before we depart, can I get you some refreshment?"

"No thank you, I'll be fine. But where are we going? I'll bet it's to L.A."

"Not necessarily, ma'am. Actually, we are headed to the North County to a place called *Tierra Bella*. Have you heard of it?"

~

The jungles of South Vietnam are undeniably the most beautiful in the world. But in 1968 they were not only the most beautiful but also the most dangerous. There were over five hundred thousand American troops in the country and there appeared to be no victory in sight for them.

Every time President Johnson increased the number of troops in country or escalated the bombing of Hanoi to encourage Ho Chi Minh to give up, the North Vietnamese army would launch a new offensive somewhere to show that they were not about to cooperate.

The U.S. was involved in a quagmire from which it did not know how to escape. It had divided the country into two political camps and tensions were high.

As the gun boat *Fiji* made its way up the Ben Hai River, Captain Jason Leyton began to reflect on his mission.

"What the hell are they thinking? They're sending me up the river fifty klicks into the DMZ which is crawling with dinks to drop a squad of Army Rangers to monitor troop movements. Far out, man. If this isn't a suicide mission, I don't know what is!"

His gunboat did have a fifty caliber machine gun and a couple of torpedoes mounted on the gunwales. But what the hell good would they be when the gooks start dropping mortars on them like snowflakes.

"Damn, only in the navy would some moronic pencil pushing officer in admin back in the safety of Saigon think of a mission like this. Let's see if we can sacrifice a squad of Rangers and a couple of frogs so I can show my commanding officer what a strategic thinker I am. Alright Leyton, let's try to get this over with. Maybe with a huge amount of luck and if the gooks are in the south of France on vacation, we can make it back alive. "Shove off" he yelled.

The Rangers were ready for action. Gung ho and silent, Lieutenant Tim Keller and his squad sat on the gunwales with their legs draped over the side, eyes peeled for *Charlie* as the gun boat started to weave its way up the Ben Hai River past Quang Tri. Dressed in poplin patterned jungle fatigues and OD camo boonies, their

M-16's were slung over their shoulders and their faces were painted in camouflage.

"Hey D'Amato, get out on the point and look for floating debris! Do it now, and if we hit any mines your ass is grass!"

Petty Officer third class Anthony D'Amato was new in country. The commanding officer at the Westport Naval Station had issued him WESPAC orders after D'Amato had attempted to blackmail him by taking photos of him and his mistress entering the Motel 6 in New London. The scheme had backfired when D'Amato discovered the CO's wife was also banging another admiral like a screen door in a hurricane. None of the involved parties cared. They all knew about each other's infidelities already. So the CO shipped him out to the 'Nam. D'Amato told himself he'd have the mo' fo' whacked when he returned. But now he knew he was in some deep shit!

"Aye aye Captain" he yelled back at Leyton.

He hated taking orders but he somehow knew it was just a matter of time before he'd have the entire Pacific Fleet chain of command in his pocket as soon as he could get back stateside. Until then he just had to stay alive, even if it meant taking orders from this ninety day wonder.

As the gun boat headed upstream into the dense jungle, little did Tony *the Bull* realize that this voyage would be the most fateful event of his entire life.

~

"The *Black Piper*" asked Tom. "It sounds like something out of a Humphrey Bogart film. You've got to be kidding."

"You are correct." said Jeremy. "The film you are thinking of is *The Maltese Falcon*. But this is not fiction. The *Black Piper* plays only second fiddle to the Holy Grail as far as mysteries goes. Its history is obscure and most of it is nothing but conjecture.

"Really" said Tom.

"Yes, no one really knows where or how it first surfaced in this modern world or what its true history is, but I can tell you what I do know about it."

"Sounds fascinating" Tom remarked. "I'm all ears."

"I have had some people do some extensive research on the subject of the *Black Piper*, mainly my art curator and advisor Peter Harrison who has a MFA in art history. He studied at Oxford and Harvard and specializes in Byzantine and far eastern ancient art and artifacts and has participated in many archaeological digs."

"You don't say?"

"Yes. I do. He is quite the art scholar I might add.

"It sounds like it."

"Let me explain about the *Piper*. According to Peter, there are references to the Piper as early as 400 BC. In the Book of Joshua in the Dead Sea Scrolls which were discovered only in this past century, there is a reference to *a dark flower that burneth in the night that shall avail one of all the world's riches but also will capture thy soul and devour it*. Of course, who knows what its real meaning is?

After all, it's a language which has been dead for twenty-two centuries.

"Interesting" said Tom.

"Yes, then in the third century BC, there is a reference in the writings of Archimedes which mentions *a glowing black orchid of divine origin so beauteous to behold one must cover one's eyes to divert its evil seduction.*"

"Hmm..."

"Anyway, it seems to have disappeared and reappeared again and again over time. It disappeared during the Dark Ages like many things and then resurfaced around the time of Charlemagne, say 714 AD."

"Ah yes... the Magna Carta..."

"Yes indeed...then once again it disappeared without a trace until the times of the Knights Templar and the Holy Grail. The crusaders never found the Holy Grail but speculatively speaking, they did find the *Piper.* Supposedly it had been discovered in a temple in Mesopotamia."

"The Middle East..."

"Yes, along with supposed knowledge of the Holy Grail, it not only had brought the Knights Templar riches beyond their wildest dreams but also had protected them from the persecution of the Catholic Church. The church feared the power of the *Piper,* then one day it vanished again. The Knights Templar were executed, their possessions acquired by the Catholic Church and the *Piper* went underground once again."

It remained a myth until 1968 when it suddenly resurfaced."

"And where was that?"

"Vietnam" replied Jeremy.

"That is most fascinating! So tell me, what is this *Black Piper*?"

"It is one of the most beautiful things the world has ever seen. It is a replica of the *Piper* flower found only in the jungles of Southeast Asia. It is in geological terms what is known as a garnetiferous amphibolite. The translation being that it is a rare combination of garnet, jade and obsidian. The intricacies of its carving are breath taking and yet as delicate as it appears to the naked eye, it is also apparently indestructible, incapable of being broken or scratched in any way."

"So what is the big deal?"

"The reason the *Piper* is such a big deal is best explained by the myth which accompanies it. Whoever has the *Piper* in his or her possession shall have both great power and acquire great wealth. A rather strong incentive to acquire it, wouldn't you agree?"

"Those are the basics" said Tom.

"Indeed. But it also reputedly has a downside. I can attest personally to the veracity of that part of the myth."

"And what might the downside be?"

"It's curse, which is inscribed in a very miniscule sort of hieroglyphics located on the bottom side of one of its leaves. Peter managed to translate it after much research."

"And it says…?"

> *"Adore the beauty, beware the power*
> *Desires fulfilled thy visage shall alter*
> *Light to darkness thy path shall be, a lesson in duality"*

"Wow… interesting. So tell me then, why is the *Piper* so important to you?"

"I own the *Piper*, Tom. It's in my vault at Tierra Bella."

~

The Battle and the Art Curator

Captain Leyton was right. About thirty-eight klicks up the river they got hit. Mortar rounds began dropping all around the gun boat. It was only a matter of time before the dinks would be all over them.

Leyton slammed the gearshift into high speed as the Rangers readied their M-16s for certain battle. Tracer bullets began to zing across the bow of the vessel. He could hear their deadly zipp....zipp sound as they passed by his head and over the gunboat. Then it happened.

There was a huge explosion at the bow. The boat lurched backward and suddenly began to lean toward the starboard side.

"D'Amato, take the helm!" yelled Leyton.

As Leyton crawled toward the bow he knew they were in trouble. One of the mortar rounds had landed just in front of the gunboat's path. Although it had not hit the vessel directly, its shrapnel had blasted open a huge hole at the waterline.

"Oh shit" Leyton exclaimed. "Now we're gonna' have to fight! Pull it over there, D'Amato."

There was what looked to be an acceptable LZ off to the starboard side about fifty meters.

"Looks like you guys are getting off the bus early today," said Leyton to the Rangers.

As soon as the vessel struck shore, the Rangers leaped off and began setting up defensive positions. The mortar strikes had intensified as had also the plethora of AK 47 rounds zinging through the jungle brush on their deadly paths.

"We're going to need air support! Lieutenant Keller, what do you think?" Leyton yelled to the Ranger squad leader.

"I'm callin' it in," Keller shouted back. "This is Bird Dog. We need air support NOW! Coordinates are BR477 east, 435 north... thirty-eight klicks south of Quang Tri. We need it now...repeat NOW!"

The firefight intensified and all hell had broken loose. But the dinks had them nearly surrounded and suddenly the squad found themselves pinned down. Leyton grabbed his sidearm and took a position next to Lieutenant Keller at the point and began firing at will. Three of the squad members had already been wounded. Two others were dead.

"If that air fire doesn't get here soon, this is not going to be pretty" Leyton screamed to Keller.

Looking around, Leyton noticed that D'Amato was missing. "Desertion in the line of fire...what a guy," he murmured to himself.

Then in the distance they began to hear the roar of jet engines. Lieutenant Tim Keller took the radio. "Hotel Echo, fire for effect, fifty meters my November tree line. I'll pop smoke" Keller screamed into the speaker as he ignited the green smoke flare.

The Marine Harriers closed in on the battle pummeling the Viet Cong positions but incoming mortars and the massive barrage of tracers had already done their jobs. Most of the squad had been wiped out. Captain Leyton and Lieutenant Keller were the only men still left fighting.

D'Amato was running as fast as his corpulent body could go. He didn't know where but somehow he had slipped through the NVA encirclement before they had tightened the noose around the doomed soldiers.

Then the Sidewinders found their mark. Explosions began to thunder all around him. He could feel the heat and smell the napalm as he continued to flee the conflagration to his rear.

He heard a roar above his head and as he looked up he could see the deadly missile heading toward a position 500 yards ahead. Suddenly he tripped. As he fell he noticed a tunnel in the hillside to his right. Picking himself up, he dove for the tunnel just as the Sidewinder hit. A huge explosion shook the earth and as the giant firestorm passed over the tunnel, D'Amato blacked out.

~

The iron gates of Tierra Bella were branded with a coat of arms that split into two upon opening. As the limo continued its journey up the winding road to the Tudor mansion in the distance, Linda reflected upon the possibility of employment there.

"This I could get used to" she thought.

As the stretch limo came to a halt in front of the mansion, Linda noticed a strikingly handsome man waiting at the bottom of the front door steps. He had a resemblance to a certain blonde Hollywood actor but was much taller. He sported black Italian loafers, cream slacks with a black belt with silver trim with a cotton black Ralph Lauren Polo shirt. She guessed him to be around fifty. As the chauffeur Ferdinand opened the door for her, the man leaned inside to take her hand.

"Ms. Squires, I presume? Welcome to Tierra Bella. I'm Peter Harrison." He spoke the Queen's English. "I trust you had a pleasant journey."

"Yes, thank you. It's a pleasure to be here. I had forgotten how beautiful the country is up here."

"Indeed it is. I suggest we have a little tour of the grounds. Would you like that?"

"Thank you, I would."

"It's a bit cheeky on foot. Would you mind terribly taking this most unusual looking mode of transportation?" Peter asked.

He gestured toward what appeared to be a golf cart made over to have the semblance of a 1957 pink Cadillac Eldorado.

"Wow! The *Pimp my Ride* crew's been here" said Linda.

"It would certainly appear that way, wouldn't it?"

Opening the suicide door for her on the shotgun side, Peter bowed slightly and said "my lady's carriage awaits her."

"Thank you, kind sir" said Linda laughing.

The grounds were magnificent. There seemed to be topiaries and mazes everywhere. Streams were connected to lakes bordered by wildflowers with neatly trimmed Bermuda grass stretching to the horizon.

Peter showed Linda the reptile barn, the Clydesdale horses, the zoo, the carousel and the roller coaster.

"Mr. Princeton did not exactly have a childhood, consequently the various and sundry forms of entertainment."

"A paradise for adult and child alike" added Linda.

"Indeed" said Peter. "But allow me to show you the main house."

"Thank you, I would like that very much."

As they approached the front entrance, Linda was awestruck by the front doors.

"Those doors need a moat in front of them" she remarked.

"Quite an accurate assessment, Peter retorted. "Those are two fourteenth century oak castle doors which once graced the façade of the castle of King Ludwig of Lichtenstein. Those indentations were made by the many arrows and axes which found their mark as the barbarians stormed the castle, no doubt."

"That's amazing" said Linda.

"Now for the interior tour, shall we?"

Peter pressed on the thick steel latches and the doors swung open.

The interior was striking in a very subtle sort of way. Earth tones and dark greens created an ambiance of elegance and charm. Big overstuffed sofas accentuated by antique leather chairs in front of numerous fireplaces gave it the look and feel of a New York men's club.

"I like it, very homey" said Linda.

"You probably expected more of a *Neo-Graceland* or *Contemporary Rapper's Delight* sort of look."

"To tell the truth, it had crossed my mind" said Linda.

"Just try to overlook the suits of armor, won't you?"

"If you insist" laughed Linda.

"Shall we continue?" suggested Peter.

Peter escorted her through many of the guest suites, the master bedroom, the game rooms and the entertainment theatre.

"The structure is nearly fifteen thousand square feet so sorry about the incomplete tour. We can't possibly see it all. But tell me, what do you think so far?"

"Really, I'm in awe. Those bedrooms are a religious experience. And I like a living room you can land a plane in."

"Yes, quite" replied Peter. "But as impressive as it is, allow me to show you something you will find breathtaking."

Peter led Linda back through a hallway and into the front foyer. On the side wall hung a gold Baroque style mirror. Peter reached over and tapped twice on the head of an ornate cherub inscribed within the frame. Suddenly a slab of the Italian marble floor began to move to the right and slide beneath the adjacent flooring, revealing a staircase. They descended the staircase and Linda felt like she was entering King Tut's Tomb. Once down, Peter approached the vault door and placed his thumb on the print verification reader. The vault door slid open with a pneumatic swish. And as her eyes focused on the interior, she could see that its contents were much more than breathtaking. They were amazing.

~

The Relic, the Heist and the Gallery

When Chief Petty Officer third class D'Amato finally regained consciousness, the sounds of battle were silent but the smell of smoke, fire and death still hung in the air. He didn't know just how long he'd been out but his body felt like it had been hit by a truck. He lifted himself up and crawled out of the tunnel.

The once dense jungle had been singed and burned and smoking twigs were the only remnants of the immediate area which previously had been so prolific. He had no idea where he was or how or if he would ever make it back to friendly troops. He knew he was in deep trouble. Then in the distance he saw a huge crater where the Sidewinder had hit. The explosion had left a mound of dirt and debris twenty feet high.

"Looks like as good a place as any to get a better view" he thought to himself.

Stumbling toward the crater, he noticed something odd protruding from the open crevice. As he got closer, he could see it was some sort of Temple or shrine which had become unearthed when the missile struck.

Upon reaching the crater, he could see a shining object that was half buried. Reflecting the sun's rays directly into his eyes, it seemed almost as if the object were beckoning him.

He climbed down and after clearing away some dirt and mud, bent down and grabbed the object. As he dusted it off, it suddenly seemed to come to life. It vibrated slightly and then seemed to glow with an incredible radiance. It was a black carving made in the likeness of what appeared to be a flower. It was the most beautifully intricate thing he had ever seen.

"Nothing stolen from any house in the Hamptons ever looked like this. I have a feeling this is going to make my life a lot easier," he thought. D'Amato stuffed the object into his fatigue shirt and as he began to climb out of the crater, he heard the unmistakable sound of the Huey choppers floating overhead. One of the choppers had already spotted him and was preparing a sling to lift him out. The Piper had already begun to work its magic.

~

On December 22, 2000, two masked thieves, one of whom was armed with an M16, held up Stockholm's *Swedish National Museum* nearing closing time. According to a BBC news article, one of the thieves stood in the lobby with the M16 pointed at the security staff while the other one set off in separate directions looking for target paintings to steal.

At the same time the robbery was in progression, two cars exploded in other parts of the city. The explosions were purposely set off to create diversions. It was a creatively deceptive tactic that had police running in different directions throughout the city, thus limiting their response to the museum robbery already in full swing.

Moreover, CNN reported that the robbers scattered spikes on the roads to further delay pursuers. It took only minutes for the art thieves to make off with two French impressionist paintings by Renoir titled *Young Parisian* and *Conversation with the Gardner* and one *Self-portrait* by the Dutch master Rembrandt.

The three paintings were valued at a staggering thirty million dollars. Unfortunately, they were uninsured.

Following the robbery, the men jumped onto what witnesses claimed looked like a stripped down military gunboat waiting for them at the waterfront museum and raced away into the darkness, the BBC reported.

Police inspector Christian Johanson was quoted by the BBC saying he believed that the robbers likely "disappeared on to any of thousands of tiny islands in the archipelago off Stockholm or into the dense forests that surround the city."

The robbers were never caught, although many suspects were apprehended. As the BBC reported, "eventually, to the museum's delight, Renoir's *Conversation with the Gardner* was recovered during a drug raid. Yet, the other two paintings remain lost. It is hoped that they will be discovered so that the public may once again enjoy their beauty. Investigators continue to look for them, believing that they are circulating somewhere on the black market."

~

Linda and Peter stepped into the vault. The room was cool and dry like a Silicon Valley microchip lab. She could hear the air cleaners and climate control systems humming as Peter reached over and waved his hand over an automated reostat. The room became illuminated with soft lights. It appeared to be around a thousand square feet and its design was magnificent.

Paintings of various sizes were hung approximately eight feet apart and separated by sculptures enshrined in walk-around wall niches. In front of each painting was a small bench, provided for the comfort of whoever was fortunate enough to be in attendance.

At the far end of the vault on the opposing wall were two paintings separated by a small Plexiglas cube under which appeared to be what looked like a dark shimmering flower.

"Oh my god, this is amazing" said Linda. "I'm not sure what all of this is, but I have this feeling….."

"You are most intuitive" Peter reassured her. "Mr. Princeton has managed to acquire quite a collection of the Bauhaus modern twentieth century masters. Some are numbered prints but most are originals."

"For example…to your left is Wassily Kandinsky's *Composition VI*, adjacent to which is his *On White II*, both painted in the early twentieth century…and over here is Georges Braque's *Billiard* followed by his *Snooker* painting. It appears he rather fancied pool halls."

"Sounds like my last few dates," quipped Linda.

"How unfortunate for you," Peter answered. "As you Americans say, perhaps it's time to move it up a notch."

"I'll be sure to join a bowling league soon, how's that sound?"

"Marvelous, I understand it's the monarchy's latest rage. You would look smashing in a bowling shirt" said Peter.

"I'll be sure to have it monogrammed."

"Please do and don't forget the velvet collar. Now where were we? Oh yes, as I was saying, the sculptures are quite priceless. In the first niche on the right is Brancusi's *The Muse* of 1932 followed by one of his most famous works *Bird in Space*.

"You have no doubt heard of Henry Moore?" asked Peter.

"Of course, I'm not quite that culturally deprived."

"Then you will no doubt appreciate the sculpture in front of you. It is his *Recumbant Figure* which was once located in the Tate Gallery in London."

"I'm impressed…I mean really impressed." said Linda.

"In that case, allow me to show you the crown jewels of the Princeton collection. Come with me, Miss" said Peter as he took Linda's hand onto his arm and began to walk her to the far side of the vault. As they approached the two paintings on the far wall and the Plexiglas box, Linda began to tremble with anticipation.

She wasn't sure what she was about to see but she was positive it was going to be awesome. She was correct. As they closed on their position she could see they were stunning.

Peter came to a halt at the velvet ropes which encircled the art.

"Ms. Squires, may I introduce to you *Mr. Rembrandt the Self Portrait* and his friend *The Young Parisian* by Renoir. And this object d' art between them is known as the *Black Piper*."

~

The Doctor, the Pass and the Bet

"You have a slight concussion but you'll be alright. Just take it easy for the next couple of days. Nurse Youngblood, will you get some aspirin for this gentleman, please?"

"You'll have a lump back there for a few days but it will heal quickly. Thank you, John. Here you are sir, take these."

"Thanks, Doctor," replied Tom.

"Please call me Courtney. Now I believe you are expected to join Mr. Princeton and his associate Peter Harrison for dinner. I have also been informed that a lady guest is also going to join you."

"The more the merrier" said Tom.

"But first Mr. Princeton has requested that you meet him in the front foyer. He wishes to show you some objects of great importance and about which he told me he will need the advice of an attorney. I understand that is your profession."

"Before I answer that, let me ask you a question." said Tom.

"Sure thing" said Courtney.

"What do lawyers use for birth control?" asked Tom.

"I'm sure I don't know".

"Their personalities!" said Tom.

"You're a comedian also. I like that. Now let me show you where to go," said Courtney as she escorted Tom to the elevator.

"Take the elevator down to the first floor and then take two lefts which will get you to where you wish to go. Have a nice evening."

"Thanks Doc, hope to not see you soon" replied Tom as the elevator doors closed.

~

"What happened, D'Amato?"

Lieutenant Colonel Wayne Jason Newell was the commanding officer of Firebase Nicki. This was his third tour of duty in 'Nam and he had seen enough combat to make John Wayne wince.

"How the hell did you survive when your captain and the Ranger squad was wiped out?" Newell growled.

"We were bushwhacked by the gooks" replied D'Amato. "They hit us with incoming and the next thing I know, we're being picked off like fish in a barrel. We were overrun, but I managed to pull one of the dead rangers over me and they didn't see me. They must have heard the air support and knew they were going to be wasted unless they got the hell out of the area fast. They ran and I ducked into a gook tunnel when the shit hit the fan! I guess I'm just lucky."

"Something doesn't add up here, D'Amato. I'm launching an investigation. In the meantime you're on report. I'm sending you back to your duty station in Saigon. If you're lying, you will be court marshaled."

"Yes sir," snapped D'Amato.

"You'll ship out at 0600 hours tomorrow. Lucky for you we have a bird heading that way for supplies. Sergeant, get this man some fresh fatigues and a sea bag."

"Yes sir, Colonel" said the sergeant. "Follow me, D'Amato."

D'Amato followed the sergeant out of the duty hut. As they passed the head D'Amato spoke up.

"Sergeant, I need to use the head."

"You just used it before you saw the colonel, D'Amato."

"Yeah, but when nature calls…"

"I'll meet you at Supply! Just get your ass in gear" said the sergeant.

D'Amato jumped into the head and went to the third latrine on the left. He reached behind the back of the throne. It was exactly where he had left it. He grabbed the *Piper* and put it back in his shirt

"This baby is my pass out of this hell hole," he thought. He was almost right.

~

"Three Patron shots, three Stellas and some tacos, doll face" said Ernie to the waitress.

"Looks like everything's comparatively calm in here" said Tom, perusing the establishment. The place was loaded with pool tables, video games, pinball machines and what looked like half of the members of the Fifth Fleet.

"Let's just keep it at one brawl tonight, okay Ernie? I think we're a little outnumbered in here."

"No worries…"

The waitress arrived with their order. Emmet lifted his patron in a toast. "To our new Swan, a safe sail back and to Ernie's new found passivity."

"I'm willing to bet number three isn't going to last long," said Tom.

"Now, now…think positive, Tom" said Emmet.

"Okay, I'm positive number three won't last long then."

"So what did you think of *Little Napoleon* out there?" Emmet asked Ernie.

"We had certain expressions in the SEALs for guys like him" said Ernie.

"Let me guess, how about if he were any more stupid he'd have to be watered twice a week" said Tom.

"If you gave him a penny for his thoughts, you'd get change back" added Emmet.

"How about, hard to believe he beat out 1,000,000 other sperm" said Ernie.

"It would take him two hours to watch sixty minutes" added Tom.

"So here's to *Louie the Lip* or whatever his name is. May we never cross paths again" toasted Emmet.

All raised their shot glasses. "Down the hatch" said Ernie as the three tossed their heads back and eased the Patron down their throats.

"Although" said Tom, "I have a feeling we haven't seen the last of him. I'll bet he is going to be a thorn in our side on this trip."

"Well, I'll bet he won't be bothering us again" said Ernie.

"Oh? And what shall we bet?" asked Tom.

"I'll bet a plane ticket to Rio I can eat more tacos than you, wimp."

"You're on, Nesto. Waitress, may we have some more tacos here please?"

"And just keep 'em coming!" said Ernie. "But first we need some rules."

"Like what?" Tom asked.

"We have to eat the same type of tacos."

"Okay, but no limit on salsa choices or number of beers."

"Done" said Ernie as the two shook hands.

"You know you can't win" said Tom.

"And why is that?"

"You have just made a bet with the University of San Diego Alpha Beta fraternity pie eating champion, fool."

"I'm not scared."

"Then prepare for defeat, knave!"

"We shall see! Are you ready?"

"Readier I have never been."

"Then go" said Ernie as the two began their food and drink debauchery.

Two hours, twenty-eight tacos, a bottle of Patron and nineteen Stellas later, Tom had won the bet. Ernie had won the waitress.

~

The Interpol Agent and the Dinner Party

Special Agent Stephanie Kensington was quite happy with her choice of careers. Not only was she pretty and intelligent, but she also had graduated with a double major in Criminology and Art history from USC followed by a Master's degree in Art History from the University of California at Santa Barbara. Consequently, she had been heavily recruited by Interpol. The job offered her a great salary and benefits plus the opportunity to travel. It was a 'dream come true'.

After training for a year at the International Criminal Police Commission's liaison office in Vienna in such things as international law, codes, protocol, detainment procedure and self- defense, she was more than ready for her first assignment. But it hadn't happened yet. First she had one more event to attend in Lyon, France.

The Interpol General Secretariat was to host its sixth international symposium on the Theft of and the Illicit Traffic in Works of Art, Cultural Property and Antiques. It was being held at headquarters in Lyon.

Over one hundred delegates from forty member countries were to be there. In addition to observers from international partner organizations such the Organization for Security and Cooperation in Europe and the International Council of Museums, private companies active in this field were also to be in attendance. The focus was to be on improvement of the international co-operation in the area of cultural property crime.

Stephanie thought it would be very informative and interesting and was looking forward to attending the event. Maybe afterwards she would be assigned a case.

"I love this city," she thought to herself as she walked by the *Hofburg* which was the former Royal Theatre located in the *Innenstadt*.

"Vienna has been good to me, I will miss it" she whispered as she unlocked the entrance of her apartment building. She had finally graduated from the Interpol Academy the previous week and was waiting for further instructions or an assignment.

But in spite of her warm feelings for the city, she still had one regret. She had fallen in love with a young orthopedic surgeon while stationed there but it didn't work out. She had caught him red handed cavorting with a prostitute in one of the clubs and when she put two and two together, she realized that his behavior was very perilous to her own health and ended the relationship. It broke her heart and she swore she would never fall in love again.

As she entered her small studio overlooking the Danube Canal and glanced over at her laptop, she saw that she had left it on that morning when she had left for the day. The *New Mail* hypertext was flashing.

"Oh goody, new mail" she said. She sat down at the desk and clicked on the *new mail* icon. It was from JB@ICPC.gov.com.

"Oh shoot, I hope this is what I think it is." She opened the email. It was from Chief Inspector Spangler in New York and the message was brief and to the point.

Ms. Kensington,
You are to report to the Stockholm Police Department immediately following the conference in Lyon. Your plane ticket is reserved on Lufthansa. Detective Christian Johanson will meet you at the Stockholm airport. Further information is attached.
Spangler

She opened the attachment and read the details of the *Swedish National Museum* heist. She couldn't believe they had not located the thieves yet. The M16, the stripped down military boat and the discipline with which the robbery was carried out all pointed to one thing. The criminals were in the military, probably the U.S. Navy.

"Maybe that's why they need an Interpol agent" she thought… "for extradition expertise. Interesting though…virtually no clues had been left at the scene of the crime other than the identification of the weapon and the description of the escape vessel."

But one thing caught her attention. It may have had nothing to do with the robbery but still it seemed odd to her. In the gallery where the *The Young Parisian* was cut from its frame, a small shirt tag had been found nearby. It had the initials RL on it and instructed the owner to wash in cold water only.

~

Upon entering the vaulted gallery, Tom's mouth had dropped like an egg from a tall chicken. He had immediately recognized some of the paintings and sculptures. Also he recalled reading about the Renoir and the Rembrandt works of art and how they had been stolen from the *Swedish National Museum*.

"Okay Mr. Princeton, just what is up with the stolen artwork?" Tom thought to himself as he, Linda, Peter and Jeremy sat down to dine.

The dinner table and chairs looked like they'd either been the property of a twelfth century monastery or Uncle Ira's 12th Street Furniture Emporium in Van Nuys. He couldn't tell the difference and wasn't about to ask.

"Ah, good old shabby chic" said Tom. "Where are the goblets?"

"They'll be here as soon as the stuffed wild boar is served" said Linda.

"I have 'dibbies' on the apple" said Tom.

"Okay, you clowns...that's enough" said Jeremy. "Now that we've all been introduced, to use an old cliché, I suppose you're wondering why I asked you all here."

A gaggle of attendants began pouring the '99 Kendall-Jackson Chardonnay and serving the foie gras and fresh oysters on the half shell.

"Don't tell me," said Tom. "It was Colonel Mustard in the conservatory with the wrench, wasn't it?"

"No, it had to be Miss Violet in the library with the lead pipe" added Linda.

"You are both very witty but fortunately no one has been murdered" added Peter.

"You should have seen my court performance today" said Tom.

"Alright, that's enough" asserted Jeremy. After the staff had served the pan roasted white fish with paella, Jeremy rang the bell on his right which sent the staff scurrying away into the kitchen.

"Now, if you will just be quiet for a few minutes while you enjoy your dinner, I would like to explain to you how I came to acquire the *Black Piper*, *The Young Parisian* and the *Rembrandt Self Portrait* and also tell you the story of how my appearance has come to be the way that it is today.

~

The Sea Bag, Stockholm
and the Black Piper

At 0600 the C-54 was ready to go. It was loaded with five gruesome body bags from the last fire fight with Charlie and also flares for the return trip in case they were fired upon after dark. The M-60 machine gun was locked and loaded.

It was also the morning of the start of the TET Offensive. There had been metal tinkling like noises all around the perimeter of the compound the previous night and there was a feeling of foreboding in the air. D'Amato didn't like it and would be glad to reach Saigon in one piece, especially considering the precious cargo he carried in his sea bag.

First Lieutenant and pilot Rod Moore exited the CP and approached the chopper. "Throw in your gear, D'Amato, it's time to fly."

D'Amato threw his sea bag into the rear door. It landed on the deck with a bang.

"And untie the rotor on my command." Moore tightened his harness and began to crank the engine.

Suddenly all hell broke loose. Motors started exploding all around the Outlaw ramp and the firebase.

"Clear!" Moore screamed as the explosions began to creep closer to the ramp.

D'Amato unhooked the tie down, but couldn't get the knot out as the engine began to scream.

"D'Amato, clear NOW!" Moore yelled.

D'Amato reached for his knife and cut the rope. At least he thought he had cut the rope.

"All clear" yelled D'Amato back. And as he dove through the rear door of the ship and looked toward the gauges, he could see tracers passing through the ship in front of Moore and his co-pilot. The Viet Cong were swarming onto the compound like Minnesota mosquitoes in an August sunset.

"Grab the M-60, D'Amato and start firing... now!" screamed Moore.

As D'Amato unlocked the safety of the M-60 and started to fire, Moore engaged the throttle to full power. But as the chopper rose into the air, for an instant the unbroken tie rope held the chopper back and tipped the ship to its starboard side. And as the unbroken tie rope pulled the chopper over, D'Amato's sea bag began to roll toward the open rear door faster than a walnut off a henhouse roof.

"Oh no!" screamed an anguished D'Amato as he lunged for the rolling sea bag. But it was too late. As the tie rope finally broke clear and as the chopper quickly regained its balance and ascended, the sea bag had shot out of the aircraft and had landed with a thud right in the middle of the skirmish fifty feet below.

As easily and as quickly as D'Amato had acquired the *Piper*, as equally easily and quickly he had lost it and had deposited it right into the hands of Defense Minister and avid coin collector General Vo Nguyen Giap and the Army of North Vietnam.

~

The flight from Lyon to Stockholm was uneventful except for some turbulence over the Baltic Sea. Stephanie had always heard what a beautiful country Sweden was and now she knew why.

Stockholm was located on Sweden's East coast, where Lake Malaren meets the Baltic Sea. As the 747 slowed in preparation for landing, she could see that the central part of the city consisted of a number of islands, all part of an archipelago. As she peered through the cabin window, she could see that the geographical city center was virtually situated on the water in a bay. It was like Venice had been moved to the far north.

As the plane landed and taxied to the main concourse, she wondered if this first assignment would prove challenging. She had gone over the details of the heist over and over again in her mind but only one thing stood out. The clues were too obvious. The M16, the PBR river patrol boat, maybe the RL label and the precision with which the events unfolded seemed staged to her, almost like a play. Somebody wasn't filling her in on the truth and she intended to find out why.

When she had exited the corridor and stepped into the concourse, she was somewhat startled. As opposed to the European countries she had visited and also the U.S., everyone seemed to be blonde with blue eyes.

"A beautiful people for sure" Stephanie thought to herself. "I wonder if they have blonde jokes here."

"Excuse me, please. You are Ms. Kensington I believe." spoke a voice from the hoard of Vikings standing before her.

A man emerged from the crowd. He was well over six feet tall and not only had thick blonde hair but also had the most shocking blue eyes she had ever seen!

"Allow me to introduce myself. I'm Inspector Christian Johanson of the Stockholm Police," he said in a heavy Swedish accent. He flashed his badge although she couldn't move her eyes to look at it.

"This guy is a god!" she thought to herself. She couldn't take her eyes off of his. After an awkward silence, she managed to find her tongue again.

"Um…yes…yes, I'm Ms. Kensington. Sorry, I'm just a little jet lagged I guess. I'm pleased to meet you, Inspector."

They shook hands.

"I understand. It's quite a long flight from France. Would you allow me to transport you to your hotel? Your reservation is at the First Hotel Reisen. I think you'll like it there. It's very close to both the *Royal Palace* and the *National Museum of Art*."

"That sounds great, thank you."

"Excellent, right this way then please." said Christian, gesturing for her to proceed first.

As they walked up the concourse she felt a little giddy. "Okay Stephanie, settle down, girl, you're supposed to be a professional so act like one." she murmured to herself.

"Sorry, what was that?"

"Oh, it's nothing. I have a bad habit of talking to myself sometimes."

"Not to worry… you are now in Sweden, where our neutrality is well known. Even if you argue with yourself, we won't take sides."

"Thank you. I'm relieved to hear that," she chuckled as they made their way to the baggage claim.

"I think you will enjoy our city" said Christian as he lifted Stephanie's luggage into the Volvo S80. "I hope you will allow me to show you some of it."

"That would be nice."

Christian turned the ignition key and slammed it into drive. "As it's quite late, it would be best for you to get some rest. Tomorrow we will meet with the Museum Director of Security to discuss the robbery."

As the Volvo sped down the Valhallagen, she suddenly realized how tired she was. That idea sounded great to her.

"I agree, thank you. But let me ask you something as long as you brought it up. Do you have any leads on the thieves who stole the art?"

"Oh no, we don't have any leads."

"How about clues, you do have a clue or two, don't you?"

"No, sorry but no clues either."

"Oookayyyy………these people may be beautiful but I can tell they're not the sharpest pencils in the drawer either" she thought.

"No leads? No clues? Surely you must have some suspects."

"No, no suspects either. You see, Ms. Kensington we know precisely who stole the art."

"What? You're joking. Then why don't you arrest them?" she asked, obviously perturbed.

'Because of three little letters, Ms. Kensington," said Christian.

"What letters might those be, Inspector? And by the way, call me Stephanie."

"Very well, call me Christian. I'll explain it all to you tomorrow, Stephanie. But so you may sleep easier tonight, I won't tell you the letters but I'll give you some hints. First, what do you do with your eyes?"

"See?"

"Good, now how does one refer to oneself?"

"I?"

"Very good, now lastly, the word apple begins with what letter?"

"I get the picture! This I can't wait to hear about."

"Just relax. There will be adequate time tomorrow to explain" said Christian.

And as the Volvo zoomed over the canal bridge by the Royal Palace enroute to the Reisen Hotel, Stephanie's intuition kicked in. This was not just an art heist. It was something much more than that.

~

"Now, as I was saying to Tom earlier on the ride up here, anyone who comes to have possession of the *Piper* not only becomes wealthy and powerful but also becomes a victim of the curse" stated Jeremy.

"Whatever you do, stay off of the Moors tonight!" said Tom to Linda.

"What curse?" asked Linda.

"There is a small inscription written on the Piper which says: *Adore the beauty, beware the power, desires fulfilled, thy visage shall alter, light to darkness thy path shall be, a lesson in duality*" said Peter.

"You don't really believe that, do you?" asked Linda.

"The evidence supports its existence" replied Peter.

"I am, along with many others, living proof that this curse exists" added Jeremy. Peter has managed to uncover several of the previous owners and all of their stories are quite convincing. Believe as you wish but the facts speak for themselves. You want to fill them in, Peter?

"My pleasure" replied Peter. "We haven't been able to determine the exact date or how it happened but around 1968 the *Piper* came to be in the possession of General Giap, Defense Minister of the North Vietnamese Army."

"And just how did you ever discover that?" asked Tom.

"Please counselor, just let me finish before you begin your cross examination."

"Objection sustained" said Jeremy.

"Okay, it's sustained then" said Tom.

"General Giap was the Commander of the People's Army of North Vietnam from 1951 through 1976. His greatest accomplishments were two fold. The first was defeating the French at Diem Bien Phu. The other one was initiating the TET Offensive during the Vietnam War. He was also a numismatic and an avid art collector."

"He was a what?" Linda asked.

"A novice transvestite Sumo wrestler" interjected Tom.

"If you please" said Peter, losing patience.

"A numismatic is a collector of rare coins. General Giap was perhaps more responsible than anyone for turning the tide of that war which eventually resulted in the withdrawal of American troops in 1975. We all know the history of Vietnam since then. It became a unified country and in 1996 Clinton dropped the embargo against it and it has most recently entered into trade agreements with the U.S."

"During that period of time, Giap became very powerful and wealthy. He evidently had amassed quite a collection of rare silver Southeast Asian coins and by 1979 was living very comfortably near the Bay of Hanoi when something happened. He suddenly lost his seat in the Politburo and was demoted. The Communist Party began to ridicule him. No one knows exactly what changed but it had something to do with the coin collection."

"And most probably the *Piper*", added Jeremy.

"Anyway, the *Piper* and the coins resurfaced in 1980 in the hands of a certain Daniel Schofield, who lives alternately in Paris, Beirut and the U.S. He is a collector and one of the world's hottest purveyors of Middle Eastern antiquities. And he is also rumored to have contacts with the mafia in southern Italy and in the U.S."

"A real Snidely Whiplash" said Tom.

"Quite...he has been in trouble with many Middle Eastern countries for attempting to export banned antiquities including a coin collection named the *Durkee Ward* collection which consisted of very rare and ancient Vietnamese and Middle Eastern coins."

"Go on."

"Anyway, reportedly his partner at some point was a certain Bruce McVail, who you may recall owned the Los Angeles Kings hockey team. McVail at some point bought the collection from Schofield for somewhere between $750,000 and a million dollars. Rumor has it that the *Piper* was included in the sale. Then at another unknown point, the collection was sold to the Hunter family of Texas."

"Sure, good old boys Duncan and Hubert" said Tom.

"Yes, those are they" replied Peter. "And are we all familiar with the fates of these three individuals?"

"Refresh my memory" said Linda.

"Very well then, I will do that. Mr. Bruce McVail made his initial fortune as a coin collector and by age sixteen, he had a collection worth $60,000 which he managed to parlay into a vast fortune. In 1987 he bought the Kings and lured Wayne Chotsky away from the Edmonton Oilers with a three million dollar salary. He was well connected in Hollywood, produced twenty films and owned thoroughbred race horses."

"Another rags to riches story" said Tom.

"Yes, but then the bottom fell out. By the 1990's, McVail's business empire was collapsing. Fraudulent transactions worth about 200 million were uncovered by federal investigators, and in 1996 McVail was sentenced to seventy months in a federal prison. His fortune is gone and he owes five million in restitution to the banks."

"And you think it was the curse of the *Piper* that put him there?" asked Linda.

"More likely a random coincidence" added Tom.

"Possibly" said Peter. "But the Hunter brothers' story adds more credibility to the curse theory. In 1979, the Hunter brothers, together with some wealthy Arabs, formed a silver commodity investment pool. In a short period of time, they had amassed more than two hundred million ounces of silver, equivalent to half the world's supply."

"I remember that" said Tom.

"Yes, when the Hunters began accumulating silver back in 1973 the price was in the $1.95 an ounce range. About the time it was rumored they had purchased the coin collections and the *Piper* from McVail, the price was about five dollars. By the very early eighties, the price was in the $50 range, peaking at $54."

"Wow… nice little profit." said Linda.

"Indeed, once the silver market was cornered, outsiders joined the chase but a combination of changed trading rules on the New York Metals Market and the intervention of the Federal Reserve put an end to the game. The price began to slide, culminating in a fifty percent one-day decline in late 1980 as the price plummeted $21 to less than $10."

"Pity, isn't it?" Tom said sarcastically.

"Countless speculators were wiped out and the Hunter brothers declared bankruptcy. By 1987 their liabilities had grown to nearly $2.5 billion against assets of 1.5 billion. In 1988 they were convicted of conspiring to manipulate the market and sentenced to prison."

"Another random coincidence," said Tom

"I can see you still doubt the existence of the curse so maybe you had better take over from here, Jeremy" replied Peter.

"Gladly, but first shall we, if you'll excuse the expression, retire to the drawing room?" asked Jeremy.

"Ah, let me guess, for some brandy and cigars" said Tom cynically.

"If you like, but I don't smoke" laughed Jeremy.

"Are ladies allowed or shall I run off to the lady's room to put on a fresh face and tighten my girdle strings?" asked Linda.

"Please do that" said Tom. "By the time you return, Holmes and Watson will have arrived."

"You Yanks certainly do have an attitude sometimes," said Peter. "Just remember that in reality you are still only subjects of the Queen."

"The only Queen I'm subject to works down at the Spearmint Rhino. But her name *is* Queenie! Does that count?" asked Tom.

"It counts I suppose. But in a perverse way and I'm quite sure *it* has very little numerical let alone any cerebral value."

"Okay children, now that's enough!" said Jeremy adamantly. "Now if you will follow me, we will finish the story where we can relax and maybe not squabble."

"But I'm an attorney, I love to squabble!" said Tom, following Jeremy. "That is my life! Squabble, squabble, squabble, squabble... Why, I even love the sound of it, don't you? Don't boggle my squabble and don't wobble my squabble either. Squabble, squabble, squabble....."

As Tom's voice began to fade ahead of him, Peter rolled his eyes and collected his notes as Jeremy led Linda and Tom out of the dining room, down the hallway and into the library.

~

The Kiss and the Altering Visage

Stephanie slept like a rock. Whether it was due to the warm ambience of the Hotel Reisen or her exhaustion from the trip she couldn't say but she hadn't had such a good night's sleep in a long time. When she finally rolled out of bed and opened the curtains, she noticed that the sky was an eerie blue-gray color, not overcast but not light either.

The views from the three huge antique windows were incredible. The hotel was located right on the waterfront and she could easily see the *Royal Palace*, the *Great Church*, the market square and across the canal, the *Swedish National Museum*.

She felt starved. She called room service and ordered some knackebrod, grot, yogurt and coffee, after which she jumped in the shower. Christian Johanson was picking her up at 9:00 and she didn't want to keep him waiting.

"What a gorgeous city" she thought to herself. "Hopefully my time here won't be spent just working, not with Christian as my associate. Easy Stephanie… first things first…we need to solve the crime before we can play" she reminded herself.

At precisely 9:00 AM, Christian's Volvo came to a halt in front of the Hotel. He reached over and pushed the door open for her to get in.

"Thank you and good morning" she said demurely as she slammed the front door.

"God morgan to you, Stephanie" said Christian. "Valkommen ombord. Did you sleep well?"

"Like the dead, thank you. It must be the lull of the canal water lapping on the docks that put me out so soundly. Of course it could have been the Ambien too!"

"Ah, very possibly" replied Christian.

"So what's on the agenda, Inspector?"

"We are meeting with the Museum Director Glenn Ostrig and his assistant Meredith Wickingham at 9:30 at Police headquarters. We want to brief you on the case, of course."

"She's American?"

"Yes, she's American but also has quite an interesting background. I'll let her explain when you meet her. Ska vidra?"

"Whatever you say, governor, drive on."

As the Volvo headed East on the *Skepps Bron* past the *Royal Palace* toward the *Kungsholmen* borough, Stephanie noticed that the sun had still not risen yet. The city was in a sort of twilight.

"Shouldn't the sun have risen by now?" she asked.

"Welcome to Sweden, Stephanie," said Christian. "The sun won't rise for another four hours, and then just barely. You see, due to the country's high northern latitude, our winter daylight is limited to six hours. In summer it becomes eighteen hours. You'll get used to it."

"No wonder it's a little brisk this morning."

"A little?" asked Christian. "In Sweden we have a word for it…*skitkalt*."

"Meaning… ?"

"Frigging cold" replied Christian. "But we Swedes also have a saying; *Det finns inget daligt vadder, bara daliga kladder*."

"Okay, don't leave me in the dark on this one."

"It simply means there is no bad weather, only bad clothing."

"I'm going to have to think about it."

"Perhaps you have to be Swedish to understand."

"I got the bad clothing part. Have you any other advice for this American girl?"

"Ja, come to think of it; don't ever ask a man for a kiss while you're here."

"Okay, now why is that?"

"In Swedish the verb to kiss means to *pee*."

"Wow, thanks for sharing!"

"You are welcome" said Christian, snickering.

As the Volvo weaved its way through morning traffic on the Karlvagen, Glenn Ostrig and Meredith Wickingham were at Police Headquarters at Kungsholmgaten 37 awaiting their arrival. In Meredith's brief case was a dossier marked *Confidential*.

As she removed it from her case and opened it, a case name and number could be seen inscribed on the inside cover. It read Case # *621A, Swedish National Museum Robbery 12/22/00*. And under it there were three names.

Anthony D'Amato
Daniel Schofield AKA Peter Harrison

~

The deep blackberry and wooden aromas of the *Remy Martin VSOP* filled the room as the foursome swished the burnished golden nectar into long dripping fingers within the confines of Jeremy's *Baccarat* crystal snifters.

As Linda sat down on the plush velour settee in front of the warm and glowing fireplace surrounded by the mahogany bookshelves, she noticed that she really did feel like she was in Sir Arthur Conan Doyle's study.

"Now, if everyone is comfortable, shall I continue with the story? I'm sure you're all wondering how I came to possess the *Piper* and the paintings, aren't you?" asked Jeremy.

"Elementary, my dear Jeremy," said Tom.

"It's getting old, Sherlock. Time to zip it" snapped Linda.

"Jolly good then" replied Tom. Peter rolled his eyes.

"Now where shall I start? In 1987 I began the *Rad World Tour*. It consisted of 123 concerts in 15 countries. Over four million people attended the concerts and the sixteen month tour grossed over $125 million.

"Nice piece of change" said Tom.

"Yes, well needless to say, at this point I needed a tax shelter rather badly to keep Uncle Sam at bay. Even though I had contributed much of the profits to charity, the IRS was drooling at the prospect of getting its hands on most of what was left. My accountant suggested I start buying art and antiquities and donating the art to museums."

"That would make sense" added Linda.

"But I knew nothing about art. So I called the curator at the Met and asked for someone who might be willing to bid for me. He suggested a young but upcoming art expert who was in New York lecturing at NYU. I flew to New York, met Peter and he has been my advisor ever since. He has not only advised me in the donation department but also has helped me acquire the collection you saw earlier this evening."

"Then the Duncan Hunter Sale of Middle Eastern Antiquities became scheduled for auction, "added Peter.

"You could say that this was the turning point of my life," stated Jeremy. "Can you elaborate, Peter?"

"Gladly... I had known of the *Duncan Hunter Collection* for some time and knew of two very valuable coin collections which I thought would be an excellent purchase for Jeremy. I contacted an antiquities dealer by the name of Daniel Schofield whom I had met once on my travels in Lebanon and who was well acquainted with the Hunter brothers. Both brothers had teenage and young children so I suggested to Schofield that he tell the Hunters that if they would give us first crack at purchasing the coins, I would arrange for Jeremy to perform for the Hunter families."

"And it worked," said Jeremy. "I did a short private concert for them and they in turn sold me the coin collections and the *Piper* at a great market discount, at which point began the nightmare of the last thirteen years."

"How so?" asked Linda.

"Well, to start with I developed a skin disorder called *Vitiligo*. Small white spots began to appear on my face which quickly grew larger. I had to start using white make-up. It kept getting worse and now you see it in the advanced stages."

"*Thy visage shall alter*," said Linda.

"Yes, it seems the *Piper* curse wasted no time once it came into my possession. But that's not all. I always had hated the look of my nose so I decided to change it. I scheduled a rhinoplasty, as it is called, with one of the top cosmetic surgeons in the world. He had done countless surgeries on many celebrities with great success so I assumed it would be a fairly minor procedure. I was wrong."

"And?" inquired Tom.

"He totally blew it! The nose became uneven and miniscule. It was as if a great artist was suddenly and mysteriously deprived of his skill. I went back two times to correct the flaws of the previous surgeries and each time the damage became worse. Then the combination of pain pills, endorphins and other hormones released into my system literally changed my facial bone structure."

"Amazing," said Tom.

"I'm sure you're all well aware of the unfortunate events in Jeremy's life after that," said Peter.

"Unfortunately, now the whole world knows about them" added Jeremy.

"And the Rembrandt and the Renoir, Jeremy?" asked Linda.

"The paintings were quite recently acquired inadvertently and in a very mysterious way. As you know, they are stolen works of art and I wish to return them to the Museum in Stockholm. But I don't want to be arrested for stealing and importing stolen art on top of all the other disasters in my life. That is one of the reasons you are here, Tom. I need legal representation to extricate me of any culpability."

"It would be my pleasure."

"Thank you, I am relieved. Now, I'm afraid the cognac has made me a little sleepy. I am going to say goodnight. Peter, can you show them how we came to acquire the paintings?"

"Yes, of course."

"Good, then perhaps I will see you all in the morning. Sleep well" said Jeremy as he exited the study.

"Now then, if you have all finished your cognacs, would you please follow me? There is something else you should see" said Peter.

As Tom placed his snifter down on the glass coffee table and started to rise to follow Peter, his eyes caught a glimpse of a large ornately inscribed book under the glass. It had Arabic inscriptions on it and as he focused his eyes he suddenly realized exactly what it was. It was a *Qur'an*.

~

The Tier Two Alert

"Stephanie Kensington, meet Glenn Ostrig and Meredith Wickingham" said Christian. "Pleasure to meet you" said Stephanie.

"Glenn is the curator of the *Swedish National Museum* and Meredith is, as far as the public knows, his assistant."

"As far as the public knows?" she asked.

"Yes, Meredith is actually undercover. Let it suffice to say that she is employed by a certain intelligence agency associated with the U.S. Department of Defense" added Christian.

"Okay, so why do you need Interpol?"

"We'll explain why to you but first things first, Stephanie. You're probably wondering who stole the paintings, right?" asked Meredith.

"Before Meredith explains the details of this case, there is one very important thing you should know first" added Glenn.

"Okay, and what might that be?" she asked.

"The paintings were never stolen."

"What?" Stephanie screamed.

"I want to show you these" said Glenn as he reached underneath the desk and grabbed two silver tubular containers. Pulling the tops off the containers and sliding the canvasses out, he laid them on the table. There in front of her eyes was Renoir's *Young Parisian* and the Rembrandt *Self Portrait*!

Stephanie was dumbfounded. "Alright, now I'm confused. Who wants to start here?"

"Let me try to explain, Ms. Kensington" said Meredith.

"Call me Stephanie, please."

"Okay, Stephanie it is." said Meredith as she handed her the dossier and fired up the Power Point on her laptop.

Stephanie opened the dossier. On the first page were two photos of what looked like the same person. Underneath the photos were two columns, each of which was a summary of their individual and joint surreptitious activities.

"Meet Mr. Anthony D'Amato and Mr. Daniel Schofield AKA Peter Harrison" said Meredith. "We have had both of them under surveillance recently. We know they are big participators in the illegal Middle Eastern art and antiquities markets and are both responsible for the *Swedish National Museum* heist. They are quite dangerous men and also have ties to the Italian and American Mafias and another group which is even more deadly."

"Which group is that?" asked Stephanie.

"Are you familiar with the group called Hizbollah?" asked Christian.

"Charming" said Stephanie.

"Let me start with Mr. D'Amato" said Meredith. "His history goes back to the sixties when he was charged with extorting college students at NYU. However, no one would testify against him so the charges were dropped.

After that he entered the Navy and served in Vietnam. He was suspected of desertion in the line of fire but once again, it couldn't be proved."

"He was just lucky?"

"Probably, but rumor has it that for a short period of time he had in his possession a legendary relic called the *Black Piper*. Supposedly, great power and wealth are its benefits. We suspect that the desire to repossess this item is what drives him."

"Is there such a thing?"

"There is no provenance anywhere supporting its existence but we cannot disprove it either" replied Meredith. "But let me tell you more."

"Okay, shoot."

"After D'Amato's service in Vietnam, he was a pariah. Considered a bad apple by his CO, the Navy wanted him out but had no proof to proceed with or warrant a court martial. So they reassigned him to the Beirut Embassy in the hopes that the danger of living in that politically chaotic part of the world would inspire a resignation."

"And did it?"

"Quite the opposite it seems. For thirty some years, D'Amato served as an attache and liaison between the Ambassador's Office and various Lebanese political factions. He bounced around between many Middle Eastern Embassies during that period. We know now that during that time he developed clandestine relations with those factions and also used these relations to smuggle art onto the black market."

"So how does he do this?"

"We think he uses his association with the U.S. Navy somehow with the help of his partner in crime, Mr. Harrison/Schofield. And that brings us to his background."

"Yes, I'd be most interested to hear about it."

"At first glance, all records indicate he is a true English blue blood. Born near London to a wealthy upper crust British family, his father was a Commander in the Royal Navy. Educated at Eaton and Oxford in art history and ancient antiquities, he received an MFA from Harvard and became an Associate Professor at NYU after receiving numerous awards for his archaeological accomplishments in the areas known as ancient Mesopotamia."

"In other words, the Middle East" said Stephanie.

"Yes, his past appeared stellar upon examination and he would have never have come up on our radar except for a certain incident which occurred around 1996."

"Which was?"

"First, let me show you this" said Meredith as she clicked on her Power Point. Two photos appeared on the computer monitor. One photo was clear and obviously professionally shot and the other was somewhat obscure and black and white.

"Okay, two photos of Peter Harrison means?"

"They're not both photos of Peter Harrison. The photo on the right is Mr. Daniel Schofield."

"But they're practically identical."

"Not practically. As far as we can tell, they are identical."

"Meaning what?"

"We can only speculate. There is very little record of Schofield ever having existed. The only thing we do know is that Mr. Harrison's father was known to frequent the Middle East on Royal Naval Diplomatic missions before his son Peter was born. There is a small village in Lebanon named Baalbak where some villagers recollect a blonde child attending the local schools until about six when he disappeared. Needless to say, with the endless violence and destruction Lebanon has endured over the last twenty-five years, there is very little record of him at all."

"So when did he make his appearance?"

"In 1996, Harrison was dispatched to Lebanon to examine and possibly purchase for the Met twenty-two silver Byzantine vessels that had been discovered that year in the northern Syrian village of Shiraz. The value of the artifacts at the time was valued at five million dollars, if authentic. We are told by Aljazeera that according to their records, despite tough sentences of up to twenty-five years for selling or smuggling Syrian antiquities, the village decided to sell to a local dealer for $200,000."

"And that dealer was Daniel Schofield?"

"That is correct" replied Meredith. "When Harrison could find no provenance supporting the vessel's legality, he assumed they were smuggled and reportedly walked away. Then something strange happened."

Meredith paused for a breath.

"Continue" said Stephanie impatiently.

"Harrison completely disappeared for four months. Neither his NYU colleagues nor any of his friends or family ever heard a word from him during that time.

All embassies in the area had been contacted which in turn had alerted the local authorities but it seemed he had vanished. In the meantime, Schofield had flown business class to London, accompanied by and using the diplomatic credentials of…. guess who?"

"Hmmm, let me guess…it was Mr. D'Amato?"

"Indeed" answered Meredith. "We have both of their signatures from check–in at the Dorchester Hotel. They remained in London for a few weeks and then returned to Lebanon. Peter Harrison suddenly had a Lebanese bank account and had purchased a home on the Euphrates River. All of these transactions were witnessed by and assisted by business associates who knew Harrison personally."

"And what happened to Harrison?"

"He reappeared out of nowhere. After four months he resurfaced in Lebanon, booked a plane ticket home and resumed his life like nothing had ever happened."

"How did he explain his absence?"

"He claimed he had been kidnapped by militant Bedouins and taken to a camp in Saudi Arabia where he was held against his will or some such nonsense."

"You don't buy it?"

"No, we know there is no such thing as a militant Bedouin. It's very suspicious. That and the other thing" said Meredith.

"And that is?"

"We have spoken with many of his NYU colleagues who worked with him on the faculty at that time and they all said the same thing".

"Which was?"

"He just didn't seem like the same person."

"Interesting…so where is he now?"

"He is presently in the employ of Mr. Jeremy Princeton as a curator of Mr. Princeton's art collection and he divides his time between California, Beirut and Paris."

"Jeremy Princeton! You mean the pop music guy?"

"Yes, the *Prince of Pop*" said Meredith. "We are not sure exactly what is going on but we have our suspicions that antiquity smuggling is not the only thing happening between Harrison, D'Amato and Princeton."

"But how did you know which paintings Harrison and D'Amato were going to steal and also from what Museum?"

"For lack of time and a better word… intelligence," Meredith replied. "We have known for some time through the Echelon Network that the two were planning a heist in Stockholm."

"Echelon Network…which is?"

"Long story short…the National Security Agency or NSA has created a global spy system, codename ECHELON, which captures and analyses every phone call, fax, email and telex message sent anywhere in the world. Operated in conjunction with the governments of Canada, Australia, England and New Zealand, the ECHELON system is fairly simple in design."

"In what way is it?"

"The idea is to position intercept stations all over the world to capture all satellite, microwave, cellular and other communications traffic. That information is then processed through the massive computer capabilities of the NSA."

"So you knew about the art heist ahead of time?"

"Yes, we have had Schofield/Harrison and D'Amato on our radar for some time. Actually we have enough evidence regarding their illegal activities to lock them up and throw away the key. But we believe there is something much bigger going on so we are simply keeping our eye on them for now."

"So, why do you need me?"

"This is where you come in, Stephanie. D'Amato must be arrested in international waters. Otherwise he is still under the auspices of the U.S. Navy. When the time comes, we need you to make the arrest."

"Okay, so let me get this straight. You learned of the heist ahead of time and prepared for it. But how did you know which paintings they would steal?"

"We knew they were targeting the *Stockholm National Museum* from cell phone conversations" added Meredith. "How we knew which paintings they were planning to steal? You care to answer that, Glenn?"

"Yes, as Museum Director of Security, I would gladly answer that question. You see, Stephanie, there are many ways to protect against thievery. Museums use various devices such as vibration sensors, false inventory numbers inscribed on the backs of paintings, environmental sensors and of course motion-detection devices. But none of these will protect against a daylight assault such as occurred that December day in 2000. So we instigated what is known as a *Tier Two* alert."

"Which is what?"

"The Tier Two consists of two directives. The first is to fully monitor all closed-circuit TV and video cameras for one week prior to the anticipated date of robbery. The second directive consists of a very simple technique which very few people outside the Museum world are aware of."

"And that is?"

"Unknown to most of the general public is that most museums have what is known as a Tier Two collection. If a museum has in its collection extremely valuable paintings, reproductions or forgeries are frequently commissioned and kept in a vault to be utilized when needed. This is done for two reasons. The first is that paintings and their frames, like a car or a washing machine, frequently require maintenance. Sometimes, when people visit a museum, a few of the paintings exhibited might be faux reproductions, but most people would never know it as it would take a trained eye and close scrutiny to ascertain when this occurs" said Glenn.

"The things you don't learn in college!" exclaimed Stephanie.

"Yes, it is generally a very well kept secret in the museum world for if this fact were ever to be made public, museum attendance could suffer. Anyway, the second reason for maintaining the Tier Two collection is for reasons such as occurred on December 22, 2000."

"Which was the date of the heist?"

"Yes, I had been monitoring the National Museum closed-circuit TV and video systems from a control room the week previous to the heist" added Christian.

"Two days before, a bearded priest, matching Schofield/Harrison's height, weight and general countenance entered the museum two days in a row previous to the robbery and spent inordinate amounts of time in one gallery."

"So up went the Tier Two Paintings of the Renoirs and the Rembrandt" added Glenn.

"We advised the security staff to cooperate and let the heist go down. We had our people in position to move on them if necessary. We could have killed them or arrested them at anytime" said Christian.

"So why didn't you and why did they need the paintings?"

"We're not sure why exactly they needed to steal the paintings. We suspect that they are both wealthy, albeit by clandestine means. But we have an idea that it has something to do with smuggling something far more sinister and evil than ancient antiquities" said Meredith.

"And that would be?"

"Parts to build a nuclear device" answered Meredith.

"But that's nothing new. As an Interpol agent I know we have been involved in intercepting nuclear parts smuggled to the middle east since the sixties."

"Yes, but in this instance there is a slight difference."

"Which is?"

"As an Interpol agent you are probably aware that between 1987 and 1996, technical analysts at the CIA became convinced that certain items from unspecified countries were shipping to Iraq thousands of specially designed aluminum tubes intended for use as components of centrifuges designed to enrich uranium."

"Not my department but in general the answer is yes."

"Well, because the parts had certain specifications and were ordered in large numbers, the analysts concluded that the parts were intended for the serial production of hundreds of centrifuges. Because each centrifuge enriches a relatively small amount of uranium, several hundred must be connected by pipes into 'cascades' in order to produce enough highly enriched uranium for a small nuclear weapon. The tubes, amongst other components are very important in this process."

"Yes, and I know Interpol has intercepted many of these shipments intended for the Middle East over the years."

"True," said Meredith, "but in the past three years something very odd has happened."

"What is that?"

"The shipments suddenly seem to have ceased. We can detect no communications implicating anyone anywhere in a scheme to smuggle these parts into that area of the world, which leads us to a very scary assumption."

"Maybe the bad guys have seen the error of their ways" said Stephanie facetiously.

"Not likely. We suspect that these parts are now somehow being smuggled into the United States."

"Meaning what?"

"Meaning, that somewhere within the borders of the United States terrorists are building a nuclear weapon!"

~

The Bang Whammers

"Now would you all please follow me?" suggested Peter to the group.

"Walk this way" said Tom hunching down and brandishing a pretend cigar like Groucho Marx.

Linda had to giggle. For an attorney he certainly did have a sense of humor.

Peter led the group down the stairs into the garage. There were seven stalls for the plethora of vintage automobiles and other vehicles gathered there.

"Nice collection" said Linda. "I'm not sure what they all are but I know a nice ride when I see one."

"Well then, allow me to identify some of them." said Peter. This one is a *2000 Ferrari Testerosa*, this is a 1974 *Jaguar XKE Roadster*, here is a *'98 Porsche Carrera*, and in this last stall is Jeremy's favorite, a 1940 *Lincoln Zephyr Continental Club Coupe.*"

"The last one Haraldo found in Al Capone's basement" Tom whispered to Linda.

"Yes, imagine what Snoop Dawg would pay for that baby!"

The group followed Peter down to the last stall which was empty. In the place of a car, a shipment container had been placed in the middle of it.

"When it positively, absolutely has to be there overnight" remarked Tom.

"That's no Fed Ex Package."

"You are absolutely correct, Miss Linda" remarked Peter. "But before I explain to you how it got here, allow me to show you the contents."

Peter lowered the front door and pulled out what appeared to be some sort of plastic musical instrument. The container seemed to be packed with hundreds of them.

"This is what is known as a *Bang Whammer*. It is the largest selling plastic percussion instrument in the world. You can do many things with them. For example, you can tie them together with this cord and use it as a xylophone or simply cap one of them and produce different octaves by hitting it on various substances. They are actually used by many musical artists including both rappers and jazz artists."

"It makes sense they should be sent to Jeremy then… maybe hoping for an endorsement?" asked Tom.

"Yes, it would make sense. But we checked with Jeremy's attorneys and they had no such agreement pending with this particular company."

"So how did it get here" asked Linda.

"It simply showed up outside the driveway one morning. It was marked musical instruments so we assumed it was band equipment. We brought it here into the garage and then opened it. This is what we found… two hundred and one corded *Bang Whammers*."

"Wow, what an ass-kicking party you could have with two hundred and one of those" remarked Tom.

"Two hundred actually, one was different."

"How so?" asked Linda.

"The packing invoice indicated two hundred of them. But I noticed that there was an extra one which was painted differently and was smaller than the others. So I removed it from the container and then started to play it... and I must admit that it was entertaining. But there was a strange muffled sound coming from the middle tube."

"Ah, a fly in the ointment, Watson" whispered Tom to Linda.

"When I removed the cap on the tube, I saw that there were something rolled up inside. I managed to shake them out and there they were...the Renoir and the Rembrandt."

"That's clever" said Linda. "So how did it get to the driveway?"

"It's unknown. As you know we are hesitant to call the authorities as we accepted the shipment and brought it onto the premises. We are now implicated. Have any suggestions, counselor?"

"Are there any shipping stickers anywhere on the container?" asked Tom.

"You can't see any stickers, but there is one barely legible stamp on the right side. It appears as if someone had tried to erase it but didn't quite get it all. Here it is" said Peter pointing to lower right hand corner of the crate. "It looks like it says U.S. Navy Rota - Coronado."

"Interesting" remarked Tom.

"But excuse me for a minute while I attend the men's room. However, feel free to play with the *Bang Whammers* while I'm gone" said Peter, turning to exit the garage.

"Okay, we might just do that." said Linda.

"These look like fun" said Tom as he picked one up and handed it to Linda. "This could be the start of a new career for me."

"I doubt it, Dizzy Gillespie" said Linda sarcastically as she examined the tubes. "Hmm… says *Made in Pakistan* on the bottom. And look, this is strange."

"What is?"

"The first two tubes appear to be plastic but this third one seems different."

"Let me see" replied Tom as he rubbed his hands over the tubes. "I think you're right. This third tube is slightly lighter, almost like it's… aluminum or titanium."

"I wonder if Peter noticed the same thing?"

"Don't know, but my instincts tell me we better not bring it up first. What do you think?"

"Let's wait to see if he comments on it."

"Okay, I agree."

After a few minutes the entrance to the garage opened and Peter reappeared.

"So how is the hootenanny coming along? Are you both accomplished Bang-Whammerers by now?"

"A couple of washboards and tubs and we're ready to tour." replied Tom.

"Splendid, I'll call Geffen tomorrow and arrange for a demo release. But in the meantime, it has grown late. Would you allow me to show you to your rooms? Your every need has been taken into consideration and I believe you will be quite comfortable for the night."

"Sounds good to me" replied Linda. "It has been a long day. What do you say, Sherlock?"

"Jolly good" replied Tom. "All I need to do is pick up my brief case in the front alcove."

"Don't worry" replied Peter. "Trust me, no one will steal it. It will be perfectly safe there for the night."

"Well alright …if you say so."

"Very good, now let me take you to the elevator to your rooms. Ah, just one thing counselor…so I may direct the chauffeur Ferdinand, will you be going home tomorrow or where?"

"No, not home come to think of it. I guess I'll just go to my friend's Emmet's house. He's my partner in the Swan which is a boat we just bought. We'll be driving to Ensenada tomorrow to sail it back to Santa Barbara."

"So you will be taking your brief case with you on the boat?"

"Yes, I guess so, why?"

"No particular reason really, It's just late and my mind is beginning to ask irrelevant questions…sorry."

"No worries" said Tom.

"Fantastic then" said Peter cheerfully. "Then this way please."

Peter walked them to the elevator.

"As I have some unfinished work in the garage, I shall bid you goodnight here. Take this to the third floor. Turn right as you exit the elevator and you will see two rooms opposite each other. The one on the right is for you, Linda and of course the one on the left is yours, counselor."

"No adjoining rooms? Curses!" said Tom.

"Sorry, but no hanky panky allowed" said Linda.

"I will not be seeing you in the morning but Ferdinand will be driving you back to Santa Barbara after your breakfasts. Linda, I hope you will accept the position for which we brought you here."

"Thank you, consider me hired."

"It is we who are grateful. I will send Ferdinand for you next Monday so you may start then."

"Whoo-hoo, a long weekend!" said Linda excitedly.

"And counselor, we will most certainly be seeing you soon. Now I bid you goodnight and wish you pleasant dreams" said Peter to the duo as the elevator doors closed.

"Well, congratulations. You're now employed again." said Tom.

"And you have a new client."

"Yes, we can now be off the welfare rolls."

"He didn't mention the aluminum tubes, did he?"

"No, he didn't…and that question regarding my brief case was rather odd, wasn't it?"

"That was random" replied Linda. "But it was probably nothing."

"Maybe" replied Tom as the elevator doors opened to the third floor. The two stepped out and turned right as instructed and proceeded ahead until the respective rooms appeared.

"Well, if a creepy mist starts to penetrate your balcony doors and suddenly a werewolf is offering you a cigarette, please feel free to come get me" said Tom.

"Or… if the revolving bookcase in your room turns into a hidden stairwell, feel free to come get me."

"Deal" said Tom as he hit Linda's upraised palm in a high five. "Sleep tight, Watson."

"You too, Sherlock" replied Linda as each turned and opened the doors to their rooms.

Both bedrooms were warm and comfy with fireplaces blazing, and neither Tom nor Linda had any problems falling asleep. All in the house seemed peaceful and quiet.

But later, as the grandfather clock in the living room chimed four bells, a dark figure appeared out of nowhere and moved quietly down the main staircase toward the mirror in the alcove. After tapping the cherub and opening the marble slab, the figure made its way to the vault. And after disarming the alarm system, it opened the gold vault and made its way to the *Piper*. Lifting the Plexiglas ever so carefully, a black gloved hand reached for and grabbed the *Piper*, replacing it with an identical replica and then while ever so carefully retracing its steps, reset the alarm upon exiting the vault. Making its way back to the front alcove, it opened Tom's brief case and placed the *Piper* at the very bottom of it before once again returning to the staircase and silently vanishing upwards into the darkness of the night.

~

The Taco Monster and U235

The smell of bacon and eggs cooking in the galley wafted its way up Ernie's nostrils and into what was left of his brain. Prying his eyes open one by one, he slowly began to emerge from his coma.

"Where the *hell* am I?" he moaned.

"It's alive, it's alive" yelled Tom.

"Cool it, Dr. Frankenstein" added Emmet. "The last thing we need right now is a gaggle of pitchfork laden serfs storming the marina with their torches demanding we turn over the *Taco Tequila Monster*."

"Oh shit" groaned Ernie. "My head, auugh…where the hell *am* I?"

"You're on the Swan, Taco Monster. Damage assessment…let me see your eyes."

Ernie opened one eye a slit as Tom took a reading.

"On second thought, you better keep them closed for a while or you'll bleed to death."

"You should see it from my side" replied Ernie. "Who put the IED into the Patron, anyway?"

"Goes with the territory when you drink the whole bottle, Mr. Alchy" added Emmet.

"He's not an alchy" said Tom. "Alchys go to meetings, he's just a drunk."

"Whatever"...Ernie replied, holding his head like it was going to explode. "Now where is the strychnine so I can end this misery?"

"I put it in here" replied Tom as he handed Ernie a bloody Mary -"hair of the dog, Ernie."

"It's not a dog, it's a mammoth elephant. Someone tell me what happened."

"You almost won the contest, champ" said Emmet. "Yep, you were almost the undisputed taco eating champion of the *First Voyage of the Swan 2001*. Congratulations!"

"Almost...what happened? I demand a rematch. The judges were biased."

"You mean Mona the waitress?" asked Emmet. "She rather did take a fancy to Ernie, didn't she?"

"I would call it more than a fancy" said Tom." She was serving him shots from her cleavage. That's not a fancy, that's a lap dance."

"Just answer one thing for me" said Ernie. "Did I have a good time?"

"Hugh Hefner would be proud, stud" added Emmet.

"Good, now explain to me how I got here, would you?"

"Well, I quit drinking after two beers while you two clowns continued with the debauchery. Then after a while, Tom quit. But you continued doing shots of Patron. Shit, Ernie you drank enough to put the Morman Tabernacle Choir into a coma for a decade!"

"After the twelfth taco, you conceded the contest. But you were like the energizer bunny. You just kept doing shots and beers and going and going" said Tom.

"After you passed out, we piled you into the Rover and drove across the border. I think the Mexican authorities thought you were a freeway dummy" said Emmet.

"I wish I were. I'd feel better! Where's the aspirin? My head feels like it's in a vice."

"Your head looks like a vice, cowboy" added Tom.

"I knew that was coming. I can read you like a book."

"Too bad you can't shut me up like one."

"This is no way to treat a man with *CRS*" groaned Ernie.

"What's *CRS*?" asked Emmet.

"*Can't Remember Shit*...now if you don't mind...the aspirin please. Just leave the bottle."

"You guys really ought to come up here, it's a beautiful day out" yelled a cheery voice from the aft deck.

"Be right up, Linda. Care for a cup of coffee?" asked Tom through the portal.

"Love one, thanks" replied Linda.

"And who might that be, Romeo?" asked Ernie.

"Her name is Linda. We met a few days ago in Santa Ynez. I'll fill you in later. She flew down to make the sail back with us. That way we'll have some beauty onboard so we don't have to just see your ugly face, Ernie."

"If my face looks as bad as my head feels, I'm in trouble."

"Right now, I can safely say that I've seen better faces on a hemorrhoid."

"Yes, how's everything in Loch Ness, champ?" quipped Emmet.

"Just dandy, thanks. Now go and let me die in peace."

"Okay shooter… mea culpa, mea culpa" said Tom as he closed the forward cabin door, leaving Ernie in his misery.

"Sometimes that guy makes Keith Richards look like the Flying Nun" said Emmet.

"Never a dull moment when Ernie's around" remarked Tom as he poured the coffee and then climbed topside to join Linda for their first day in Ensenada.

~

"So what makes you think a nuclear device is being built within the borders of the United States?" asked Stephanie.

"Military encryption codes" answered Meredith. "There has been a heavy flow of a foreign type of encryptions between the Middle East and certain European cities over the last few years but we cannot decode them."

"I thought you said earlier that they had ceased."

"They have ceased flowing into that area but not out entirely. There are communications coming out of Beirut, but only Beirut as far as we can tell. But, as I said, we can't decode them."

"Why not?" asked Stephanie.

"Because of fiber optic cable…it is the one medium that renders Echelon almost impotent."

"Really?" said Stephanie.

"Yes, decoding over fiber optic cable is the one thing Echelon finds difficult but we do know one very important thing."

"And that is?"

"We can tell that they are technical instructions of some type."

"Maybe they're just engineering specs or something."

"No, we're pretty sure what they are" responded Meredith. We can't interpret the code alphabetically but numerically we have been able to make some sense of it."

"Numerically?" asked Stephanie.

"Yes, numbers are more easily decoded than alphabetical ones. Don't ask me why, they just are."

"So what numbers are you talking about?"

"The numbers two, three and five, are you familiar with these numbers?"

"As in, say U235?"

"Yes, you may recall from your high school science class that a very small percentage of all natural uranium is uranium-235, the rest being mostly uranium-238. In order to produce a nuclear device, the U-238 must be enriched. Simply stated, this is done through aluminum or titanium tubes used as components in centrifuges. The process is really quite simple. Given one physicist and the correct parts, almost anyone can build such a device. It is a grave concern in these times."

"So you translated the numerals 235 frequently in the encryptions?"

"Yes, frequently…that and only one other word which was translatable only because of its rhythmical phonetic alliteration."

"Which was?"

"N-SEN-ADA" answered Meredith.

"Ensenada, that's a place in Mexico, isn't it?"

"Yes, it is. And for reasons I won't explain now, we believe that it has significance but we are not sure exactly in what way. But suffice it to say that we believe the components of such a device are making their way into the U.S. via Mexico."

"And what has all that to do with the art heist?"

"We know that this whole thing has something to do with the paintings and perhaps the phantom *Black Piper* but in what way we are clueless."

"Is there any record or history of this supposed *Black Piper* anywhere?"

"There may be. Our company sometimes employs certain rare individuals to do psychic and paranormal research in cases like this."

"You're joking!"

"It sounds preposterous but certain governments of the world have been involved with this sort of thing for decades now. Supposedly there are people in this world who have not only psychic qualities but also an innate ability to project themselves onto the astral plane in search of answers to the questions involving cases such as this."

"Astral plane, what is that?"

"We'll get to that later. Anyway, we contacted such a person over a week ago. Her name is Lynne Northland. She works for the company and she has been researching this case. She is flying here from the states this afternoon."

"Amazing, do you really believe in that sort of thing?"

"I can't knock it. As crazy as it seems, I have seen it produce results. And considering the stakes here, we must use every conceivable option."

"Well then" said Christian. "Perhaps we shall have some answers this afternoon when she arrives. In the meantime, may I offer anyone some coffee and knackebrod and then perhaps a tour of the scene of the crime, the *Swedish National Museum*?"

"Both sound good to me" answered Stephanie.

"I could certainly use a break to catch my breath" said Meredith.

"And I would be delighted to give you a personal tour of the world's finest art museum" added Glenn.

"Mer senare" said Christian as he hit the speaker phone button and ordered some morning sustenance for the group. "May this day be what we call in Sweden a *stor succe!*"

"And what might that mean?" asked Stephanie.

"It means a great success! I have a feeling that very soon we may just solve this case."

~

The Twins and the Psychic

D'Amato thought the briefing had gone well. As usual the status quo had been maintained. The reports were the same as they had been for years now. Navy and Coast Guard Cutter patrols were maintaining vigilance and successfully stopping the flow of illegal aliens and smuggling off the California Coast.

Of course, everyone knew it was bullshit. But as is common in the military, most times it is easier to let things stay as they are rather than rock the boat and create more work for the officer above you. That was a sure way to end your career or be passed up for future promotion.

And D'Amato wasn't about to rock the boat which he now knew would make him wealthy beyond his wildest dreams. All the centrifuge tubes, disguised as musical instruments, had been shipped and received according to plan. Now there was only one more shipment left and then he was done. The ten million dollar payoff from the CFAF was to be placed in the Swiss bank account as soon as the last component had arrived at the Santa Ynez estate.

It was brilliant, he didn't mind telling himself. Who would ever suspect that such a device was to be built in the garage of a fading and controversial pop star that would soon be off to Bahrain for months or even years before returning?

Schofield had done his work well. His impersonation of Harrison was perfect. No one suspected he was not Harrison, his identical twin brother, from whom he was separated at birth.

Commander Samuel Harrison had planned it that way. He had sired two illegitimate twin children in an affair with a French Ambassador's secretary in Beirut in the late-fifties. And when she died in childbirth, he had "adopted" one of the twins as a 'Lebanese orphan' and after returning to England, had secretly and simultaneously supported the other through surrogate nannies in small villages around Lebanon.

He had sent money to his son's Lebanese guardians and made sure his education was paid for but never had any association with him. Given the name Erimanc Feyad by his Lebanese guardians, he grew up an outcast in a sea of Sunnis and Shiites, Christian Maronites and other Muslim sects and had not adopted his English name until his twenty-second year.

But Erimanc had heard things over the years. More than once he had listened to a Lebanese banker or a teacher refer to the 'other one' while speaking to a mysterious voice on the other end of the telephone.

The twins had grown up not only looking identical but also had nearly identical educations. While one was at Oxford studying art history, the other was at the American University in Beirut studying similar subjects. For all intents and purposes, one was a nearly identical reproduction of the other except for one thing.

Erimanc Feyad had become a militant Muslim. Growing up amidst the tragic events that had shaped the hostilities of the region and the plentitude of death and misery, he advocated the destruction of Israel and the United States and he was determined to do something about it.

That desire became a reality the day he met Tony *the bull* D'Amato. Together they had become the most prolific art and antiquities smugglers to ever have operated out of the Middle East. It was a perfect union. Each had something to offer the other. Schofield was fluent in all the native languages. And because he grew up among the local villagers, he was always the first to hear when a new archeological site hit pay dirt or if an art thief needed a fence.

Anthony D'Amato had the connections to smuggle any art anywhere in the world through his network of naval supply officers and enlisted men, all on the take. Money talked in this world of Navy blue and gray. He knew military men did not make great livings so bribing most of them was easy. He also knew that none of them would talk as long as the money kept coming. By the time the flow of payoffs stopped, he would be long gone.

His network consisted of innumerable ships, trucks, other vehicles and shipping containers. And it was all accomplished under the auspices of the United States Navy. It was an organization which operated clandestinely within one of the branches of the most powerful military machines in the world.

When Harrison appeared in Syria as the representative of the Metropolitan Museum, D'Amato was shocked to see this identical likeness of Schofield in front of him but didn't say anything. When he told Schofield of the identical likeness, they immediately put two and two together and saw this as an incredible opportunity.

Kidnap Harrison, assume his identity and return to the U.S. to determine the best location to assemble the device. When Jeremy Princeton hired him to become his curator, Schofield thought it was almost too good to be true. The perfect location and situation had manifested itself and now the United States could experience the most cataclysmic disaster in its entire history.

~

"And how was your flight, Ms. Northland?" asked Meredith.

"It was very long but I had a layover in New York so I'm not too tired, thank you. And please, call me Lynne."

"Thank you, and call me Meredith. This is Inspector Johanson of the Stockholm Police, Glenn Ostrig who is the museum's curator and Stephanie Kensington who is with Interpol."

"I am pleased to meet you all" said Lynne. "Now we don't have much time so let me tell you what I am and why I am here. I am what is known as a 'paranormal psychologist'. Paranormal refers to anything which is unable to be explained or understood in terms of scientific knowledge."

"You're psychic in other words" added Stephanie.

"Yes, that I can be at times."

"Fascinating" said Glenn.

"Now, as you all now know the company suspects that parts to build centrifuges to enrich uranium are somehow being smuggled into the U.S. Needless to say, this is very serious. In such cases as this, the company uses every possible means to obtain any knowledge to thwart these attempts."

"Including using a psychic" said Glenn.

"Yes, in this case, the company has requested I use my special abilities to determine the connection between the paintings and another mysterious work of art called the *Black Piper*" replied Lynne. "We believe that they are all interconnected."

"So what did you find out about the *Black Piper* and why were the paintings stolen?" asked Meredith.

"I did find many references to the *Piper* in our computer data base, albeit they were quite nebulous ones. It is a mythical sphere which supposedly grants the owner great wealth and power but at the same time at some point during or after the ownership period its blessings become a curse. After much research, I did manage to find the wording of the curse in an ancient Aramaic language which has long been lost to modern mankind. It took our computers some time to translate three lines."

"And they are?" asked Christian.

"Something like; *Adore the beauty, beware the power, desires fulfilled thy visage shall alter. Light to darkness thy path shall be, a lesson in duality*" answered Lynne.

"Light to darkness?" asked Stephanie. What exactly is a curse, anyway?"

"Good question and I shall tell you. Curses are highly negative emotional charges which manifest themselves on the astral plane."

"Astral plane?" asked Christian.

"Yes, suffice it to say that the astral plane is a different dimension consisting of many different levels of vibration, very high to very low. Some think it is where we go when we die. Now what occurs when a curse is manifested is that the negative emotional charge finds its appropriate level on the astral plane and there it stays for eternity. It cannot be destroyed except by divine intervention."

"But how does it work?" asked Meredith.

"For example, let's say I kill your cat or your dog and your hatred of me grows to become so intense over time that the hatred begins to have a life of its own. Eventually, you die but that negative emotion does not, and instead seeks a new existence in the lower realms of the astral plane. Now if you have put the curse into words, the essence of the curse must follow its literal interpretation."

"*Light to darkness thy path shall be*?" asked Stephanie.

"Yes, in this case the receiver of the curse would be the owner of the object. But once again it is important to remember that although the curse cannot be destroyed, it can be neutralized" said Lynne.

"Neutralized, how?" asked Stephanie.

"We're not sure but we believe it is the motive for stealing the paintings. Somehow the paintings have the ability to either neutralize the curse or render it impotent.

And we presume now that the two reproductions are together somewhere with the *Piper* and the owner or perhaps a new owner wants all the benefits of the curse but of course none of the drawbacks."

"But how?" asked Stephanie again.

"As I said, the curse must follow the literal translation of the wording. In this case the wording *Light to darkness thy path shall be* is directed at the owner. But, if an object can be produced which changes the direction of the curse without changing the literal translation, the curse could be neutralized."

"What sort of object?" asked Christian.

"Like a talisman or a voodoo doll, something that would change the meaning of *Light to darkness thy path shall be* without changing the wording. The key to this mystery is somewhere in the paintings. But we can't find anything of any relevance to our theory in the paintings themselves" sighed Lynne.

"Light to darkness!!" screamed Stephanie suddenly. "Holy smokes, the key isn't in the paintings. The key is in the painters! Why didn't I think of it earlier? Oh my gawd, it is so obvious! Don't you see? It's something any art history student could tell you about."

"Well, let us in on it then" Meredith replied.

"Oh my god, I can't believe it, I can't believe it" yelled Stephanie eagerly.

"Calm down, please! Ta det lugnt!" said Christian.

"Okay, okay then... let me put on my art history professor hat and explain a few things to you. You see,

Rembrandt and Renoir are two of the world's most prolific and greatest masters" said Stephanie.

"So what do they have in common?" asked Christian.

"It's not what they have in common but rather what they don't. Let me explain briefly about each artist. First, Rembrandt was what is known as a *Baroque* master. His style is defined as painterly, meaning he painted vigorously with a heavily loaded brush. But more importantly, his innovation was the ability to substitute exact imitation of form with the suggestion of it."

"Very true... go on" said Glenn.

"Now, Rembrandt, like Leonardo DaVinci, was a master of a painting technique known as *chiaroscuro* which is Italian for 'light dark'. The technique uses a method where three dimensional volume is suggested though highlights and dark shadows. Objects are dramatically lifted from a dark shadowy background and then lit by a shaft or explosion of light. In other words, his paintings emerged from total darkness to radiant light."

"Of course, why didn't I see it earlier?" said Glenn hitting his forehead with his palm.

"Now Renoir, as you probably know was an *Impressionist*. They were rebels in their time and also broke the rules of the academic painting of their time. Long story short, the most conspicuous characteristic of the *Impressionistic Movement* was an attempt to accurately and objectively record visual reality in terms of the transient effects of light. In fact, light was the focus almost to the absolute exclusion of darkness and shadows."

"One a painter of darkness, the other a painter of light" added Christian.

"And now I understand also" said Lynne. "Thank you, Stephanie for clearing it up for us."

"Well then perhaps someone would be kind enough to clear this up for me" said Christian.

"Alright" said Stephanie. "Here we have two paintings. One's focus is upon light emerging from the darkness and the other's focus is the display of light to the exclusion of darkness altogether."

"*Light to darkness thy path shall be*" said Meredith.

"Yes, by possessing these two paintings with the *Piper*, the owner refocuses the intent of the curse away from him and onto the paintings. Remember that the curse's negative energy must follow the wording of the most literal translation. The paintings would act like a lightning rod. The energy is redirected onto a detour away from the owner of the *Piper* and onto the objects themselves, in this case the paintings."

"Unbelievable" said Christian.

"But it does make sense" added Lynne. "As I see it, in addition every original painting encapsulates or shall we say, reflects the soul of the painter. It is the painter's genius or the inspiration of the divine that becomes manifest in these original pieces."

"The divine?" asked Christian.

"Yes, and because it is a positive manifestation of the divine and because the curse is a negative emotional charge that can only be destroyed or neutralized by divine intervention, these two paintings, if kept together with the *Piper*, would comply with that curse. In this way, not only has the literal wording of the curse been literally carried out but it also has been effectively negated through divine intervention" said Lynne.

"So the energy is eternally trapped in an endless quest traveling from one painting to the other in its mission to fulfill the most literal wording of the curse, correct?" asked Glenn.

"Exactly… it is on an eternal merry-go-round, going from the Renoir back to the Rembrandt, proceeding from *light to darkness* over and over again, evil intentions of the curse being divinely neutralized by the paintings" said Lynne.

"Most fascinating" said Christian.

"But Schofield and D'Amato don't have the real paintings in their possession so the curse will still be in force, correct?" asked Stephanie.

"Yes, well then they are in for a surprise without a doubt. They presume they are now immune from the curse and they are not. And something else just occurred to me" said Lynne. "There is another possibility as to the meaning of why the paintings were stolen."

"And that is" asked Meredith.

"To divert attention away from the paintings so the focus of the investigation would be more on the heist itself" she replied.

"Why would they do that?" Christian asked.

"Not sure" said Lynne. "But as I recall, both artists spent their entire lives in either Paris or Amsterdam. Maybe that has something to do with it."

"With what...what are we looking for here?" asked Christian.

"If nuclear parts are being smuggled from the Middle East to the U.S., what would be the most obvious routes?" Lynne asked. "Is anyone familiar with European or Middle Eastern geography?"

"If I remember correctly, if something were to make its way to Amsterdam from say, Iraq... it would have to go through Turkey and Eastern Europe...not exactly a pleasure cruise" added Christian.

"And if something were to go from the Middle East to Paris it would be on a route just a little further south. It would not be a picnic going through the Ukraine, Slovakia and Germany. Whatever they are shipping, it would never make it without being discovered somewhere" said Stephanie.

"Christian, do you have a pen and piece of paper?" Lynne asked.

"Yes, right here" said Christian passing the items to Lynne.

"Just guessing the parts are being shipped from Pakistan, let's just jot down a few routes."

"Why Pakistan?" asked Christian.

"I'm psychic, remember?"

Taking the pen, Lynne wrote four lines.

Pakistan to Paris
Pakistan to Amsterdam
Paris to Amsterdam
Amsterdam to Paris

"Now what do you see?" Lynne asked.

"Lots of P's and A's?" said Christian.

"Well, this is what I see" said Lynne, circling and then enlarging the letters.

pakistAn TO paRis
pakistAn TO amsteRdam
pAris TO amsteRdam
amsterdAm TO paRis

"You mean that is what you actually see right now? I don't see that" asked Christian.

"I have ways of seeing that you do not, my friend."

"Obviously, so what does it mean?" Christian asked.

"Well, all of the letters I see spell *ATOR*."

"What do you think it means?

"It could be an anagram of some sort but it's also a partial mirror image" answered Lynne.

"Mirror image?" asked Christian.

"In the mirror, except for the R in the wrong direction, it would spell *ROTA*" answered Lynne.

"Let me see what the possible anagrams are for these four letters" said Meredith.

"I'd say TORA or TARO and that's about it" added Stephanie. "TORA is a Japanese word so it must be TARO or ROTA."

"It could be, let me see what the office says about ROTA" said Meredith as she pushed the buttons on her cell phone.

"What is ROTA, do you suppose?' asked Stephanie.

"Not sure but I sense water and ships" answered Lynne. "Let's see what Meredith can find out."

After a few minutes Meredith put the cell phone away after a short conversation.

"Well, here's our answer. There is a U.S. Naval base in Spain near Cadiz and it is named *Rota*. And it appears to be on the most direct shipping route from Beirut via the Mediterranean."

"Tack sa mycket!" said Christian. "I do believe this psychic thing works. What else do you know that we don't?"

"I know that we need to start booking transportation now and that we all will be hearing a lot of Spanish very soon."

~

La Cucaracha and New Orders

"Gosh, what a gorgeous day" said Linda to Tom as he handed her a coffee and some carrot cake.

"Si señorita, esta un buen dia. Quieres a bailar con mio anoche y mas tarde coochee coochee?" asked Tom as he bent Linda backwards as if dancing a Tango.

"Easy caballero, I speak Spanish. Sorry, but no '*coochee coochee*' for you, amigo."   "Porque no, señorita? Mexico is the *Land of Enchantment*."

"I don't know what land it is but I am not that enchanted just yet, tiger. But it was a nice try."

"Oh well, as someone once said, the position is ridiculous, the pleasure is momentary and the price you pay is for the rest of your life."

"Now that's a romantic little love sonnet sure to win the heart of any girl."

"How about the shortest sentence is 'I am' but the longest sentence is 'I do'?"

"How nice…take me now, I'm yours."

"The direct approach is always the best."

"I swear that you men haven't a clue."

"We haven't a clue about what?"

"About love…..amore…"

"Well, I love dogs. I'm thinking about getting one."

"Why would *you* want to get a dog?"

"I can't take a fish for a walk?"

"Oh, that's funny" Linda replied sarcastically.

"By the way, eat this carrot cake we bought for breakfast. Carrots are good for your eyes" said Tom.

"How do you know carrots are good for your eyes?"

"Have you ever seen a rabbit with glasses?"

"I think my mother used to tell me that one, Mr. Comedian" said Linda.

"Your mother must have had a great sense of humor."

"Let's leave my mother out of this."

"Whatever you say, Watson…so it looks like we've got a day or so to kill here while Ernie recovers. What do you think about exploring Ensenada a little?" asked Tom.

"Absolutely, it looks like a beautiful city."

"Emmet, you want to go explore a little today?" Tom yelled into the hatch.

"I'm up for it."

"Good, then let's head up to Hussong's for a bloody Mary."

"This time of the morning?" asked Emmet through the hatch. "It'll be as empty as a chapel in a whorehouse right now."

"This is Mexico, partner…probably still people there from last night."

"Okay then, be right up."

"That means another half hour" said Tom to Linda. "The guy's got a heart of gold but sometimes he's slower than a grandma on a freeway."

"Supposedly, there is a tourist attraction called *La Bufadora* which I would like to see" said Linda.

"What is it?"

"It's a huge blowhole where the ocean spews its waters up and out of some rock. I read about it and it's supposed to be quite impressive."

"A blowhole...sounds like some ninth circuit judges I've known."

"Then you'll feel right at home" Linda chuckled.

"Sounds better than a poke in the ass with a frozen dishrag" said Tom with a sneer.

"Oh stop it, you'll enjoy it."

"Okay, let's go then. Emmet, we'll meet you at Hussong's." Tom yelled into the galley.

"Okay, I'll be right there."

"And don't forget your wallet."

"Why did you tell him that?" asked Linda.

"Because he always forgets his wallet...the guy is overly generous but it must be passive aggressive. Not that money's a problem, but I always end up paying which puts him in the 'tighter than a bull's ass in fly season' category sometimes."

"Gawd, where do you get these expressions? They are funny, I must admit."

"Glad you approve, I hear them... I say them."

"You are a bad boy sometimes."

"Oh Lord, make me good but not just yet."

"Let's go before we're struck by lightning" said Linda as she grabbed Tom's arm and escorted him down the gangway as Emmet's baritone voice sang from the galley *"La cucaracha, la cucaracha... ya no puede caminar."*

~

Chief Warrant Officer D'Amato was late for an appointment at the Admiralty Office. The CO had issued him a 'Change of Status' directive which meant he was to be reassigned on a new mission. It couldn't have happened at a worse time. The last shipment of aluminum tubes was due to arrive at Coronado from Ensenada via Rota in five days and he had to be present to be sure the tubes were unloaded and dispersed before the supply officer found them.

As he walked along the naval dockyards approaching Admiralty Headquarters he knew he may have to invent a reason as to why he couldn't leave his present duty station. Once the CFAF check was certified in Zurich he could disappear and never be seen again but this was more than inconvenient and could definitely ruin his scheme.

"Shit, I didn't serve all those years in that hell hole of the Middle East to see my plans go up in smoke now" he thought to himself. "I need to think of an excuse to tell the old man."

"The Admiral is waiting for you, D'Amato" said Ensign Whiff outside the CO's office. He entered Admiral Roberts' office and immediately could see that he was not in a good mood.

"Chief Warrant Officer D'Amato reporting as ordered, sir" snapped D'Amato in a salute.

"You're late again, D'Amato" growled Admiral Roberts. One more time being tardy and I'm writing you up...at ease. Here are your new orders. The U.S. Navy needs you to make a delivery. You will be disembarking today."

"A delivery?" asked D'Amato.

"The United States Navy has sold an 'E' class Bronstein frigate and two 'C' class Halcyon patrol corvette boats to the Mexican Navy. You will be joining Captain Dehnel on another corvette and you will embark today at 1500 hours to see that the other ones are safely delivered into the hands Mexican Rear Admiral Jose Gonzales within seventy-two hours. The crews will be returning on your vessel."

"Might I ask where they are taking delivery, sir?" D'Amato asked.

"Yes, but let me tell you something first. Three days after tomorrow is Mexican Navy Day. It's one of their biggest celebrations and President Vicente Pero will be attending the festivities. They're going to stage a mock terrorist attack which will be thwarted by the Mexican Special Forces."

"Yes sir?"

"The vessels you are to deliver will be participating in the ceremonies. It's a big deal so don't screw it up. We want those ships delivered within 72 hours. Pick up your charts from Ensign Whiff on your way out."

"Aye, aye sir, but might I ask where this is all going to happen?"

"Ensenada, D'Amato… now get your ass in gear and ship out! That is all."

As D'Amato saluted and turned to exit the CO's office only one thought crossed his mind. "This is too good to be true. The *Vice President* will be very pleased!"

~

The Train to Cadiz

Christian and Stephanie boarded the AVE high speed train to Seville at the Atocha station in Madrid. It was to be a two and one half hour trip to Seville and another one hour to Cadiz across the bay from Rota Naval Station where they would try to meet with the base commander.

Stephanie and Meredith had both reported their findings to Interpol and Company headquarters and Stephanie had been issued a travel directive to Rota Naval Base in Andalucia via Eurostar from Madrid to investigate any possibilities of illicit smuggling happening on the blue line.

As the investigation directly affected the Stockholm Museum heist, Christian had been issued orders to accompany Stephanie on the train trip. Meredith and Lynne had also been assigned to investigate and flew ahead to scout for any surreptitious smuggling operations in Cadiz.

"Well, this should be a fine trip" remarked Christian. "I have never seen southern Spain. It is supposed to be very beautiful country."

"Just remember we're on assignment" said Stephanie. "We really need to keep our eyes peeled for any suspicious activities. If indeed there are parts moving to Cadiz via land it would be on this train."

"Ja, something out of the ordinary…such as what?" asked Christian.

"Just keep your eyes open" she said as they both took their coach seats near the windows.

"Varsagod, there's a rather strange sight" said Christian pointing to three very loud and disheveled youths all piling into one of the washrooms."

"I wonder what's up with that?" asked Stephanie. "Let's keep our eyes on them."

As the train began to move forward out of the station, the conductor began collecting tickets. "Billete, por favor" he said as he approached their seats.

Stephanie and Christian were the only passengers in the car. After handing him their tickets, they turned to see him walk toward the washroom and knock on the door which flashed an *in use* sign. "Billete, por favor" he said as he knocked on the door. The door opened a crack and an outstretched hand though the crack in the door delivered one ticket to the conductor before he continued on his journey through the cars.

"Well, well…stowaways" said Stephanie. "Shall we turn them in?"

"I have an idea to teach them a lesson" said Christian. "We have to change trains at Seville so let us see if they try the same thing on the next train."

"Just what did you have in mind?"

"Wait and see" answered Christian.

As the train rocketed its way to Seville and the Costa de la Luz, Stephanie noticed how breathtaking the country was. The villages that could be seen from the train seemed to be delightful and untouched places surrounded by ancient forts and hills which exhibited a wealth of flora, fauna and natural beauty.

The Muslim youths had long since exited the washroom and were generally being loud, rowdy and obnoxious, much to the irritation of Stephanie and Christian and the other passengers walking through the car.

"Time for security" said Stephanie. "We're out of our jurisdiction here but we can turn them into the local authorities in Seville."

"Ja, but we can also tell them to behave now!"

Christian got up and as he approached the youths, one of them reached into his coat pocket and pulled out a Jambiya dagger.

"And what do you want, infidel pig?" the youth snapped at Christian.

"I want you to shut up and behave like decent human beings, Abdullah!"

"Screw off and leave us alone" said the youth brandishing the dagger.

"I'll take that" said Christian as he gingerly pulled his 357 Magnum out of its side holster and pushed the end of the gun barrel flat against the youth's forehead. Cocking the weapon, he snapped back "go ahead and make my day, Ahab!"

The youth dropped the dagger and as Christian kicked it back to Stephanie, one of the other youths grabbed for Christian's arm. As if holding a squash racquet, Christian backhanded the 357 muzzle across the youth's face knocking the youth back against the window seat.

And as the third youth leapt up to do battle, Christian stepped back and kicked the youth in the throat, sending him backward over the seat, landing face down with a splat in the aisle.

Within seconds, the conductor and a security guard burst through the door.

"Que es esto? Que pasa agui?" yelled the guard.

Christian flashed his badge and holstered his weapon. "We have some very loud and disrespectful children here. This one pulled a knife on me", said Christian pointing to the seated delinquent. "The others attacked. I was simply defending myself."

"And here is the weapon" said Stephanie handing the dagger to the security guard.

"Entonces, venga con mio ahora, jovenes!" said the guard with his Lugar drawn. After handcuffing the trio, he began to move them forward to the detention cabin with a swift kick to the butt.

"What are you going to do with them?" Stephanie asked the conductor.

"Unfortunately, there is nothing much we can do. Muslim youths like these with their bellicose and aggressive attitudes are all over Europe now, particularly in Paris and Amsterdam. They hate the world. If we file charges in Seville, the police will just let them go anyway."

"You can't send them to jail?"

"No, and if they could ever find them again to put them on trial, which they wouldn't, we would have to be witnesses which is most inconvenient. There are just too many of them and the jails cannot hold them all. They would probably just get probation anyway. It is fruitless. The best lesson they will ever have is what you have just shown them."

"Ja, I am aware of the growing problem in those cities. It is most unfortunate."

"We will watch them and escort them off the train in Seville. That is the best we can do. May I apologize for this incident and wish you a pleasant trip for the rest of your journey? Buenos Dias" the conductor said as he turned and left the car.

"Well, that was impressive, Harry Callahan" said Stephanie. "Next assignment, find the *Scorpio Killer*!"

"Ja, I have never had a chance to use that line before. It *was* rather fun."

"Okay, Dirty Harry, enough of that. What say we go to the bar car and get a glass of wine? After that little episode I need to calm my nerves."

"Good idea, although you know you have a dalig mage" answered Christian.

"And that means?"

"You have a weak stomach."

"Oh is that so, Mr. Viking man? We'll see about that."

"But on the other hand, you also look skitsnygg today."

"Meaning?" asked Stephanie.

"You look gorgeous" answered Christian.

"Okay, the second one cancels the first. Now that you're back to where you started, let's go get that drink."

Once in the bar car, Stephanie ordered a glass of *San Semillon* and Christian a glass of *Chateaneuf de Pape* after which they leaned back in the comfy sofas to enjoy the views and their glasses of wine.

"I had no idea the Muslim youth were so prone to lawlessness and violence" said Stephanie.

"I know in Paris, one has to be most careful now not to wander into the wrong places such as the 'cities' which are nothing but ghettos for the unemployed Muslim youth. They would kill you in an instant just for being an American" replied Christian.

"Yes, it is a huge problem worldwide. But then poverty and ignorance are the parents of violence."

"Ja, there are no simple solutions. I can tell you I am glad to be Swedish. So far we have managed to insulate ourselves from these foreboding developments."

"Your *weather* keeps people away. It has nothing to do with insulation. It's just *too damn cold* where you live!" Stephanie laughed.

Christian laughed also. "Perhaps you are right. But let's not solve the world's problems right now. This is my chance to get to know you a little better."

"Back at you, Thor" replied Stephanie, and as she turned to him and gazed upward into his eyes, he leaned forward to kiss her.

"Let's wait" she said, placing her finger tips on Christian's lips. "We're on duty. I promise I will make it up to you later."

"Promises, promises, not even one little kiss?" replied Christian.

"Down boy, we'll see about that later. Right now, let's keep our energies focused on the mission, okay?"

Christian sighed and leaned back into the sofa. "You are correct. Our mission is first... *fan ocksa.*"

Stephanie laughed and lifted her glass in a toast. "May our mission be successful in more ways than one" she said as her eyes burned into his.

"Garna" said Christian meeting her gaze with an equal passion. Raising his glass to meet hers he said "ja, in more ways than one."

~

The Stowaways and the Bartender

Except for the one clash with the Muslim youths, Christian and Stephanie noticed nothing out of the ordinary on their journey. The remainder of the rail trip to Seville was uneventful although the surrounding countryside was breathtaking.

As they exited the train upon arrival in Seville, Christian noticed the same youths were boarding the Eurostar for Medina Sedonia on the next rail platform.

"Well, looks like those 'javla idioters' are changing trains. Watch my bags for a minute. I will be back shortly" Christian said to Stephanie as he ran for the platform.

"Um...okay" said Stephanie.

Trailing behind the youths at a safe distance, he could see through the car windows that the three of them once again were squeezing into the washroom. Jumping onboard, Christian approached the restroom and knocked on the door as the train began to pull away.

"Billete, por favor!" Christian said in an authoritative voice.

As the restroom door opened a crack Christian took the ticket from the extended hand, stuffed it into his pocket and walked toward the exit door of the car. And after exiting, he proceeded to jump off the side step onto the platform as the train slowly pulled away and the conductor entered the car and began to check tickets.

Rejoining Stephanie in the terminal, she noticed he had a huge smirk on his face.

"And what sort of mischief have you been up to?" she asked.

"Oh, nothing much, but let's just say we will be needing only one ticket for the remainder of our journey, but three Muslim youths will very likely be thrown off of their train much earlier than they ever expected."

"You are incorrigible but I think I love it" said Stephanie as she turned and walked hand in hand with Christian toward the loading platform for the train to Cadiz.

~

"Three bloody Mary's please" said Tom to the bartender.

"Wow, I guess you were right, Tom. This place is still jumping" Emmet said.

"We almost never close" said the bartender to the trio as she began to make their drinks. "People come here to party and we accommodate them as best we can."

Tom noticed that the female bartender was very attractive although a little on the slim side.

"Where are you guys from?" she asked.

"Santa Barbara" answered Emmet. "We're here to sail a boat back."

"Well, welcome to Hussong's, mateys. My name is Janae and I'll be your bartender."

"Thanks" said Tom. "This is quite a crowd for nine in the morning."

"This is the second shift. The midnight to nine is the real killer."

"You have to work those hours?" asked Tom.

"Only occasionally...I'm usually the day bartender" she answered.

"Whatever brought an attractive girl like you down here south of the border?" asked Emmet.

"Well handsome, as long as you ask... long story short... Smith grad, ex-model, New York club owner... got tired of the phony wannabes and flew down here for a vacation. Never went back, it's been nearly ten years."

"New York to Ensenada... like night and day" added Linda.

"That it is" said Janae. "But after growing up in Connecticut and then doing the New York thing for far too long, I was ready for the polar opposite."

"You said you were a club owner?" asked Linda.

"Yes, started something called the *Model Café*. It was a business venture for five ex-models who needed to capitalize on their notoriety while they still could. It never flew."

Just then someone from the kitchen began gesturing for Janae's attention.

"What is it?" Janae yelled.

"It's your roomie on the phone! She lost the key again."

"Be right back. It's my roommate Suzanne. She's always getting locked out. I have to tell her where I hid the spare key…excuse me for a sec" she said as she turned and strolled to the kitchen phone.

"Wow…that girl is beautiful but very thin" said Linda.

"Maybe she has a summer house in Somalia" added Tom.

"Are you kidding me, she's skinnier than a Tijuana crack whore" added Emmet.

"That girl could walk through a harp" added Tom while gazing at the lean beauty.

"Model Café…can you imagine?" asked Emmet. "Busiest room in the house would be the restroom where they're all throwing up after dinner."

"And I wonder what they order for desert?" Tom asked. "I'll have a double espresso and a TicTac please. No wait, make that a TicTac and two forks."

"Shut up you two!! There you guys go again. Doesn't anything but looks matter to you? I swear… men are so shallow."

"We're not shallow, we're practical" added Emmet.

"Then you mean you're practically shallow" added Linda.

"Why… just because we noticed she's so flat you could plant wheat on her chest?" asked Tom.

"Boobs, golf and football… men can't think of anything else, can they?" asked Linda.

"Sure, there's beer too" Tom replied.

"The point is that in spite of the fact she's beautiful, although a little thin, she also seems like a very nice girl. Doesn't that thought cross your small minds?"

Tom and Emmet looked at each other and then simultaneously turned to Linda.

"NAH" was the dual response.

"But I will say that she's sure cuter than the other bartender. She's so ugly she'd have to sneak up on a glass of water to get a drink." Tom replied.

"That rear is so big the space shuttle could circle her moon" laughed Emmet.

"Stop it right now. You two are impossible! Like you two are a couple of Greek Gods or something."

"Hey, how a guy looks doesn't matter to a woman. You're all attracted to money and power. Besides, you brought it up, Squires" said Tom teasingly.

"I was just making an observation, not a judgment. And we are all NOT!"

"Yes you are. But we weren't judging her either, just stating facts. Actually, come to think of it, she'd be a perfect match for Emmet" said Tom.

"And why is that?" asked Emmet.

"Well, she's so thin and you're a light eater."

"I am?" asked Emmet.

"Yep, as soon as it's light you start eating."

"That's an old joke, counselor" said Emmet.

"But poignant."

"I may be a tad overweight but at least I don't date bimbos."

"I don't date bimbos" Tom said adamantly.

"Oh give me a break. That last one you dated practically had a sign on her forehead."

"What sign was that?" asked Tom.

"It said: *Space to Let - Long and Short Term Leasing Available.*"

"For your information, she was very intelligent. She was matriculating at City College."

"Matriculating? You call *stripping* matriculating? She was a city college dropout."

"She'd had a difficult semester and needed a change."

"That girl couldn't *change a quarter.*"

"Alright, children, that's enough, no more bickering" Linda interrupted.

Just then Janae returned from the other end of the bar. "So what are you sailors up to today?" she asked

"We thought we might go see La Bufadora. That is, if I can stand being with these two fifteen year olds for a full day" answered Linda.

"It's a beautiful thing to see. Need a guide? I'm actually off in an hour, just filling in on my day off until the regular barkeep returns."

"That would be great. I would love to have some female company to offset the effects of having to be with these two Neanderthals. You're hired."

"Right on, sister, it would be my pleasure."

"The more the merrier" added Tom. "But did you mean to say you're not the regular bartender?"

"Nope" answered Janae. "I'm the regular *owner*...now how about having another round on me?"

"Really, well in that case, how could we say no? Digame tres mas, senorita... por favor!"

Janae made four Margaritas and raised her glass in a toast. "Here's to amigos, amore and luz de la luna."

"Friends, love and moonlight?" asked Tom.

"Down here it means friends, love and Tequila" replied Janae.

"How about adding one thing?" said Tom.

"Sure what would that be?

"*Good wind*…after all we are sailors."

"Okay then, here's to amigos, amore, luz de la luna y buen viento."

"Salud and to good wind" said the foursome as they all raised their glasses in a toast to the eventful stay yet to come in Ensenada.

~

The Monk and the Chapel

"Wow, what a killer view" said Meredith.

The room at the Parador Hotel in Cadiz stood next to the Genoves Park and was built on the promontory overlooking the Bay of Cadiz. The palm trees swayed in the breeze along the boardwalk. The bougainvillea seemed to be in full bloom in spite of the winter season. The white sandy beaches were filled with colorful umbrellas and the boardwalks hosted a multitude of bicycles, surreys and carts selling lattes and sangrias. Locals were strolling and playing volleyball. It could have almost been summertime.

"Really awesome, I guess it's been quite warm for it being winter. That's okay with me. After Stockholm, I could use some sunshine" Lynne said.

"I'm with you on that and I think we've earned this view and a little sun after all the schlepping we did today" Meredith replied. "Five ports here in Cadiz and we struck out. Nothing out of the ordinary and the Port Authority assured us there was no possibility of anyone smuggling nuclear parts without detection. What do you think, do you believe them?"

"I didn't sense any duplicity and it seems like all the security checks were efficiently in order but I don't know. I just have this feeling that there is something here that has been waiting for us. I don't know what it is but I have this intense feeling that whatever it may be, it is going to find us" Lynne replied.

"Well, whatever it is, it will have to wait because I am famished. What say we go get something to eat?"

"Sounds good, the restaurant downstairs looked interesting."

"Let's go then, I could use a glass of wine."

"I could use a martini" said Lynne as the two grabbed their room cards and headed for the door.

Shutting the door briskly behind her, Lynne noticed as the door slammed that one of the screws holding the door numerals upright suddenly had fallen off causing the room number to turn 180 degrees, inverting the numerals.

"Whoa, this is not a good sign" she exclaimed.

"Why is that?" asked Meredith.

"Look what happened to our room number."

"So it's upside down, so what? Looks like room ninety-nine just became room sixty-six. We'll let them know downstairs, let's go."

"Meredith, have you noticed we are also on the sixth floor?" asked Lynne.

"Yes, I told you the view was awesome."

"Room number sixty-six on the sixth floor. That makes three sixes, Meredith. Three sixes is the mark of the devil!"

"It's just a coincidence, Lynne."

"No, I don't think so. I think it's an omen. I can feel something happening now. Something is trying to communicate and it's not the good fairy."

"Well, I think it's just a coincidence. Can we go eat now, please? You can fill me on the recent communiqué over a martini. Lucifer will have to wait."

"Alright, I'm right behind you." replied Lynne.

Lynne and Meredith entered the elevator and pushed the button for the first floor. The generators kicked in and the car began its downward journey. Suddenly between the third and the second floor the lights flickered and the power disappeared, bringing the car to a sudden halt while leaving the two in total darkness.

"Oh shit, this is not good" exclaimed Lynne.

"Push the emergency button" said Meredith.

Just as Lynne reached for where she thought the red button might be, the power suddenly seemed to reactivate, turning the lights on and pulling the elevator downward with a shudder.

As the elevator car reached the first floor and the door opened, a handsome young man in a gray suit was waiting for them. He had a look of panic on his face.

"I am so sorry, señoritas. I hope you were not frightened. It is the *Levante Wind* which causes these power failures. Please forgive us and allow me to make it up to you. I am Señor Dustin Lambada and I am the hotel manager. What can I do to make this experience go away?"

"Well, as a matter of fact, we were just going to have a bite to eat in the restaurant" said Meredith.

"In that case, allow me to show you the way" said Dustin as he led the girls down the brightly tiled hallway filled with flowers to the restaurant which overlooked the pool and the Atlantic.

"Jean Pablo, these ladies are very special. Todo es complimetario, entiende?" said Dustin to the Maitre D'.

"Si, Senor" said the Maitre D'.

"Why, thank you, Senor Lambada" said Lynne. "Usted es muy amable."

"It is my pleasure, Señoritas! If there is anything I can do for you while you are here, do not hesitate to call me. I am at your service."

"Thank you" said Lynne and Meredith in unison as Dustin bowed and returned to the lobby area.

The Restaurante del Parador was elegant but at the same time seemed relaxed and casual. The Moorish influence of the region was evident in the ambience of the interior décor. Bright and intricately inlaid Spanish tiles decorated the floor and walls and Mosharabia chairs with Moroccan cushions made the room comfortable and warm amidst elaborate iron work.

"Interior o en el patio?" asked the Maitre D'.

"It's a beautiful evening" said Lynne. "Is the patio okay with you, Meredith?"

"Absolutely" she answered.

The patio of the restaurant was open aired and was surrounded by beautiful Moroccan Palm trees. A warm breeze caressed the guests as they sipped their early evening sangrias and munched on seafood tapas.

As the Maitre D' escorted the two ladies to an outside patio table, Lynne noticed a very unusual looking man dressed in a monk's robe sitting nearby. He was short, bald and had a gray beard growing beneath his half spectacles which balanced on the end of a rather large nose. He was nursing a Sangria and spoke with a British accent as he conversed with an older lady.

"Well, it is nice to see at least one of the church's chosen practicing heterosexuality for a change, isn't it?" asked Meredith.

"And imbibing at the same time... now that is an enlightened monk" said Lynne.

"Buenos tardes, Señoritas, my name is Luis and I am your server this evening" said a tall dark Spaniard in his early twenties. "May I help you with your menu selections?"

"If Enrique Inglesias had a twin" thought Meredith to herself.

"Yes, thank you, what do you suggest?" asked Lynne.

"The Fritura Gaditana is excellent if you like spicy seafood and the Lenguado Segun is so light it will melt in your mouth."

"Excellent, we will have one of each...okay Meredith?"

"Sounds good, and what would you suggest for vino?"

"May I suggest the *Candado de Huelva*. It is a very dry light wine with just the slightest hint of grapefruit and lemon. It is delicious with seafood."

"Absolutely then, we will have a bottle."

"And also one dry Kettle One martini with one olive, please...shaken but not stirred" giggled Lynne.

"Muy bien, Señoritas" replied Luis as he gathered their menus and hurried off to the kitchen.

"Well, now this is nice" said Meredith taking a sip of her Peregrino.

"Yes, it is but I have this uneasy feeling that I just can't seem to shake" Lynne replied.

Lynne glanced over at the next table and the monk seemed to be smiling at her.

"Well, well, looks like friar Tuck is flirting" Lynne remarked. "That old guy should be ashamed of himself" she said laughingly. "Let's see what happens, shall we?"

With that, Lynne put her chin on her fist and returning the monk's gaze, gave him a big wink.

"Now we'll see how serious he is about his vows" Lynne said jokingly.

"Oh, you are too funny" Meredith replied as she turned to see the monk's response.

The monk beamed and smiling broadly while peering over his glasses, he threw each of them a kiss.

"Oh my gawd, he is totally gay, dude. How funny" said Meredith.

The monk, giggling, lifted his glass to toast the girls. Meredith and Lynne lifted theirs in mutual admiration.

"Well, it looks like we've made a friend, doesn't it?" said Lynne. "I needed a bit of joviality to take my mind off the paintings and the *Piper*."

And as she said the word *Piper*, the eyes of the monk which had been focused on her lips opened wide as if suddenly gripped in terror. His mouth dropped open and his body seemed frozen in fear as his wine glass slipped from his hand and crashed on the tiles beneath him.

Then something very strange happened. Within seconds the warm sun disappeared behind what looked like a huge black layer of ashen fog. The warm breeze suddenly turned cold and gusty and hail began to fall on the patrons. Covering their heads with menus and table cloths, the once comfortable diners ran for the main building as the winds increased in ferocity. Tables and chairs were being overturned and just as Lynne and Meredith got up to join the other people in retreat, a wrought iron gate near the pool was lifted off its hinges and was propelled by the gusts directly toward Lynne and Meredith as they ran for shelter.

But just before the gate could strike the two women, a deft pair of sinewy hands gripped the two by their arms and pulled them out of the gate's flight path as it sailed by their heads, striking the stucco wall of the patio before crashing to the ground.

"What the hell is going on?" asked Meredith. And as the two turned around in shock, there stood the monk.

"You both are now in danger, please come with me immediately!" he screamed above the howl of the gale.

Lynne and Meredith got to their feet and scurried after the monk who hustled them into the lobby of the hotel and then down a flight of stairs to an elevator door which had a sticker marked *Out of Service*. There stood Dustin Lambada.

"We must hurry, Brother Bob" said Dustin, and as he pushed the button in a sequence, the door opened into a tunnel which was illuminated by electric lighting.

"What is this and who are you?" asked Lynne.

"Please, you must trust me. Your lives are in danger. Now quickly, please follow me" exclaimed the monk.

Lynne and Meredith followed the monk who ran nimbly like a wide receiver through a labyrinth of tunnels and caves until they reached what looked like an ancient chapel. Dustin trailed them, all the while looking over his shoulder.

The chapel contained a very old wooden staircase which rose in a circular fashion to a series of platforms connected by wooden ladders to a steel door which had been fitted into the surrounding rock above. The chapel itself was run down with an old crucifix mounted above another ancient door which had been sealed with chains. The wood of the altar was rotting and torches on the walls of the ancient priory burned intensely.

Finally able to stop, the two tried to catch their breath. They felt like they had just sprinted a 440.

"What is this and who are you?" Lynne asked between gasps of breath.

"I am so sorry to have met you in this manner, ladies. But your lives were in great danger. Welcome to the original Oratorio De Santa Cruz. But may I introduce myself? I am Brother Robert with the Franciscan Order. Please call me Brother Bob."

Dustin stood at the rear on alert in case they had been followed by anything.

"But what is this place and why were our lives in danger?" asked Meredith.

"This is one of the original chapels of Cadiz. It was built in the fourth century and remained buried until twenty-eight years ago when the Order had it excavated. It is located strategically directly beneath the Cathedral and is a secret, needless to say."

"But what was with that wind and the sudden gale? Is that what they call the Levante wind? And why do you say we were or are in danger?"

"That was not the Levante, not even close. What just happened has been predicted for centuries. We just didn't know what circumstances would bring it to life again."

"What... what is *it*?" asked Meredith.

"You spoke the WORD which *it* has been waiting for" said the Brother.

"What word? Who's *it*?" Lynne asked.

"*Piper*" said Brother Robert

"The word *Piper* caused a storm? I don't think so" said Meredith.

"I shall explain all to you" said Brother Bob." But that was no mere storm. That was what we call in the Order *El Viento de Satano.*"

"The wind of Satan" said Lynne.

"Yes" said Brother Bob. "And now that it knows you are here, it will seek to destroy both of you."

~

The Cab Driver and the Buffalo Snort

"Taxi!" yelled Stephanie as Christian hustled their bags out of the claim area of the Cadiz train station which was situated by the port of Cadiz. A rather shabby old blue Citroen Cab screeched to a halt at the curb. On its doors was painted *Muy Baritisimo*.

"Hola Señor y Señorita" said the cabby in a friendly manner while hopping out of the cab to retrieve their luggage. "Me llamo Antonio. Donde quiere a ir?"

The driver appeared to be in his early twenties and was dressed in linen trousers and a freshly washed white shirt. He had dark olive skin, was cleanly shaven and his hair was black and neatly trimmed.

"Very nice," Stephanie thought to herself.

"What does baritisimo mean, amigo" she asked.

"You are American. Welcome to Cadiz, Señorita. It means that with my cab you will get the very best service at the least expensive price."

"Sounds good to me" answered Stephanie. "Let's go, vamonos Christian."

"And where are you going, Señorita?"

"Parador Hotel, por favor" she replied.

The Taxi driver suddenly froze in his tracks. His face, which moments before was deeply tanned, turned white as a ghost.

"Muy bien" said Antonio almost as if in a trance. After a few deep breaths and a shake of his head, he seemed to regain his composure and threw their bags into the trunk.

"Something wrong?" asked Stephanie.

"No Señorita, nada" he replied as he loaded their luggage and then began the drive to the hotel.

A warm breeze caressed the faces of Stephanie and Christian and as the sunlight danced across the surface of the clear turquoise ocean like a million diamonds, the cab exited the train station and began its drive along the tranquil bay lined with parks, boardwalks and beachcombers.

"This is so nice" said Stephanie. "No offense, Christian, but I think I much prefer this to your Scandinavian winter."

"Ja, I agree and no offense taken, Stephanie. It is very beautiful here. Antonio, has the weather been this beautiful all week?"

"Si Senor, it has been very beautiful."

"Tach och lov" answered Christian. "We are here for a few days and are hoping it remains this nice."

"It should be...unless it happens again" replied the cabby.

"Unless what happens?" asked Christian.

"Yesterday something muy curioso happened, Señor. I was driving my taxi by the bay. One minute it was calm and beautiful with a nice breeze. Then out of nowhere, a black dust covered the sky and los vientos almost blew my taxi into the sea. It has never happened before. I do not understand it."

"But Cadiz is well known for its Levante winds. Don't you think it was just a very powerful one?" asked Stephanie.

"No Señorita, this was different. I have lived here all my life and I have never seen anything like this. One minute the weather was magnifico and the next minute it was horroroso! The winds blew like a hurricane. There was much destruction all around the bay. Palm trees were uprooted and windows were broken by the lluvio de escombros. Many of the boats in the harbor were blown over or beached and a sticky ash was everywhere. It was like something evil had come to life, I tell you."

"I wonder ... do you think Meredith and Lynne saw the same thing?" Stephanie asked Christian.

"May I ask where your amigos were staying?" asked Antonio.

"At the Hotel Parador" answered Stephanie.

Hearing that, Antonio suddenly pulled over to the side road and slammed on the brakes. He crossed himself and turned to Christian and Meredith in the rear seat. His face had grown sheet white and sweat had begun to pour down his face.

"What is it, Antonio?" asked Stephanie.

"You must swear to me that you will never tell anyone this."

"Okay" answered Stephanie.

"When the wind almost blew my taxi off the road and into the sea, I stopped and got out to try to see what was happening. The wind was blowing hard and there was mucho sand and dirt in the air. It was difficult to see but I did see something and it was muy terrible!"

"And what was that?" asked Christian.

"The black ash and wind had taken a form, Señor. It was huge like a…how shall I say…like a……giant head and it had the hornillos of a goat. It had the most horrible yellow eyes that shone in the ash and as I looked up, it glanced my way before it started to whirl and descend on the city. It was El Diablo, I tell you."

"And just where did it descend? Did you see?" asked Stephanie.

"Si, I was in clear view of where it descended, Señorita."

"Yes, so where was that?"

The driver sobbed and crossed himself again. Pointing in the direction of the beach hotels he said "alli, it came down right over there, right at the Hotel Parador!"

~

"This place looks like a swap meet gone Latin" said Linda as the barrage of churro vendors in the alley began their assault on the foursome.

"Yes, it's a little touristy but we're not far from *La Bufadora*" said Janae. Once we get there you'll be impressed. I guarantee it."

"And just what does La Bufadora mean" asked Tom.

"The Buffalo Snort" Janae replied.

"Phew…some of the aromas from these Taco stands would be enough to stun a buffalo" Tom remarked. "I see where they got the name."

"Here in Punta Banda they don't have a lot of refrigeration. I'd stay away from these stands but in Ensenada you're probably okay" said Janae.

After a short hike away from the vendor area and around the point, the four arrived at their destination. The beauty of the small scalloped bay and rocky shores nestled in the hills rushing down to the sea was breathtaking.

Rounding a corner on the trail, a fountain of water spraying into the air in the distance alerted the group that they had almost reached their journey's end. Arriving at a wooden platform with stairs descending to another platform near the natural attraction, they ran down the stairs in anxious anticipation of the next show. Finally reaching the bottom platform, they stopped to rest and take in the beauty of the cliffs and ocean.

La Bufadora blew another small geyser and the resulting mist drenched their faces.

"Wow, this is truly amazing" said Linda. "Can we go closer?"

"Absolutely" said Janae. "Here, jump the fence and move a little closer so you can see just how beautiful the geyser can be up close." As the trio jumped the fence and advanced cautiously toward the hole, Janae stealthily began to move backwards.

Suddenly a huge wave crashed against the cliff forcing the water into a gigantic geyser thirty feet tall which moments later became a flowing waterfall cascading back down upon Tom, Emmet and Linda.

"Oh shit!" the trio yelled in unison as they turned in an attempt to escape the shower of sea water. Safe under the shelter, Janae was laughing hysterically. "You three look like drowned rats."

"We won't forget this, gringo girl" said Emmet.

"Okay Janae, this is war, you know" said Tom reaching for the towels which she had stuffed into her backpack.

"Relax guys" Janae replied still chuckling. "I'm sure you'll have your chance to get even. It's a warm day, you'll dry off."

"Actually, that was fantastic" said Tom. "Come on, Linda, we're already wet so let's go again."

"Uh…I think the Park Ranger might not like that" said Janae. "Look up there," she said, pointing to the top platform.

Looking up, there was a Mexican Ranger with aviator glasses peering down at them.

"Okay, maybe next time" said Tom, drying himself off.

"So, that was fun" said Emmet. "Where are we going next?"

"We're going to *Papa's and Beers* for lunch and tequila, gringos." Janae replied while turning to ascend the platform to start the hike back to her Jeep. "They have a very unique way of serving tequila shots. You'll enjoy it."

"Tequila shots for lunch? I think not" said Linda.

"Come on Squires, loosen up" replied Tom. "You're on vacation… when in Rome."

"We'll see" Linda replied.

And as the foursome began their hike back to Janae's Wrangler, Ernie began to stir once again back at the Swan. The heat and sunlight of the late morning had awakened him from his alcohol induced comatose slumber. And as he began to regain consciousness and turn over in his berth, a flat tin key fell from his cargo shorts' pocket and onto the cabin deck with a clink.

"What was that?" he said, awakening from his stupor. Pulling himself up on his elbows and holding his head, he crawled over to the side of the berth where the noise had come from. Peering over the side, he saw a flat tin key attached to a chain lying on the deck. Reaching down, he grabbed the key and then turned over on his back with a groan. Blinking and focusing his eyes, he read the inscription. It said:

> *U.S. Navy Munitions Facility*
> *Ensenada, Mexico*
> *Property of U.S. Government*

"Holy shit" Ernie muttered to himself. "Now how in the hell did I ever end up with this?"

~

The Black Paintings

As the trio's cab approached Parador Hotel, Stephanie and Christian could see in the distance an army of workers busy white washing the sidewalks and the entrance façade of the hotel.

"Looks like spring cleaning time" said Stephanie.

"They have been busy washing the area since yesterday, senorita! The ash is muy dificil to remove. You will see when we get there" said Antonio.

The cab rounded the corner and began to make its way up the long circular driveway that led to the Grand Parking area. The putting greens and croquet course located on the front lawn, normally a verdant green, were covered with a soot-like substance that gardeners were attempting to wash away with powerful water hoses.

"Looks like black snow" said Christian.

"Except it doesn't melt" added Stephanie.

Antonio pulled the Citroen into the Valet area and stopped alongside a *Bentley Continental GT* and an *Aston Martin Vantage*. Bellmen were busy loading luggage into both vehicles.

"Looks like some people are leaving" said Stephanie.

"Si, Senorita, since yesterday's diablo storm, many of the hotel guests have decided to leave. As you can see, the hotel is not el mismo ahora."

"Ja, we can see that" said Christian as he opened the Citroen door and stepped out onto the sooty pavement.

"Ewwww, it doesn't smell so great either! What the hell could have caused this, do you suppose, Christian?"

"Some sort of strange weather phenomenon having to do with global warming, perhaps?" he answered.

"Let's see if we can find Lynne and Meredith. Maybe they can shed some light on this" said Stephanie.

"Ja, but I wonder why they are not answering their cell phones."

"Probably has something to do with the storm. Let's go see if we can find them. Antonio, wait here while we check in. It may be awhile."

"Si, Senorita, no problema!"

The hotel entrance was comprised of two large double glass doors with a gold embossed *PH on each*, and as the doorman pulled one of them open for the pair, Stephanie noticed that inside a group of workmen and security guards seemed to be carefully beginning to take down paintings from what appeared to be an art exhibition which had been showing in the main lobby.

"Let's go see what all the commotion is about, shall we, Christian?"

The two strolled over to the start of the exhibition where mounted on the wall were fourteen paintings in a row.

"Oh my god, this is macabre" said Stephanie arriving at the first painting on exhibit. "What's with this one of a man eating a small dead body? This is grotesque."

"A skrackfilm, this is. Or as you Americans say, this looks like it's from a horror film" said Christian.

"They are known as the *Black Paintings*, Señor Y Señorita" said a voice from behind them.

Stephanie and Christian turned around. There was Dustin Lambada.

"Allow me to introduce myself. I am Dustin Lambada, the manager of this establishment."

"Oh, ah...hi... I'm Stephanie and this is Christian" said Stephanie offering her hand.

"A pleasure" said Dustin, bowing and returning the handshake.

"So what is the story with these?" asked Stephanie as she and Christian began to move down the line of the exhibition. "Oh my god, these are morose, almost evil."

"Si Señorita, these paintings are indeed macabre and terrifying. We are removing them as many people think they had something to do with the terrible storm yesterday."

"Who painted them?" asked Stephanie.

"They were painted by Fransisco Goya and yes, they portray very intense, haunting and dark themes."

"Of course, Goya...I am aware of his work but not these ones. These are like a nightmare, Senor. What's the story here?"

"Well then, as you probably remember, Goya is known as the last of the old masters and the first of the moderns. His paintings broke out of neoclassicism into a sort of realism."

"Yes, as I recall from my art history courses, his paintings gave him a nice life."

"Yes and no… he became a portrait painter to the Spanish aristocracy at one point, and then during the Napoleonic wars with Spain he ironically served as a court painter to the French."

"Sounds like a nice cushy life."

"It was, until the French invaded Spain. Then he began to see the atrocities and horrors of war. His paintings and drawings began to reflect these characteristics."

"Yes, I can certainly see that."

"That in combination with his going deaf at the age of forty-six, began a downward spiral into deep depression over the rest of his life."

"Too bad Prozac wasn't available then."

"Yes, from what you see here, he could have used some" said Dustin. "He continued to paint and was quite prolific in spite of this illness. And in 1819, at the age of seventy-two, Goya moved into a house outside of Madrid called *Quinta Del Sordo* or *A Deaf Man's Villa*. It was there that he painted these on the walls of the house. They were later converted to canvas as you see here.

"Outside Madrid, sounds pastoral to me, so what happened?"

"As I said, after the Napoleonic wars, he had developed an embittered attitude about humanity. He had an acute awareness of panic, terror, fear and hysteria. Today we would define it as post-traumatic stress syndrome. He also had barely survived two illnesses. The result is what you see in front of you."

"These are *gnarly*."

"What is the word *gnarly*, Stephanie?" asked Christian.

"It means creepy, Christian."

"Ah ja… laskigt."

"So what is with this delightful one?" asked Stephanie.

"This is known as *Saturn Devouring His Son*. It portrays the Roman god Saturn eating one of his children. Fearing a prophecy that one of his children would overthrow him, according to the myth, Saturn ate each of his children."

"How enchanting" Stephanie remarked sarcastically.

"Yes indeed… here he depicts this act of cannibalism with startling savagery."

"Ok, moving on" said Stephanie looking to her right.

"Very well, as you can see as we go in this direction, each painting becomes more morose and dark."

"What's this one about, it's eerie?"

"It's called *Fight with Clubs*" answered Dustin. "Two men fight to the death but neither can escape the blows of the other due to their knee-deep entrapment in quagmire. Some think it is a premonition of what is happening between the United States and the Middle East today or perhaps between the two extremist factions of the Christian and Islamic religions."

"Most interesting" said Christian.

"Yes, most interesting" Stephanie agreed.

As they moved down the line of fourteen paintings, Stephanie noticed one was much larger than the others. Walking quickly toward it and stopping in front, her face suddenly became aghast with horror.

"What is it, Stephanie?" asked Christian.

Arriving where she stood, Christian turned and looked at the painting. "Otrolig!" he exclaimed.

"Yes, quite a coincidence, isn't it?"

"Skit ocksa, this is unbelievable."

The image was ominous and gloomy. It depicted a silhouette in front of a crowd of grotesque human beings with sunken eyes and horrifying features. The figures huddled together, leaning inward toward the silhouette. Only one dark haired woman seemed resistant to the crowd, and she sat at the far right, dressed in navy blue and holding some sort of key on what appeared to be a chain.

And toward the forefront of the painting was the image of a being dressed in a dark robe. It appeared to be directing its supplicants, who knelt in submission. It held a black sphere and had what looked like a snout emerging from its head, on top of which were horns.

"The horns of a goat... Christian, it's Antonio's hallucination!

"Ja, it would seem that way."

"It is titled *The Great He-Goat* or *Witches Sabbath*" said Dustin. "Tell me please, someone saw this diablo?" he asked, pointing to the devil-like image.

"Yes, our taxi driver saw it yesterday before the storm. He told us about it on the cab ride over here."

"May I ask you something, por favor?"

"Sure, fire away!" replied Stephanie.

"What brings you to the Hotel Parador?"

"Two of our friends are supposed to be staying here."

"May I ask what they're names are?"

"Sure, why not? Their names are Meredith and Lynne."

"*Three and one, the riders come*" said Dustin.

"Vad?" asked Christian.

"Yes, what does that mean?" asked Stephanie.

"Perdoneme, Senor Y Senorita, it is a verse from a very ancient document."

"Do you know where our friends are?"

"Yes, they are hiding."

"Hiding... from what?"

"I will answer that question soon but in the meantime they are fine, trust me." I can take you to them but not just now. I am expecting a visitor. Can we meet back here in say, two hours?" asked Dustin.

"Okay, that will give us the time to go visit Rota Naval Base."

"Muy bien, Señor Y Señorita...entonces, let us meet in Café Los Arcos here in two hours."

"Ja...in two hours" said Christian.

And as Christian and Stephanie returned to the taxi and Dustin returned to his office with the TV monitor of the hotel lobby, a very tall and sinister figure entered the hotel and approached the front desk. It wore a black trench coat and a black Fedora. Sunglasses covered its eyes and gloves covered its hands. And as it approached the front desk, activity in the vicinity seemed to cease as all eyes were drawn to its presence.

"I need a room, anything will do" he said to the front desk agent. He spoke in a strange almost indiscernible way that frightened the girl at the desk.

"Yes sir, we have a double king available for..."

"Yes, that will do" barked the figure.

"Very good, just sign here please" said the girl politely. "Will you be paying with a credit card, sir?"

Slapping a 500 Euro note on the desk, the figure removed its glasses to sign the hotel register. And as it did so, the girl gasped. And after she handed the figure the room card, it turned and quickly walked to the stairs as the girl turned sheet white.

"What's wrong?" asked the other front desk agent.

"His eyes...did you see his eyes?"

"No...why...?"

"They.....they..."

"What, what is it?"

"They were yellow!"

"Yellow, are you sure?"

"Yes, yellow! When he looked at me....it.....it was...... terrifying!"

"Here, sit down" she said, pulling a stool up behind her. "I wonder what he signed on the register."

Pulling the register over, she looked at the signature and gasped.

"What did he write?" asked Nicki.

"This is creepy!" "It's signed *Wx*...what is that?"

And as the girls tried to shake off the eerie feelings, Dustin Lambada had been observing the front desk on the monitor. "He's here...right on time...just as predicted" he said to himself. And within seconds he was on his way down the stairwell leading to the tunnel connected to the Oratorio de Santa Cruz.

~

The Guardian

"Here's the email from Interpol" said Stephanie to Christian. "This should be interesting." Stephanie clicked on the attachment on her laptop. The email had arrived just in time as she and Christian were on their way to Naval Base Rota to make inquiries that probably were not welcome.

"Ja, so what does it say?" asked Christian.

"Okay, here it is".

January 23, 2006
Special Agent Stephanie Kensington
Interpol
Agent Kensington,

FOR YOUR EYES ONLY

Transcription procured from US General Accounting Office website email Implications will be obvious. Proceed to Rota and see Commander Ferguson. Attempt to procure all cargo manifests for the last three months. Do not expect cooperation.

Special Agent J. Cristen – Headquarters Vienna

Okay cool…It is addressed to Rear Admiral A.S.Crane, Department of the Navy. Washington DC. And it says:

Dear Admiral,

This letter is part of our continuing effort to address inventory management activities within the Department of Defense (DOD) as a high-risk area. We recently reported that the Navy used unauthorized activity codes to requisition over 2.6 billion in new government property and 100 million in excess government property over the last five years. As a consequence, this property was vulnerable to fraud, waste and abuse.

No shit, duh! Okay, so blah, blah…*as discussed with your office, this letter focuses on the U.S. Navy's use of unauthorized activity codes from January 2004 to December 2006.*

Okay, this is good. It says:

Scope and Methodology

We interviewed Navy service point personnel and obtained a list of Navy activity codes identified as unauthorized to acquisition. We provided the codes to the Defense Automatic Addressing System Center and the Defense Reutilization…. blah blah….oh god, is this bureaucratic bullshit or what? Next it says:

Results in Brief

As of December 2000, the Navy maintained 4239 activity codes identified as unauthorized to requisition government property. In addition, safeguards to prevent unauthorized activity codes from being used to requisition government property failed.

Hmm….can you imagine that? Okay, next we have…

Background

Okay, blah blah blah…..*An activity code is a six position alphanumeric code that provides a uniform method for recording the receipt and disposition of property.* Okay, so yahdee yahdee yahdee….. *An activity within a military service that is assigned the responsibility of controlling activity code data is known as the service* point.

Now let's see….it says *there are three codes not authorized to requisition and they are activity codes beginning with FA, FY and JM.* Oh, here we are… *as of June 2004, there were 1239 FA, FY and JM codes used.*

This is good…. *It was determined that of the 1239 activity codes that should not have been used to requisition, 65 had been inappropriately used to requisition $19.6 million in new property and of this number 98.1 % was associated with two Naval base supply depots, namely Rota, Spain and Coronado, U.S.A.*

Bingo! Next……

Conclusions and Recommendations for Executive Action
We recommend that the Secretary of Defense direct the Secretary of the Navy to:

1.) *Verify whether the requisitioning authority for all Navy activity codes is categorized accurately and review procedures to ensure* blah blah…oh my God, this is such bullshit…listen to this.

2.) *Evaluate current safeguards in appropriate databases to ensure that unauthorized activity codes are not used to requisition government property.*

And listen to this ....

Agency Comments and Our Evaluation
Regarding our recommendation to verify the accuracy of
requisitioning activity codes and review the procedures, the
following actions were sited:

   1.) *The Navy will review procedures to ensure...*blah
       blah blah....*more specific policies will be developed.*
   2.) *The Defense Automatic Addressing System Center*
       will be asked to edit all incoming transactions blah
       blah....
   3.) *The Navy will propose significant changes to the*
       DOD Activity Address Directory Admin"istrator...
       yahdee yahdee yahdeee. And then it ends with:

As arranged with your office, we plan no further distribution
of this letter and it is signed:

Sincerely Yours,
H. Robert Harkin II
Managing Director
Office of Special Investigations GAO

And
Sheldon Gages
Director Defense Capabilities and Management GAO

   Do you believe this crap, Christian? Looks like
they're using government funds to purchase illegal goods

with American taxpayer dollars and then the Naval and governmental authorities are turning their heads. What the hell is going on here?"

"I believe in America you call this a conspiracy, ja?"

"More than a conspiracy, Christian…for the GAO to cover up this sort of activity, it would need to have the nod of someone very high up in the government."

"Ja, it would certainly seem that way!"

Just then the taxi rounded a curve and straight ahead appeared the entry gates of Naval Base Rota. The cab pulled up to the white gate that stretched across the road and came to a stop. A very tall but stout Marine guard popped out of the guard shack.

"May I help you, sir" asked the Marine.

"Si, señor, this señor and señorita have an appointment" answered the cabby.

"Who is your appointment with, please?" asked the Marine.

"The Base Commander" answered Stephanie.

"May I see some IDs please?"

Stephanie and Christian handed him their Interpol and Stockholm Police badges.

The Marine took them and after looking them over and handing them back he said "wait here please" and reentered the guard house.

Stephanie and Christian could see him dialing the phone and appearing slightly uneasy in his conversation. After several minutes he returned to the taxi.

"Commander Ferguson is not available but Chief Petty Officer Nicholski will see you instead. Proceed through the gate past the barracks and go left. Then go two blocks to the Administration building on your right. Here are your passes. But do not, I repeat *DO NOT* at any time leave your vehicle except to access the Administration building. Is that perfectly clear?"

"Perfectly" answered Stephanie.

Handing the trio the passes, he reentered the guard house and opened the gate. Antonio put the taxi in gear and roared ahead.

It seemed like a pretty typical Navy base. Everything was painted gray and there was no grass and no plants anywhere. The dirt outside the billets had been raked and everything seemed spotless. But something just wasn't quite right. The base appeared to be without life. There were no people. And except for an occasional parked military jeep or deuce and a half troop transport, the place was devoid of activity.

"Where is everyone?" asked Christian.

"Good question, the place looks deserted" said Stephanie. "This is very odd. Antonio, have you been here before?"

"I was here many years ago, Señorita. In my youth, this base was very busy always. Military ships in and out toda la vez and always many sailors were here. I was here once with my father to attend a base carnival celebration for children."

"So what happened?"

"No one knows, Señorita!" answered Antonio. "As the years passed, activities on this base became more secretive and it is rumored that any sailors who come here now are not allowed off the base. No one knows why. It has hurt the local economy mucho."

"Too bad" said Stephanie as the taxi passed a transport carrier parked by the curb. "That's weird Antonio, stop! Back up to that truck back there."

"Why, Stephanie?" asked Christian.

"I saw something very strange back there. I'm going to take a look."

Antonio backed the cab up to the deuce and a half truck and Stephanie jumped out.

"So much for not exiting the cab" said Christian.

Hopping out also, he approached the vehicle with Stephanie and peered into the interior through the window.

"Shit, there are no guts to this vehicle" said Stephanie.

"Tokig" said Christian. There is no steering wheel, seat, transmission, nothing."

"Bizarre," said Stephanie. "There's another truck. Let's check it out."

Running over to the other vehicle on the next block, they once again peered through the window.

"Same thing" said Stephanie. "What is going on here?"

"It would appear that these vehicles are for appearance only. And judging from the lack of personnel on this base, I'd say this place is just a shell…a, how do you say in America…a paper tiger?"

"Yes, an American Naval base used for some other purpose. And look at that truck over there."

One block away was a newly built billet next to which was parked a huge flat- bed hauler. Its bed had been lowered at a 45 degree angle to the fence encircling the compound and it appeared as if the billet were going to be loaded unto the flat bed to be transported somewhere else.

To the casual observer it would appear as if construction activity and transportation were happening but upon closer scrutiny, one might notice that the tires were a little too black to be real.

"Those tires look odd to me" said Stephanie.

"Let's take a look" Christian replied.

Jogging over to the truck they peered into the cab of the flat bed.

"Same thing again, Christian, said Stephanie. "And look at these tires."

Christian bent down and put his hand on the front tires. "Skitkalt, Stephanie, they're cement."

"Now that's a rough ride. What the hell is up with this, Christian?"

"Well, perhaps this Nicholski can answer some questions. Let's go see him, shall we?"

"Absolutely," Stephanie replied and with that both she and Christian jumped back into the taxi. "Let's go, Antonio."

Antonio slammed the Citroen into gear and sped off toward the Administration building. Another Marine guard stood at ease in front of the administration building and officer's headquarters. He was in dress blues and had a cell phone on his hip next to his sidearm. The marine opened the taxi door.

"Good afternoon, Chief Petty Officer Nicholski is located on the second floor. Please proceed there and go to the second door on the right. Do not, I repeat, do not waiver from this course. Is that understood?"

"If you say so, Marine" Stephanie saluted as she and Christian exited the cab and began to walk up the stairs leading to the entrance.

Entering the building, they could see four offices on the first floor. Each office had an embossed emblem on the door indicating various departmental officers. The office on the left was marked *Commanding Officer Ferguson*.

"Christian, start to walk slowly up the stairs, I'm going to check something." Then pretending to drop her bag, Stephanie ducked and crawled over to the first office marked 'Ferguson' and turned the doorknob.

"Locked" she whispered to herself and proceeded to each of the other three offices. All were locked.

"Very strange" she said to Christian as she rejoined him and the two once again began to ascend the stairs. Reaching the top, the two turned right and saw a door marked *Chief Petty Officer Nicholski* and underneath read *OPERATIONS*.

Inside, another Marine in dress blues sat behind a gray desk scattered with papers. As they entered, he stood up and said brusquely, "wait here, please", and turned to knock on what apparently was Nicholski's office door.

"Yes" barked a voice from the interior.

"The people are here to see you, sir".

"Alright, send them in and go to chow, Sergeant."

"Aye, aye, sir" replied the Marine.

Stephanie and Christian entered the office.

"I'm Senior Chief Petty Officer Nicholski, what do you want?"

The Navy lifer who stood in front of Stephanie and Christian projected more than an air of gruffness and inhospitality. He appeared almost hostile. He was middle-aged and balding. And he had a gray goatee growing out of more chins than a Chinese phone book. He was fairly tall but had a huge belly that made him look like a huge greasy pear dressed in Khaki.

"I'm Chief Inspector Johansson of the Stockholm Police and this is Special Agent Stephanie Kensington with Interpol" answered Christian. "I believe your CO here at Rota has briefed you as to why we're here."

"Okay, sit down" he growled as he took his chair and then lit up a half smoked stogie which had been smoldering in a dirty military ash tray half filled with cigarette butts.

Stephanie perused the room. It was painted all gray and the walls were bare except for two drawings of what looked like two separate Navy battleships which flanked a photograph of Nicholski shaking Vice President Ernst Lamply's hand at some sort of ship christening ceremony. The furniture was Spartan and consisted of Navy requisitioned chairs and a desk. It could have been a room right out of a World War II Fred MacMurry movie except for a computer on the gray steel desk.

"Something about smuggling nuclear parts or some other bullshit, I think that's what he said."

"Yes, we have reason to believe that the Naval base here at Rota is being used as a way station for smuggling via Beirut and the Middle East" Stephanie answered.

"And what the hell makes you think that? As the supply officer her at Rota, I'm gonna' tell ya', nothing gets by me. If that were happening I'd know about it, and it ain't, so good afternoon" barked Nicholski.

"Chief Petty Officer Nicholski, would you mind if we looked over your cargo manifests and supply requisition orders for the last three months?" asked Stephanie.

"Would I mind? Oh please do, anything your little hearts desire. Whad'ya think I'm crazy? The only way you're getting those records is with a gun and a mask. And even then, you wouldn't get off this base alive!"

"I'm sure your CO Captain Ferguson would see it differently" replied Christian.

"Well, we'll just see about that! Now if you'll excuse me, I'm taking inventory, so good afternoon."

With that, Nicholski rose and strutted over to the office door which he opened for Stephanie and Christian. He then turned and returned to his desk chair. After he had sat down again, he snickered; "don't let the door hit you on the way out" without looking up.

Stephanie and Christian looked at each other in disbelief.

"Mister Nicholski, if you don't cooperate we will get official clearance for the release of that information" said Stephanie.

"Don't break a leg, now get out of here. I'm busy."

With that, Stephanie rose and angrily headed toward the door. And as Christian began to follow her out of the office, he turned and said to Nicholski "du ar inte klok!"

"And what the hell is that supposed to mean? Is that some sort of threat or something?"

"It means that on my word, you will regret this!" And with that, Christian picked up the ashtray on Nicholski's desk and threw it against the back wall where it connected with a crash, shattering the glass and tearing the photo of Nicholski and the Vice President.

"Well, you son of a bitch!" yelled Nicholski. And as he reached for his side drawer, Christian drew his magnum and aimed it with both hands directly between Nicholski's legs.

"All right, cowboy, you made your point, now get out" said Nicholski, holding his hands high.

"Ja, we will leave, *COWBOY*, but not until I see what's in that drawer! Now, very slowly move away from the desk with your hands behind your head."

Nicholski hesitated.

"NOW!" yelled Christian.

As Nicholski moved backwards, Christian handed Stephanie the Magnum and moved to open the drawer. Inside was a Beretta M9 and as Christian grabbed the pistol and removed the cartridge, he also noticed an envelope with a waving American flag and an eagle in the upper left hand corner.

"Hmmm, marklig, what might this be?" he said to himself as he picked up the envelope, pulled out the letter within and began to read it. At the top of the cover page was a header marked by the same waving American flag and eagle.

"You read that and you're a dead man!" shouted Nicholski. "I guarantee your life will end soon if you do!"

Nicholski made a slight move toward Christian and Stephanie immediately cocked the hammer on the Magnum. "Don't even think about it, Gomer Pyle!" she yelled.

"We'll see about that" Christian replied. And as his eyes moved down the page and began to read the document, a slight smile began to cross his face.

"Skamlig, skamlig!" he said shaking his head. "This is quite astounding, ja."

"You bastard, you are dead, DEAD!" yelled Nicholski.

"What is it, Christian?" Stephanie asked.

"It is a requisition order, Stephanie. A most interesting requisition order, indeed!"

"So what, what is so interesting?"

"It's an order for centrifuges."

"Centrifuges… let me see!"

Giving the magnum to Christian who turned and pointed it at Nicholski's head, she began to peruse the document.

"Holy shit, a requisition for FA: 500 titanium tubes for centrifuges from Pakistan marked *Bang Whammers*… point of delivery Rota – Ensenada via CFAF 19, Departure date 1/22/06. That's four days ago. This is frigging huge! Those things are on their way to Ensenada now."

Nicholski had broken out in a cold sweat.

"And read the last line, Stephanie" said Christian.

"It says: *DESTROY IMMEDIATELY-FOR YOUR EYES ONLY...* and it's signed, *Ernst Lamply, Vice President, United States of America.*"

And with that statement, Nicholski had snapped open a ring on his right finger with his thumb and within moments had deposited a small capsule into his mouth. Biting down on it, Stephanie and Christian could hear a crack and smell the aroma of bitter almonds and within seconds the Chief Petty Officer had dropped to the floor, dead.

~

The Brief Case and the Committee

"Good morning, Peter, did you sleep well?" asked Jeremy, pouring a cup of coffee.

"Marvelously, Jeremy, thank you…and you?"

"The Ambien always helps, but still my sleep is restless" Jeremy replied. "I guess I'm worried about my finances too much and all the other disasters the *Piper* has caused in my life. There must be someone who is interested in purchasing it. It needs to be gone, care for some coffee?"

"Yes, thank you" Peter replied, pouring himself some. "I have a feeling that Linda Squires is going to be our good luck charm. With her pre-qualifying our buyers, we can put together some irresistible packages that collectors will find most interesting. We can include the *Piper* in the sale of those packages. Consider it out of your life."

"I wish I could. With all of this negative publicity I'm getting, I need to change what is happening to my life. I agree with you, leaving Tierra Bella would be best now. Is that palace in Bahrain still available?"

"Not only is it available, but I have made arrangements for you to live there for the next few years. You're right. You need to escape this barrage of negative publicity which the media has concocted. Once you are gone a few years, everything will be forgotten. The American public has the attention span of a lightning bolt."

"I hope you're right" said Jeremy. "But how did you arrange for the palace when my financial condition is so well known?"

"Let's just say, as you know, I have certain Middle Eastern connections. Actually, I have arranged for you to leave tomorrow. A certain entity from that area of the world has sent their private jet and it will be in Santa Barbara tomorrow to transport you."

"Tomorrow, when did all this come about?"

"I thought that in light of the fact that you now had in your possession two stolen paintings from the Stockholm Museum, it would be best if you left the country until we can determine the best way to return them without implication" said Peter. "I made arrangements within the last few days, actually."

"But what about the curse, Peter, what does the curse have yet in store for me?"

"Trust me... I truly believe that the curse can no longer harm you."

"But how do you know this, Peter?"

"You are just going to have to believe me, Jeremy. That is all I can tell you now."

"You know I have always trusted your advice, Peter. I hope you are right."

"You can be quite sure the curse can no longer affect your life. Now go devote your day to packing your things. The sooner you can leave the U.S. the better."

"That is fantastic. Then I will pack up my things today. What a relief to be free again" said Jeremy as he turned to find the day butler to help him pack. "I'll see you later."

"Very well, Jeremy" answered Peter.

"Yes, very well," Jeremy thought to himself as he turned away from Peter and left the kitchen. "Now that the *Piper* is in that attorney's *brief case*, this is all going to work out very well indeed."

~

"All ahead full" said Captain Dehnel looking out from the bridge. "Steady on course."

"Aye aye, Captain" replied the helmsman.

"Look at that gorgeous coastline, seaman" said Dehnel.

"Yes, sir, it's absolutely awesome, sir."

"We're approaching Ensenada harbor. D'Amato, take the helm... we'll dock at the Navy Piers. Tomorrow Admiral Gonzales will take possession of the other vessels for the Mexican Navy. A couple of days of R and R for the crews and then we'll be haze gray and underway again."

"Yes, sir," D'Amato replied. "Not that I can remember how to navigate anymore" he thought to himself. "This is bullshit. I think it's time for an attack."

"AGGGHHHH" shouted D'Amato suddenly doubling over and holding his stomach.

"What the hell is with you, D'Amato?" asked the captain.

"I'm sorry, sir" said D'Amato, pretending to be writhing in pain. "It's a pancreatic virus I picked up in Lebanon. It never goes away, just comes and goes."

"Brennan, take over" yelled Dehnel. "D'Amato, get your ass to sick bay now."

"Aye, aye sir" said D'Amato heading for the bulkhead hatch.

Exiting the bridge, D'Amato made his way to the stairs connecting the bridge to the boat deck. Climbing the stairs, he then proceeded to the flag deck where he situated himself between the two Lewis .303 caliber machine guns.

"Not much chance of any of the Feds getting this text message down here in Mexico" he chuckled to himself as he removed his Blackberry from his pocket. Punching in the international numbers, he began his text message.

Brubaker, Italy is landing at Ensenada Navy Pier #8. Meet me at Papas and Beers at 1300 hours.

"This smuggling scheme is working like a friggin' charm" D'Amato thought to himself.

The scheme had all come about when Vice President Lamply and the other neo cons in Washington had formed the group known as the CFAF or the *Committee for American Freedom* long before the 2000 election. The group had formulated certain ideological goals for the country which were both rapacious and grandiose. The committee's main objectives were to advance the economic and military domination of the U.S. and to use its military might as the only remaining superpower to implement the plan. When the election was won, these goals would become realities.

Because the Committee's plans were legally questionable, there were a few obstacles to overcome. The U.S. Congress was first one and the U.S. Constitution was the other. In order for them to be implemented, a catastrophic *event* would need to occur, one that would not only threaten the economic stability of the country but also the safety of its population.

After America had been attacked by an invisible combatant and had declared interminable war on an ambiguous enemy, enacting legislation to circumvent these obstacles would become politically expedient for both parties of Congress and the Senate. The Constitution would become a moot point.

But what event would accomplish these objectives? And who would be the architect of it? Enter Mr. A.Q. Khan. The Pakistani metallurgist who was once the head of Pakistan's nuclear program was the perfect answer for the Committee. The CIA and other countries of the Nuclear Non-Proliferation Treaty had long suspected Khan of passing nuclear secrets and parts to Iran, Libya and North Korea. Recently, two separate shipments of centrifuges which had been hidden under cement bags in the holds of tramp tankers destined for Iran had been boarded and seized by NATO inspectors in the Persian Gulf. Khan was the prime suspect.

Consequently he would serve the Committee's ambitions perfectly. The Committee had secretly contacted Khan though the Pakistani Directorate for Inter-Services

Intelligence or ISI. Like the Committee, the ISI had become a state within a state, answerable neither to the leadership of the military or their respective governments. They each had their own agendas independent of their government's one. Khan had accepted the Committee's offer to become their parts supplier and for an astronomical price, he would build the centrifuges and smuggle them into the U.S.

The question was how to escape detection? He needed a new way of disguising and transporting the centrifuges. Then the answer came to him while attending a jazz concert in the Netherlands. A band member was playing a curious instrument. It consisted of various sizes of tubes which were remarkably close to the same dimensions as those of the centrifuges he was attempting to smuggle to rogue nations.

After the concert was over, he found out the name of the company which made the instrument from one of the band members. Contacting the company, he portrayed himself as a music rep and ordered 500 of the instruments. Then he had them shipped to a UPS mail box in Paris, the owner of which was an ISI agent. The company never questioned the order. The agent then shipped them to Pakistan.

His method was brilliant. The centrifuges were assembled into the instruments in Islamabad and then smuggled over the Khyber Pass from Peshawar to Kabul. And the ironic thing was that, in exchange for money from the Committee, the local tribesmen who escorted the shipments over the pass to safety in Kabul were actually allies of the Taliban, the very same people the U.S. government would soon claim as the enemy.

The *event* would result in collateral damage of a great magnitude but it was necessary so the Committee could accomplish its goals. Triggering such an *event* would become possible when all the centrifuges arrived undetected within the borders of the U.S. Then it would be possible to begin the enrichment process necessary to construct a dirty nuclear device to explode within an American city.

But Khan faced a challenge. Moving the shipments out of Pakistan into Afghanistan was easy. The tricky part would be moving them from Kabul to a seaport or airport from which they could be smuggled into the U.S. undetected.

Even disguised as they were, the titanium elements in the centrifuges could set off alerts in American ports or airports. Then he met the ISI agent in Paris. He would solve Khan's problem. He had access to the most fool proof way of smuggling in the world. His name was Daniel Schofield and that *way* was Tony *the bull* D'Amato, Chief Warrant Officer, United States Navy.

~

The Friendly Skies

"Oh my god!!" screamed Stephanie.

"Javlar, satan och helvete!" exclaimed Christian running over to the body slumped on the floor.

"He's dead as a post" said Christian, feeling for Nickolski's pulse.

"That's dumb as a post, Christian, try dead as a doornail!"

"Ja, whatever… skit ocksa!"

"What do we do, Christian?"

"I think we better be leaving now, Stephanie."

"That would not seem appropriate under the circumstances. Shouldn't we stay and explain what happened here?"

"Trust me, Stephanie, let's go now. I do not want to spend any time in a U.S. Navy brig. We have other things to do."

"But we're innocent here" she pleaded.

"Don't be javla dum, Stephanie. Let's go now" said Christian grabbing Stephanie's arm and escorting her toward the door.

"Now walk slowly like nothing has happened" said Christian opening the door of the Administration building and heading toward Antonio's taxi parked by the Marine guard.

And as luck would have it, who was passing in the opposite direction? It was the Sergeant, returning for his cover which he had left on his desk.

"Have a good day, ma'am" he said passing the two on the steps.

"I think we better hurry a bit" whispered Stephanie to Christian.

The Marine guard opened the cab door and bid them a similar ovation.

"Que paso, amigos?" said Antonio to the duo as they entered the cab.

"We'll tell you later, Antonio, right now es necessario to drive rapidamente" said Stephanie.

"Seguro, señorita" Antonio replied, firing up the engine and burning rubber just as Corporal Shumacher came charging out the Admin building doors waving his pistol.

"I think we're in deep doodoo now" said Stephanie. "We may have a little problem getting back through the front gate. Go as fast as you can, Antonio!"

"Si, Señorita!" he replied. Rounding the corner on two wheels they could see the guard house dead ahead and there was the Marine guard mounting a tripod with a 50 caliber machine gun aimed in their direction.

"I think he got the memo" said Stephanie. "Better turn around, Antonio!"

Antonio turned the wheel and slammed on the brakes just enough to turn the Citroen into a 180 degree skid.

"Wow, nice job, Parnelli. Where did you learn that one?" Stephanie asked just as the bullets from the 50 cal began to fly by the cab.

"It would not be the first time I have had to change directions quickly, Senorita. I have mucho Cadiz parking tickets and I have learned to avoid police cars quickly when I see them heading my way."

Retreating back toward the Admin building to avoid the barrage of bullets from the front gate, Antonio put the pedal to the metal only to see the sergeant and the Marine guard headed straight toward them in a Jeep that actually was moving.

"Oh oh, que pasa ahora?" Anotonio screamed.

"Antonio, you were here as a child…there must be another way off this base!" Stephanie screamed back.

"No, Senorita, the front gate is the only way that I can remember."

"Well, Christian, any ideas?" asked Stephanie as the two Marines started emptying their M9's into the rear of the Citroen.

"Skit Ocksa" let me think a minute" he replied.

"Christian, I don't think we have a minute here!"

Then it hit him. "The truck, Antonio, head toward the flat hauler."

"Que, Senor?"

"Antonio, just pull over, quickly!" yelled Christian.

Antonio screeched to a halt as Christian jumped out and tore open the front door of the cab.

"Move over, please" he sternly told Antonio. "We're going for a little flight."

"What...what are you doing?" screamed Stephanie.

"You'll see" Christian yelled back as he floored the Citroen and peeled out. And as the two Marines closed in, he headed right for the flatbed hauler with its cement tires and its bed tilted at 45 degrees.

"Christian, are you frigging crazy?" screamed Stephanie.

"Ay yi yi ....mia madre...ayudeme" whined Antonio.

With the bullets zinging by the windows and the Citroen reaching 75 mph, Christian headed directly for the flatbed.

"Fasten your seat belts" he yelled.

And as Stephanie and Antonio clipped their belts, the tires of the Citroen hit the truck bed like a ton of bricks. But amazingly, the little French taxi stayed level with the bed and after flying up the ramp, was launched into a twenty-five foot high arch and catapulted over the base wall before turning once in a 360 degree perfect flip and then landing with a slam on the pavement and continuing ahead, almost as if nothing had happened.

"Did that just really happen?" said Stephanie, breathing heavily. "Fly the friendly skies of Naval Base Rota! You are one crazy mother fucker, Christian Johanson!"

"I was a ski flyer in the Olympics", he answered steering the taxi through the Puerta Tierra and back toward the Hotel Parador. "Flying is natural to me."

"Well, I've had enough of flying for one day. Can we slow down and give the cab back to Antonio now?"

"Ja...and I think we owe Antonio a very large tip."

Antonio was frozen and speechless in the rear seat. Coming out of his stupor he managed to speak a few words. "Ah... is okay senor. From now on... only I drive... okay, por favor?"

Stephanie and Christian suddenly burst out in uncontrollable laughter.

"Ja...okay, Antonio...but you're not done yet. We'll need you for the rest of our stay. We will make it worth your while."

"Whatever you think, senor! It's okay now...I mean what else could happen?"

Stephanie and Christian laughed again as Christian steered the little Citroen back to the hotel to meet with Dustin Lambada and reunite with Lynne and Meredith.

And as they ascended the drive leading to the entrance of the hotel, a dark and loathsome figure gazed out the window from room 99. It had ransacked the room and as it moved closer to the window its mouth drew back in a hideous snarl. Removing its dark glasses, it focused two yellow eyes on the threesome approaching in the taxi.

"These mortals shall not thwart my plans" he growled to himself. "I have waited centuries for this time to come and now the *Disciples* will pay for their treachery."

~

The Louis Vuitton Bag, Ginko Viagra and the Pilot

"That should do it" D'Amato thought to himself. "Now I think I'll just go have a little nap in sick bay." But as he began to head aft of the engine room under the flag deck, he lifted his hand to feel for the rectangular key which he never, ever removed from around his neck.

It wasn't there. He pulled his shirt off thinking it had just been mixed in with the other confederation of dangling chains and medallions which embellished his tattooed and hairy chest.

"Frickin' A, it's not there!" D'Amato said to himself as he started to panic. Then he remembered. When his men had gotten into that brawl at Turtle's, that one guy who had decked two of his men had grabbed his shirt before his mates had pulled him off. He remembered hearing a clink but being caught in the moment, his mind had dismissed it.

"Damn, the ammunition dump key chain must have been ripped off my neck that night," he thought to himself. "This could present a problem. Shit, I need that key to close this deal!"

And at that same very moment that D'Amato began to panic, Ernie had picked up the key from the deck of the Swan's aft cabin.

"I guess I must have picked this up at some point. I wonder where?" Ernie thought to himself as he stuffed it into his pocket. "Wow, am I hungry. I guess I'll head up to Papas and Beers for some chow. That should make me feel better."

And at the same time D'Amato was text messaging agent CFAF Brubaker.

Urgent — meet P's and Beers asap.

Ernie made his way to the head to brush his teeth and splash some water on his face, and upon exiting the head he stumbled on something that had been left in the galley. Righting himself on the sink, he looked down to see a briefcase which he had turned on its side. The buckle had been left askew and something round and black had rolled out onto the deck of the galley.

"What the hell is this?" he asked himself. "This is frigging awesome, dude!"

And as he picked the item up, it began to vibrate and throb as if it had come to life.

"This is beautiful" he thought to himself. "What the hell is this doing in Tom's briefcase? This isn't safe here. I'd better take it with me."

And with that, Ernie climbed the galley ladder to the cockpit deck where he placed the dark globe into the empty *Louis Vuitton* bag that Linda had accidently left on deck. Then after locking the cabin and engaging the stanchion gate clips, he headed up Costero Blvd. to Ruiz Avenue where Papas and Beers awaited a most interesting situation.

~

"Well, that was fun!" said Linda climbing into the Wrangler. "Do you think we could stop to change clothes before heading to Papas and Beers? I'm still soaked."

"Don't worry, Linda, you'll dry off on the way back to town. It's a hot day and I'll put the top down" said Janae.

"*Okey dokey*" Linda replied.

"*Okey dokey*...wow, Squires... I haven't heard that one since I asked Mary Beth Mcguire for a goodnight kiss after the Junior Prom" said Tom.

"Her name was Mary Beth? And she said *okey dokey*?" asked Emmet. "Did you two grow up in a Norman Rockwell painting or something?"

"It's a mid-west thing, Mr. Cool. I guess where you grew up in Encino you just had really intelligent expressions like *bitchin'*."

"Well, yes... but as a matter of fact I always preferred *tubular*" said Emmet.

"Ah yes, the crowning linguistic achievement of modern man, the adjective *tubular*. Tom replied. "And I presume the girls you dated had really all American names like *Moon Unit* or *Dwezil*?"

"Not those ones, but my high school girlfriend was named *Sunshine*."

"I rest my case...only in California, land of fruits and nuts" replied Tom.

"Land of fruits?" asked Emmet, putting his arm around Tom in the back seat of the Wrangler. "Like me, handsome?"

"Yes, like you, sweet boy!"

"Does this mean I'm your bitch?"

"You're starting to make me as nervous as a grasshopper in a henhouse, Emmet. Janae, you got an ejector seat back here for this guy?"

"No, but here are some reading materials to distract him" she said, handing Tom some comic books.

"Ah...a fan of the classics... let's, see here, Emmet... here's one to match your California intellect...*Daffy Duck*! Luckily it even has pictures too."

"What's wrong with my intellect?" asked Emmet. Growing up in California made me what I am today."

"What's that, a rich *surfing* avatar of yuppie greed?"

"No, it made me a successful entrepreneur and man of wealth and taste."

"Oh puleeease, spare me! You may be a rich dude but the only taste I've ever seen from you is this morning at breakfast when you chose oatmeal over your *Count Chocula*."

"I think the latest research shows that chocolate is very high in antioxidants" Emmet replied.

"I think that's cocoa, Emmet...not processed chocolate" added Linda.

"So what's the difference, I forget."

"You'd forget your nose if it wasn't on the front of your face, Emmet. What you need is some *Ginko Viagra*" said Tom.

"*Ginko Viagra*? What's that for?"

"So you can remember what the frick you're thinking. Now let's roll, Janae" exclaimed Tom as Janae and Linda tried to control their laughter.

Firing up the engine, Janae put the Wrangler into four wheel drive and floored it. And as the little Jeep kicked up a cloud of dust and began to wind its way back to Ensenada, two destined men sauntered into Papas and Beers and unknowingly took seats at opposite ends of the bar from each other.

~

Pilot Rod Moore started his walk around the Citation Jet. Everything seemed to be in ship shape. The ailerons, flaps, landing gear and elevators seemed ready to go and so was he, this hopefully being his last flight before retiring.

After his harrowing escape from the VC at *Firebase Leslie* in the '*Nam*, he had completed his WESPAC duty and then had sworn off piloting choppers. Returning to the states, he decided the career of a commercial jet pilot was more to his liking. Jets had two engines and the power to get you out of trouble if necessary. It took him less than three years to get his commercial jet license and since that time he had logged more than 50,000 hours flying around the world piloting small commercial jets.

He had worked for both commercial airlines and private jet leasing companies. His present position was as Captain of a Citation X which was owned by a jet leasing company out of Bahrain. It was an Arab company and this was his sixth year in their employ. But this was his last assignment. He was tired of flying and he was starting to develop blood clots in his legs. Bahrain was a beautiful place but face it, the Middle East was still the Middle East.

Now in his fifties, he had managed to sock away close to a million dollars for his retirement and he longed for a nice peaceful life back in Santa Barbara where he could substitute a sail boat for his planes. Maybe even find some nice coochee mama to spend weekends with sailing out to the islands with her and his buds.

"So hopefully this is the last flight" he thought to himself as he flipped the elevators.

"I wonder who my last passengers are going to be. Funny, they wouldn't tell me. It must be someone either who thinks they're important or a celebrity. You'd think they'd realize that those people don't impress me anymore. Not after the megalomaniacs I've flown around the world. But the Santa Barbara airport sure is beautiful this morning" he thought to himself as he watched the sun rising over the Santa Ynez Mountains. There was a nice breeze, five knots across the runway. "What a beautiful morning to fly. This is going to be an awesome swan song to my flying career, I can feel it."

Just then the Hummer Stretch Limo pulled onto the tarmac. It was pretentious but probably indicative of the personality riding within it. "Anyone who can ride in one of those these days without extreme pangs of guilt is either living in a dream world or is totally ignorant of the world's environmental crisis" he thought to himself. "But then, how many times have I seen this before?"

As the Hummer pulled next to the Citation and came to a stop, Rod positioned himself by the gangway to welcome his passengers and introduce himself as their captain.

Ferdinand the driver jumped out and proceeded to open the rear door of the limo. Out popped Jeremy in his signature white gloves and a black suit followed by Peter who could have been mistaken for an older Ralph Lauren model.

As Ferdinand unloaded the luggage, the two approached the airplane. "Good morning. My name is Rod Moore and I'll be your Captain on this flight. Welcome aboard" he said as he bowed slightly to Jeremy and Peter.

"I'm Jeremy, and thank you" said Jeremy, returning the gesture. "We should only be a few minutes unloading and then we're ready to go." Two bag handlers took the luggage from Ferdinand and started to load it into the cargo hold of the plane.

"So Peter, you will take care of Tierra Bella, won't you?" asked Jeremy.

"Of course, trust me, Jeremy, all will be fine. I'll look after the estate and in a year or so when you return, all will have been forgotten by the public. It's all going to work out just fine."

"And you'll be sure the *Piper* is sold and the paintings returned to the Stockholm Museum, won't you?"

"Jeremy, how many times have we discussed this? Yes, all will be taken care of, I promise." Just then Peter's cell phone rang.

Peter looked at the number display. "Shit, it's D'Amato" he mumbled under his breath. "He knows he's not supposed to call me on this number."

"Uh, excuse me, Jeremy. It's NYU calling, I'll have to take this" said Peter, turning away and walking toward the terminal.

"Hello, D'Amato, you know you're not supposed to call this cell number. What the hell are you thinking?"

"It's an emergency, Schofield. The fricking key to the Ensenada ammo dump is missing" answered D'Amato.

"What, what do you mean it's missing?"

"I carry the damn thing around my neck at all times. Today I noticed it's not there. I think it got ripped off of my neck in a brawl."

"Listen, D'Amato, I don't care where or how you lost it but you better damn well find it or Lamply is going to roast our asses on a stick! We have to get the uranium dioxide from those torpedoes."

"What the hell, we got the *Piper* and we got the two paintings. We don't have to worry about that anymore. Let's just deliver the last of the centrifuges as promised and let him find the uranium dioxide by himself."

"D'Amato, you forget about our Swiss bank accounts that are not going to have squat in them if we don't deliver as promised."

"Shit, this is bad luck. Are you sure about the Renoir and the Rembrandt doing away with the curse? This seems like a very bad turn of events" said D'Amato.

"The *Piper* and paintings are together at Tierra Bella, D'Amato. The curse has been negated, believe me. So where are you now?"

"I'm sitting at the bar at Papas and Beers in Ensenada. I'm meeting my contact here any time now."

And as D'Amato looked around for the agent, his eyes were drawn to what seemed like a familiar person seated at the other end of the bar. Focusing his eyes on the individual, he saw that the man had ordered a Stella Artois and upon reaching into his pocket to get the money to pay, had emptied its contents on the bar. There, on the bar, appeared to be exactly what he was looking for. A shaft of sunlight from the skylight had illuminated a rectangular key shaped object.

"Holy shit, it's him. And he has the friggin' key!" D'Amato exclaimed to himself.

"What the hell is happening, D'Amato?" asked Schofield.

"The key is here" said D'Amato. "The guy who was messin' with us the other night is right here. And he just laid the key on the bar."

"Do NOT let that guy out of your sight. I'll be there in two hours."

"Oh trust me, I won't" D'Amato replied. "You're coming down here, how?"

"Never mind, I'll call you when I get there" And with that, Schofield hung up and turned to walk back to the Citation. The luggage had been loaded and Jeremy was on board.

And as Jeremy began to locate his seat belt, he thought to himself… "Finally I will have peace again now that the *Piper* is no longer in my possession. Peter was dragging his feet. Sometimes you just have to do things yourself. Too bad though, Tom seemed like a nice guy but now the curse is his problem, and better he than me. Now that the *Piper* is in Ensenada on his boat, I hope I never see it again."

And as Jeremy clicked himself into the seat belt of the Corinthian leather cabin seat, Peter was walking quickly back to the Citation.

"Yes sir," said Rod as Peter approached the plane.

"There's been a change in the flight plan, Captain."

"Really, how so, where are we going then? We're not going to Bahrain?"

"Oh, you'll be going to Bahrain eventually. But first we're going to take a little detour. How do you like Mexican food, Captain?"

"Ah… love it… meaning?"

"Viva Zapata, Captain…we're going to *Ensenada*."

~

The Sarcophagus

Dustin Lambada stood waiting outside the main foyer for Stephanie and Christian's return. Exactly two hours had passed since they had left for Rota and it was most important that he intercept them before they could set foot back in the hotel. Looking down the driveway, he could see the Citroen approaching and just as the little taxi zoomed into the porte-cochere, he ran out, waving his arms in the air.

"What's up, Dustin?" asked Stephanie through the rolled down window.

"I will explain it to you but you cannot go back into the hotel" said Dustin opening the back door of the vehicle and sliding in beside Antonio. "We have to go back to the Oratorio de Santa Cruz. We can join your friends there. Now hurry, we must leave now."

Christian slammed the little taxi into first gear and floored it, leaving the bellhops in a cloud of smoke. "Where are we going, Dustin" he asked.

"Follow the boulevard Parque Genoves until we see the Puerta Tierra. The church is near there."

"I know where it is, Señor. Can I drive now? I would like to live through this day, Senor Christian" said Antonio.

"Pardon me, Antonio, I almost forgot whose cab this is...tack ska du ha" replied Christian as he pulled the cab over just outside the hotel grounds where he and Antonio then exchanged seats.

"Why are we not going via the tunnel like we did before?" asked Stephanie as the cab pulled back into the fast lane of the boulevard.

"Let us just say that now your lives are also in danger. It will all be explained to you when we reach the underground chapel."

'It is the devil storm, si? Esta es todo el trabajo del Diablo, verdad?" asked Antonio.

"Tranquilo, Antonio… just drive… quickly. I better text message brother Bob to let him know we will be there soon." said Dustin as he fumbled through his pockets for his cell phone.

"Not too quickly, Antonio. I don't think I've recovered from the aerial circus at Rota yet" said Stephanie. "My heart is still pounding."

"Si, Señorita Stephanie, yo entiendo" replied Antonio as Dustin started his text message.

BB-will b there 10 mns open sarcophagus DL

"Hopefully he'll get the message" said Dustin. And as Brother Bob's phone rang in the underground chapel, Meredith and Lynne were playing cards, anxiously awaiting their arrival.

"Hopefully that's Stephanie and Christian" said Lynne as she laid her hand on the table. "*Gin* again, Meredith!"

"Sugar, that's the tenth game in a row I've lost. How do you do it?"

"I'm psychic, Meredith, remember? You'll never beat me. You must learn to control your thoughts before you'll ever have a chance. You're like a billboard to me."

"Well then, I give up. How can you beat someone at cards who knows what your cards are all the time?" said Meredith.

"You can't, Meredith, until you learn to stop broadcasting them."

"You should be in Vegas playing blackjack rather than here in an old underground chapel in Cadiz, Spain. Brother Bob, I'm getting bored sitting around here like a clove on a ham. When are we meeting up with Stephanie and Christian?" asked Meredith.

"It should be any time now, ladies" answered Bob. And just then his cell phone rang. The ring tone was set on the hymn *Onward Christian Soldiers*.

"That's apropos" said Meredith.

"Yes, and I have a feeling it's going to take on some real meaning in the days ahead" said Lynne emphatically.

"Jolly good... I say, it's a text message from Dustin and they're on their way, ladies. Who wants to help me unlatch the sarcophagus?" asked brother Bob.

"Uh...sarcophagus...where, what sarcophagus?" asked Meredith.

"Why, that one, my dear" said Brother Bob pointing to the very highest platform.

"Up there? You expect me to climb up there? I think NOT" said Meredith. "I get vertigo way too easily."

"There's a sarcophagus up there?" asked Lynne. "Why are we unlatching a sarcophagus, may I ask?"

"But of course, you may, my dear. Up there is an entrance to this cavern through the sarcophagus of an ancient Phoenician male. It was discovered under the church altar in the year 1887. It is the entrance to the sepulcher through which your friends shall enter this chapel to join us. However, we must unlatch it from this side. Someone must hold the ladder while I tend to this endeavor from the top. Lynne, what do you say? You don't let heights bother you, do you now?"

"No, I guess not. But can I get a parachute just in case?"

Brother Bob giggled and said "not to worry, I'll see to your safety and the view is simply smashing up there. Now, what say you?"

"So you want me to climb up there to help you unlatch the sarcophagus in the sepulcher?"

"Exactly" answered Bob.

"Well, let me ask you this. Once we unlock the sarcophagus in the sepulcher, how will our friends find us?"

"They'll find us through the Sanctuary" Bob snickered.

"Okay, now that I know you're joking, I guess if one of us has to help you" said Lynne.

"Jolly good, then shall we?" said Bob. And with that he started to climb the ladder to the first platform. He began to leap from step to step effortlessly, nimbly negotiating every step with the grace of a chimpanzee. In a matter of seconds, he had reached the third of five platforms leading to the ceiling of the chapel.

Huffing and puffing, Lynne had barely reached the top of the first platform. Looking up at Bob, she could see him giggling at her climbing ability.

"Come on Lynne, just pretend you're climbing the Matterhorn" yelled Bob from two platforms above her.

"Welcome to the Cirque du Soleil" Lynne thought to herself. "Who is this guy? He must be a former member of the *Flying Wallendas*! How does he climb so fast?"

"Jolly good, Lynne... but watch the second platform, it's a bit cheeky."

"Gee, thanks for the warning, Spiderman" Lynne thought to herself. "Now don't look down. Just take it step by step."

Brother Bob turned and continued to climb effortlessly just like Tarzan, swinging his arms step by step, platform to platform until he sprightly reached the final one 100 feet above the chapel floor.

"Hurry Lynne, you can help me plant the flag. You can do it!"

Finally after five minutes more of climbing, Lynne reached the final platform and, breathing heavily, climbed onto the deck to join the monastic alpinist.

"Okay Bob, I made it. What's next, the flying trapeze?"

Bob giggled. "Oh I love your Yank's sense of sarcasm. But no trapezes up here, my dear. Just this box with a few knickknacks, I'm afraid."

As Bob bent over to open the box, Lynne looked down to see an assortment of rather strange objects.

"What in the world are those things" she asked.

Opening the box, Bob began to remove its contents and said "just a few simple tools to help us along in our task. These, my dear, are what are known as *Bigfoot Super Jacks*. They are pneumatic, revolving, two ton, double plunger, super low profile truck jacks which are strong enough to lift an M-1 Abrams tank off the ground to change the tread."

"Oh, well that's good to know" said Lynne with a quizzical look. "And what is that long pool cue for?"

"Well, it's not a pool cue actually, but there is a close resemblance. This is what is known as a *Big Green Monster Tailgate Telescoping Holder*.

"Uh... okay, if you say so...and the trolley?"

"It's not a trolley but close....this is my *Horizontal Streamlined Creeper*."

"Two jacks, a tailgate holder and a creeper...I thought we were going to unlatch the sarcophagus, not change its oil."

"You are too bloody funny, my dear. Now, when I reach the top of the ladder, would you be so kind as to pass these items to me please?"

"You get me off this platform alive and I'll be your humble servant forever, Brother Bob!"

"Not necessary but jolly good" said Bob as he began to climb the ladder.

As he neared the top, Lynne could see that the steel door attached to the ceiling of the cavern had a wheel with a handle like those on the hatches of navy ships and submarines. When he was within grasping distance, Bob grabbed the handle and turned it in a clockwise motion until a resounding clank was audible.

"Aye matey, reminds me of me seafarin' days whenever I do this" said Bob as he began to whistle *God Save the Queen*. "Now Lynne, would you pass me the '*Big Green Monster*' please?"

Lynne reached own and grabbed the 'Monster' and passed it up the ladder where Bob took it and with a whistle, twirled it twice like a baton before pushing the hatch up to a vertical position and securing it.

"Which is next?" asked Lynne.

"Now pass the jacks and then the creeper, my dear, if you please."

"Here's one, Bob" she answered while passing up a jack to him. "Do you mind if I ask you what all this is for?"

"Not at all, my dear, you see, the sarcophagus lid weighs almost 800 kilos. We learned to improvise in order to get the top to move with as little effort as possible. You will see, now pass me the other 'Bigfoot' and then the creeper and you can come up for a look-see."

Lynne passed the jack and creeper up the ladder. "This I have to see" she thought to herself.

Grabbing the creeper, Bob turned it sideways and slid it up through the manhole. He then took one of the *Bigfoot* jacks and mounted it on the creeper. Disappearing into the hole, she could hear Bob moving on the creeper to the left and then after another moment, moving it back to the entrance and then grabbing the other jack which was perched on the top ladder rung before once again disappearing into the hole.

"What is going on up there? I never knew unlatching a door could be so intricate" Lynne thought to herself.

Still whistling *God Save the Queen*, Bob then reemerged from the manhole with the creeper and descended the ladder.

"Jolly good, Lynne, your turn…now pop up there and have a look-see."

Lynne ascended the ladder and poked her head through the manhole. The sarcophagus was lit by two holes in each end of it. It was dark but she could make out what Bob had done. He had placed the jacks at opposite ends of the sarcophagus with their plungers flat against the top.

"Now I see there is a method to his madness" she thought to herself descending the ladder.

Upon reaching the bottom rung, Bob took her arm to steady her.

"Well, Brother Bob, I must admit that it is a very clever way to lift the top of the sarcophagus in the sepulcher off the sanctuary, but I have just one question for you."

"Fire when ready, Gridley" responded Bob.

"I presume the whole idea is for people to squeeze into the sarcophagus and crawl down here, correct?"

"Absolutely" he replied.

"But how can anyone squeeze into the sarcophagus without knocking over one of the jacks? It looks like a tight squeeze to me."

"Jolly good question, Lynne, and here is your answer" said Bob while reaching into his pocket and producing two electronic devices.

"Wala!" said Bob enthusiastically.

Handing one of them to Lynne, she could see that it was some sort of remote control.

"Ah, let me guess…this is for the home theatre in the sepulcher off the sanctuary, right?"

Bob laughed loudly. "No Lynne, this is the remote for one of the 'Bigfoot' jacks. Remember, they are revolving jacks. See here, this button is for lift and this one is to initiate revolution. Once we lift the sarcophagus top up a few feet, it is then possible to turn the top ninety degrees, leaving both ends more accessible to enter without disturbing the jacks."

"Very ingenious, I must admit" said Lynne.

"Thank you very much" said Bob just as his cell phone tone began *Onward Christian Soldiers*.

"It's Dustin, he's up there. Here Lynne, push this lift button when I say so."

Positioning the other remote in his left hand, Bob said "I'm going to count to three and then push this button. We will hold it down for five seconds to lift the lid, and then you will push this button for eight seconds to turn the lid."

"Got it, Bob, I'm ready."

"One, two, three, now" said Bob. Pushing the button, Lynne could hear the hum of the jacks initiating lift off. There was a slight shudder above and then she could see streams of light filling the void of the manhole.

After five seconds, Bob said "stop. Now, on three push the revolve button. Are you ready …one, two three."

Lynne pushed the other button and suddenly she could hear voices. After eight seconds, Bob shouted "stop." And after a few more seconds she could see Dustin Lambada coming through the manhole, followed by Stephanie, Christian and Antonio.

"Welcome to *The Cavern Bar and Grill*, ladies and gentlemen." said Bob. "May I see some IDs please?"

"Hi guys" Lynne said to the group. "Welcome to the real *Raiders of the Lost Ark*."

"My god, what the hell is this place" asked Stephanie. "My gawd, we're 100 feet off the ground here!"

"I hope you like ladders" said Lynne.

"Skit ocksa" said Christian. "This place is amazing!"

"Ai yi yi…and I thought nothing else could happen to me today" whined Antonio.

"We must hurry, Brother Bob" said Dustin. "Wegreog is searching the hotel. It is only a matter of time now."

"Yes, all levity aside, we should hurry. Now if you will all be very careful, allow me to show you the way down" said Bob as he began descending the labyrinth of ladders. Lynne, Stephanie, Christian and Antonio followed while Dustin closed the lid of the sarcophagus but left the manhole hatch propped open. "Just in case we have to exit this way" he thought to himself.

Bob stopped at each platform to ensure the group's safety. When they all had reached the floor of the cavern, Antonio was the first to speak. Perdoneme, senor, but where is el baño, por favor?"

"Third stalactite on the right" snickered Bob. "Va a la derecha, señor, pero tenga prisa."

"Gracias, señor, I will hurry" answered Antonio. And after a few minutes Dustin slid down the last ladder faster than a fireman on a pole, landing on the ground with a thud.

"Now that you all are here, allow me to introduce myself" said Bob. "We don't have much time so I will be brief. I am Brother Bob of the Franciscan Order. This is an ancient chapel that dates back to the fourth century. We discovered it almost thirty years ago while researching the sarcophagus above. We excavated it and have had it preserved somewhat. What you see here is mostly original. We are not sure exactly whose chapel this was but after a great deal of excavation we discovered what you see before you. It is a secret, needless to say."

After a minute, Antonio returned from the restroom.

"As I was saying, Señor" said Bob addressing Antonio, "this cavern is a secret and you must not tell anyone."

"I promise, Father" said Antonio.

"Bueno, now I am going to show you what we discovered here almost thirty years ago. It has predicted exactly the events that have happened recently and some more that may occur in the future. You will be quite astounded as to their accuracy."

And with that Bob turned and walked briskly to the burning torch on the side wall. Reaching up, he pulled downward on the handle and as the torch was lowered, a hole in the wall underneath opened up like a Burger King drive through window. A light went on and there on a flat surface was a key ring with approximately ten ancient keys.

"You're kidding, that's right out of a *Mummy's Curse* movie" exclaimed Stephanie.

"Yes, it's so cornball that no one would ever consider it. Sometimes the most obvious can be the most furtive" Bob replied.

Taking the key ring, Bob walked over to the ancient wooden door that appeared to be secured with chains and locks. As Bob proceeded to unlock each one, they fell to the floor with a resounding clank before Dustin pulled them away from the threshold.

Once they all were cleared away, Bob turned toward the group and took a deep breath. "What you are about to see, few men or women have seen since the fourth century and perhaps even long before that time. What you are about to see dates back to as early as 50,000 B.C. and is of astronomical importance now, meaning right now. Whether you like it or not, you're being here has been predicted for centuries and you are about to find yourselves some of the major players in a drama of life and death for civilization that is about to unfold in the next few weeks."

And with that said, Bob turned around and pulled on the great door, swinging it open and letting it crash with a bang on the surrounding rock.

As light filled the void of the previously black space, sparkles of bright energy began to dance and shimmer off what appeared to be tablets lain on an altar. As the light filled the room, the tablets seemed to take on a beautiful bright glow and also seemed to emit a sort of vibration, almost as if angels were singing. Soon the room had filled with the most splendiferous light and heavenly music.

The group was speechless, numb with awe. Antonio crossed himself. Finally Christian spoke. "God Jul" what are these things?"

For the first time, Brother Bob had a reverenced countenance. Gesturing for the group to enter, he said "enter the chamber and behold the *Emerald Tablets of Troth the Atlantean!*"

The Beautiful Ensign

Ernie had just ordered his second Stella and was nursing a shot of *Chopin*. The huevos rancheros were probably not the best thing to order to cure his hangover but as he had been starved, it did cure him of his hunger.

"Are you drowning your sorrows or just taking them out for a little swim, handsome?" said a melodious voice from behind him.

Ernie turned around on the barstool. There stood a curvy brown haired girl with one hand on her hip gazing down at Ernie through deep green eyes that that looked like shimmering emeralds. She had on a halter top which barely covered what Ernie would classify as *hooters par excellence* and a thin little waist curving outward onto perfectly proportioned hips which were adorned with the tightest low rise jeans he had ever seen.

"No sorrows to speak of… just curing a hangover" Ernie replied.

"Well, are you drunk yet, sailor?" she asked inquisitively.

"Not sure, but let's just say both of you are very beautiful" Ernie replied.

"Good answer, mind if I sit down?"

"Be my guest" Ernie answered, gesturing to the neighboring barstool. "What's your name?"

"Diana" she said as she took a seat next to Ernie and extended her hand. "And you are?"

"Ernie" he responded, taking her hand and kissing it, obviously delighted with this unexpected development. "Can I buy you a drink?"

"I was hoping you'd ask, thank you" she responded.

"What would you like?" asked Ernie.

"To drink?" she replied.

"Um, not necessarily" said Ernie.

"How about we'll start with that?" answered Diana.

"Sounds good, what can I get you?"

"How about having an iced tea?"

"Okay, not indulging today?" asked Ernie.

"It's a bit early for me. I only indulge my alcoholism after six o'clock." she replied.

"Ah...a sense of discipline, I like that in a girl. Bartender, can we get a couple of drinks down here?" Ernie shouted to the barkeep.

"Be right there" he answered.

"So let me ask you something, Diana" said Ernie.

"Ask away, sailor.".

"Exactly that, how did you know I am a sailor?"

"The anchor on your forearm was a dead giveaway, Popeye."

"Ah...the anchor...of course... now if I only had an anchor on my forearm."

"Okay, to tell the truth, let's just say I know a sailor when I see one. I've had some experience at it."

The bartender brought the drinks and Ernie threw a quarter onto the bar as a tip.

"Wow, a whole quarter!" exclaimed Diana. "Now he can afford the down payment on the Ferrari."

"A sense of humor and a sense of sarcasm... I like that." Ernie said as he took the quarter back and threw down a five note.

"That's much better, don't you feel better now?"

"Sorry, I guess I wasn't thinking! You've obviously been in either the sailing industry or the service industry?"

"In a manner of speaking, yes, you could say that" said Diana smiling with gorgeous teeth that sparkled like polished ivory.

"And what manner are we referring to here, may I ask?"

"Yes you may ask. And shall we say service as in service to my country" she answered.

"Really, well whatever service you're in, I'm reenlisting. I love your uniforms!"

"Needless to say, this isn't exactly the uniform of the day" said Diana laughing.

"Well then, I love your tailor. Seriously, what service are you in?"

"Let's just say that we're both sailors."

"Really, what service to what country is it? If I can't reenlist I'm repatriating" Ernie said enthusiastically.

"You won't have to...we're both on the same side."

Ernie paused to think for a second. "No way" he thought to himself. "Not the U.S. Navy?"

Diana held out her hand once again..."Ensign Diana Williams, United States Navy."

"Oh really" said Ernie. "Well then, maybe you better make that handshake a salute, Ensign... Lieutenant Ernest Walters, *United States Navy, Special Ops, Navy SEALs*."

"Inactive status I presume, however."

"True, but once a SEAL always a SEAL. It's a brotherhood. The SEAL part is always active."

"I'm impressed. See, I knew you were a sailor." said Diana raising her glass in a toast. "Here's to the Blue and Gray."

"Anchors away" replied Ernie, clinking her glass with the Stella bottle and then chugging the remaining brew.

"So obviously you're on a little *R and R*, I presume" asked Ernie.

"You presume correctly, Lieutenant Ernie. I had two weeks of it coming and I'm not going to miss Coronado one bit either."

"Coronado you say... that's where I did my SEAL training...well, some of it anyway."

"Silver Strand?" asked Diana.

"We called it the *Elephant Cage*."

"Oh yes, those lovely circular antenna there make for such a lovely view" said Diana.

"450 acres of sheer recreational delight" added Ernie.

"So what year are we talking about here?"

"Don't ask and I won't lie to you" Ernie answered.

"Oh, come on Ernie, give me a hint."

"Like what?"

"Ok, like what weapons did you use? Yes, what side arms did you carry then? Let's see, judging from your appearance I'd say it was *muskets*. Am I right?" asked Diana laughing.

"Very funny, I'm really not as old as I look today."

"Just giving you a hard time, sailor" answered Diana. Putting her index finger on Ernie's nose flirtingly, she said "you're plenty cute enough for me sailor, don't go away. I'll be back in five minutes. I have to attend the little girl's room."

"I'll be here, Ensign Williams."

"Good, then I'll be right back." Rising from the bar stool, she put her hand on Ernie's knee and gave it a quick squeeze. "I'm feeling a little frisky this morning, Mr. SEAL. You just may get lucky." And with that, she turned and walked away, swaying her hips and bum in a slow sexy walk that turned a bar full of male heads all at once.

"Awesome, dude" thought Ernie. "Is this really happening? That lady is a total babe."

And as Diana rounded the corner of the bar and proceeded to the ladies room, another navy serviceman waited by the door.

"So what's the deal, Brubaker?" asked Tony *the bull* D'Amato.

"It's a done deal, D'Amato. I'll have that key back to you within the hour. You men are really something. If it was raining brains, you guys wouldn't even get wet. Your brains are in your peckers, I swear."

"Good" D'Amato responded. "Lamply is expecting delivery in the next three days. We have to get those torpedoes loaded onto the Corvette boat soon and the sooner the better."

"Piece of cake" answered Diana. "The raid will still go down tonight as planned. The necessary preparations have been made."

"Well then, see that you're there as usual." said D'Amato. "By the way, the centrifuges sailed in today. We'll transport them and the torpedoes back to the Corvette after nightfall. With any luck, we can set sail day after tomorrow after the Mexican Navy Day."

"Good, I like this. Instead of using one of those Mexican freighters and bribing the officials in order to move our wares out of Mexican waters, we get an escort of none other than Uncle Sam."

"The Mexican gun boats can stop every other friggin' non Mexican vessel like they always do and we'll just motor right on by them" replied D'Amato.

"And no more unloading and loading cargo twenty-five miles out at sea. I'm glad this will be the last trip."

"Yep, one more trip and then I can just quietly disappear, never to be seen again" said D'Amato. "By the way, Brubaker, what assurances do I have that Lamply and your CFAF will make good on your promises?"

"I've told you, D'Amato, you'll have half the money put into your Swiss account upon delivery to Coronado and the other half upon delivery to Tierra Bella."

"I don't trust you bastards...not one iota. You can tell Lamply that Schofield is on top of this. If there is any hanky panky going on, we deep six the cargo."

"Don't worry, D'Amato. You'll get your money. Now I better get back to lover boy out there so I can get that key."

Diana turned and walked back the way she had come followed by D'Amato at a distance. Taking a seat at the opposite end of the bar, he was in full view of Ernie and his backpack which he had placed on the bar in front of him.

"Did you miss me, handsome?" asked Diana, sauntering up close to Ernie and putting her arms around his neck.

"More than ever" said Ernie with a grin ear to ear.

"What say we blow this pop stand and go relax a little at my hotel?"

"Whatever you say, cupcake" answered Ernie.

And as they both got up to leave, Ernie, in his excitement, grabbed the *Luis Vuitton* bag by the wrong end. The top flap opened and out rolled onto the bar the black sphere, glowing and vibrating slightly.

"What is that?" asked Diana? "That is beautiful!"

"I'm not sure" Ernie replied. Holding it up in his hand so they both could see it better, he said; "I found it in Tom's brief case a while ago. I didn't think it would be safe on the boat so I put it in this bag I found on the deck."

"Well, put it away before some bandido sees it" said Diana. "That thing looks valuable."

"Yeah, I suppose. But I wonder what it is," said Ernie stuffing it back into the bag. "Oh well, no harm done, no one saw it…let's go."

But someone had seen it and that someone had reached into his jacket to undo the safety on his .45 caliber revolver. "I can't believe it, that son of a bitch. He has the key and the sphere. Thirty years I've been searching for it and it turns up in the hands of that mooch. I don't need either of those two but I want that sphere back now. A bullet in the back of the head ought to do it. No one will know, they'll just think it was a bandido" D'Amato thought to himself.

And as Ernie and Diana opened the door of the saloon to leave, D'Amato began to follow close behind, waiting for the perfect moment to put a bullet into both their brains.

Strolling arm in arm down Avenue Ruiz, the two rounded the corner onto Juarez Street where D'Amato saw the perfect opportunity. The street was deserted. No one would see the murders. It would be chalked up to bandidos and both the key and the *Piper* would be his again.

Stealthily walking behind the two, D'Amato pulled the revolver from his jacket and slowly and quietly cocked the hammer of the firearm. Lost in conversation, Ernie and Diana were oblivious to his approach.

"I can't believe it, the *Piper* will be mine once again" thought D'Amato. Elated over this opportunity, he pulled the gun from his jacket. Now it was just a matter of seconds before his life's greatest desire would be fulfilled.

Closing to within ten feet of the two, he began to raise the weapon to fire when all of a sudden a Jeep Wrangler holding four people careened around the corner and sped right in their direction.

Tom saw him first. "Emmet, look, isn't that Ernie?"

Emmet held his hand over his eyes to block the sun. "I'll be *ding-danged*, sure looks like him."

"Janae, stop by that couple up there" yelled Tom from the back seat.

"No problema" said Janae as the Wrangler screeched to a halt right next to Ernie and Diana.

"Shit" thought D'Amato, placing the weapon into his jacket and ducking into an alleyway. "Damnit" he murmured to himself.

"Well, well, look who's here" said Ernie, dropping his arm from around Diana's waist.

"Well I'll be a monkey's uncle, look who's awake" said Tom. "He has *risen*! Hallelujah!" he yelled from the back seat.

"The *Taco Tequila Monster* walks amongst us again" added Emmet.

"Someone rolled away the rock of the tomb on the Swan… it's a miracle!" Tom said sarcastically. "Hmmm… looks like we're interrupting something here."

"You could say that, yes" said Ernie, obviously annoyed. "This is Diana. Diana, meet the crew. This is Moe, Larry and Curly and their driver……"

"Janae" she said from the driver's seat.

"Hello" said Diana.

"And I'm Linda."

Where are you two headed?" asked Tom.

"Nunya" said Ernie.

"What's nunya?" asked Emmet.

"Nunya frickin' business…now get lost, will ya?" said Ernie. "I'll meet up with you later on the Swan."

"Can we give you a lift?" asked Janae. "Where are you headed?"

"The Hotel Coral and Marina" Diana replied.

"That's eight blocks away" said Janae. "Hop in and we'll run you up there. We're just heading up to 'Pappas and Beers' for lunch. Why don't you join us?"

"Just came from there... now goodbye" said Ernie, turning and grabbing Diana's arm to continue their walk."

"Wait, Ernie. She's right. It's a long walk in the sun. Let's ride instead."

"Well...alright then, Diana" grumbled Ernie.

"I'll hop in back" said Linda.

Ernie jumped into the front seat with the *Louis Vuitton* bag followed by Diana who sat on his lap.

"Hmm, it looks like someone borrowed my bag" said Linda.

"Sorry Linda" said Ernie. "It was just there on the deck and I needed a bag. I would have asked had I known it was yours."

"No worries" said Linda. "It's an old *Louis Vuitton* bag."

"It fits you, Ernie" said Tom. "After all, you are kind of an old bag, aren't you?"

"Oh that's funny" Ernie jeered.

"Is everyone strapped in and ready?" asked Janae.

"Ready and able" said Tom.

"Well then blast off" she yelled as she slammed the Wrangler into gear and floored it, leaving Chief Warrant Officer Anthony D'Amato extremely aggravated and seething in the dust.

~

A Death in Beirut

On April 13, 1975, members of the Lebanese Phalange Party were caught in a drive-by shooting as they left a church ceremony in Beirut. Four people died. Hours later, Christian Phalangist militiamen pulled over a bus carrying Palestinian and other Muslim workers back to the refugee camps. The workers were ordered out at gunpoint and then had their throats slit. Twenty-seven people in all were murdered. One of the workers was named Abdul Feyad.

As news of the murders spread, Palestinian militias went on a rampage through Beirut. Armed clashes with Phalange erupted throughout the city. Soon Lebanese National Movement militias entered the battle. Numerous ceasefires and political talks proved fruitless. It was the beginning of a long and bloody war that was to last fifteen years.

Then on Saturday, December 6, 1975, the bodies of four members of the right wing Kataeb Party, an organization grouping of primarily Maronite Christians, were found dead in an abandoned car outside the state-owned power plant in Christian dominated East Beirut.

The Phalange's militia men in the city went into a frenzied rage, blaming the killings on the Lebanese National Movement (LNM) dominated by leftist Muslims and Palestinians. Phalange forces attacked

Muslims throughout Christian-dominated East Beirut, indiscriminately firing into crowds.

In an orgy of bloodletting, several hundred people were murdered in a few hours, most of them civilian. Estimations of the total number of victims range between 200 and 600, much of the slaughter taking place in a marketplace where a sixteen year old blond boy accompanied his guardian to buy groceries.

When the Phalange had opened fire, the woman had been standing in front of the boy, accidentally protecting him from taking direct hits. After the turmoil had ceased and the area was secured by the authorities, the police had found the boy unconscious, but alive. A bullet had passed through his upper chest and exited through his back. The woman did not survive. She had received six bullet wounds in the back and head. The boy had an identification chain around his neck. It said his name was Erimanc Feyad.

Seven years later, on June 6, 1982, Israel invaded Lebanon with 60,000 troops in an act condemned by the UN Security Council. Two months later, under a U.S. sponsored cease-fire agreement, the PLO agreed to leave Lebanon and Israel agreed not to advance further into Beirut.

On September 1, the expulsion of the PLO fighters from Beirut was completed. Two days later, Israel deployed its armed forces around the refugee camps in West Beirut. The next day Ariel Sharon, the Israeli defense minister at the time, claimed that 2000 PLO fighters still remained in that area.

On September 14, 1982, the President of Lebanon, Bachir Gemayel, was assassinated. In response, the Israeli army reoccupied West Beirut. Israel's occupation breached its peace agreements with Muslim forces in Beirut and with Syria. Israel justified its move into West Beirut by a need to maintain order and stability.

The Israeli army then disarmed, as far as they were able, anti-Israeli militia in West Beirut, while leaving the Christian Phalangist militias in East Beirut fully armed. The United States had given written guarantee that it would ensure the protection of the Muslims of West Beirut.

Within the next ten days, the Israeli military had completely surrounded and sealed off all refugee camps and set up observation points on the roofs of nearby tall buildings. On September 15, they met throughout the day with top Phalangist leaders to arrange the details of the operation.

On the evening of September 16, the Phalangist militia entered the camps armed with guns, knives and hatchets. A Phalangist officer reported 300 killings, including civilians, to the Israeli command post at 8 PM, and further reports of these killings followed throughout the night. Robert Fisk, one of the first journalists to visit the scene quotes unnamed Phalangist officers as saying that 2000 terrorists, women as well as men, had been killed.

On Saturday, September 18, the Phalangists were ordered to continue action mopping up. They forced the remaining survivors to march out of the camps, randomly killing individuals. The first foreign journalists were allowed into the camps at 9 AM Sunday and there they found hundreds of dead bodies scattered about, many of them mutilated, among which were found were thirty-five women and children.

Among the dead was a teenaged girl. She had been bludgeoned and shot. A note written in Lebanese was found in her jacket. It read:

Dearest Nashiba,

It is with the greatest of love and affection that I write this note to you on your eighteenth birthday. You are truly the light of my life. Every moment that we are apart seems an eternity. Every moment I live, I do so with you in my heart.

You have brought me back to life. I have never felt this way before. The spirit of my departed and beloved guardian and adopted father Abdul Feyad has brought us together.

I cannot wait to see you again this Sunday. Together we can escape this war which endangers both of our lives. It is the very thought of being with you again which sustains me and my soul.

Allah willing, we will be together again soon. With all my love and deepest devotion, I am always and forever yours!

All my love,
Erimanc Feyad

PS. By the way, two years ago my instructor advised me to take a western name if I was to become an art dealer. I chose one that is pleasing to the ear. It is a common name in America and I hope you like it. My western name is Daniel Schofield."

~

The Darkness

"What? What the hell do you mean, there's been a delay?" yelled Ernst Lamply. "That shipment is supposed to be at Coronado in two days. And if it isn't, I am going to kick some serious ass around here! Do you understand, Colonel?"

"Yes, sir, I do, sir!"

"Without that shipment the *event* will not happen. You DO understand the significance of that, don't you, Colonel?"

"Yes sir, Mr. Vice President." said Colonel Graham. "I understand perfectly."

"Then what is the friggin' problem, Graham?" asked Lamply.

'No problem, sir. All I know is that we got a text message from the CFAF operative saying that the shipment may be delayed. It has something to do with a lost ammo bunker key. The agent in Ensenada said they were in the process of rectifying the problem as we speak."

"Lost ammo bunker key? You gotta' be kidding. What kind of an incompetent idiot is this guy, what's his name – Tomato?"

"D'Amato, sir, and actually he has been quite effective in helping to implement *Operation Stranglehold*. I'm sure it's just a temporary setback, sir."

"Well, see that it is, Graham. If you want to be the first in command for FEMA after the *event*, then you had better get on top of this. I want that shipment at Coronado within two days, as planned. Is that perfectly clear, Colonel?" screamed Lamply.

"It's crystal clear, sir. I will get right on it. There's just one more thing, sir."

"What is it, Graham? I'm a very busy man" yelled Lamply.

"The operative wants to be sure that he will be paid as agreed. He is threatening to jettison the shipment out at sea if the ten million is not in his Swiss account upon docking at Coronado."

Lamply turned bright red as his temper started to flare into one of his signature tantrums.

"You tell that son of a bitch Tomato or whatever his name is that he'll get his money, alright. Just remind him that he wouldn't be losing an ammo dump key if it was up his ass. And that is where he'll find his head if he dares question me again. Do you understand, Colonel Graham?"

"Yes sir, Mr. Vice President. I'll take care of it, sir!."

"And if those supposed *operatives* dare to screw this up, he'll be at Guantanamo the next day. And for life too, you might remind him. And who's that other Muslim terrorist he's working with… what's his name…*Hatfield*?"

"Schofield, sir, his name is Daniel Schofield." answered Graham.

"Well the same goes for him" screamed Lamply while suddenly gripping his chest.

"Shall I notify the President, sir?" asked Graham.

"Screw the President. If his IQ were any lower he'd be a geranium. I'm running this operation. President Black is dumb as a sack of hammers. Hopefully, he's in Oklahoma, clearing brush. That's about all his brain can ever handle." The chest pains were obviously getting worse as Lamply began to grimace.

"Those fools" thought Lamply to himself. "If they think I'm going to actually pay each of them ten million dollars they are in for a big surprise. I can use that money in other ways. Guantanamo could use a couple more inmates."

"Sir, are you alright?" asked Graham.

"No, I'm not alright, Graham" said Lamply as he opened his desk drawer and tore the top off a prescription bottle and grabbed a handful of amyl nitrate pills.

"Sir, I'll call the doctor" said Graham apprehensively. Picking up the phone on Lamply's desk, he hit "O" and screamed "get the doctor in here, now!"

And as the operator rang the White House infirmary, a perfectly coiffed and sartorially splendid middle-aged man was fidgeting with his hair and perusing his reflection in the James Monroe mirror adorning a wall of the infirmary lobby.

"This is Doctor Reno" he said, slightly annoyed at the interruption. And as he answered the red phone, he slipped the comb back into his rear pocket without taking his eyes off the mirror.

"The Vice President needs you now, Doctor. It's an emergency."

Sighing deeply, he replied *"on my way"*, and with one last turn of his head he spit on his finger to smooth one slightly disheveled graying sideburn which had been brushed out of place when the phone touched his ear.

"I have to go, you gorgeous guy" he said to his reflection with a wink. Then after straightening his shirt about his belt, he grabbed his little black bag and proceeded just quickly enough to the West Wing.

"These Washington big shots, everything is always an emergency with them" he thought to himself. Then, rushing just enough to appear impressively busy, he dawdled long enough to straighten those annoying tucks and observe his reflection once more in the polished brass doors of the elevator.

And minutes later, he marched into Lamply's office with the air of a *good ol' boy* slightly annoyed for being called away from his self-produced tete-a-tete. Pulling a syringe from his bag, he began to prepare a remedy to inject into a vein of the Vice President.

"Reno, I am getting pretty goddamn sick of these attacks" screamed Lamply, holding his chest and sweating profusely as the doctor injected the specially concocted preparation into his arm.

"Well, Ernst" answered Reno with an assumed familiarity, "there's not much we can do, sir, short of replacing your ticker. You got more miles on this than a Dallas Cowboy cheerleader!" Reno was a Texan and knew all the good ol' boy jokes but also knew when not to cross the line.

"Shut up, Reno!" declared the VP. And as the preparation began to shoot through Lamply's veins to his heart and brain, the Vice President began to relax.

Obviously relieved, Lamply took some deep breaths. "That's better. Now get out, both of you."

And as the two rose quickly to exit the office, another gold gilded mirror hanging over the Regency sofa caught Reno's eye. Drifting his gaze to his reflection and then on to the administrative assistant in the doorway, he didn't see the ottoman which lay directly in his path stationed beneath his horizontal field of vision. And as his eyes locked on the reflection, his legs hit the ottoman and he went head over highly polished heels.

"Reno, watch where you're going, damnit" yelled the VP. "I'm the one who needs attention here. Now get out!"

Not the least bit embarrassed, the vain doctor picked himself up and began once again to smooth out the tucks in his shirt. "Ah, sorry Ernst, it looks like I got tackled" he chuckled in a sort of jock vernacular.

And as Reno and Graham once again turned to exit the office, Graham's cell phone jingled. Pulling it from his belt casing and looking at it while walking toward the exit, he suddenly muttered "oh shit!"

"Now what is it, Graham?" Lamply asked.

"Ah, it's a text message, sir. It's from D'Amato."

"So what does it say, Graham?"

"It's not good news, sir" answered the Colonel.

"What is it, Graham? Tell me now" said Lamply threateningly.

"Well sir, it looks like we've got another little setback."

"What the hell is it, Graham?" screamed Lamply.

"Well sir, it appears one of the CFAF agents has been kidnapped."

"Kidnapped… you are fricking joking!"

"No sir, he says that Special Agent Brubaker was kidnapped by the same guy who has the ammo dump key. And he is part of a terrorist group consisting of two women and two other men. He thinks they are an Islamic terrorist organization. He heard something about the *Swan*.

"Damn it all", yelled Lamply! "I guess if you want something done you have to do it yourself. Graham, contact intelligence and see what they have on a gang called *The Swans*. We can't have them ruining *Operation Stranglehold*."

Picking up the phone, Lamply punched a few numbers. "Hello, get me the Secretary of State now. Yes, get her now."

After a few moments, Lamply had someone on the other end of the line.

"Hello, Wheaton… Drop what you're doing, we have an emergency. I want you to call Vicente Pero and tell him he is going to have a few visitors very soon. Also contact Andrews Air Force Base. We'll need *Air Force 2*. Arrange the usual fighter escorts and security. Where are we going? Well Miss Wheaton, we are going to pay our south of the border friends a little visit.

There was a pause in the conversation. "Yes, I will take medical with me. Doc Reno and his staff will be accompanying me. There are some important things I need to tend to down there in beaner land."

There was another pause. "Where are we going? Suffice it to say, Secretary of State Wheaton that we are going on a mission to ensure the success of *Operation Stranglehold*. We're going to Ensenada, Mexico!"

The Shadow Government

Some people claim there is a shadow government in the United States. It is not an elected body, it has a secret budget in the billions of dollars and it does not have public disclosures and has more power than the President or Congress.

It has the power to suspend laws, arrest and detain citizens without a warrant and hold them without trial. It can seize property, food supplies and any transportation systems. It can also suspend the constitution. It is not the CIA or the military. It is called FEMA or the Federal Emergency Management Agency.

It is the most powerful entity in the United States and was not created under constitutional law by Congress. It was the product of a Presidential Executive order originally created to assure the survival of the U.S. in the event of nuclear attack or a natural disaster. It has grown into something quite different.

FEMA was created in a series of Executive Orders, something that becomes law simply by its publication in the Federal Registry. Congress is by-passed. Originally conceived in the Nixon Administration, it was refined by President Jimmy Carter and given substance in the Ronald Reagan Administration. The present Administration has given it omnipotence. It incorporates:

- The National Security Act of 1947 which allows for strategic relocation of industries, services and government and other essential economic activities.
- The 1950 Defense Production Act which gives the President sweeping powers over all aspects of the economy.
- The Act of August 29, 1916 which authorizes the Secretary of the Army, in time of war, to take possession of any or all transportation systems in the United States.
- The International Emergency Economic Powers Act, which enables the President to seize the property of a foreign country or national.

Here are just a few executive orders associated with FEMA that would result in a suspension of the Constitution and the Bill of Rights and could be enacted by the stroke of a Presidential pen.

- Executive Order 10990 allows the government to take over any highways, seaports and modes of transportation.
- Order 10995 allows seizing and controlling all media.
- Order 10997 allows taking over all electrical power, gas, petroleum etc.
- Order 10998 allows all farms to be taken over.
- Order 1100 allows mobilization of civilians into worker brigades.

- Order 1101 allows the takeover of all health, education and welfare.
- Order 1102 designates the Postmaster General to operate a national registry.
- Order 1103 allows the takeover of all aircraft.
- Order 1104 allows the relocation of communities.
- Order 11051 gives the authorization to put all Executive Orders into effect in times of increased international tensions.
- Order 11310 grants authority to the Department of Justice to enforce the plans set out in Executive Orders.
- Order 11921 allows the Federal Emergency Preparedness Agency to develop plans to establish control over energy resources, wages, salaries, credit and the money flow in any U.S. financial institution. It also provides that when a state of emergency is declared by the President, Congress cannot review the action for six months.

All in all, a pretty scary scenario if an "event" were to occur which might trigger these orders.

After Hurricane Andrew called attention to FEMA, the media and Congress commenced to study the agency. Some very interesting facts were uncovered. For example, it was found that FEMA was spending twelve times more for *black operations* than for disaster relief. It spent 1.3 billion constructing secret bunkers throughout the U.S. Yet fewer than 20 members of Congress, only members with top security clearance, knew of its expenditures. In other words, 1.3 billion dollars has been appropriated by FEMA for situations that do not qualify as disaster situations.

Congressional leaders state that FEMA has built a *black curtain* around its operations. For example, it was discovered that the agency has developed 300 sophisticated mobile units that are capable of sustaining themselves for over a month. They are located in five areas of the U.S. Each contains huge generators but none have ever been used for disaster relief. *Black helicopters* have been sighted around these areas raising questions as to whether or not the agency has its own military equipment and army.

FEMA's enormous powers can be triggered easily. In the event of any foreign or domestic problem, emergency powers can be enacted. Martial law can now be declared by the President with the stroke of a pen, activating FEMA's awesome powers. Under emergency plans already in existence, the power to overturn the Constitution and hand the reins of government to FEMA and military commanders is firmly in place.

If an *event* were to occur, FEMA then would have the right to order the detention of anyone questioning its authority and could authorize the arrest and internment of any perceived dissident for an undetermined amount of time without a trial.

The heart of this frightening scenario is that FEMA has the power to turn the United States into a police state in times of either a real or manufactured crisis. Intelligence reports indicate that FEMA has a folder with

22 Executive Orders ready for the President to sign in case of an emergency.

The potential scenarios which could trigger FEMA into action are easily found in the world today. Economic collapse, civil unrest, terrorist attacks, and protests against American Imperialism all could serve as FEMA triggers. All these premises exist and it could only be a matter of time before an event activates FEMA's powers and then it may be too late, because under the FEMA plan, there is no contingent possibility of restoring Constitutional power.

It was James Madison's worst nightmare that a self-righteous faction of a country could someday be strong enough to sweep away the Constitutional restraints designed by the Framers to prevent the tyranny of centralized power, excessive privilege and an arbitrary governmental authority designed to wipe out individual freedoms.

It may have been James Madison's worst nightmare, but it was also Vice President Ernst Lamply's greatest dream.

The Emerald Tablets of Troth

"My God, what are these?" asked Meredith stepping first into the cavern. They are so beautiful and why do they glow like this? And what is that? Is it music?"

Christian and Lynne then entered followed by Brother Bob and Antonio.

"I never, ever thought I would be so fortunate as to see these" said Lynne. What I sense here is beyond words, something not of this world. I have read about the *Emerald Tablets* but thought they were a myth. And here they are. They actually exist."

"Otrolig" said Christian, his mouth agape in total awe. "I am supremely humbled to be in their presence. What are they?"

Joy Stephanie was speechless. She could only stare at the magnificence of the ethereal light reflecting and surrounding each tablet.

Antonio crossed himself and muttered a prayer.

"These are the *Emerald Tablets of Troth*" said Bob. They were discovered here in this very cave twenty-eight years ago. All who have witnessed their existence here have sworn vows of silence. If anyone knew they were here, we would all be murdered and they would undoubtedly fall into evil hands. Be forewarned about this."

"So what are they?" asked Stephanie, suddenly finding her voice again.

"Let me tell you who Troth was first and then I will explain to you about the supernatural powers of the tablets. First of all, the Tablet's antiquity is stupendous, dating back some 36,000 to 50,000 years B.C. The writer is Troth, an Atlantean Priest-King who founded a colony in ancient Egypt after the island was destroyed and sank into the depths of the ocean."

"Atlantis was really a country?" asked Meredith.

"Yes indeed, my dear… Troth was the builder of the Great Pyramid of Giza, erroneously attributed to Cheops. In it he incorporated his knowledge of the ancient wisdom and also securely secreted records and instruments of ancient Atlantis."

"Most interesting" Christian commented.

"Yes, isn't it" said Bob. "Anyway…as I was saying… for some 16,000 years, Troth ruled the ancient race of Egypt from around 50,000 to 36,000 B.C. By that time, the ancient barbarous race among which he and his followers had settled had been raised to a high degree of civilization."

"How could he have lived so long?" asked Stephanie.

"He was immortal" said Bob. "As in many ancient religious and pagan myths, he supposedly conquered death. Modern Christianity purports the same myths. He passed into the highest realm or plane only when he willed it and even then it was not through death."

"Helt fascinerande" Christian commented.

"So what do they say and how do they glow like that and what is that heavenly music I hear?" asked Meredith.

"I'll explain their radiance and resonance in a minute. What they say is, of course, open to interpretation. But some of it is quite specific in its explicitness. I shall show you the parts that apply to all of us now, at this time. The Tablets have very accurately predicted many events that have already occurred in this century and some of its predictions, even though cloaked in mysterious metaphors and symbolism, seem to insinuate that an impending cataclysmic disaster is imminent for mankind."

"Imminent?" asked Lynne.

"Well, imminent only if the designated players don't change it!" answered Bob.

"Players?" asked Lynne. "I have a feeling that the players are right here, am I correct?."

"You *are* psychic, Lynne. But only half right. Some of the players are here but the others are on a different continent" said Bob.

"Which continent" asked Christian?

"Let me tell you this first" Bob replied. "Long after Troth passed into the upper planes of existence, Egypt fell back into turmoil around 1300 B.C. Many delegations of priests were sent to other parts of the world. Each of them took a tablet as a talisman by which they could exercise authority over the less advanced priests of races descended from other Atlantean colonies."

"The tablets became scattered?" asked Stephanie.

"Yes, temporarily" said Bob." But that is irrelevant right now. Now, as I was saying, one group of priests went to what is now South America and settled there. From these settlements grew the Mayan civilization which inhabited the Yucatan and at one time spread all the way up into what is now Baja, California."

"So the other players are in South America?" asked Christian.

"Well, more specifically, as you will see, a place in Baja, Mexico actually" answered Bob. "But I am getting way ahead of myself here."

"Are these a new discovery, I mean did anyone know they existed before twenty-eight years ago?" asked Meredith.

"No, no one knew. Like the Holy Graile, they were a myth. Secret societies throughout the ages have searched for them. You noticed the Goya paintings in the hotel lobby? Goya was one of many artists along with others such as Rembrandt, Renoir and Van Gogh who belonged to a secret society called the *Freemasons*. They somehow knew of the tablets and their contents."

"And the 'Freemasons' were?" asked Christian.

"Long story short…the 'Freemasons' was an extension of the 'Knights Templar'. As you may know, the *Knights Templars'* claim to fame was their pursuit of the Holy Graile, which was never found, although they did discover something else which they thought was of great value but actually turned out to be quite the opposite. But I shall get to that in a moment."

"How do you know all this" asked Christian?"

"I have spent most of my life in pursuit of the answers to these myths. You could call me a religious historian, I suppose" answered Bob.

"Tell us more about the *Knights Templar*" said Lynne. "I have read many things about them, but it is all very nebulous."

"Quite so, they were a secret society so much of their ways and beliefs are lost although the *Freemasons* still exist today, but in a much more secular way. Now, where was I? Oh yes, the Templars.....the Templars started out as crusaders and protectors of pilgrims escorting the devoted on their holy pilgrimages. Their original intentions were all good but as they became rich and powerful, like many human institutions do, they eventually became corrupt and also blasphemous in the eyes of the Church."

"As I recall, they came under the influences of various pagan religions, right?" asked Lynne.

"Yes, indeed they did, Lynne. I see we have a scholar in our midst here" said Bob.

"I've done some reading" said Lynne.

"Jolly good, now, as Lynne was saying, the Templars became corrupt and blasphemous. They tried to control the wealth of Europe at that time but were valiantly stopped by Philip the Fair of France in the 14th century. When put to the question about their beliefs, the leaders of the Templars revealed that they worshipped a goat-like creature, which sometimes also had a serpent's head, called Baphomet."

"The Devil?" asked Lynne.

"We are not sure whether he is the devil or just an agent of the Devil. He has many names, some others of which are Lucifer, Wegreog and Beelzebub" said Bob.

"And he signs his mark as *Wx*" came a comment from behind the group. It was Dustin, who had been on point keeping watch while the group was inside the cavern.

"And here it is" Dustin said while holding out a page of the hotel registry. There was the same signature scrawled on the paper.

"Uh, oh," said Meredith. "I think I'm beginning to get a picture here."

"Yes, we must hurry. But first let me finish." said Bob calmly.

"Mia madre, why didn't I stay in bed today?" murmured Antonio, crossing himself once again.

"As I was saying, conspiracy theorists make the claim that the Templars were the beginning of an international secret society whose wealth and prominence and banking system made them the real creditors of that time. And now they have evolved into the powers behind what is happening in the world today. These secret societies are known as the Bilderbergs, Tri-lateral Commission, the Committee on Foreign Relations and many others. Those of us who think we live in free societies are sadly mistaken. Much is planned and executed long before the average man has anything to say about it. But these secret societies do all have one thing in common."

"Which is" asked Meredith.

"They all practice to some extent satanic rites and are members of the Kingdom of the Beast. Did you see the film *Eyes Wide Shut*?

"I wondered what that film was about" Meredith commented.

"Yes, in order to keep their power, they have…well… what could be termed a pact with the devil. And in order to keep their power, they seek to find these tablets and another black sphere, which circulates in this world, referred to in these tablets as *Pi-ei-per*."

"The *Black Piper*!" exclaimed Lynne.

"Yes, that is the contemporary name. You know of this, do you?" asked Brother Bob.

"We are aware that it supposedly exists" answered Lynne.

"Oh yes, my dear, it exists alright. It is all explained in these tablets."

"Okay, this is cool….so we got Beelzebub or whoever up there looking for the *Black Piper* and also wants to kill us….why?" asked Lynne. "I had a bad feeling about all this!"

"It is all explained here so listen carefully. I have marked the crucial parts. It has taken years to translate them as they are written in the ancient Atlantean language" said Bob.

"Just one more question, why do they glow and what is that music?" asked Meredith.

"These tablets are not of a definable mineral element. They are formed from a substance created through alchemical transmutation. They are imperishable, resistant to all elements and substances. In effect, the atomic and cellular structure is fixed, no change ever taking place. In this respect, they violate the material law of ionization. They glow because of this unique cellular structure's interaction with the spectrum of light."

"Fascinating, and the music is?" asked Meredith.

"The characters of the language are responsive to attuned thought waves. What you hear has been referred to as the *Music of the Spheres* or the planets. It is the voices of angels that a mortal hears upon transformation to the next dimension."

"But how is it that we hear it now?" asked Lynne.

It is attuned to your thoughts, Lynne, and all of you also. Being in the Tablet's presence, shall we say, allows us to *see* and *hear* what is not normally allowed us" Bob replied. "That is what makes it so valuable. It gives the person or people in its presence great wisdom and power. To those that dwell in the lower realms like Wegreog, these tablets are a threat. Evil cannot triumph over good with these Tablets on earth."

"So he wants to find these tablets and destroy them?" asked Christian.

"They cannot be destroyed by him or anyone else. It can only be used for good. Wegreog or Beelzebub, take your pick, knew this so he devised a means to deal with this obstacle. He knew that man could be easily tempted so he assembled a similar indestructible artifact which gives the person who possesses it great power and wealth to begin with, but which inevitably slowly destroys the that individual's life."

"The *Black Piper*" said Lynne.

"Yes…*from light to darkness thy path shall be, a lesson in duality*" added Stephanie.

"You know of this, do you?" asked Bob.

"Lynne told us" said Stephanie.

"Excellent then" said Bob. "You are already educated in this matter."

"Only a little" said Stephanie. "What does Wegreog want and how or why does he appear now? Where has he been?"

Wegreog seeks revenge and to seize the Tablets so his *Piper* can triumph in this rivalry" Bob replied. "But his reappearance has been predicted in the Tablets, you will see."

"But why is he after us?" asked Stephanie. "What did we ever do to him?"

"You did much to him. In previous incarnations you were Troth's disciples. You were the ones who sent him back into the realm of darkness. He has a score to settle with you."

"Oh, how nice…said Lynne. "You are telling us that he knew who we were in previous lifetimes? What a memory he must have. I can't even remember what I did the day before yesterday."

"It is all written in the Tablets. You see, we stand in the way of his mission to retrieve the Tablets and take them to the lower realms. There, they cannot influence man to deviate away from the path of evil the powers of this world have chosen and his victory will be easier to achieve."

"So what are we going to do?" asked Meredith. "I don't relish the idea of fighting with the Devil."

"Neither do I but I have a plan by which using the power of the Tablets hopefully will send him back to where he came from. It is what banished him before" said Bob.

"So what brought him back?" asked Lynne.

A set of circumstances just happened to come about at the perfect time which opened a hole in the fourth dimension. These circumstances with your utterance of the *word* allowed him in again."

"What *word*, Brother Bob?" asked Meredith.

"The *word Pi-ei-per* or as you spoke it *Piper*" answered Bob. "The astrological and metaphysical circumstances of that precise moment in time in combination with that precise second you spoke the *word* opened a dimensional portal on the other side of which he has waited for centuries. It is written in the Tablets."

"Ooookaaayy" said Lynne. "Now that he's here, how do we destroy him before he does us?"

"We cannot destroy him, but with the help of the Tablets we can send him back again" answered Bob.

"Well then, let's get this show on the road, shall we?" asked Stephanie. "I'm all for that plan, the sooner the better."

"Jolly good then, let us begin. Dustin, keep your eyes open for intruders and use this if you must." Bob tossed Dustin an ancient relic which resembled a crucifix but upon which the top was encircled.

"What is that?" asked Christian.

"It is an ancient Egyptian relic called an *ankh* used to keep the wolves at bay, shall we say. Now then, let me explain the contents of the Tablets. The tablets are twelve and are divided into thirteen parts for the sake of convenience. The last two are so great and far-reaching in their importance that at present it is forbidden to release them to the world. But let us start with the first and I will point out the pertinent passages."

And with that, Bob opened the first volume and began to read as Dustin closed the cavern door on the group. Gripping the ankh tightly, he turned apprehensively toward the entrance in case any unwelcome fourth dimensional visitor was to appear suddenly.

~

The Hotel and the Club

After a brief stop at customs in San Diego, the Citation made the Ensenada airport in less than fifteen minutes.

"Permisso to land, por favor" said the co-pilot Dan Maris to the control tower as Rod Moore adjusted the flaps for landing and began his approach.

"My gawd, will you look at that! If the runway were any shorter it would be a patio" said Rod.

"Well, this is Mexico and not La Guardia, after all" said the co-pilot.

"True, thank god for reverse thrust" said Rod as he put the jet down as softly as a feather on the tarmac and engaged the thrusters, bringing the jet to a slow stop. Rod grabbed the intercom and pushed the talk button. "This is your captain. Welcome to Ensenada. Please remain seated until we come to a full stop, thank you."

As the jet came to a halt, the cabin door popped open.

"Looks like a beautiful evening tonight" said the flight attendant.

"Yes, it does, Maryanna. Maybe we can stay a few days down here. Is there any word on that from our passengers?" asked Rod.

"None yet, but a few days down here would be nice. It's Carnival, you know?"

"No, I didn't know but it sounds like fun. That would rock!"

"There is a great bar here called O'Malleys. I think we better go."

"I'm up for it" Rod replied enthusiastically.

"Nice landing, Captain" said Peter sticking his head into the pilot's cabin.

"Thank you, sir" said Rod. "Might I ask if we will be staying overnight or flying on to our destination?"

"I'm afraid that's an unknown at this point. Jeremy is on the phone with his travel agent to see how the room situation is down here. We have been informed that it's Carnival starting tonight. It just may not be possible to find lodging."

"I would think the town is fairly well booked" said Rod.

"Indeed, and another concern is security for Jeremy. If anyone finds out he's down here, there could be riots or attempts on his life. I mean, who knows what might occur."

"That's true" added Maryanna.

"But I will say that we will be here for at least a few hours" said Peter. "I have some urgent business to attend to. But let me check with Jeremy to see if he found out anything" said Peter, turning to walk back to the passenger cabin to consult with Jeremy.

As Peter approached Jeremy, he noticed that he was off the cell phone and was scribbling on a notepad.

"So what did your travel agent say, Jeremy?"

"All the hotels down here are booked except for one. I'm too tired to fly anymore tonight so I booked it. They had enough rooms for all of us thanks to a cancellation."

"Very well, Jeremy, but how may I ask are we going to keep your identity a secret? If people find out you're here there will be chaos" said Peter.

"There's an extra uniform here in the Captain's closet" said Rod. I think Captain Maris is just about Jeremy's size. He could wear that."

"The white gloves will have to go so people don't think it's just another one of his performance costumes. But if he tucks his hair under the hat, he may just get away with it."

"Jeremy, how do you feel about wearing a Captain's uniform to the hotel?" yelled Peter.

"Hmmm…why not, I think I'd like that" Jeremy replied.

"Very well then, I'll be off and will meet you later at the hotel. Which one is it?" asked Peter.

"It's called the *Hotel Coral and Marina* and it supposed to be quite nice. I reserved the suite for us and rooms for the others" said Jeremy.

"Excellent, then I shall see you later at the hotel" said Peter.

But where are you going?" asked Jeremy.

"To a club called *Pappas and Beers*" Peter replied.

"What's there?" asked Jeremy.

"I need to find a *key*" said Peter as he exited the aircraft and headed toward the main terminal to hail a cab.

~

The Nine

"Now as I was saying, the Tablets consist of thirteen volumes. Obviously, we don't have the time to read all of them but I have compiled a sort of outline that should give you an idea of what they say and how you fit into the scheme of its predictions" said Bob as he opened the first tablet.

The Tablets were fastened together with hoops of a golden-colored alloy attached to a rod of the same material and as Bob opened and turned to the beginning of each Tablet, the group could see that he had inserted a summary of each one's contents into the pages. Gathering them together, he reached into his robe pocket and produced a pair of bifocals. Turning towards the group he donned his spectacles like a college professor beginning a lecture.

"Now, the outline consists of random sentences extracted from the text of the various pages. Needless to say, there are probably many interpretations of the Tablets on many levels. But after having studied them for a great while, I believe these are the passages which are pertinent to our present day situation as I believe them to be. And as I read them, you will see that they begin to paint a picture."

"Wow, this is deep" said Stephanie as the vibrant streams of colored light danced and weaved to the vibrations of the celestial music emanating from the Tablets.

"Yes, that it is, Stephanie" said Bob. "Now, these passages are open to group discussion so feel free to comment when you think it necessary."

"Skitbra" said Christian.

"The first three Tablets are about the history of Troth and what he calls the *Halls of Amenti*. Keep in mind that these writings may have provided much of the basis for the grounds for modern day Christianity but we won't concern ourselves with those aspects now."

"Coming from a Franciscan monk, that's quite a statement" said Lynne.

"Yes, let's just say my beliefs are somewhat antithetical to most others in the order."

"I'd rather know how to deal with that fourth dimensional thug up there who is looking to kill us" said Christian.

"Right with you there, old chap" said Bob. "Now, Tablet three is entitled *The Key of Wisdom* and he begins to speak of earth at a time in the far future. These are sentences which I have selected to elucidate us."

"*Many in this new time are so filled with darkness and seek to fill all with their darkness.*" Okay, that applies to just about any time in the last 2000 years. Do we all agree?" asked Bob.

"Yes" the group answered.

"Very good then, next we have: *Called He the Dweller the Three Mighty Messengers*. Anyone have ideas?"

"In Christianity it would mean the Father, Son and Holy Spirit" said Lynne.

'Possibly, but in this instance on a more mundane level, it would refer to three who have the power to save the world from a cataclysmic event. Anyone have any ideas here?"

The group remained silent.

Hmm… we better leave that an unknown for now" said Lynne.

"Very good, then that is an unknown. Next at one point he speaks of the Tablets becoming buried, which they were when we found them here. It says: *Hidden and buried these Tablets shall become, lost to man until the NINE. Name them by name, Untanas, Quretjas, Chietal, Goyana, Huiertal, Semretan and Aridan, Theros and Tianem.*

"Can't say I've ever met anyone with those names" said Stephanie.

"They're not Swedish either" said Christian.

"But there is something most unusual about these names, I can sense it" said Lynne.

"Okay, moving on it says: *By their names I call them to aid me and free me from the darkness of the light giver.*"

"The light giver, does he mean the sun in our solar system?" asked Christian.

"No, I don't believe so. I think it refers to an individual, someone who is mortal. Let me give you an example. One thing I recall from my Latin classes is that the name Lucifer means *giver of light* for without the darkness he brings, metaphysically speaking, we would not know what light is. So let me ask you this. On a more worldly level referencing a prominent player on the world scene, can we think of a similar instance in which this metaphor can be used?" asked Bob.

The group turned their heads to look at each other.

"Lamply" said Lynne. "It's Vice President Ernst Lamply, isn't it?"

"It's a good bet" said Bob. "The metaphor fits. A lamp gives off light and yet that individual's motives could definitely be classified by many people today as being on the dark side."

"Most interesting" said Christian.

"Yes, provocative isn't it?" said Bob. "And next it says: *Dark is the way of the DARK BROTHERS who lead a great nation. Turn not to the DARK BROTHERS. One's name speaks of light but he is a master of darkness. The other's speaks of night.*"

"Fascinating" said Lynne.

"Yes and next we have: *Use they the DARK MAGIC, banded together as a secret order, magic that enshrouds man's soul with darkness.*"

"Mork magic" said Christian.

"And then we have: *Many are there a PARTY who walk in the DARK BRIGHTNESS and yet are not the children of LIGHT.* Are there any comments?"

"These statements could be construed as many things" said Meredith. The DARK BROTHERS could be President Black and Vice President Lamply and the members of the neo-conservative movement. Or how about including the radical evangelical Christian movement in America?"

"Radical Islam is also a possibility" said Stephanie. "Or are the DARK BROTHERS the leaders of Israel or Hamas?

"Yes, they are all opposite faces of the same coin, I'm afraid" said Bob. "But let me ask you this. What is meant here by the DARK MAGIC?"

"The promises of great wealth and power if one does evil in order to achieve economic and military domination of the entire world." said Meredith.

"That is an excellent guess, Meredith. But what enables the DARK MAGIC?" asked Bob.

The group drew a blank.

"Well then, let me tell you this. In the last few Tablets Troth refers to the *dark fluid* and the end of mankind. It is quite explicit. Here is a passage from Tablet XII called *The Law of Cause and Effect and the Key of Prophesy*. It states: *There shall come onto man a time when the black fluid shall begin to cease. Then shall the DARK BROTHERS cause the event that shall make the earth tremble and shake. They shall open the warfare between light and the night and the great warfare shall begin. When man shall conquer the ocean and fly in the air on wings like birds, when he has learned to harness the lightening, then shall the time of warfare begin."*

"It sounds very much like the Book of Revelations" said Lynne.

"Yes, as the Evangelicals won't let us forget, the rhapsody and all that" added Stephanie.

"Yes, ladies… predicting the *end of days* is nothing new. But as opposed to those particular religious dogmas, Troth provides a scenario whereby mankind can be saved" said Bob.

"In that case, I do believe I prefer to hear Troth's predictions about this" said Christian.

"Ayudeme, Dios amable" whimpered Antonio from the background.

"It also states" said Bob "that also there exists BROTHERS OF LIGHT who walk amongst men secretly."

"Like you, Brother Bob" said Meredith.

"Thank you for that compliment but I believe he refers to entities of great supernatural power, those who are not mortal" said Bob.

"Angels?" asked Lynne.

"Yes, that would be my guess."

"Well, that's encouraging!" said Stephanie.

"Yes, let us hope it's true because from judging from the next passage, we will need all the help we can get" said Bob. "And here it is, it says: *Far in the future, the evil invader shall arise from the deep and walk again amongst mankind. He shall be called forth from the portal by the word and he rides the wind. The portal shall be opened with the word spoken by the two sisters of law as the great light sets over the place where Atlantis once thrived. The evil one bears the head of a goat and comes to claim the Tablets and seek revenge.*"

"Well, that will teach you to keep your big mouth shut, Lynne" said Meredith facetiously. "It would appear that we are the two sisters of law."

"Then it would follow that Cadiz would have to have been at one time the place where Atlantis existed" added Lynne.

"Logically, it would appear that way" said Bob.

"Well, Wegreog or whatever his name is sure made a grand entrance on the wind, alright" said Meredith.

"And it seems as if the *word* is the *P* word which I won't repeat." said Lynne.

"And that painting up in the lobby" said Stephanie. "The figure had the head of a goat."

"Yes it did, and as Goya knew of these Tablets, he painted certain elements of that painting symbolically. As you may recall, there were other elements in that painting evocative of the Tablet's words. For example, listen to this. It says *Three and one the riders come. Follow the KEY to the new waters. There the FAIR LADY holds the KEY. Take the Tablets and flee to the Three Lords of Nse'n'aTa on the new sea where the finger divides the waters. They alone can shift the earth's balance. But beware and shun the dark flower that tempts man.*"

"The dark flower is obviously the *Piper*" said Meredith. "And I guess the *three* and *one* refers to Christian, Lynne, Stephanie and me. But the new sea, what do you suppose that means?"

"Obviously, in those days the earth's geography was quite different. The new sea could be anywhere" said Stephanie.

"Yes, I believe the three and one *does* refer to you four and obviously the name Nse'n'aTa on the finger which divides the waters can only mean one place" added Brother Bob.

"Yes, Ensenada on the Baja peninsula would be my guess" said Lynne.

"Makes sense to me" said Meredith.

"Unless there is something in Sweden you know of, Christian" said Stephanie.

"Tyvarr inte" said Christian. "There are many fingers but nothing with a name like that."

"So assuming, Troth means Ensenada, what do we do now?" asked Stephanie.

"First we have to lose that creature from Hell" said Bob.

"Yes, how does Troth suggest we do that?" asked Lynne.

"I'm not entirely sure" said Bob. "But here are some more excerpts cloaked in mysterious imagery.

Lift the veil from the He-Goat and send him back from whence he came.

Seek ye within the circle, use the WORD to open the gateway.

Seek ye to find the path through the barriers, away from the light giver.

Speak the WORD and pass the evil one to the lower realm. Use my name three times; Chequetet, Arelich, Volmalites.

Beware the Dwellers in Angles. Only the Circle will give protection. Well, anyone have any ideas here?"

"There is safety in the circle, find the path through the barriers, avoid the Dwellers in Angles, say the magic words and send Satan back to Hell! Ooookkaayyy" said Lynne. "Sounds like a piece of cake to me!"

"Tvartom" said Christian. "Or as you Americans say, on the contrary. What do you suggest we do next, Bob?"

"Well, the Tablets do tell us to take them and flee to the people of the New Sea, whoever they may be. I suggest we do exactly that" said Bob.

"It's a little late to arrange airline tickets, isn't it? I mean, with old Beelzebub up there searching for us, I don't think a stroll to the concierge desk is in order" said Stephanie.

"I have taken the liberty of arranging some transportation for all of us. Antonio… is your cab ready to go outside the Oratorio?" asked Bob.

"Si, Señor… it is very ready to leave this place and the sooner the better."

"Good, now let's see here. There are six of us here so if we each take two of the Tablets, we can start our climb to the sepulcher" said Bob, opening the door of the cavern where Dustin stood guard.

"But aren't they heavy?" asked Lynne.

"No, Lynne, they are extremely light. You will find them light as paper. Dustin, distribute the Tablets. We will be leaving through the sepulcher. But we must hurry!"

"Yes, Brother Bob" said Dustin as he began to hand each of the group two of the Tablets.

And as the group carried the Tablets up the ladders, through the manhole and out of the Oratorio de Santa

Cruz to the Citroen, a dark figure with yellow eyes had found its way to the Hotel's basement elevator. And as the little cab sped toward the Cadiz airport, a cloud of ashen fog began drifting through the labyrinth of tunnels that would eventually lead to what used to be the resting place of the *Emerald Tablets of Troth*.

~

The Bar Room Brawl and the Darkness and the Light

"D'Amato, where in the hell are you?" screamed Schofield into his cell phone in an obviously irritated tone of voice.

"I'm walking back to Pappas and Beers, Schofield" said D'Amato. "Where in the frick are you?"

"I'm in a cab heading for the same place. I'll be there in five minutes. Meet me there. We have a big surprise headed our way and we better have our act together by the time it arrives in Ensenada."

"And just what friggin' surprise might that be?" asked D'Amato.

"I got a call from Colonel Graham. I'll tell you what it is when I get there. Just meet me at the bar."

"Alright, I'm practically there already!" replied D'Amato.

Meanwhile, the Wrangler with the *Swan Gang* had found its way to the entrance of the Hotel Coral and Marina.

"Come on, Ernie. Don't be such a wuss" said Tom. "Come on back to *Pappas* with us."

"Yeh, Ernie, you can't wimp out on us now" said Emmet.

"Sorry guys, no offense but as you can see, we have other plans" said Ernie, in anticipation of the afternoon delight which he thought lay ahead. "Let's go, Diana" said Ernie, hopping out of the Wrangler with the bag and offering his hand to his newly found companion.

Diana hesitated. "Okay, think fast Williams. I have to get that key but I can't have these people knowing I was with him when I steal it" she thought to herself. "There has to be another way."

"Come on, Diana, let's go" said Ernie pleadingly.

"Um…on second thought, Ernie, I think I've changed my mind. What the heck, it's still early and I feel like partying with your friends."

Ernie's face suddenly drooped like a hound dog's in a rainstorm. "Aw, come on, Diana. We can catch up with these clowns later" he exclaimed dejectedly.

"Get back in, Lieutenant. I've decided you're just going to have to work a little harder "said Diana laughing. "Now let's go get some chow with your friends."

"Damn" said Ernie to himself, hopping back into the Jeep with the bag. "Alright, let's go" he said as Janae popped the clutch on the Wrangler and headed back to the bar.

"Whoo hoo, Patron shots are on me!" she yelled as the Jeep peeled out and sped back up Ruiz Avenue to the same establishment where D'Amato and Schofield were now rendezvousing.

"So what's the surprise, Schofield?" asked D'Amato.

"Lamply is headed this way on *Air Force 2*."

"What, are you shitting me?"

"No, unfortunately I am not. He should be here in a few hours. We have to get that uranium dioxide from those torpedoes before then and have it ready to go back on the Corvette boat or we can kiss our ten million dollar paychecks goodbye. So where's the key, D'Amato?"

"A certain CFAF agent named Twyla Brubaker is with the guy who has the key. I almost got it back but I was interrupted by the *Swan Gang.*"

"So where is this gang now?"

"I heard them say that they were headed to the Hotel Coral and Marina. Hopefully Brubaker has him tied up by now and has gotten the key back. When they left he looked hornier than a ten-peckered goat! He was drooling so bad he could have watered the front lawn."

"Can't you call her?"

"I don't want to blow her cover, Schofield. How hard can it be for a hot bitch like that to get a key from a guy?"

"Where's the Coral and Marina?"

"It's a cab ride" D'Amato answered.

"Well then, we better get our behinds over there and make sure she's doing her job. Let's go."

And as the two turned to walk to the exit, a Jeep Wrangler had pulled in and parked in front of *Papas and Beers.* And just as the duo had reached the saloon doors to exit, in walked the *Swan Gang.*

Ernie, Tom and Emmet stopped dead in their tracks, as did D'Amato.

"Well, well, look who's here" said Ernie. "If it isn't the little Don of the United States Navy, the same one who said if he ever saw us again we'd be dead meat. And this time he has no Navy goons with him either."

"You're still gonna' be dead meat, mister!" said D'Amato. And with that statement he started to barge right through Ernie and Tom. But as he tried to pass, Ernie had decided it was time to deck the little Napoleon. Dropping the Louis Vuitton bag momentarily, he grabbed D'Amato by the shoulder, swung him around and fired off a right cross. But as he swung, D'Amato's short stature made him miscalculate the height of his punch.

And being slightly drunk, his intended punch went right over D'Amato's head and landed smack in the face of Admiral Gonzales of the Mexican Navy, who was just coming through the doors and who had stopped by with his staff for a leisurely lunch.

When the punch landed, it knocked the Admiral out cold and into the arms of his aids. And as he fell backwards, his side arm was knocked out of his holster and crashed to the floor. Landing on its hammer, the weapon's safety was disengaged, resulting in a bullet discharge which hit the brass bar and ricocheted off of the wall. Zinging wildly, it then struck the chandelier cable on the ceiling which then broke, whereupon the circular chandelier cascaded downward directly onto the band of roving mariachi's who had been serenading the customers.

Initially shocked but unhurt, the mariachis were not pleased that their instruments had been damaged by the falling light fixture. And assuming they were being attacked by the Mexican sailors, they grabbed what was left of their instruments and charged the group to retaliate.

Then the two bouncers who were rushing to break up the skirmish, knocked over a table of bloody Mary's onto a group of bikers who had ridden their Harley's down for the weekend. Being shit-faced drunk, one of them picked up a chair and threw it at one of the bouncers who ducked. The hurled chair then hit the mirror behind the bar, breaking it into a thousand pieces which caused the barkeeps to leap over the bar and confront the bikers with swinging fists.

As chaos began to reign inside the bar, two waitresses who were carrying trays of food orders slipped on the spilled vodka and tomato juice and the trays went flying, landing in a messy heap on the Mayor of Ensensda, Cristobal La Rosa who was there to meet with the Admiral to discuss the Mexican Navy Day festivities.

"I think we best be leaving now, Ernie" said Tom sensing the erupting chaos.

"That's probably a good idea" Ernie replied.

And as the group turned to leave, it occurred to Ernie that D'Amato had exited the saloon already and just could be waiting in ambush outside the front doors.

"Let's cut through the kitchen" said Ernie to Tom as he picked up the bag again and quickly led the group towards the back where he plowed his way through the swinging kitchen doors. But as Ernie pushed both doors open, one of them knocked a waiter back on his heels. And in an attempt to prevent a fall, the waiter grabbed the handle of a frying pan which was sautéing mushrooms. Flipping the pan skyward, the mushrooms and grease were launched out of the pan and right on to a copy of the latest *Gringo Gazette* which had been left by the grill. Being in a highly flammable state after being near the heat for hours, the *Gazette* then burst into flames and leapt onto a cleaning rag which the chef had been using to clean the grill.

"Oh my god, look" said Linda turning around and seeing the potential conflagration unfolding before her eyes.

Turning around to look, the group saw that the rag had in turn ignited a trail of spilled Reposada tequila which the cook had been using to flavor the Camarones Borrachos. And as the trail of burning tequila found its way to the source of the leak, the pineapple into which the Reposada had been decanted to age exploded like a Fallujah IED, scattering incendiary fragments of the fruit to all points of the compass which sent the cooks and kitchen staff scurrying toward the exits like heifers in a Texas Longhorn stampede.

"Oh shit, Ernie, I think we're in some deep doo-doo now. Let's get the hell out of here!" shouted Tom.

Grabbing Diana by one hand and with the bag in the other, Ernie and the crew scooted out the back door and rounded the corner of Avenue Ruiz just in time to see five Ensenada police cars and a fire truck screech to a halt in front of the restaurant blocking any sort of getaway in the Wrangler.

"I think we best leave the area" said Emmet.

"Everyone split up and walk on separate sides of the street. We need to get back to the boat and out of Mexico fast" said Tom.

"Shoot, I've got to get that key first" thought Diana.

"I believe I'll just mosey on back to Hussong's, mates. I can get the Wrangler back later." said Janae.

'Stay in touch, Janae. You may be bailing us out of jail before this is all over" said Tom as he, Emmet and Linda began to make their way back to Calle Primera to hail a cab before the police dragnet commenced.

"Diana, you better go back to the Coral and Marina. I've got a little errand to attend to before we meet back at the boat" said Ernie.

"I think we're in enough trouble, Ernie. What is that sinister brain of yours thinking of now?" Tom asked.

"If we want to get out of this area, we're gonna' need a little firepower to negotiate with. I'm going to pay a little visit to an ammo dump" said Ernie as he reached into his pocket to be sure the key was still there.

"Firepower?" asked Tom. "Like what kind of firepower, John Wayne Walters?"

"Oh, I dunno, maybe a torpedo or two."

"Are you frickin' nuts, Ernie?" asked Tom. The Mexicans are already going to lock us up for life. Now you also want to become classified as a terrorist against the U.S. government by stealing some torpedoes?"

"Well then, we have nothing to lose, do we? It should just take me an hour or so. I know my way around these installations and how to get into them. Go back to the boat and get ready to make sail. Trust me, if you want to get out of here, we'll need some bargaining chips. Diana, go back to the hotel" said Ernie.

"This is too good to be true" Diana thought to herself. "This guy is going to steal the torpedoes for me. How convenient is that?"

"No, Ernie, I want to come with you. You'll need someone to watch for guards and things. I'm coming with you" pleaded Diana.

"Hmm, this chic must really dig me to risk her Navy career like this. I guess I still got it" Ernie thought to himself.

"Please Ernie, I don't want to see anything happen to you" pleaded Diana.

"Well alright, being in the Navy, you could be helpful to me. In fact, you're going to be most helpful. The sooner we can get this done and shove off the better. We'll meet you guys back at the boat in an hour or so."

And as the group prepared to scatter and head back to the Marina, Linda looked back and could see flames darting out of the kitchen windows as a handcuffed Anthony D'Amato and Daniel Schofield were being put into a squad car while an irate Mayor La Rosa stood by, drenched in guacamole and tortilla sauce and screaming in Spanish that the gringo who started this fracas would never leave Ensenada alive.

Meanwhile, at the Ensenada airport, two planes were making preparations for landing. And as both would be arriving at approximately the same time, it was causing the traffic controller more than a little consternation. Ottavio Gomez, the traffic controller of the day was on the line with the Ensenada Chief of Police Manuel Diaz.

"Señor Diaz, we have a slight problem and we need you to make a decision" said Ottavio, obviously agitated.

"Why me, Gomez, I have nada to do with airport landings."

"Senor Chief, we have two airplanes approaching the airport and they are both muy importante aircraft. They will both be arriving at almost the same minute" said Gomez.

"So what, can't they land one after the other?" asked the Chief.

"Si Senor Chief, they can, but that is not the problem" answered Gomez.

"Well then, what is it, Gomez?"

"The problem is not landing both planes but which one to land first, Senor Chief."

"What is the problem? I don't understand, Gomez. What planes are they?"

"The first is *Air Force 2*, Senor Chief."

"Well, obviously that would get priority, wouldn't it, Gomez?"

"Si, Senor Chief, but the second plane will probably not like waiting to land either"

"Why is that, Gomez" asked the Chief, obviously irritated.

"It is the *Papal Jet*, Senor, the private airplane of Pope John Paul II."

"Caramba!" said the Chief. "I'll be right there."

"Can you bring some extra security, Senor Chief?"

"I'll see you in a few minutes" the Police Chief screamed into the phone. "Lupe, I'll be at the airport. I'll be back later" he said as he grabbed his hat and gun belt.

"Will you need backup, Chief?" asked the office assistant.

"Caramba, si, I will need it but I won't get it."

"Why Chief" asked Lupe.

"Why? I'll tell you why, because all my cars are up at *Papas and Beers*. Some gringo started a brawl and a fire and all my men are there now making arrests. And if I ever find him I'm going to lock him up for the rest of his life!"

And with that statement, the police Chief strapped on his gun belt, donned his hat and flew out the door of the police station to make his way to the Ensenada airport to witness the arrivals of *the darkness* and *the light*.

~

Winston Churchill

"Well, I must admit that this is the only way to travel" said Meredith leaning back into the Corinthian leathered bucket seat centered in front of the mahogany backgammon table. "What kind of jet is this again, Brother Bob?"

"It's a Gulfstream G550, my dear, the latest model. The Vatican wants to be sure his Holiness has the latest aircraft available in order to speed the spiritual salvation of mankind to wherever it is needed as quickly as possible."

"Otrolig" said Christian.

"What does that mean, Viking man?" asked Stephanie.

"It means unbelievable, Stephanie" said Christian. "We must be at 50,000 feet. I can hardly see the ocean from up here."

"We are at 51,000 feet, actually" Bob commented. "You heard the pilot say that is where we'd be cruising today."

"This is truly awesome, Brother Bob. But let me ask you, how is it that you can fly in the *Pope plane* on a moment's notice?" asked Lynne. "I have a feeling that you know something about him, am I right?"

"Well, Woji and I have known each other for many years."

"Woji...you call the Pope Woji?" asked Meredith.

"Yes, indeed, Meredith, it is short for Jozef Wojtyla, his real name."

"Well, come one, Brother Bob, let us in on the dirt." said Stephanie.

"There is no dirt, Stephanie" replied Bob laughing. "Let's just say that we are....well, sort of related."

"Oh, come on, Brother Bob... let us in on it. I mean we're all already up to our necks in mystery and intrigue" said Stephanie. "You're amongst your brothers and sisters here, Brother Bob."

"Very well, it is quite a fascinating story actually. You may have read about it on the Internet already."

"Okay, fill us in then" said Lynne from the suede divan across the cabin aisle.

"Very good, well...let's just start by saying once there was a man named Fleming who was a rather poor Scottish farmer. One day, while toiling to make a living for his family, he heard a cry for help coming from a nearby bog. So he dropped his tools and ran to the bog. There, mired to his waist in black muck, was a terrified boy, screaming and struggling to free himself. So farmer Fleming saved the lad from what could have been a slow and terrifying death.

"Not a pleasant way to go" said Stephanie.

"Indeed, so the next day a rather fancy coach pulled up to the farmer's humble abode and an elegantly dressed nobleman stepped out and introduced himself as the father of the boy Fleming had saved. The man said he desired to repay the farmer as he had saved his·son's life"

"A noble gesture, but these days I doubt you would ever see that happen. And even if it did, they'd just take the money and head to Vegas after buying a new wide screen TV for the double-wide" said Lynne.

Brother Bob laughed. "Perhaps Lynne, but in any event the farmer would not accept payment for what he did and waived off the offer, whereupon the farmer's own son appeared at the door next to his father. And when the nobleman asked if the boy was his son, the farmer proudly replied yes."

"The plot thickens" Stephanie remarked.

"Yes, it does, Stephanie. So then, the nobleman made an offer which was to let him provide the son with the same level of education his own son would receive. Then, the nobleman said, if the lad was anything like his father, he would no doubt grow up to be a man they would both be proud of."

"It sounds like a Mark Twain story" said Meredith.

"Or perhaps *Dickens*" Bob replied. "But this story is true, so hear me out. Subsequently, farmer Fleming's son attended the very best schools and in time graduated from medical school and went on to become known throughout the world as the noted Sir Alexander Fleming, the discoverer of Penicillin."

"Interesting" remarked Lynne.

"Yes, and years later, the same nobleman's son who was saved from the bog was stricken with pneumonia. And guess what saved his life?"

"No are you serious?" asked Meredith.

"Yes, it was penicillin" said Bob. "And guess what the name of the nobleman was... anyone?" asked Bob.

No one had an answer.

"So tell us then," demanded Christian.

"The name of the nobleman was Lord Randolph Churchill. His son's name was Sir Winston Churchill" replied Bob.

"Wow... that is quite a story. But how does that connect you and the Pope?" asked Lynne.

"Let's just say that the two families have never lost touch and an unstated fealty exists between the two families to this day. The two families are quite close, actually. They even vacation together when possible."

"But what is the Pope's connection with Fleming? I don't understand" said Lynne.

"Well...you see, for whatever reasons, Alexander Fleming was not able to father any children. But once on a trip to Poland, he visited an orphanage and took a fancy to a child there and adopted him. Can you guess the child's name?" asked Bob.

"Jozef Wojtyla" Lynne answered.

"Yes indeed, you are correct, my dear."

"So then, what is your connection?" asked Christian.

"My connection is, dear boy, that I have quite a famous grandfather."

"No, no way" said Stephanie. "You're not saying that..."

"Indeed I am, my dear. I am the grandson of Sir Winston Churchill."

Everyone's mouth had dropped like anvils in either disbelief or awe.

"Oh no, we're not buying that one, Brother Bob!" said Stephanie. "No" she said chuckling. "Come on, we weren't born yesterday."

"Yes, I understand your reservations, but it is the truth and believe me, you would not be the first to question my veracity."

'Well, true or not, Churchill sure was a character" said Stephanie. "What were the stories about him at dinner parties?"

The myths are numerous but the two that come to my mind are the dinner parties at Balmoral for Notting Hill Carnival and Harvest Festival in 1943. On those dates, his dinner partners were Lady Mountbatten and Lady Bessie Braddock, Duchess of Kent. He was not very fond of either one."

"As I remember, his insults were quite witty" said Stephanie.

"Yes indeed, when he was drunk you had to watch yourself. Lady Mountbatten had had quite enough of him one night and told him "if you were my husband, I would poison your wine." To which he replied: "Madam, if I were your husband I would drink it!"

"That is so funny" said Lynne laughing. "What happened on the other occasion?"

"Ah, the Lady Braddock" said Bob. "Surprisingly, I remember her quite well. She was this insufferable old hag who used to pinch my cheek and ask for a kiss. Her face was as ugly as sin and she walked as if she had a wicket up her butt. Anyway, one night at the Harvest Festival Party, she got into a little war of words with my grandfather. She accused him of being drunk and he responded to the accusation by telling her: "Madam, I may be drunk but tomorrow when I arise I shall be sober while you will still be ugly."

The group broke into laughter.

"Oh my gawd, that is hysterical" said Meredith.

"Not to doubt you, Brother Bob, but what proof do you have of this family relationship?" asked Lynne.

"But of course, my dear" said Bob. "Dustin, would you be so kind as to retrieve the *History of World War II* A-C from the Pope's literary cabinet over there?"

"Con gusto, Brother Bob!" answered Dustin, opening the small built-in book shelf, removing the volume and handing it to Bob.

Taking the volume, Brother Bob licked his fingers and started to move to the 'C' section.

"Here it is" said Bob. "Have a gander at this."

The group gathered around the prodigious literary volume and focused on a photo which adorned the page. There was Sir Winston Churchill sitting in a seat in full regalia, his medals in full review, with a small boy in his lap. The caption beneath the photo read *Sir Winston Churchill and grandson Robert circa.1955*.

"Wow, you had more hair then, Brother Bob" said Stephanie.

"Indeed I did, my dear" said Bob. "But if you will notice the medal third from the left on his chest."

"Yes, quite a stunning array of medals there" said Meredith.

"Well, my dears, the medal third from the left is known as the *African Star* and was awarded to my grandfather in 1945 for his participation in the North African Campaign at that time."

"A handsome medal" said Lynne.

"Yes, he had thirty-three in all, amongst other numerous titles bestowed upon him. Now I would like to show you something. And with that Bob pulled down the front of his robe to reveal a medallion on a chain which hung around his neck.

"Oh my God," said Lynne. "It's the same *African Star* as in the photo!"

"It was one of his gifts to me" said Bob.

"Wow, I guess we're really in front of an awesome heritage here" said Lynne.

"Well, I'm not so sure I could ever live up to Grandpa Churchill but I do know one thing at this moment."

"What's that?" asked Meredith.

"At this moment I do believe I know a really superb Chardonnay when I see one and I saw quite a few in the Papal refrigerator in the galley just a few minutes ago."

"Ooh, that sounds good" said Meredith.

"Very well then, Dustin, would you please pop the cork on a few of the bottles and pour us some glasses, thank you. What do you say, chaps?"

"Jolly good" they all said in unison.

"Jolly good, indeed, now then, let's all sit back, relax and enjoy the rest of our journey? We have much work cut out for us when we arrive at *the New Sea*."

And as the jet hit mach 0.885 and Dustin began to pour the wine, the pilot of the Gulfstream noticed something strange on his radar screen.

"What the hell is that, Ruggles?" asked the Captain.

"I don't know but it's right on our tail and it doesn't seem to be falling off. It looks like a mini storm system or something. It's thick like a massive fog bank but small and it's keeping right up with us five miles behind."

"Strange, but we've seen a lot of odd phenomenon up here. Alert the FAA to be sure to cover our rears."

"Aye, aye Captain" said the co-pilot. "But this is really weird, take a look."

"Wow…that cloud formation… it's…it almost looks like a… a, well, the head of an animal" said the captain. "Keep your eye on it."

And as the Gulfstream sped across the Atlantic toward Ensenada, the unknown climactic aberration slowly seemed to lose its speed and dissipate.

"Now it's gone, Captain" said the co-pilot. "It looks like we just had another UFO sighting."

"Yes, it would appear that way, wouldn't it? Still, something else was odd for a moment" said the captain.

"What's that, captain?" asked the co-pilot.

"Well, unless you have a bad case of gas, I'd say there was a very strange smell in this cabin for a few seconds."

"I noticed it too but didn't want to say anything. But now it's gone… weird."

And as the plane streaked along the stratosphere, its passengers tried to relax and sipped their Chardonnay and contemplated the situation they now found themselves in and the events that were predicted to unfold in the very near future. And just overhead of the jet, just far enough to be off the radar, a curious cloud formation followed it right along as it made its way to *the land where the finger divides the waters.*

~

The Smirking Storm

"What, what the frick do you mean they're in jail?" Vice President Ernst Lamply screamed into the phone. "How in the hell did that happen, Graham?"

"I'm not sure, sir. There was some kind of a barroom brawl and fire and the Ensenada police just took everyone into custody. D'Amato and Schofield were in the vicinity when it happened, sir."

"Well, those two imbeciles are going to be in trouble big time if they don't get that key! I want that uranium dioxide ready to ship by tomorrow. Get it done, Graham and keep me updated!" yelled Lamply, slamming the phone in Air Force 2 down with a bang.

"Yes sir, Mr. Vice President, I'll take care of it right away, sir." snapped Colonel Graham. "Lieutenant Longaberger, get in here" Graham screamed into the speaker on the desk.

"Yes sir, Colonel, right away" answered the Lieutenant as he proceeded into Graham's office. "Aye, aye sir" he said as he stopped in front of the Colonel's desk.

"Lieutenant, there are two people in the Ensenada Mexico jail that need to be bailed out. Their names are Anthony D'Amato and Daniel Schofield. They are instrumental to *Operation Stranglehold*. Contact the Mexican authorities and get them out. I don't care how you do it but get them out. They need to be out before

Lamply lands there and that should happen in the next few hours."

"No offense, sir, but that's not a lot of time" answered the lieutenant.

"Just get it done, Lieutenant. I suggest you start contacting the Mexican authorities now or Lamply will have our asses in a sling before morning Colors. Now go to it!"

"Yes sir, Colonel, I'll get on it right away, sir!" And with that statement, Longaberger turned to begin making the calls to attempt to extricate the two from the Mexican jail.

Meanwhile, at the Ensenada airport, Jeremy Princeton had put on his airline pilot's uniform and was ready to accompany Rod Moore to the Hotel Coral and Marina.

"Well Mr. Princeton, now that you've removed the white gloves, I would say you look just like a real pilot. No one will even know it's you under that hat with your hair tucked in like that. For once, your fans won't recognize you" said Rod.

"I hope not. There are mobs of people out there because of Carnival."

And as Jeremy adjusted his pilot's hat, a sinister ashen fog had suddenly begun to accumulate in and around the plane and at the same time a slightly putrid odor had penetrated its way into the passenger cabin. And as Rod Moore and Maryanna began to empty the storage bins, she turned to Rod with a wrinkled nose.

"What did you eat for lunch, Captain?" asked Maryannna. "Ewww, the *restroom* is back there, Rod!" she said gesturing toward the back of the cabin.

"Don't look at me, Maryanna. She who smelt it, delt it!" he answered covering his mouth and nose.

And as the two waved their hands in front of their faces, a raspy and mysterious voice came from outside the aircraft.

"Excuse me, señor" said the voice.

"Yes, what is it?" asked Rod.

"Señor Captain, could you taxi this plane across the runway and into the field over there? Two more grande planes will be landing in a few hours. We will need more room for them when they land."

"Just a minute" said Rod as he poked his head out of the cabin door to speak with the mysterious voice. "Who are you?"

There at the base of the stairs was a very tall and dark individual dressed in a pilot's uniform not unlike Jeremy's. His pilot's hat was pulled down over his forehead as if to hide his face and he wore black gloves.

"I am Captain Rodriquez, with Acapulco Airways. I have just come from the tower and the controller asked me if I would relay the message to you, Captain. The runways are clear now and it would be an opportune time for you to do this."

"Hmm…well, I guess so" said Moore. "No worries, I'll move it now. Jeremy, why don't you go on ahead and I'll meet you at the Coral and Marina. This could take a few minutes" said Rod as the mysterious captain turned and disappeared into the night.

"I think I'll do that. See you at the hotel" replied Jeremy who grabbed his *Louis Vuitton* flight bag and began his exit from the aircraft.

"Wait, I'll go with you Jeremy" said co-pilot Maris.

And as Captain Moore started the engine, he shouted to Maryanna in the rear who was straightening the passenger cabin. "Maryannna, did you think there was something weird about that guy?"

"I didn't see him" she replied. "Why do you ask?"

"Oh, I don't know. It's probably just my imagination but even with his cap pulled down I caught a glimpse of one of his eyes."

"So?" she asked.

"It looked yellow and it seemed like it glowed" he answered.

"You've been reading UFO reports again, haven't you? I think we better leave now. Let's just get this plane moved so we can get to the hotel and start enjoying Carnival."

And up above in the skies of Ensenada airspace, two aircraft prepared their approaches at six nautical miles out from opposing directions.

"Ensenada tower, this is *Air Force VC-2* one niner, Captain Coleman requesting permission to land. We are on final approach six nautical miles south southwest of the rabbit, descending at 2.5 degrees. Do we have clearance?"

And moments later, Captain Heinrich was contacting the tower also. "Ensenada tower, this is Gulfstream CB five two requesting permission to land. We are on final approach eight miles north northeast of the field descending at three degrees, request clearance and runway designation please."

"Well, Señor Chief, which one do I allow to land first?" asked Ottavio Gomez.

"I think Air Force 2 is more important, Gomez. The Pope will not mind landing afterwards, por seguro" replied Chief Diaz.

"Bueno, Senor Chief, I will do that." And with that, he clicked on the intercom and hailed the jet.

"Gulfstream CB fiver two, abort approach landing. Initiate *go around* and maintain decision altitude at 600 feet. Do you copy?"

"Roger" said Captain Heinrich. "Ten four, locking in at 600 feet and holding altitude heading zero two zero."

"There's a big bird on approach dead ahead, Captain" said co-pilot Ruggles. "Look at the vector reading here. That's a 707 putting down. No wonder he waived us off."

"Wow, that's a huge airplane for this runway. I wonder if they can accommodate an aircraft that size. We better check with the tower" said Heinrich. "Ensenada tower, what's with the 707? Can you land the big bird on approach? Repeat, can you land the 707, over?"

"Gulfstream CB, this is Ensenada tower. Roger, the 707 is cleared for landing, maintain heading and altitude until further instructions, over."

"Well, I guess he seems to know what he's doing. We can just observe from up here. I don't want to play a game of chicken with a 707" said Heinrich to the co-pilot.

"I certainly agree, Captain" said Ruggles. "Especially considering the size of that band-aid they call a landing strip down there. Let's listen in, shall we, Captain?"

"Yep, crank the squawker, this should be interesting. Man, I love flying so doggone much!" said Heinrich as he slowed the Gulfstream's speed down to 120 knots.

"Air Force 2, this is Ensenada tower. You are cleared for landing on runway number one, over" said the controller Gomez.

"Air Force 2, you have to be kidding me" said Heinrich. "What the hell is the Vice President of the United States doing landing at Ensenada? This is incredible!"

Just as Heinrich said those words, three F-15 fighter jets zoomed by in formation flying just 200 feet above the aircraft that was the personal jet of the second most powerful man in the world. And after visual assurance that no hostile aircraft were in the vicinity, they split off in three separate directions and disappeared back into the stratosphere.

"Wow, how amazing is this, Captain?" asked Ruggles. "How often does somebody get to see the airplane Air Force 2 landing?"

"This should be interesting, Ruggles" said Heinrich. And as he adjusted the volume on the radio, the voice of controller Gomez could be heard clearly and distinctly.

"Air Force 2, this is Ensenada tower, you are cleared for final approach on runway one. Do you copy, over?"

"Roger, Ensenada tower" said the 707 pilot. "Initiating ILS and descending glidescope to decision altitude of 200 feet, over."

And as the big jet began its descent onto the runway, Captain Rod Moore had begun his taxi across the very same runway, unaware that a 300,000 lb. jet representing the most powerful nation in the modern world had begun its descent and also unaware that the descent path which it had chosen would land it directly on top of the passenger cabin of the jet which Peter Harrison had leased for Jeremy Princeton's flight to Bahrain.

But as Air Force 2 descended to 400 feet, the pilot suddenly realized that the smaller jet was directly in its path of descent and in serious jeopardy of being crushed under the weight of the behemoth aircraft.

"Holy shit, Ensenada tower, what is that aircraft doing in the middle of the runway?" yelled Captain Coleman.

"Aye, caramaba, Chief, who told that airplane to move now?" screamed Gomez.

"Ah, Gomez, may I suggest you tell the Presidential plane to abort their landing," said Chief Diaz.

"Si, Señor chief… esta es muy peligroso ahora" Gomez shot back. "Air Force 2, abort landing now, do you read me, abort landing NOW!" Gomez screamed into the transmitter.

"Oh my gawd" yelled Coleman. "Reverse flaps, full forward power" he yelled to his co-pilot. "Roger, we're aborting the landing! Tower, we have an emergency situation here, *red alert*" he yelled into the radio.

Pushing the thrusters into full power, Coleman braced himself for a crash landing and as the 707 bore down on the smaller aircraft, he turned on the intercom. "Mr. Vice President, please be sure your seat belt is tight, we have an emergency situation up here. Prepare for a crash landing, sir!"

"What!!"…Lamply screamed. "If I find out who is responsible for this, he'll be in Guantanamo by tomorrow morning" he yelled as he tightened his seat belt around his overly indulged extended belly and began to sweat bullets. Reno stood up to tuck in his shirt before taking his seat once again to adjust the belt. Removing a comb from his back pocket he began to rake it through his hair like Danny Zucko in a house of mirrors.

"Sit down, Reno, what the frick are you doing?" screamed Lamply as his chubby hands clasped the leather armrests causing his knuckles to go white.

"Well, Ernst" said Reno insouciantly. "If I'm going to die, I want to look good, that's all!"

"Sit the hell down and shut up, Reno…NOW!" yelled Lamply.

And up front, Captain Coleman had readjusted the flaps and was struggling to pull the huge aircraft upward before it landed on the smaller plane taxiing across the runway, crushing it like an aluminum beer can in a vice.

"Come on, baby, up, up!!" screamed Coleman as he pushed on the thrusters as hard as he could. "You can do it" he yelled as the behemoth plane descended toward the runway on a direct path to crush the smaller jet.

"*Air Force 2* pull up *now*!" yelled Gomez into the speaker.

And just as the 707's landing gear was within inches of the smaller jet's tail wing, the thrusters kicked in and the 707 began to ascend once again into airspace clearing the smaller plane by only a few feet.

"Thank God" said Coleman, relieved that the crash had been avoided. "Mr. Vice President" he spoke into the intercom. "The danger has passed, sir. Sorry about the false alarm."

"Well, I am pissed off" screamed Lamply. "I'm going up to the front cabin and rip some heads off!" he yelled as he undid his seat belt and began to rise from his plush leathered armchair.

"Ah, Ernst, don't be all gettin' in a tizzy now. You have to watch your ticker, sir."

"Shut up, Reno and prepare another shot! I'll be right back" he snapped as he headed for the front cabin.

"Ensenada Tower, requesting missed approach procedure, we are initiating a *go around*...request new heading and altitude for new approach, over" said Coleman.

"*Air Force 2*, this is the tower" replied Gomez. "Initiate a *go around* at 800 feet heading zero two zero. There is another plane at 600 feet in a holding pattern. Keep a visual alert, over."

"We read you, tower" replied Coleman. "We have aircraft in sight, over" he said as he peered off to the port side of the plane.

And as Lamply burst through the cabin door to perform one of his notorious tantrums, an unusual cloud formation began to gather over the Ensenada airport.

"Alright Coleman, what is your frickin' excuse. You almost killed me, the Vice President of the United States. I want an explanation now, mister!"

"There was another unexpected plane taxiing on the runway, sir. I'm sorry but we had to abort the landing."

"Well, find out who the hell it was and I'll have him arrested for endangering the life of the Vice President, do you understand?" he screamed.

"Yes sir, we'll do that, sir" Coleman snapped back.

"Captain, what is that cloud build-up up over there?" asked the co-pilot. "It looks like some sort of a cumulus cloud formation. And it seems to be heading this way."

"You had better take your seat again, sir" said Coleman to the VP. "It looks like we're not in the clear yet. That could be a nasty weather system and it might get bumpy, sir."

"Alright, but let's get this plane landed ASAP, understand? I have some very important business to attend to down there" Lamply growled as he turned to exit the cabin.

And as the plane ascended to 600 feet, the cloud formation had totally engulfed the aircraft.

"Wow, Captain, we are totally flying blind. This fog just came out of nowhere, didn't it? And what is that odd smell?"

"I don't know but it's not a pleasant odor, is it? That happened fast. I'll have the tower vector us to our final approach. Tower, this is Air Force 2. We will need a ground controlled approach. We are ascending to 800 feet and initiating a *go around,* over" Coleman said into the headset.

There was no response from the tower, just static.

"Ensenada tower, do you read me, over."

Only static could be heard.

"What the hell is going on here?" said Coleman. "I better try to reach the other bird that's up here with us" said Coleman changing channels on the communicator. "This is *Air Force 2* hailing all aircraft. Please acknowledge and identify altitude and heading, over. *Come in*, please, over!"

There was no response.

"What the hell is going on here" screamed Coleman. "Ensenada tower, come in! Tower, do you read me, over!"

There was nothing.

"Captain, look at our altimeter. It says we're still at 600 feet. We better climb out of here fast. That other aircraft is up here with us somewhere nearby" shouted the co-pilot.

Captain Coleman increased thrust and adjusted the flaps but the controls were not responding.

"What the hell is going on here?" Coleman yelled. "None of our systems are responding. Red alert, prepare emergency procedures now!"

And as Coleman and his co-pilot began evasive maneuvers to no avail, traffic controller Gomez and Chief Diaz were on the radio trying desperately to reach either aircraft.

"*Air Force 2*, do you read me, come in, *Air Force 2*."

There was only static to be heard.

"*Gulfstream CB*, do you read me, over, come in *Gulfstream*, do you read me?"

There was only more static.

"What do we do now, Senor Chief? Look at the radar screen here. We are going to be in big trouble, señor if we do not do something."

"They'll be at different altitudes, Gomez. Lets' just hope this weather clears up soon. Let them circle until it disperses" said Chief Diaz.

"They could do that but there is something else going on here, Senor Chief."

"What's that, Gomez?" asked the Chief.

Gomez took another look at the radar screen.

"I told Air Force 2 to ascend to 800 feet!"

"Si, so what is the problema?"

"Oh blessed Jesus, help us!" said Gomez.

"What is it, Gomez?"

"Look aqui! Air Force 2 has *stopped climbing* at 600 feet heading zero two zero. And the Gulfstream…..ay dios mio, no, no please!

"What Gomez, what is it?"

"The Gulfstream is also at 600 feet."

"They'll maintain distance, won't they?" asked the Chief.

"No Señor…the Gulfstream is at 600 feet and is proceeding at two zero zero."

"What the hell does that mean, Gomez?"

"It means…oh my God, help us…it means they are closing on each other…oh my God, no!"

And as air controller Gomez continued to try to alert the two aircrafts, the storm had taken what could be called a form of sorts. As Gomez and the Chief cast their gazes toward the skies in grim anticipation of the impending disaster, they could have sworn they saw what resembled the head of a goat. It seemed to have two yellow eyes and it appeared to be smirking.

~

The Giraffe and the Elephant

"Wait Ernie, before you go...just one more question" said Tom.

"Okay, shoot" said Ernie.

"How in the hell do you ever think you're going to break into a U.S. Navy ammo dump?"

"Who says I'm breaking in, Tom? Oh by the way, I think you better take this back to the Swan" said Ernie as he tossed Tom the Louis Vuitton bag.

"Damn, what do you have in here" asked Tom, grabbing the pack in mid-air.

"Oh yeah, I guess I forgot to tell you...there's some sort of sculpture in there."

"Sculpture... what sculpture?" Tom asked as he unzipped the pack and looked inside.

"It's the sculpture that rolled out of your briefcase this morning when I tripped over it."

"It's the *Piper*" Tom exclaimed as he fished it out of the pack and held it up to be sure. "How in the hell did this get in my brief case?"

"It must have been Peter" said Linda. "Remember, he asked if you were taking your brief case to the Swan."

"Dang, he must have slipped it in the case during the night when it was in the front hallway of Tierra Bella. But why, I wonder?" asked Tom.

"The curse, Tom…he must have figured if he gave you the *Piper*, Jeremy could escape the curse." said Linda.

"And that I would inherit his bad luck, I suppose. I still think it's all a lot of coincidental nonsense. But still, we better keep an eye on this. I have a feeling it's going to come in handy."

"That won't be safe on the boat, Tom" said Linda.

"She's right, Tom" agreed Emmet. "With the Ensenada police and the Mexican Navy Admiral looking for us, it would be better off somewhere else."

"Yeah, I guess you're right" answered Ernie. "Diana, you're going back to the hotel. Take the Louis Vuitton bag and put it in the hotel safe."

"You certainly are trusting, Ernie" said Diana. "What makes you think I won't disappear with it?"

"I'd find you" Ernie replied. "Need I say more?"

"No, you needn't" said Diana. "Okay, I'll put it in the hotel safe at the Hotel Coral and Marina."

"Good girl" said Ernie as he handed the Louis Vuitton bag over to Ensign Williams. "Now come on, Diana, you're going back to the hotel and then we're going to pay a little visit to Uncle Sam's local armory down here."

"Ernie, I have to agree with Tom. How in the hell are you ever going to get into an armory?" asked Emmet. "You're hallucinating if you think you can ever do that."

"Emmet, let me ask you two very simple questions."

"Okay, you can do that."

"First question; how do you put a giraffe in a refrigerator?"

"Are you on crack or something? What has that got to do with anything?"

"Just answer the question, Emmet. My nine year old niece Ava got these answers right. Certainly a man of your great intellect can equal her feat. Now, how do you put a giraffe in a refrigerator?"

"Is this a trick question?"

"Not really" Ernie answered.

"Umm…I don't know…I guess you bend its neck and put him in that way, right?"

"Wrong, Emmet…what you do is simply open the refrigerator door and put him in, that's all."

"What, well……I don't think…"

"Now, let me ask you this. How do you put an elephant in the same refrigerator?"

"Ah, let me guess…you open the door and put him in just like the giraffe" replied Emmet, obviously bored with Ernie's puerile questions.

"No, Emmet, that is incorrect, although you're half right. The correct answer is you open the refrigerator door, take out the giraffe and then put the elephant in."

"It is a trick question then."

"No it's not… it's basic Zen."

"You're obviously the Zen Master here, Ernie" said Tom. "But what do those questions have to do with breaking into a United States Navy ammo dump?"

"Very well, Grasshopper, I will tell you" replied Ernie. "You see, all of us tend to complicate things unnecessarily." And with that statement, Ernie reached into his pocket, withdrew the flat silver key to the ammo dump and held it up for the group to behold.

"And what is that?" Linda asked.

"This is the key to the ammo dump" Ernie replied. "And with this key, I shall open the refrigerator door, remove the giraffe and put in the elephant, so to speak. Now we had better disperse before the Ensenada police head this way. I'm going to catch a cab and I'll meet you back at the Swan in an hour or two."

"I'm not even going to ask how you ever got that. So I'll just say good luck, Ernie" said Tom. "I can't wait to see your *Wanted, Dead or Alive* poster at the Anacapa post office."

"Not to worry, Tom. I learned a thing or two in the SEALs….piece of cake really…see you later." said Ernie as he grabbed Diana's arm and turned to hustle her and the Louis Vuitton bag up Ruiz Avenue to find a cab.

"Diana, by any chance, did you bring a uniform with you?' he asked.

"As a matter of fact, yes… I have to go straight back to Coronado when I return. I didn't think I'd have time to get back to my condo in La Jolla with the traffic so I brought one with me."

"Excellent, so this is what I need you to do. Go back to your hotel room, stash the bag in the hotel safe and then change into your uniform. Then I want you to catch the launch to D'Amato's ship and tell the duty officer that D'Amato has spilled something on his uniform so he needs some work utilities."

"They'll never buy that, Ernie. They probably have his cell phone number anyway. They'll just call him to check it out" said Diana.

"Diana, the guy is in jail. I don't think he'll want the U.S. Navy to know that. I have a feeling that he is involved in some heavy shit. I'll bet he wants to keep his name clear and not call attention to himself. Besides, you're an active Navy officer with the military ID's and everything. They won't question you, trust me."

"Let me think about this for a minute" said Diana as she took a deep breath and paused to ponder the situation. "I'm not sure what this guy is thinking but I'd better play along. Maybe he has a better plan than the assault raid the CFAF has organized. If I go back to the hotel I can alert the other agents to abort the mission or at least postpone it" Diana thought to herself. "Okay, so what is the plan, Ernie?"

"Don't worry about it, Diana. Just do as I said and I'll meet you at the Navy Piers where the launch is, at say 1600 hours."

"He seems to be sure of himself. I guess I'll play along" she then thought to herself. "Ernie, don't forget that it's Carnival. The traffic and crowds are horrendous."

"I'm planning on them being horrendous, Diana... the more so the better. There's a cab" said Ernie, hailing the roving taxi with both arms.

And as the taxi pulled to a stop, Ernie opened the door and gently pushed Diana and the Louis Vuitton bag into the back seat.

"But Ernie, what about......."

"No worries, Williams, just do as I say and I'll meet you at 1600 hours."

And with that, Ernie slammed the rear door of the cab, and after hitting it twice on the roof signaling the driver to proceed, he turned and made his way back to Costero Blvd. where the Carnival parade was also proceeding down to the Navy Piers.

As the floats and revelers created a resounding chaos, the Mexican Navy was busy at the Navy Piers preparing for the mock terrorist attack which was to take place the next day. Turning onto Costero Blvd., Ernie could see the Mexican Naval vessels in Todos Santos Bay were staging the next day's performance.

"Good, they'll be busy tonight when we sail" thought Ernie. "Now, to go get that elephant" he said with a slight smirk as he turned up Ruiz Avenue and slipped off stealthily into the night.

~

The Boomerang

"Wow, this is quite a celebration, isn't it, Captain Maris?" Jeremy asked as the taxi weaved its way through the Carnival revelers en route to the Hotel Coral and Marina.

"Call me Dan" the co-pilot replied. "It certainly seems like everyone is having a good time, doesn't it?"

"Driver, tell me, who are all these people? Where do they all come from?" asked Jeremy.

"They are many college estudiantes, señor. These are the ones who want to celebrate Carnival but cannot go to Brazil so they come here. It is a great excuse for them all to party and get drunk."

And as the cab pulled into the porte-cochere of the Hotel Coral and Marina, Jeremy noticed that a group of young girls and photographers had gathered at the hotel entrance.

"Shoot, paprrazzi!" exclaimed Jeremy. "Someone in reservations must have tipped off the locals."

And as the taxi pulled in front of the hotel entrance, another cab with a very attractive passenger and a Louis Vuitton bag had already stopped a few feet ahead. Opening the taxi door and climbing out, she began to walk to the hotel entrance just as Jeremy Princeton had simultaneously opened his cab door. And in an attempt to make his way to what he thought would be the safety of the hotel's interior before the swarm of fans and the paparazzi could engulf him, he burst into a sprint toward the front entrance. Co-Captain Maris tried to follow but was absorbed by the mob.

"Señor, don't forget your bag!" yelled the cab driver, who had grabbed the Louis Vuitton bag Jeremy had forgotten in the back seat. "Senor, your bag!" he yelled again, running after him.

As Jeremy and Diana reached the front entrance at the same time, another wall of adoring fans burst through the double doors and gushed out, screaming Jeremy's name. And as the crowd pushed forward, Diana became frightened and began to swing her bag alternately sideways and in an upward arc in an attempt to keep the crowd at bay.

But as she swung the bag upwards on her third swing, her grip on the handles slipped and her Louis Vuitton bag was flung backwards with the speed of a cannon ball. The flying bag zoomed in on the taxi driver's head with the accuracy of a laser, blindsiding him as he looked left and right at the gathering mob and nailing him directly on his cerebral cortex. Dazed and stumbling backwards, he proceeded to drop Jeremy's bag on the pavement exactly where Diana's bag had landed moments before. And as the herd of screaming fans encircled the two, the identical Louis Vuitton carry-ons were bounced around like two bingo balls in a collender.

"My bag!" screamed Diana who had turned around and now was nose to nose with Jeremy as the throngs of admirers shoved pens and papers in front of Jeremy for his autograph.

"Bag.... oh damn, I forgot mine too...its back in the cab" said Jeremy. "By the way, I'm Jeremy" he shouted as the two were suddenly sandwiched together like a grilled cheese.

"Yes, I know, I'm Diana" she screamed back as a herd of bellmen, front desk agents, car parkers and concierges intervened to separate and hold the crowd back. And as the crowd was eventually pushed back enough to give Jeremy and Diana some breathing room, Diana saw her chance to escape and ran back down the steps and grabbed one of the Louis Vuitton bags that lay on the pavement. Streaking by Jeremy, she yelled "nice to meet you" and raced through the entrance doors on her way to the front desk.

Breathing heavily, she reached the front desk and said' "Room 411, Diana Williams and I'd like to put this in the hotel safe."

"Yes, ma'am, right away" said the front desk agent, who promptly took the bag and headed to the back to secure the Louis Vuitton bag inside the safe.

"Thank you" she replied as she hurried to catch the elevator to her room to change into her uniform. And as the elevator doors swallowed her and the crowd was pushed back, Jeremy turned to look for his own bag which he had forgotten in the taxi. Dazed and confused, the cab driver had regained consciousness and began also to search for Jeremy's bag.

"Aqui esta, Señor" he said after groping around on the pavement and finally looking under the taxi. Grabbing the bag, he handed it to Jeremy who quickly sprinted up the stairs through the hotel entrance where the fans and paparazzi still were waving and pleading for autographs.

Making his way to the front desk to check in, he noticed that his jacket had been torn by the screaming fans. Co-captain Maris reappeared looking equally disheveled.

"So much for the disguise idea" said Jeremy to the co-pilot as he and Maris stumbled to the front desk.

"We are very sorry about the disturbance, Mr. Princeton" said the front desk agent from behind the desk. "There was a carnival party here earlier and somehow, someone must have found out you were on your way here. I assure you we would not divulge such information ever, señor. But none the less, please accept this suite at no charge to you and your party" he said as he handed the room card to Jeremy. "Now security will escort you to your suite. May I carry your bag for you, señor?"

"Thank you" said Jeremy "but no, I can manage the bag myself."

"Very well, Señor Princeton, it is our great honor to have you as our guest. Security, please escort Senor Princeton and Senor Maris to suite # 412."

And as the hotel staff held the crowds at bay, Franco and Juan from *Security* escorted Jeremy and the co-pilot to the suite and unlocked the door. And after checking the room for intuders, they bowed slightly and wished them a *buenas noches*.

"That was quite a welcome, Mr. Princeton. After all that, I guess I'll just grab the bedroom down the hall and say goodnight" said Maris.

"Yes, it was, wasn't it?" said Jeremy. "I understand, goodnight Dan."

"Goodnight, sir" said Maris as he walked to one of the bedrooms of the four bedroom suite.

Finally alone, Jeremy flopped down on the sofa to decompress. "Who would have ever thought this would happen down here" he thought, "Oh well, such is the life of a celebrity. Still, I wonder who that girl was. She was very attractive. Maybe I can find out tomorrow. Right now I feel like brushing my teeth and having a shower."

And pulling himself to his feet, he took a deep breath and strolled over to the *Louis Vuitton* flight bag which lay on the coffee table. Unzipping the flap, he glanced inside and turned white as a ghost.

"Oh, my gawd... no!" he screamed. "How can this be? Oh, no...no, no" he cried.

Reaching his hand into the bag, he shuddered as he removed the contents. Holding the contents up to the light, he couldn't believe his eyes. In his hand he held the familiar black sphere that looked like a flower. And as he held it up to the light, it began to throb and vibrate as if it had just come back to life.

~

Wegreog

B ob was staring out the window of the plane. He had a look of horror on his face.

"Bob, do you recognize that odor?" asked Lynne, awakening from her nap. "I have a very bad feeling just like I felt at the Hotel Parador in Cadiz. What is going on and what is that smell?"

"Wegreog is back I'm afraid. I thought we could lose him but evidently it's not going to be that easy. Quickly Lynne, the tablets, get them out of the storage bins! I'll be right back" said Bob as he headed for the pilot's cabin.

"What…what's going on?" asked Christian as he and the others awakened from their slumber.

"It looks like we all dozed off" said Meredith.

"What is that smell?" asked Stephanie.

"We will need the tablets" said Dustin. We have no time to lose!" he yelled, as he quickly reached for the over-head bins and began to remove the Tablets one by one, handing them to the group.

And as Brother Bob entered the Captain's cabin, he could see that Captain Heinrich and his co-pilot were obviously struggling with the controls.

"What's going on, Captain?" asked Brother Bob.

"This fog, it's done something to the controls. We're stuck in a circular heading and can't seem to move the rudder. It's almost as if an invisible hand is guiding the plane."

And as the plane began to shudder while the captain tried to maintain control, Brother Bob realized what he had to do.

"I'll be back, Captain" he yelled as he returned to the passenger cabin. "Quickly Dustin, we must hurry!" he said urgently.

"What is going on here, Brother Bob?" asked Meredith.

"Wegreog has found us, Meredith. And he will destroy us unless we can send him back from where he came. Now is the time to try to *Lift the Veil from the He-Goat*."

And in the meantime Captain Rod Moore and Maryanna, obviously shaken over their close brush with death, had joined the Controller Gomez and Chief Diaz in the tower.

"What the hell happened out there?" asked Rod. "We were almost crushed to death by that 707! Why did you tell that other Captain from Acapulco Airways to have me taxi across the runway when the 707 was going to land? Are you totally incompetent?" asked Rod furiously.

"What Captain from Acapulco Airways?" Gomez answered. "I never told anyone to tell you that!"

"Well, who did then?" asked Maryanna.

"No one from in here, Señor" said the Chief. "I have been here for the last hour. No one else has been here, senor."

Rod Moore shook his head in total bewilderment.

"Right now, we have another very big problem, Captain" said Gomez to the duo.

"What's that?" asked Rod.

"We have two planes on a collision course and one of them is the Pope's private jet. We have lost communications with both planes due to this strange fog that has appeared out of nowhere. I've tried all channels and there is no response."

"Two planes?" asked Maryanna. "What is the other one?"

"*Air Force 2*" the Chief replied.

"Oh my God" said Rod.

"Oh my God" echoed Maryanna as she and Rod joined Gomez and the Chief in searching the skies for any signs of the two planes.

And 600 feet above, Brother Bob and Dustin had removed the Tablets and swiftly began paging through Volume Nine.

"Here it is" said Dustin, pointing to one of the passages. "*Seek ye within the circle, use the WORD to open the gateway Speak the WORD and pass the evil to the lower realm. Use my name three times Chequetet, Arelich, Volmalites.*"

"Okay, that's cool" said Stephanie. "But what does it mean?"

"The circle....the circle....what could it be referring to?" Bob asked, holding the sides of his head in deep concentration.

"It's the symbol for infinity, isn't it?" asked Meredith.

"Or is it the symbol for oblivion, or rather nothing?" asked Christian.

"Something with no beginning and no end?" asked Stephanie.

"Lynne, what do you think?" asked Bob.

"Yes, it is all of those things but I feel it means something else here. It refers to a power of some sort, something we already have in our possession now at this moment."

"Very well, but we need to tap that power soon. We are now in grave danger" said Bob.

"Well then, there is one thing we are forgetting about and that is that the circle is also the sign for the eternal feminine, the goddess or the mother earth. I have an idea. Meredith, Stephanie… let's form a circle around the Tablets. I want to try something." said Lynne.

And as the three made a circle around the Emerald Tablets and joined hands, the Tablets suddenly came to life. An ethereal vibration began to emanate outward in all directions as a celestial light began to fill the cabin.

And up in the cockpit, Captains Heinrich and Ruggles fought to try to somehow control the aircraft. Straining their eyes to see through the dense fog they saw a large object on the same heading moving directly toward their plane.

"Holy shit, Ruggles, *Air Force 2* is coming right towards us!" Heinrich screamed as he tried in vain to regain control of the rudder. I can't get off this heading!"

And as the captain pushed on the thrusters and attempted to bank the plane to no avail, the two planes drew ever closer as the two pilots thought their deaths were now imminent.

Captain Coleman in the 707 had also seen the Gulfstream and was also attempting to regain control of Air Force 2. "Oh my God, no!" he screamed as he raised his hands in front of his face in a futile attempt to protect his face from the inevitable crash that was about to occur.

But as the planes closed within 500 yards of each other, something miraculous happened. The ethereal light which pulsated from the Tablets began to transform the molecular densities of the three women. Their physical bodies started to lose their cohesiveness and viscosity. As if in a *Pointillistic* painting by *Seurat*, their molecular structures were broken up into minute globes of matter floating freely like tiny marbles in space.

And as the light continued to emanate outward, it suddenly seemed to explode like a supernova and the molecular composition of the superstructure of the plane and its passengers changed in a similar fashion, so that what would normally be classified as solid became modular-like tiny circular fragments, attached yet not attached. And as the explosion of light energy transformed the plane and its passengers, time seemed to slow down to a snail's pace.

As the planes closed and began to crash, the consciousness of the passengers of the smaller plane were transported from the interior cabin to a place outside in space. Like angels, they could see the whole crash sequence in slow motion. And as the 707's nose hit the front of the Gulfstream, the smaller plane became engulfed in total radiance as the tiny beads of matter from the plane and the passengers separated like miniscule billiard balls and then drew back together as soon as the solid matter of the 707 had passed through them.

After the 707 had slowly spread apart the fuselage of the Gulfstream, the minds of Bob, Dustin, Meredith, Lynne, Christian and Stephanie and the pilots all witnessed the same parts of the fuselage coming back together, as if a slow motion video camera were in reverse. And they also saw their corporeal bodies behaving in an identical fashion. As soon as the huge jet had passed through the Gulfstream, the consciousness of each passenger was snapped back like a slingshot into each body exactly as it had been before the crash.

Stunned to be back in the cabin once again, the group looked at each other in total amazement as the intensity of the celestial light decreased and was reabsorbed by the Tablets.

"What just happened?" asked Stephanie.

"Oh my God, did we all see the same thing?" asked Christian.

"That was miraculous, the Emerald Tablets did something to save us!" said Meredith.

And then the cabin door burst open. It was Captain Heinrich. "Holy moley, can someone tell me what just happened?"

"Your psychic intuition was correct, Lynne" said Bob. "Captain, I cannot explain now. Please just continue to try to regain control of the plane! We will explain later."

"Now there is no time to lose!" said Bob. "Meredith, Lynne...join hands about the Tablets and speak the *word* that opened the portal. But you must hurry!"

Meredith and Lynne quickly moved and stood over the Tablets and joined hands.

"Are you ready, Meredith" asked Lynne.

"Yes, I'm ready, on three...one, two, three..." And on three they both spoke the same *word* that they had spoken in Cadiz at the Hotel Parador Restaurant.

Meanwhile, Bob had reached into his carry on and withdrew a large Egyption ankh. Holding it above his head, he slowly turned clockwise in a circle and shouted *Chequetet, Arelich, Volmalites, Chequetet, Arelich, Volmalites, Chequetet, Arelich......*

But before he could finish the words, there was a loud clunk and then the group heard a roar as if ten locomotives were converging on one spot. Suddenly a high pitched piercing wail resonated through the plane that sounded like it came from the mouth of Satan himself.

"What is that" screamed Stephanie, covering her ears.

"I don't know but look" shouted Lynne, pointing to the window of the plane. The fog had begun to disperse and streams of light could be seen entering the cabin. And as the group felt the plane start to climb, free once again from the force which held it on the collision course, Captain Heinrich spoke over the intercom.

"This is the captain. We have regained control of our rudder and are ascending to 800 feet, please fasten your seat belts."

"Tack och lov" said Christian. "I think I've changed my mind about flying. Hopefully we are safe now."

I have a feeling we're not quite out of danger yet" said Bob, listening intently as if he expected something else to happen.

And as he said that, the malodorous aroma which they had all smelled earlier became a rancid ubiquitous stench. And as the plane ascended and banked to starboard, the cabin air vents began to emit a sickly green vapor. Covering their mouths and noses, the group could see the putrid mist begin to coalesce and take form in the front of the cabin.

"Oh my God, no!" exclaimed Bob. "Dustin, take this ankh and hold it high" he said with great trepidation. "Everyone, move to the other side of the Tablets, NOW!"

Moving quickly to the other side of the Emerald Tablets as the plane leveled off, they turned in terror to see a fourth dimensional monster that would have sent Freddy Krueger scurrying. It was the size of a very large man but it was not a man. Instead of skin, it had scales like a lizard and it had a long tail which draped behind it and undulated back and forth like a snake. Moving forward slowly, it hunched over like a T-Rex ready to attack. And as it held its scaly claws up, long jagged fingernails glistened in the light like daggers as it spoke in a guttural vile monotone that pierced their ears like chalk scraping on a blackboard. . It had the head of a goat and yellow eyes that blazed pure evil. And as the group froze in sheer terror, it spoke.

It said: "I am Wegreog, and now the Disciples of Troth will join me in Hell!"

~

The Homey

"Did you get the utilities, Diana?" Ernie asked.

"Yes, here's a naval work uniform" she said, handing Ernie the standard work fatigues. They didn't bat an eye. I guess when they saw me in my service khaki, they didn't need an explanation. The Officer of the Day walked me to the Chief's cabin and gave me this set of utilities, no questions asked.

"Hopefully they'll fit" said Ernie. "Let me duck behind this cargo container and slip them on."

A few minutes later Ernie reemerged from the shadows. "Well, it's a little short but I guess no one will notice."

Diana put her hand to her face to cover her more than obvious amusement. "A *little* short, you look like you're ready for the Great Flood" she said giggling.

"So is it my fault that guy's a little twerp? I'll roll up the sleeves and no one will know the difference."

'No one will notice unless they look down there" said Diana pointing to his ankles. 'It looks like you've got a pair of Capri pants on" she said laughing hysterically. "You look like a U.S. Navy homey. A couple of tats, a shaved head and your cover on backwards and you could pass for Eminem."

"Shut up, Williams...so my usual sartorial splendor is being compromised here. Just remember we're on a mission. Let's keep focused on our objective here, Ensign."

"Aye, aye sir" said Diana, snapping to attention and saluting. "What are my orders, sir? Just make it *short*, sir" she said doubling over with laughter.

"Alright Williams, that's enough. Now there are three things we have to do and the first is to get back to the hotel. We need to print out a Navy requisition form. Then we are going to get ourselves some transportation and visit a construction project I noticed near the airport.

"A construction project..." said Diana sardonically.

'Oh, you're a real doubting Thomas, aren't you, Ensign Williams. Let's just hold off on the jokes for now and see if we can't get ourselves a cab so we can get ourselves some firepower if we need it, okay?"

"What's this *we* shit, Kemosabee?" said Diana. "Or do you have a frog in your pocket? Just remember I'm only here to keep you out of trouble, Mr. SEAL."

"Alright, point taken" said Ernie. "Now can we get this show on the road?" he asked as he grabbed her arm and hustled back off the pier to hail a cab.

And back at the Ensenada jail, two American inmates, one with a U.S. Navy uniform and one not, were being processed when the phone rang.

"Policia de Ensenada, como puedo ayudarle?" asked the receptionist Elmarie. "What...who is this ...once more....si señor, uno momento, por favor."

Placing the caller on hold, she summoned the guard and led him around the corner. "Sergeant, it is the Office of Presidente Pero. They say there are two Americans who we arrested who need to be released immediately."

"They must be down in the tank. Where is the chief?" the guard asked.

"He is out at the airport and he told me not to disturb him as he was in an emergency situation. What shall we do?"

"They said they were faxing the release papers now. We'll have to let them go" said the sergeant. "Como se llaman?"

"Anthony D'Amato and Daniel Schofield" Elmarie answered.

"The Chief will not be happy when he finds out they were released. He said he needed them to find the gringo who started the brawl at *Pappas*."

"We have no choice, do we, Sergeant?"

"No, but find out where they are staying while they are here if the Chief needs to find them."

"I think one is with the U.S. Navy and the other said he was going to stay at the Hotel Coral and Marina. Mira, aqui estan los papeles ahora" she said picking up the release orders as they spit out of the fax machine.

At the top of the first page was the emblem of an eagle on a cactus holding a snake in its beak and it was titled *Officia del Presidente de Mexico*.

"It looks official, and it says to release those two Americanos immediately and it's signed by Presidente Pero" said the receptionist Elmarie. "I guess it's their lucky day. Go let them loose, sergeant. I'll go get their personal items we confiscated."

"Si, señorita" said the sergeant as he walked down the stairs to the holding tank where the participants of the brawl were incarcerated.

Removing the keys from his belt, he opened up the jail cell door and yelled "Senores Schofield and D'Amato."

And as the two men made their way through the wall of inmates, Elmarie retrieved the two clear plastic envelopes into which she had placed the billfolds and pocket contents of the pair. But when she unzipped one of the bags to reach in, an errant fly began buzzing her head and landed on her nose. Waving it off with her hand, the personal affects bag tipped and spilled unto the desk. And looking down, she saw something that caught her eye.

"Caramba, this is weird" she said to herself.

An international driver's license had spilled out unto the desk and landed in such a way that it rested at a 45 degree diagonal angle with its side resting on the log book. Upon first glance she noticed that in direct light the license said its owner was Daniel Schofield. But as she turned her head slightly she thought she saw the image change. Picking the license up, she turned it slightly so the light hit it differently.

"Mia madre, what is this?" she thought.

The photo was still in the same place but the letters were different. It was like a hologram and it betrayed the claim of the card in flat light. Turning the card ever so slightly, the letters flickered off and on like a candle but eventually she could began to decipher what it said. It was also an ID card but it had a strong military look to it and across the top it read:

Office of Inspector General - Intelligence Oversight
Special Agent Peter Harrison

~

The Transformation and Four More!

"What the hell just happened?" screamed Captain Coleman to his co-pilot.

"I'm not sure, Captain. I thought we were going to crash for sure and then nothing happened" he replied as he felt his body to make sure it was still in one piece.

"What the frick is happening here?" Ernst Lamply screamed as he burst through the cabin door. "Coleman, I am going to have your pilot's license revoked and you're going to prison for endangering the life of the Vice President of the United States, you hear me, dipshit!"

'I'm sorry, sir but we have now regained control of the aircraft so if you would be kind enough to be seated I'll put her down and we'll all be safe from any further turbulence."

"You do that, Coleman, and do it *NOW*!" Lamply shouted as he turned to take his seat once again, slamming the door as he exited the cabin.

"Right away, your highness" whispered Coleman sarcastically as he readjusted his headset to reconnect communications with the Ensenada tower. "Ensenada tower, do you read me, this is *Air Force 2,* over."

"Gracias a Dios, the radio is working again" cried air traffic controller Gomez to the group which had been surrounding him and his screen, frozen in fear anticipating a crash.

"Roger Air Force 2, I read you loud and clear. Proceed on approach to runway number one, runway lights are on. You are clear to land, over."

"I see the rabbit, tower…descending to land, over" the co-pilot replied.

And as a great sense of relief overcame the passengers and crew of the 707 and the group in the tower that had been observing the potential disaster, a very different scene was taking place on the Gulfstream.

"I am *Wegreog* and now the Disciples of Troth will join me in *Hell*!"

And as Meredith, Stephanie, Lynne, Dustin and Christian, fearing for their lives, scurried behind the Emerald Tablets which lay in the aisle of the plane, the creature from Satan's realm began to slowly move menacingly forward toward the group. And as it came within yards of the troupe, Bob suddenly raised the Ankh and shrieked at the top of his lungs "VOLMALIT…"

But before he could finish enunciating the last word of the incantation he had begun before the appearance of the demon, the same deafening roar which had shaken the aircraft moments before, again ripped through the cabin. And as the creature heard the beginning of the last word, it emitted a dreadfully horrid high pitched scream and instantaneously dissolved into a green mist which drifted back into the air vents from where it had entered the Gulfstream.

And at the same time on the 707, Vice President Ernst Lamply had decided to relieve himself after all the excitement and had walked past Doc Reno to the rear of the plane where the executive washroom was located.

"Ernst, don't you think you ought to sit down and fasten your seat belt for landing?" asked Reno as Lamply walked briskly by the luxurious Corinthian leathered chair which had been expressly contoured for the Vice President's corpulent body.

"Shut up, Reno and prepare another shot. I've got just enough time to take a leak before landing. Now do as you're told and I'll be right back."

Opening the washroom door, Lamply put one hand up to brace himself against the bulkhead as he began to lean over the loo. And as he removed his glasses for a moment to wipe his forehead of the sweat which had accumulated there, a green mist began to penetrate the vents of the aircraft and drift into the washroom where he stood.

"What the frick is that smell?" Lamply asked himself, looking around. Turning to look at his reflection in the mirror, he could see that a greenish fog had permeated the room, surrounding him and immediately beginning to seep its way into his cranial cavities. Totally in shock at the realization that this was happening, he futilely tried to cover his ears and nose. But before he could scream for help, he felt a surge of power and well- being like he had never felt before in his life. And as he began to delight in the thrill of this feeling, he looked into the mirror and saw himself as a young man, strong and handsome.

"My God, what is happening?" he said. Standing in front of the mirror, entranced with his transformation, he began to feel a presence which was reading his mind and thoughts. "What….stop it, stop this…you can't do this… what are you doing?"

As a sinister and evil laugh pervaded his consciousness, he saw the image of the young man dissipate and in its place another form was emerging. It had the head of a goat and its eyes were fiendishly yellow and it was laughing diabolically. And as Ernst Lamply became a prisoner in his own body, he felt the presence scan his memory and become infused in his brain.

When the evil laughter finally ceased, blackness began to permeate his being and a hideously resonant voice spoke to him from within. And as he felt the presence take over his self-will and awareness, it spoke to him in an eerie, spine-chilling monotone. It said "Now, Vice President Ernst Lamply, *together* we will *destroy* the world and *avenge* the Disciples of Troth!"

~

"How in the world will we ever sail out of here with the Chief of Police *and* the Ensenada Mayor *and* a Mexican Admiral all looking for us at the same time?" asked Linda as the trio made their way down Costero Blvd. to the Marina.

"Well, they know we're here somewhere but they don't know exactly where just yet. If Ernie gets his butt back here in a reasonable amount of time, we can set sail before they can find us" answered Tom.

"We're just lucky that it's Carnival" said Emmet. "They may not be able to find us with all the commotion and partying going on. What's all that happening out in the harbor?" he asked pointing toward the Navy Pier where Mexican gun boats appeared to be practicing some sort of maneuvers.

"Those boats are hauling ass. I wonder what kind of boats they are" asked Tom.

"They sure are angular looking" added Linda.

"Ernie would know, being the sailor extraordinaire that he is" commented Emmet.

"You mean the sailor extraordinaire that he *thinks* he is" said Tom.

"Ah, that too" Emmet replied. "And look at that, some of those boats have lights on their masts. There must be some sort of boat parade happening tonight."

"It sure looks like a crowded harbor out there. Aren't those U.S. Navy ships out there also?" asked Linda.

"I think you're right Linda" said Tom. "That gives me an idea, Emmet. You and Linda head down to the Swan and get her ready to sail. I'll be back in a few minutes."

"Where are you going, Tom" asked Linda.

"To get some lights, we are going to be in a boat parade." And with that, he turned and began to jog back up Costero Blvd. back to where the parade had started as Linda and Emmet looked at each other quizzically.

Meanwhile Ernie and Diana had also found their way to the beginning of the parade where a familiar U.S. Navy gray and blue Jeep was parked on a dark part of Avenida Lopez Mateos by Hussong's Cantina. There, standing closeby, two U.S. Navy Seaman Second Class were taking in the sights of the parade.

"That's what I'm looking for" said Ernie.

"I've got a bad feeling about this, Ernie" said Diana.

"Don't worry, I've got it all figured out. This is what I want you to do, Diana. See where those Navy guys are standing? I want you to go up to them and start flirting. Talk them into buying you a drink and get them into Hussong's. Then meet me in the back after, say ten minutes. I'll be waiting there."

"You're going to steal that jeep, aren't you, Ernie?"

"We're just going to borrow it for a while, Williams. Now get moving."

"As if you haven't gotten us into enough trouble" Diana replied. "Now you're going to steal a United States Navy Jeep."

"They'll never even know it's gone, now go." said Ernie.

"Aye, aye sir, straight away" said Diana, snapping to attention and saluting sarcastically.

And as Diana turned and began her walk to the sailors, she thought to herself that even though Ernie's methods were questionable, she had to get the uranium dioxide for the CFAF if she had any hope for her career. She had her orders and it was not her place to question them. Ernie was serving a purpose and as long as he seemed to have a plan, she just might complete her mission soon. As much as Ernie was growing on her, he would just have to be collateral damage. Her mission came first.

Within five minutes, Diana had coerced the navy personnel into having a drink inside Hussong's. And after they had all entered the establishment, Ernie went to work. Hopping into the driver's seat, he located the ignition and after opening the correct tool on his Swiss Army Knife, he began to remove the covers from around the ignition. Locating the panel of ignition wires, he separated the "on" positive and negative wires in the steering column. As they were color coded, he pulled and separated the different colored wires from the ignition column, stripped a portion of each and twisted them together. He then found the starter wires and pulled them from the ignition tumbler as well. He then stripped the ends and touched the wires together briefly.

"VROOOOOM" went the engine and as Ernie slammed the shifter into first gear and floored it, leaving the scene in a cloud of dust, Diana and the two sailors were already getting cozy. With arms around each other and both seamen drooling over the prospect of landing Diana, the trio had ordered two shots each of Patron and Coronas. And when the shots and beers arrived, Diana made the two a bet.

"I'll bet you two guys can't chug both shots and the Coronas before I count to ten" she challenged them.

"Easy" said the two in unison as they tossed back both shots and chugged the beers as Diana reached the count of eight.

"Wow, I'm impressed" said Diana, goading them on. "I love men who can handle their liquor! But I'll bet you can't do it again" she said to them, smiling widely and batting her eyelashes.

"Bartender, four more here" screamed the taller of the two guys. "That's not a problem, ma'am" he said to Diana as the thought of making time with the beautiful Ensign started to heat up his bloodstream.

And as the next round of shots and beers were consumed by the sailors, Diana challenged them again. "That's only two rounds, guys. Surely you can do better than that!"

"Ensign, are you trying to get us drunk?" asked the shorter sailor.

"I'm just trying to loosen you two up" she said flirtingly. "I was thinking of taking you both back to my hotel room."

"Bartender, *four more*!" screamed the sailors.

"Boys, I'll be right back" she said excusing herself. "I have to attend the little girl's room. And if you really want to impress me, have another round by the time I get back. By the way, I have to call the base. I may be a few minutes so y'all don't go away now."

"No Ma'am, we sure won't" the two sailors answered together. And as the two ordered another round, Diana sashayed down the aisle toward the ladies room and walked right on by it and out the back door where Ernie was waiting with the Jeep.

"Did you manage to buy us some time, Williams?" asked Ernie.

"Like I've said before, if it were raining brains you men wouldn't even get wet. Those two in there are practically passed out already. They'll be waiting for a good hour before they realize I've gone and by then they'll be too shit-faced to drive or walk anywhere. Where are we headed now, Eminem?" giggled Diana after glancing once more at Ernie's ill- fitting utilities.

"Back to your hotel" said Ernie. "I need to print out a U.S. Navy work order form on the internet. And then we're going to get ourselves some PVC pipe."

"You can download those forms off the internet?" asked Diana.

"Yep, good old *Google*…does it every time. The *Order for Work and Service Form 2275*…that's what we're going to download. And then we are going to fill it out."

"What will you fill it out with?" asked Diana.

"It will be a standard *Mark 46 Mod 5 Torpedo Service Replacement Requisition Order*" answered Ernie.

"What the hell does that mean?" asked Diana.

"It means I'm going to take out the giraffe and put in the elephant" Ernie replied as he floored the accelerator and headed back to the Hotel Coral and Marina.

And while Ernie and Diana were speeding back to the hotel, Daniel Schofield and Anthony D'amato had been released from the Ensenada jail and were attempting to call CFAF agent Brubaker on her cell phone.

"Damnit Schofield, she doesn't answer. We have to get that ammo dump key back or we can't make that delivery to Coronado. Lamply will hang us by our nuts and we'll both be out ten million dollars!"

"We'll find them, D'Amato. This town is not that big. They're here somewhere." said Schofield.

"I thought those paintings we stole in Stockholm were supposed to neutralize the curse of the *Piper*. It doesn't seem like things are exactly going smoothly here, does it, Schofield?"

"Shut up, D'Amato, this was just a temporary setback. The curse has been neutralized, believe me. I'm the art expert here. You're just supposed to be the smuggler so zip it! Everything is going to be just fine."

"So where do we start looking, Mr. Art Genius?" asked D'Amato.

"Keep trying to call Twyla Brubaker. I'm heading over to the Hotel Coral and Marina. I need a shower after spending two hours in a Mexican jail. Keep your eyes open and I'll meet you at the Navy Pier in one hour, got it?"

"The Coral and Marina, that's where I heard Brubaker and that other guy who has the key say they were headed" exclaimed D'Amato.

"Well in that case maybe we had both better head over there to see if we can find them" Schofield replied. "Jeremy Princeton is also over there."

"He still doesn't realize you're Daniel Schofield. He may be talented but he sure is clueless."

"Shut up, D'Amato, it's my brilliant acting that's making this whole thing possible for us. We just need to get the uranium dioxide from the torpedoes and we're home free so let's go find the two of them."

"I'm sure by now that the real Peter Harrison is dead. Once we turned him over to Hizbollah, his days were numbered" said D'Amato.

"Not necessarily, D'Amato. They told me they were keeping him alive as a hostage for prisoner exchange with the Israelis" declared Schofield.

"Whatever, at least he won't be in our way. Who gives a shit about his sorry ass! When I get my ten million, I guarantee he is the last friggin' person on earth I'll be thinking about" chuckled D'Amato.

"You never know, D'Amato" said Schofield.

"What the frick is that supposed to mean, Schofield?"

"Nothing, now let's get over to the hotel" said Schofield as he raised his arm to hail the cab which was driving by.

And as the cab pulled over and the pair climbed into the back seat, Schofield smiled slightly and thought to himself "you never know D'Amato because you and the Vice President of the United States and the whole CFAF are going down, you fool."

~

The Three Mighty Messengers

"**O**kay, so let's just Google U.S. Navy Requisition forms" said Ernie as he sat in front of the Hotel business center's computer. "Here it is: *ORDER FOR WORK AND SERVICES-NAVCOMPT FORM 2275 (REV.8-81)*."

"And you're just going to fill it in, just like that" asked Diana.

"Yes-sir-ee Bob, just like that" said Ernie.

"You mean that you are just going to fill in the spaces with whatever it is you're going to requisition and you think no one is going to question it?"

"Yep, I sure do."

"And how can you be so sure, Mister SEAL?"

"Because this is a Navy requisition form and no one on earth, much less anyone in the United States Navy can understand it. Surely you've dealt with a few of these forms yourself, Ensign?"

"Well, yes, a few" Diana replied.

'Check this out, Ensign" said Ernie, holding the form up to the light to read.

"THIS ORDER IS ISSUED AS A: (CHECK THE BOX), PROJECT ORDER AND/OR AN ECONOMY ACT ORDER AND IS TO BE ACCOMPLISHED ON A, CHECK THE BOX, FIXED PRICES AND/OR COST REIMBURSEMENT BASIS. WHEN THE FIRST

BLOCK IS CHECKED, THIS ORDER IS PLACED IN ACCORDANCE WITH THE PROVISIONS OF 41U.S.CODE 23 AND DOD DIRECTIVE 7220.1. THE FOLLOWING SUPPLEMENTARY ITEMS ON REVERSE ALSO APPLY AND ARE AN INTEGRAL PART OF THIS ORDER: 1-5, 7, 8."

"I believe it's called *Navalese*, the usual bunch of gobbledygook" said Diana.

"My point exactly" said Ernie. "No one ever understands this stuff so I'll just fill it in as I need to. Even if the information is incorrect, those guards at the ammo dump won't ever know" Ernie replied.

"You hope not, anyway" said Diana. "I know nothing of this. If I am implicated in any way I will deny everything, just so you know."

"No worries, Ensign. If we're busted, I'll tell them I kidnapped you and was going to turn you into a slave in my basement."

"Just so we both have the same story before they throw us into Leavenworth" replied Diana. "Now what information are you going to put in the boxes?"

"Hmm...okay, let's see here. REFERENCE NUMBER; Make one up, Williams."

"Okay, I'll play. Um, let's see... how about 7665/JC54...how's that?"

"Perfect, now WORK COMPLETION DATE; today, FOR DETAILS CONTACT; Lets' see, we'll put USN TECH POC ORDNANCE ADMIN 6632/JCS CORONADO CALIFORNIA. Whada'ya think?"

"Sounds convincing enough to me, let's move on."

"Okay, now let's see here. TO: We'll put DIRECTOR OF ORDNANCE, UNITED STATES NAVAL AMMO DUMP 24685, ENSENADA MEXICO. What else?"

"Umm...how about writing Naval FAC JX 25 ORDNANCE REQUSITION OFFICER, ENSENADA MEXICO, how's that sound?"

"Very impressive, does it mean anything?"

"Yes, I'm quite certain it does."

"How do you know these things, Williams?"

"Let's just chalk it up to women's intuition for now. What's next?"

"It says: ACCOUNTING DATA TO BE CITED ON RESULTING BILLINGS and then APPROPRIATION, SUB-HEAD, OBJ CLASS, BU CONTROL, COST CODE and AMOUNT" said Ernie. "What shall we put here?"

"Put CCV43, CCV42, NJ7, ADNOV, and MSXC2" Diana replied.

"Wow...how do you know these things, Williams?" Ernie asked, amazed by her answers.

"Maybe I've seen this form before" Diana replied.

"You have? So what shall we put in this box here?" asked Ernie. "It says DESCRIPTION OF WORK TO BE PERFORMED AND OTHER INSTRUCTIONS."

"You're on a roll, go for it!" said Diana.

"Okay, how about this: RECALL ALL STANDARD MARK 46 MOD 5 TORPEDO MAINFRAMES ENSENADA AMMO DUMP # 24685 ENSENADA MEXICO."

"Wow, you're slick, ace!" said Diana sarcastically. "Just let me ask you a couple things here, Ernie. First of all, how do you know how many torpedoes are in the ammo dump?"

"Good question, I guess I don't know, do I?"

"And do you know how much each torpedo weighs?"

"Well...uh, hopefully not that much?" said Ernie.

"Ernie, a fricking MOD 5 MARK 46 Torpedo weighs 500 lbs!" shouted Diana. "Now, how in the world do you plan on lifting a 500 lb. torpedo, much less ten of them or however many you think are in the Armory.?"

"I guess we don't really need the torpedoes, Williams. We just need to get through the gate." But I guess I never considered that, did I? There might be quite a few in there, right?"

"What was your first clue?" asked Diana sarcastically.

"Okay, Wonder Woman, what do you suggest?"

And with that question, Diana reached into her pocket and removed two pieces of paper. Unfolding them, she snapped them sharply and threw them down on the computer keyboard. "Try these" she said.

Ernie picked it up with both hands and his eyes grew as large as saucers at a World Wrestling Federation tea party. "What the hell is this, Williams? Where the hell did you ever get these?" Ernie asked in disbelief, his mouth on the floor.

"I believe its FORM 2275 and you will note that it's filled out correctly with all official authorization codes and signatures" answered Diana.

"And what is this other list?" Ernie asked incredulously.

"I believe that its official designation is *INVENTORY.*"

"Yes, but this is the inventory at the ammo dump. What ….how…what are you doing with these and how did you get them?" asked Ernie in disbelief.

"Let's just say I know people in high places."

"And I know high people in low places but that doesn't explain……"

"You're just going to have to trust me for a while, Ernie. I have all the information we will need to get into the Ammunitions Armory here. And I also have these things which you will find helpful" said Diana reaching into her handbag and grabbing some documents and a sealed letter, tossing them down on the keyboard.

"Now what are these?" asked Ernie picking them up, one by one.

"It's called *How to get into a U.S. Navy Armory A101,* Mr. SEAL. If you are going to be successful in your mission, you will very probably need these to avoid arrest."

"So what is this?" asked Ernie.

"It's known as a Torpedo man Mate's Designation and ID Badge."

"Very handy, tell me, Ensign Williams, just what is your MOS anyway?"

"2012" Diana replied.

"And that is what?"

"Drum Majorette, what did you think it was?"

"Actually I was thinking more along the lines of *Military Intelligence.*"

"Once again, what was your first clue, Einstein?"

"You want to tell me what's going on here, Ensign?"

"I don't have time right now, but suffice it to say we can help each other out. These items were for Plan A but now we're doing Plan B. Now let's be a little more professional about this, shall we? Now, may I have the envelope please?"

Ernie handed her the envelope, still stunned by it all.

"And the winner is…YOU!" said Diana, tearing open the envelope and handing the paper to Ernie.

"Well, well…a *Security Clearance*, now how about that, sports fans!" said Ernie incredulously. "It's even in my name, Torpedo man's Mate R4 Luis Salgado."

"It will get us through the gates to the armory. No one will know it's not you. It will be dark."

"I don't believe this, Williams. You have all this documentation, so what do you need me for?"

"You're forgetting one thing, aren't you?"

"I am, and what might that be?"

"You have the key to the armory. I can get us through the gate. You can get us through the vault door."

"So what are you after here, Williams?"

"The same thing you are, Ernie…armaments. But I need certain torpedoes…only a slightly different version of the MOD 5 Mark 46."

"Which is….." asked Ernie.

"If you look under Incendiary Weapons subsection C where it lists torpedoes, you will see that two Mini SHKVAL Torpedoes are listed there."

"And just what is a SHKVAL Torpedo?" asked Ernie.

"It's a mini torpedo weighing approximately only sixty lbs. which was originally designed by the Russians as a countermeasure against torpedoes launched by undetected enemy submarines. They are capable of speeds up to 200 knots in the water due to something called *super-cavitation*." replied Diana.

"Which is?" asked Ernie.

"It means that the torpedo is, in effect, flying in a gas bubble created by outward deflection of water by a specially shaped nose cone and the expansion of gases from its engine. By keeping water from contacting the body of the torpedo, drag is reduced significantly and allows extremely high speeds. In effect, the SHKVAL is an underwater missile."

"Okay" said Ernie. "Next question, just what do you want with these torpedoes?"

"Sorry, Bubba, but that's *Top Secret*. Even I don't know that. But my mission is to somehow remove them from the Ensenada armory and get them back to the Corvette boat in the harbor. But I do know one thing that's curious."

"And that is?" asked Ernie.

"It has something to do with the nose cone and the uranium dioxide it uses as fuel."

"Uranium dioxide!!" shouted Ernie, jumping to his feet. "It's a frigging nuclear torpedo, woman!! You are going to steal two nuclear torpedoes and you want me to help you?"

"Shhhh…shutup will you? We're in a hotel lobby here. Just relax. They're not armed, if that helps."

"Not armed? Oh, well, then no problem, consider it done! Are you kidding me? All I need is a little something for protection assurance to get us and the Swan out of here. But smuggling nuclear missiles, that's a whole different ballgame, Williams!" said Ernie adamantly.

Placing her arm around Ernie's shoulder and her other hand on Ernie's thigh, she cooed in his ear; "Ernie, you're already in enough doodoo here in Mexico to put you away for the rest of your life. All I have to do is blow the whistle, my dear, and you're history. I'm not involved one little tiny bit in this as far as the authorities know. If you don't help me with this mission, I will have no choice. Now do we understand each other, Lieutenant?" she purred while nibbling on his ear.

"Okay, I get the picture, Ensign. It looks like I've been shanghai-ed. So what's your plan of action, Williams?"

"You're now a *Torpedo man's mate*, Ernie. Your official function is to maintain underwater weapons such as these torpedoes here on the inventory and the systems used to launch them."

"Sounds important" said Ernie.

"It is. You are also responsible for, and I quote here, 'inventory torpedo components, tools and test equipment and requisition replacements'. You'll notice on the official *FORM 2275* which I have, it states in the DESCRIPTION OF WORK TO BE PERFORMED that we are to REMOVE FAULTY SHKVAL TORPEDOES NOSE CONES AND REPLACE WITH NOSE CONES HEREWITH."

"Okay, but one question here. With all this documentation, why do we need my key? Won't the guards just open it up for us?" asked Ernie.

"No, that is part of the security procedure. If we are authentic, we will have our own key issued to us by Naval Security at Coronado. The guards are at no time to admit anyone into the ammo storage facility without one. There is just one problem though."

"And that is?" asked Ernie.

"The gate guards will want to see the replacements that go with these orders."

"So we need something that will pass for two nose cones, right?"

"That's right" said Diana. "You have any ideas?"

Ernie chuckled to himself. "Back to the original plan, Diana, we're going to take out the giraffe and put in the elephant."

"Meaning?" asked Diana.

"Meaning we'll need some PVC pipe and a few ripe melons and maybe some gray paint."

"I'm not even going to ask. Can we just get on with it?"

"I'm ready to roll but I just have to print out one more little thing" said Ernie.

"And that is?"

"The passenger manifest for the Harbor Master. I have to make a list of all passengers leaving Ensenada on the Swan and leave it at his office."

"Ernie, you're wanted by every law enforcement agency in Ensenada and you're going to file a passenger manifest with the Harbor Master? Now I ask you, what sense does that make?"

"Oh it makes a lot of sense. See, he has the key to the engine. The sailor who sailed it down from Santa Barbara left it with him. Hopefully we can get it before the news of the fiasco at Hussong's reaches his office. This will just take a second."

"Okay, but hurry it up."

"Okay, let's see here. This will just take a minute. Trip Date: 01/27/06, Destination: Santa Barbara, California. Boat Description and Slip #: Swan 44 ft. Sloop Sail # 060947, Marina 1, slip 5P. Passengers: Tom Dunsmore, Emmet McQuire, Ernie Walters. I don't know Linda's last name so I'll skip it.

"I'm sure she'll be eternally grateful to be excluded" said Diana.

"Ah, I love your sincerity, thank you" replied Ernie.

"You're welcome, not!"

"Okay so last thing here, it says *Party's Designation*. How shall we designate ourselves? Let's see here, what comes in three?"

"The *Three Stooges* is fitting but over used. How about a three way light bulb? No, on second thought, you're not that bright," said Diana.

"Ha ha" said Ernie sarcastically. "Ripped to shreds by that rapier like wit of yours again. Seriously, think of something. How about writing *three-bean chili*?"

"Now that's better, all of you being as full of hot air as you all no doubt are."

"Oh that's funny, Williams. I think we need a more serious designation here."

"Hmm... well then how about the *Three Kings*, she asked. You know the ones that were the messengers to the manger with the frankincense and myrrh, whatever that was."

"You know, I like that. *The Three Messengers*, what do you think?" said Ernie.

"Equating yourselves with three kings, now that's mighty grandiose of you" said Diana.

"Hmm...*mighty*.....I like that too. It has a nice ring to it. So be it, our designation is now *The Three Mighty Messengers*. There we go, now I'll just make two copies and print it."

Diana shook her head and rolled her eyes incredulously.

And as the copies printed out, Ernie grabbed them, folded each one and stuffed one into each breast pocket.

"We're done here" said Ernie. "Now let's go shopping for that PVC pipe. I remember seeing some out by the Ensenada airport."

And as Ernie and Diana exited the hotel lobby to drive the Navy Jeep to the airport, Jeremy Princeton was upstairs in hotel suite # 412, sitting stunned and shocked, gazing on the *Piper* which had returned to him like a boomerang.

"How could this have happened?" he thought to himself. "I can't tell Peter. He'll know I switched the *Pipers*. He thinks it's still at Tierra Bella. I refuse to be cursed by this object the rest of my life. What can I do with it?"

Then just at that moment there was a knock at the door. ""Yes" yelled Jeremy, grabbing the *Piper* and hiding it under his airline pilot's jacket.

"Maid, Senor" came the answer. "Do you want me to turn down the beds?"

"Sure, why not?" Jeremy answered, starting toward the door. "Come on in" he said as he opened the door.

"Gracias, senor" said the maid.

And as the maid entered the suite, Jeremy saw that on her cart outside the room was a master key card on a chain which she had left on the top of the towels. And as Jeremy saw the key, an idea flashed in his brain.

"Desperate times call for desperate measures" he thought to himself as he grabbed the key and stealthily strolled down to the next suite which was designated # 413.

"Perfect" he thought as he slipped the key card into the slot and turned the lever when the green light flashed. "This unlucky number is a perfect match for this unlucky object which haunts my life."

Entering the suite, he quickly looked around for a hiding place, preferably one that would preclude its return to him forever. Scanning the room quickly, he noticed some Mexican object d'art situated on a shelf over the mini bar. There he saw three bowls resting on the glass shelf. And in front of each one was a placard explaining its purpose and date of creation. The one in the middle read *Replica Mayan Ceremonial Bowl Dated 512 BC*. It was made of a substance which resembled obsidian and Jeremy noticed that its circumference appeared slightly larger than the size of the circumference of the *Piper*. Taking the *Piper* from beneath his coat he placed it over the top of the bowl where it slid in perfectly, forming a sort of sculpture which resembled a black setting sun but yet obscured the essence of the *Piper's* seductive beauty.

"That should do it" thought Jeremy. "By the time anyone notices the *Piper* doesn't belong with the bowl, I'll be on my way to Bahrain where it will never catch up with me again and the curse will then be someone else's problem."

Exiting the suite he returned to key to the top of the maid's cart exactly where he had found it just as the maid returned from her duties inside Jeremy's suite.

"Gracias, señora" he said to the maid and as he turned to enter his suite he heard a commotion towards the end of the hallway. Ten or so men in suits and wearing sunglasses had come up the stairs and also had gotten off the elevator and were heading in Jeremy's direction. Flying by Jeremy like a herd of stampeding wildebeasts they came to a halt at suite 413 and opened the door quickly, closing it behind them with a sense of great urgency.

'Que pasa agui, señora?" asked Jeremy.

"No seguro, señor", the maid answered with what seemed to be a sense of trepidation. "But the word among the staff is that a very important person will be staying in suite 413."

"Very important," Jeremy asked," like who?"

"Señor, the word is that it is the *Vice President of the United States*," she replied as she resumed her duties and pushed the cart across the hallway.

And as Jeremy closed the door to his suite, contemplating this bizarre turn of events, Ernie and Diana had arrived at the airport where Ernie had spotted a pile of discarded plastic pipes laying near the tarmac on the group's return from La Bufadora earlier in the day.

"There they are" said Ernie, steering the Navy Jeep off the main road toward a construction site close to the tarmac.

"Ernie, there are people over there" said Diana pointing to the Gulfstream which seemed to be deplaning a group of people. "Won't they see us?"

"Nah, they're too busy getting their bags together. And besides, we're U.S. Navy personnel. They won't think twice about this" he said with complete confidence.

Pulling the Jeep alongside a pile of plumbing pipes, Ernie began shuffling through the pile of discarded plastic pipes.

"What size are the nose cones, Williams?"

"To be exact, they are eight inches in diameter and forty-one inches in length."

Examining the pipe's lengths, Ernie spotted two smaller ones at the bottom of the pile. "These should do" he said to Diana as he pulled them from beneath the pile and threw them into the back of the Jeep.

But as he bent over to pick up the pipes, his left breast pocket was brushed open and out fell one of the manifests onto the top of the pile. Not noticing this occurrence, he hopped back into the driver's seat and sped off back to the main road just as another jet was taking off on an adjacent runway.

As the Jeep sped off and the jet became air born, the combination of the thrust from the jet and the exhaust from the Jeep blew the manifest directly over to the Gulfsream where Dustin Lambada noticed it and picked it up. Unfolding it, he read it to himself and then screamed at Bob.

"Brother Bob, look at this!" he shouted.

"What is it, Dustin" said Bob, dropping his bags and taking the paper from Dustin.

Lynne, Meredith, Stephanie and Christian all gathered around him, curious about what Dustin had read that was so earth shattering.

"What is it?" Lynne asked.

"Goodness gracious, this is a divine epiphany" said Bob, hardly able to believe his eyes.

"What, what is it, Brother Bob?" the group asked.

"The Emerald Tablets predicted if we came to the land of *Nse'n'aTa where the fingers part the sea* we would find them. And here they are. Dustin, what do the Tablets say again?"

"They say *Called He the Dweller the Three Mighty Messengers.*"

"And here they are" exclaimed Bob jubilantly

"Here who are, Bob?" asked Meredith.

"*The Three Mighty Messengers*, that's who, and we can find them at the Ensenada Harbor, Marina 1, Slip 5P. Quickly, place the Emerald Tablets into your laptop bag, Dustin. We'll need a van to get us there so hurry everyone. We all have a rendezvous with destiny. We must find the *Three Mighty Messengers* before Wegreog does."

And as the group hurriedly assembled their gear and made their way to the terminal to arrange transportation to the marina, the Vice President of the United States and his entourage boarded a limo headed for the Hotel Coral and Marina overlooking the Ensenada Harbor where the Battle of the Light and the Darkness was about to commence.

~

The Parade Lights

"Here, Emmett, grab these" said Tom, passing a coiled string of lights over the stanchions.

"Looks like Christmas" said Emmet.

"And hopefully our big gift will be getting out of here safely without incarceration" said Linda.

"You worry too much, Linda" said Emmet. "With Ernie on top of our escape plans, you have nothing to worry about."

"Yes, nothing" said Tom. "With Ernie planning our escape we'll all be in jail within the hour! Now run these lights up the halyard, you two. We're going to be in the boat parade. Hopefully it will disguise the Swan enough to avoid the authorities."

"Where does the parade start?" asked Linda, wrapping the halyard line around the winch.

"It starts at the sport fishing pier and goes around in a circle by the cruise ships dock and then on to the navy piers dock and then back" Tom answered.

"Then what are all those angular vessels out there?" asked Linda.

"I asked the people at the boat parade registration. They said they're old Navy SEAL gun boats which were sold to the Mexican Navy. They're going to stage a mock terrorist attack tomorrow so they're practicing their

341

maneuvers. They'll be further out in the open water so they won't interfere with the boat parade."

"Let's just hope they don't find out just who we are before we have a chance to make our exit back to American waters" said Linda.

"We'll sneak off into the darkness where the circle exits the harbor and hopefully no one will notice we're even gone" said Tom. "If not, we may need some of your clever business negotiation skills to win our freedom, Emmet."

"Move over *the Donald* and just call me the *Emmet*."

"Don't joke about it. With Ernie out there somewhere, anything could happen" said Tom. "Now get busy with those lights and let's hope Ernie shows up soon so we can get the hell out of here. The parade starts in one hour so let's move it."

And as the trio scrambled to get the parade lights onto the shrouds of the Swan, Bob, Dustin, Lynne, Meredith, Christian and Stephanie had hailed a van cab and were making their way down to the marina from the airport.

"So, Brother Bob, what will we do once we find the *Three Mighty Messengers?*" asked Stephanie.

"I'm not really sure, Stephanie. But we will find out once we find them" Bob answered. "Dustin, what do the Tablets say about the NINE once again?"

"Yes, I wonder who exactly the NINE are?" asked Christian.

Dustin removed the tablets from his laptop computer case and began to page through the ancient documents.

"Here it is Brother Bob. It says: *Hidden and buried these Tablets shall become, lost to man until the NINE. Name them by name; Untanas, Querjtas, Chietal, Goyana, Huiertal, Semertan, Aridian, Theros and Tianem. Only the power of the nine Lords can shift the earth's balance and the power of the DARK BROTHERS.*"

"Curious" said Lynne. "I have a feeling there's something more to those names. May I see that Tablet for a minute, Dustin?"

"Aqui estan" said Dustin, passing the Tablet over. And as Lynne took the Tablet, once again sparkles of bright energy began to dance and shimmer off of the Tablet and it began to emit the same glow and vibration that it had while in the cavern in Cadiz.

"It is attuning to your thought waves, Lynne" said Bob anxiously, "Tell us what you see."

As Lynne looked down upon the page of the Tablet, a look of sheer amazement and great amusement came over her face.

"It appears to have answered your question, Christian. Here, take a look" she said, laughing and holding the Tablet up for all to see.

The group gasped and then after a minute they all started to chuckle.

"It appears that the *Emerald Tablets of Troth* have a sense of humor" said Bob.

"It certainly would seem that way, wouldn't it?" said Lynne.

And as she held up the page for everyone to observe, different letters of the names leapt off the page like a holograph or images in a 3D movie, flashing off and on like a Times Square billboard.

"Oh my God, this is so cool!" said Meredith.

Certain letters of the names which Dustin had read just moments before had become extended beacons of bright green light and had been transcribed in front of the page where they jumped out alternately like a flashing neon sign, their illumination obscuring the underlying letters which were not applicable to the new wording.

First the letters un*T*anas, chietal, g*O*yana, se*M*ertan projected into the name *TOM*.

Then the letters qu*ER*jtas, goya*N*a, hu*IE*rtal projected into the name *ERNIE*.

Next the letters s*EME*re*T*an, *T*heros projected into the name *EMETT*.

And then the letters chieta*L*j, hu*I*ertal, ar*I*dia*N*, Ari*DA*n projected into *LINDA*.

The letters chieta*L*, go*Ya*N*a, semereta*N*, th*E*ros projected into *LYNNE*.

Then the letters Quert*J*as, *GOY*ana, c*Hi*Et*A*l, huier*T*al, t*HER*os projected into *JOY STEPHANIE*.

After which the letters se*MERE*tan, ari*DI*an, *TH*eros projected into *MEREDITH*.

Next the letters *CH*ietal, huie*R*tal, ar*I*dian, thero*S*, *TIAN*em projected into the name *CHRISTIAN*.

And finally the letters unt*A*na*S*, c*H*ieta*L*, go*Y*ana projected into *ASHLY*.

But the most surprising anagram came from underneath this alternating lineup of names. There, in a larger and bolder font, another sentence flashed off and on and read *and how 'bout them Dodgers, Buster Brown?*

"It would appear that Troth is a Dodgers fan, wouldn't it?" asked Stephanie laughing.

"It would seem so" said Meredith. "It's comforting to know Troth has the time to follow baseball."

"I think it may have another meaning" said Lynne. "But I'm not sure what it is."

"So we know who seven of the nine are, but who are Linda and Diana?" asked Christian.

"We don't know, do we?" replied Bob. "And evidently we didn't make the cut, Dustin."

"I guess not, Bob" said Dustin disappointedly. But just as he said that, two more separate projections alternately leapt out from the question *and how 'bout them Dodgers, Buster Brown* and flashed in front of the group. They read *AND* how *'BO*ut those dodgers, *B*uster Brown; the letters projecting into the words AND BOB. And then in addition, the letters intermittently flashed off and on with *AND* how about those *D*odgers, b*UST*er brow*N*; these letters projecting into the words AND DUSTN.

"AND BOB AND DUSTN" said Lynne. "It appears that Troth not only has a sense of humor but also needs some spelling lessons."

"His syntax could use some improvement as well" added Stephanie.

"Troth may be slightly dyslexic but at least we know he is communicating with us, albeit in the American tongue. Still, it is a very good thing" said Bob.

"Great, at least we made the roster anyway" said Dustin.

"Absolutely, this is jolly good" said Bob. And as the van wound its way to the marina, the Vice President of the United States and his doctor were checking into the Hotel Coral and Marina.

"Reno, when we get to the suite, prepare for me another shot and make it a double this time. I'm going to need some extra energy to see that our mission here is accomplished" Lamply grunted at the doctor.

"Sure thing, Ernst, but don't you think a double dose might be a little bit too much? You have to watch your ticker, sir" Reno replied as he checked himself out in the mirror located on the hallway wall.

"Just shut up and do as I say" said Lamply, following the secret service agents into the elevator. Upon reaching the suite, one of the agents unlocked the door.

"Sir, we have cleared the suite and it is free of any listening or visual devices" said the agent. "We will, as usual, be here outside the door."

"Good" snarled Lamply, slamming the door behind him and entering the suite with Reno. "Now get that shot ready, Reno. I'm going to see if I can't find that CFAF agent. What was her name?"

"Brubaker, Ernst, her name is Twyla Brubaker" Reno replied. "That little filly was supposed to be in touch with Colonel Graham, wasn't she Ernst?"

"Get him on the phone now, Reno. I want to know if he spoke with her or found out anything" growled Lamply.

"Reno took out his blackberry and speed dialed Graham and after a few minutes of chatting, turned to the Vice President.

"Sorry, Ernst, Graham says he hasn't heard anything from her and there is absolutely no intel on a gang called the *Swans*. He presumes she is still being held as a hostage."

"Well, what about Tomato and Hershfield or whatever their names are?" asked Lamply, obviously perturbed.

"I believe that's D'Amato and Schofield, sir. And Graham says that they can't be reached either" said Reno, running a comb through his hair.

"Damnit!" yelled Lamply. Launching himself into one of his signature tantrums, he picked up one of the candle sticks on the dining table and heaved it against the wall with the Mayan object d'art where Jeremy had placed the Piper minutes before. And as the candle stick struck the Mayan object d'art on the shelf, the obsidian bowl shattered with a crash, and as it fell to the ground in pieces, the black sphere which had been partially hidden within it struck the floor with a thump and rolled to Lamply's feet.

"What the hell is this?" he asked, picking the sphere up in his hands. Immediately mesmerized by the great beauty of the *Piper*, he began to caress it adoringly as it started to vibrate and glow.

"Wow Ernst" said Reno. "That's just about the 'purtiest thing I've ever seen this side of the Pecos!"

"Yes, it really is something isn't it?" Lamply said, gazing upon it with total adoration. And as he held the black sphere in his hands, entranced by its beauty, a very evil and sinister laugh began to reverberate within his being. And as Lamply swooned into a coma like state, his eyes momentarily turned a yellow color and began to radiate. And although the voice spoke to an unconscious person, the words seared their way into what was left of Lamply's soul. The voice spoke in a slow and modulated tone and it said:

"Adore the beauty, beware the power. Desires fulfilled thy visage shall alter, Light to darkness thy path shall be, a lesson in duality."

And as Lamply began to return to consciousness, the voice became a terrifying screech. It said: "Now you fool, my creation has returned to me and you, Vice President Ernst Lamply will become the beneficiary of its powers and its curse. *Together we will destroy the Disciples of Troth and the world!*"

And as the fiendish laugh subsided and Lamply began to regain consciousness, his eyes returned to their normal state and he seemed to awaken from what seemed a moment of sleep.

"What, what was that you said, Reno?" he asked.

"Ah, I said, sir, that that there object is about the purtiest......."

"Shut up, Reno, I heard what you said. I'm not sure just what this object is but I have a feeling it's going to help us in our endeavors. Now get that shot ready, I'm going to unpack some things."

And as Lamply turned away and strolled down the hallway and entered the bedroom with the *Piper*, he laid his bag on the bed. But something distracted him and looking up momentarily, he saw his reflection in a mirror hanging on the wall.

"That's weird" he thought to himself. Stopping what he was doing, he strolled over to the mirror and looked closely at his reflection.

"This is fricking strange" he thought. "What the hell is going on here?"

It was hardly noticeable, but something about his face looked different. It had become slightly thinner and his nose seemed somewhat larger. His lips were broader somehow. His eyes looked different also. They had become more deeply set and darker. The changes were subtle but there they were.

Suddenly there was a knock at the bathroom door. It was Reno.

"Ernst, President Vicente Pero's people are on the phone. They say *El Presidente* would like you to meet him down at the Marina in one hour to see the boat parade and the Mexican Navy practicing maneuvers for tomorrow's mock terrorist attack."

"Damnit" thought Lamply. "I need to find those torpedoes, not go sip on a margarita with some two bit beaner despot who masquerades as a president. On the other hand, he does send us very cheap labor. I guess I'll have to placate him this once and begin the search tomorrow."

"What shall I tell them, Ernst?" shouted Reno through the door.

"Alright, Reno, tell him I'll meet him. Now get my shot ready! I'll need it and don't forget to make it a double."

"Whatever you say, Ernst" Reno replied, tucking and smoothing his shirttails into his trousers. "Whatever you say" he mumbled as he shuffled his way back to the phone.

And as Reno returned to the phone to arrange the rendezvous with Pero, Lamply looked in the mirror once more.

"Hmm, I can't quite put my finger on it but something strange is going on here" he thought as he scrutinized his face in the mirror. "Something very, very strange….."

~

The Bell Captain

"I've got two voice mails and three text messages from Graham here on my cell" said D'Amato. "He wants to know the status of the torpedoes and the whereabouts of agent Brubaker. He also says that the Vice President has arrived here in town."

"I think we better find that key to the ammo dump fast or we can kiss our ten million 'goodbye'! Hopefully we won't have to deal with him personally. He's probably staying in one of the mansions outside of town" Schofield replied. "We're almost at the Hotel. Hopefully we can find our agent and her kidnapper there."

"What about Princeton?" D'Amato asked. "Maybe he's seen something."

"Jeremy knows nothing about this so keep your distance when we get to the hotel. I'll have to check in with him anyway." said Schofield.

And as the taxi pulled into the driveway of the Hotel Coral and Marina, Schofield noticed that four men in suits were standing behind the valet stand and next to the front doors.

"Hmm…people wearing suits in Ensenada…that's weird….no, it couldn't be" exclaimed Schofield.

And as the taxi stopped at the front door, he could see that a caravan of black stretch limousines was parked off to the side of the porte-cochere.

351

"Looks like you have some important guests" said Schofield to the doorman as the driver unloaded their bags from the trunk.

"Si señor, we have some very important guests staying here with us" he said with a smile. "Let me get the door for you, senor."

"Thank you" Schofield replied. "D'Amato, make yourself scarce and get lost somewhere in the lobby and make sure your cell is on. I'll check in and see what's up with Princeton."

"I'll do that."

"And keep your eyes peeled for our kidnapper and hostage."

"I'm on it."

"Good" said Schofield. Approaching the front desk, agent Ronando greeted him with a smile.

"Welcome to the Hotel Coral and Marina, sir. You have a reservation?"

"Yes I do. Peter Harrison is the name and I'm with Jeremy Princeton."

"Ah yes, here it is, Señor Harrison. "Noussa, would you escort this gentleman to his suite please?"

"At your service" the bell captain replied, putting Schofield's bag on a cart and gesturing toward the elevator.

"Just one thing, Senor Harrison" Ronando interjected.

"Yes" said Schofield.

"There are secret service agents at the elevator on the fourth floor. You can expect to be frisked. I am sorry about the inconvenience, señor."

"Thank you for the warning."

"You're most welcome. Have a wonderful stay with us, Senor Harrison!"

"Thank you very much."

"This way Mr. Harrison" gestured Noussa toward the elevator. And as the elevator door closed, Peter turned to the Bell Captain.

"May I ask who this very special guest is, Captain?" asked Schofield.

"I am sorry, Señor, but we are not at liberty to disclose that fact."

Peter reached into his pocket and pulled out a fifty dollar bill.

"Would Mr. Ulysses S. Grant change your mind?" he asked.

"Ah yes, Mr. Grant is one of my favorite American presidents, senor. But I could never take a bribe like that" said the Bell Captain as he held out his hand and looked the other way.

Peter placed the bill in the bell captain's hand.

"For the Ensenada Fireman's fund!" said Noussa as he grabbed the bill and shoved it into his jacket pocket. "Now señor, it did not come from me but it appears we have a most important dignitary staying with us. I still cannot say who it is exactly but suffice it to say that I helped him with his bags and his doctor referred to him as *Mr. Vice President.*"

"That's what I suspected" said Peter. "Anything else I should know?"

"Perhaps, perhaps not, señorr" said Noussa.

Schofield pulled a twenty out of his pocket which was quickly snapped out of his hand by the philanthropic bell captain.

"Well, perhaps it is nothing but I overheard one of the secret service agents say they needed to clear the area down by the marina so he could meet with *El Presidente Pero* for the Carnival boat parade. By the way, your suite is right next to his."

"Most interesting" said Schofield. And as the elevator doors opened two men in suits stepped forward. And as they walked forward one of the men spoke.

"Sorry, sir, but we'll have to frisk you and search your bag."

"Be my guest, gentlemen" said Schofield while scanning the hallway for any other unusual activities. And as the agents frisked him and searched his bag, suddenly a door opened from down the hallway and out strode Vice President Ernst Lamply and another man who Schofield didn't recognize.

"Alright, make way please, gentlemen" barked one of the agents as the Vice President arrogantly pushed his way through the group without so much as a nod or a sorry or a 'pardon me' spoken.

And as the elevator doors closed on the two men, Peter turned to the agents who had finished their task.

"Friendly sort of chap, isn't he" Schofield said sarcastically.

'Alright sir, you may go" said the agent handing the bag back to Nousa.

'Thank you" said Schofield.

Arriving at the door of suite 412, Noussa knocked and then inserted the key card into the slot. But before he could open it, the handle had turned and the door swung open. It was Jeremy.

'Peter, where have you been?" asked Jeremy.

"Let's just say I had a slight delay, Jeremy. Thank you, Noussa" said Peter, entering the suite and starting to close the door behind him.

"Wait" shouted Jeremy. "Noussa, did you find out who that girl was like I asked?"

"Perhaps, perhaps not, Senor Princeton" he replied.

"Peter, do you have some money?" asked Jeremy.

"General Grant most certainly is losing the war today, I must say" said Schofield reassuming his role as Peter and reaching once again for his wallet and handing another fifty to Noussa…"for the fireman's fund, Senor Noussa?"

"The Ensenada Fire Department can now afford new hoses, Senor, thank you" said Noussa. "Now Senor Princeton, I am at your service. The girl's name is Diana Williams and she is staying next to you in suite 411. The cab driver said he took her down to the navy pier but had said something about maybe needing a cab later to go to the Marina."

"Thank you, Noussa" said Jeremy, closing the door.

"What is going on here, Jeremy?" Peter asked.

"Peter, I met the most wonderful and beautiful girl checking in here. I didn't get her name so I offered Noussa a little something extra if he could find out who she was and he did!"

"Diana Williams …who is Diana Williams?" thought Schofield.

And before Peter could unpack his bag, Jeremy had grabbed his airline pilot's hat and was heading toward the door.

"Come on, Peter. I have to see this beautiful girl again. It's time to do *Carnival* here in Ensenada. Hurry, we're going down to the marina."

~

The Oblong Melons

"Okay, Ernie, we've got the PVC pipe, now what?" Diana asked as Ernie punched the accelerator and grinded the jeep into fourth gear.

"We just need some gray paint and a couple of small melons and we're ready to rock and roll" he said as the navy vehicle careened around the corner

"I'm not going to ask" said Diana, hanging onto the seat with both hands.

"Trust me, I know what I'm doing here!"

"Why do I doubt that?" Diana replied apprehensively. "So, what bank are we holding up next?"

"No bank, but we will need to purchase a few items from the farmer's market. And then of course, we'll need a little paint so we'll pay a little visit to the parade prep tent on Calle Primera."

"Cased it all out already, eh Mr. Dillinger?"

"Every move I make is very carefully planned" said Ernie in his best Jacque Clouseau accent as the jeep screeched to a halt by the fresh fruit stand at the nightly farmer's market. "Come on. Diana. We need to find an oblong melon."

"Find a what?" Diana asked.

"There are round melons and then there are oblong melons. We need to find two oblong melons that will fit

357

into these PVC pipes" said Ernie as he grabbed the pipes from the rear seat.

"Okay, I'll bite. What is the difference between an oblong and a round melon and how do you know these things?"

"Tom told me. He used to work at a kibbutz in Israel. He was actually a chicken flinger but he learned all about melons also."

"A chicken flinger…what the hell is a chicken flinger?"

"You don't want to know" said Ernie grabbing Diana's hand and pulling her down the melon aisle. "But let me show you a thing or two about melons."

Ernie stopped at a very large table with six different bins, all holding a different variety of melon.

"For example, Diana, this is what's known as a *muskmelon*" he said picking up one of the varieties. "As you can see, it is round with *orange* flesh and a ruddy beige *netted* skin. It combines the desirable characteristics of both the cantaloupe and the muskmelon."

"Ah yes… subtle aromas of cranberry and spice with a hint of forest floor."

"Exactly, Williams" said Ernie moving on to the next bin. "Now here we have the *Canary melon*. It is *fragrant* when ripe and has bright yellow rinds and sweet, *off white flesh*."

"Indeed, the hint of violet and cherry blossom is augmented by the deep, rich tones of blackberry, clove and pomegranate" Diana added sarcastically. "I must admit that I'm impressed. I'm with a guy who can break down and rebuild his M-16 in eight seconds and is also a melon connoisseur!"

"Is that a note of sarcasm I detect, Ensign?"

"It's not a note, Ernie, it's a movement. So what the hell are we doing here, watermelon man?"

"Ah, here we have the perfect melons" said Ernie picking up an orange melon with green ends. "These will do perfectly. This is known as a *Casaba melon*. You will note its rather unusual oblong characteristics."

"I'll alert the media" said Diana. "So?"

"You will observe the *supple smoothness* of the exterior, the *netted yet penetrable exterior* of its casing and the unusual egg like shape."

"Are you going to eat it or make love to it? Now get to the point will you, Emeril?"

"Ah yes, the point...that is exactly the point" said Ernie as he picked up one of the melons and lined its end up with the top of the PVC pipe before dropping it into the tubing where it sped to the bottom with a swish and wedged itself neatly into the other end, its nose protruding outward like a pregnant mother's bosom.

"Wow, congratulations Mr. Newton" said Diana. "There really is a force called gravity! I'm numb with awe."

"I thought you would be, Williams. Endless years of grueling research went into this project. The Nobel Prize will be mine at last" said Ernie as he picked up another melon and slid it into the second PVC pipe where it fell to the bottom with a thump.

"Okay, now we have two stuffed pipes. What next? No wait, don't tell me…don't tell me. You're going to put them into the magic box and saw them in half?"

"You just don't appreciate my ingenuity, do you, Williams?" asked Ernie as he laid a dollar bill on the counter.

"Is there ingenuity involved here? I hadn't noticed."

"We geniuses are never appreciated until we're dead. Now let's go, Diana" said Ernie grabbing the two tubes and throwing them into the back of the jeep. "Now, one more stop and we're ready for the siege."

And as Ernie once again slammed the jeep into first and peeled out, Diana's cell rang. It was D'Amato. "Not a good time" she thought as she let the three ring tones dissolve into the voice mail.

"Screening your calls today?" asked Ernie as he flew around the corner onto Calle Primera where the Carnival parade prep tent was located.

"Not in the mood" Diana replied as Ernie pulled the jeep into the drive off of the street where the parade floats had exited twenty minutes earlier.

"Ah, perfect timing. Let's check it out, Diana" said Ernie jumping out of the jeep and entering the tent. The place was in shambles with streamers, cardboard and old glue and paint canisters adorning the tables where the floats had been constructed. A few men were sweeping up and attempting to remove the debris.

"Over there, Diana" said Ernie scanning the chaos and pointing to a table with used and partially used paint brushes and cans. "Let's grab the tubes. They'll need a little customizing."

"Excuse me, señor" said Ernie to one of the sweepers. "Is it *bueno* if I use some of this left over paint?"

"Is it *bueno*? Wow, you're bilingual on top of everything else!" exclaimed Diana.

"Seguro, senor" said the man. "Help yourself."

"Shut up Williams and you might learn something" Ernie replied as he reached for a can of black paint and some duct tape. Wrapping the tape around both tubes' necks twelve inches from the top, he grabbed a black paint can and proceeded to spray the casaba melon nose cones black down to the tape.

"Hmm" muttered Diana. "I think I'm beginning to see a method to your madness."

"Hold these on the bottom Diana" said Ernie, passing the tubes to her.

Grasping the tubes and holding them out, Ernie grabbed a can of green paint and sprayed the bottoms of the tubes while Diana rotated them in her hands.

"Voila!" said Ernie, removing the tape and then smiling like he had just finished painting the Mona Diana. "How do you say, they are fantastique, oui madame?"

"Veritable masterpieces, Ernie," admitted Diana, pondering the creations. "I have to admit they actually sort of resemble torpedoes. So now what happens?"

"Now we go to take out the giraffe and put in the elephant and this key is going to be our pass" Ernie replied as he took the key on the chain out of his side pocket and draped it around Diana's neck. "Here you are, my lady" he said. "*Now the fair lady holds the key.*"

"Imagine my relief" said Diana.

"Yes, and I guess we could use this too" said Ernie, grabbing a wooden packing crate that had been left in the area.

"Ernie, that's a frigging orange crate…almost. You think the gate guards won't notice? Are you on crack or something?"

"Ah…but voila…this will make it official" Ernie replied, pulling some sort of rolled up paper out of his fatigue pocket.

"And what, may I ask is that, David Copperfield?"

"It is, Miss Marple, what is commonly known as a U.S. Navy decal. And watch what I do with it" said Ernie.

"And just where did you get that, may I ask?"

"It just happened to be in the jeep that we borrowed."

"Why do I doubt that?" asked Diana.

"Okay, never mind where I got it from. Just watch" he said as he laid the decal across the top of the crate and taped it in place. Picking up a can of spray paint marked *Cerulean Blue*, Ernie sprayed the paint across the decal until the paint had thoroughly left its mark on the surface.

"Da Da!" said Ernie as he peeled the decal off, leaving a clean and vibrant blue *Property of U.S. Navy* brandished across the cover.

"It'll never fly" said Diana.

"It doesn't have to fly, Diana" Ernie replied. "It only has to get us through the ammo dump gates."

"The things I do for my country" Diana sighed. "Well then, let's give it a shot."

"Piece of cake" said Ernie.

And as the two returned to the jeep with the faux crate and the two torpedoes in Diana's hands held up to dry, Ernie looked over at her with a smug sort of grin from ear to ear.

"Don't even think of saying it, Ernie."

"I wouldn't dare, Williams" Ernie laughed. "Now let's go finish our mission."

And with that comment, once again he slammed the jeep into gear and sped off into the night.

~

A Couple of Crusty Old Dudes

"Excuse me, sir?" asked Stephanie. "Can you tell us how to get to Marina One?"

"Sure thing, lady" said a young and thin man with a hooked nose who was on his knees scrubbing the sidewalk with a toothbrush.

"Go to the end of the breakwater and it's on your left" he barked back without looking up.

"Thank you" Stephanie replied.

"What a strange man" Lynne remarked. "Did you see what he was doing?"

"He was scrubbing the sidewalk with a toothbrush. Why on earth do you suppose he was scrubbing the sidewalk with a toothbrush?" Meredith asked the group.

"Maybe he's just a clean kind of guy" said Dustin.

"Or he's an out of work dentist" added Bob.

"His name is *Lang* suddenly added a voice from behind the group.

"Pardon me?" asked Stephanie, turning around.

"Lang…his name is *Lang*" said a handsome man from behind the group who was dressed in a Polo shirt, shorts and Topsiders and resembled Tom Selleck. "He brushes the sidewalks here every night."

"But whatever for?" asked Stephanie.

"No one really knows for sure" added the stranger. "But rumor has it that he once had aspirations of becoming a U.S. Marine but supposedly in boot camp he had a bit of a problem with his drill instructor."

"I wonder what it was" Stephanie remarked.

"Supposedly while in boot camp, he smuggled a beer into his billet and the drill instructor caught him. Of course he denied the charges so the DI made him scrub the grinder with his toothbrush all night!"

"Wow, it must have been a squeaky clean piece of pavement in the morning."

"It would have been if he had stayed on the base."

"What do you mean?" asked Dustin.

"No one knows what really happened but once again, supposedly at some time during the night something dropped out of the sky and banged him on his head. They supposedly found a frozen brick of something or another near where he was supposed to be the next morning. They guessed it was something from a passing jet."

"Ewwwwww!" cried the group in unison.

"He's lucky he lived" laughed Lynne.

"Yes he is" said the man. "The brick must have hit his head and knocked his marbles around a bit. But somehow or another he escaped the base and hopped a bus down here to Ensenada with his toothbrush and he's been scrubbing the sidewalks ever since. We call him the *Lang Banger*.

"Poor guy" said Stephanie. "That's kind of sad, isn't it?"

"Well, he's happy as a pig in you know what doing it, so who's to say? We all help him out with food and lodging so he's not destitute. It all works out for him. By the way, my name is Phil, Phil Smythe" said the mystery man holding out his hand for Stephanie to shake. "Let me show you the way to Marina One. I'm headed that way."

"Alright" Stephanie replied, shaking the man's hand. "By the way, these are my friends. This is Bob, Meredith, Lynne, Dustin and Christian."

"A pleasure" replied Phil politely, nodding to the group but unable to take his eyes off Stephanie. "What brings you all to Ensenada?"

"You want to handle that question, Bob?" asked Stephanie.

"Jolly good, Stephanie, I shall. Let it suffice to say that we are seeking three individuals who need to alter the course of the world."

"Are you serious or delirious? How are they going to do that?"

"It's complicated" Bob replied as the group descended the marina ramp and made their way out to the slips.

"And what brings you to Ensenada?" Meredith asked Phil.

"I've been here for almost a year now. Just came down from the states to do a little fishing. Having spent my life on the frozen tundra of Minnesota and never having been to Mexico, I thought I'd pay this berg a little visit. I was surfing the internet one day looking for great fishing spots and up came a deep sea fishing tour in Ensenada run by a couple of Vietnam era vets. I booked a tour a year ago and haven't returned yet. I like the pace of things here"

"Yes, it seems like life here is at a slower tempo, doesn't it?" remarked Lynne.

"That's for sure" Phil replied. "Of course, now that I'm part owner of the fishing tour company, I have a vested interest in this place."

"Well then, congratulations!" said Christian.

"Yep, it works out well. The tour operation was owned by a couple of old guys who had both spent time in the Hanoi Hilton during the Vietnam War. They know all the best fishing spots but are a little too laid back and more than a little crazy too. Long story short, they needed a cash infusion and some young blood to keep it going. They're really characters, I have to tell you! Well, here's my slip. Nice meeting you all" said Phil as he stopped at finger P.

"Nice to meet you" replied the group.

"Good luck with your mission and saving the world. By the way, there's a boat parade tonight. We're in it if you want to come with us and have a little fun."

"Love to but we do have some things to attend to here, but thank you" replied Stephanie.

"Suit yourselves" said Phil. "But if you change your mind, we're right here, the sixth boat on the left."

"Thank you" replied the group.

"You're welcome and good luck" said Phil, still leering at Stephanie.

"Oh, while I think of it, if you change your mind and I'm not here just come on aboard and introduce yourselves to the other captains. They're a couple of crusty old dudes but they're harmless. Just tell them you're my friends. This whole marina knows them like a couple of rock stars. They're real celebrities down here."

"Doubtful but thanks" said Bob.

"Alright then, maybe I'll see you later" said Phil.

"But wait, just in case, what are their names?" asked Dustin.

'Oh yeah, I almost forgot to tell you" Phil replied. "Their names are Captains Leyton and Keller."

And with that comment he turned and began to whistle Earth Wind and Fire's *After the Love Has Gone* as he made his way down the dock to his slip.

~

Camp Enchilada

The Ensenada Munitions and Fuel Storage Facility was a Defense Department white elephant left over from Teddy Roosevelt's administration during the *Spanish American War*. Leased from the Mexican government in 1905 for ninety-nine years, the facility was located in the Valle de San Antonio de Las Minas off Highway 3, sixteen miles south of the town of Ensenada.

Dubbed *Camp Enchilada* by the Navy and Marine personnel stationed there, it had originally been used for nothing more than fuel storage for American ships with military contracts on their way to the Panama Canal. Nothing of any real consequence had found its way to the facility in the last fifty years with the exception of diesel fuel and some engine parts. But due to the rising hostilities with the Venezuelan government and Colombian drug lords, the facility had been resuscitated in recent years.

It was located on fifty-two butt-ugly acres situated in the hot Mexican Baja desert but was considered pretty much a country club by the MSG Marines and Navy personnel lucky enough to pull duty this close to a south of the border paradise.

A chain link fence encircled the area and created a buffer zone of one kilometer surrounding the main facility which consisted of the storage bunkers, a loading area and a recreation area with a couple of billets for sleeping. The living areas were separated from the magazines by blast barriers ten feet high, just in case any of the munitions ever broke down and detonated. But there wasn't much chance of that happening in a facility that stored no munitions. That is, it stored no munitions until the last few months.

"May I help you, ma'am?" asked the Marine guard as the Navy jeep came to a halt at the front gate.

"Ensign Brubaker, Marine" said Diana with an air of authority. "I'm the EOD Officer for METL Operations, Coronado Naval Base. This is torpedo man's mate Salgado. He is the EOD Tech and we have been assigned orders to implement MET NAVMC Directive 3500-EOD 6626."

"Ma'am?" the Marine asked, obviously confused.

"Here are our orders, clearances and IDs. We are here to perform upgrade maintenance on two MK 44 Mod 5 ADCAP torpedo heads. You *are* aware of the directive regarding this, aren't you sergeant?" said Diana with great emphasis on the word *are*.

"Wait here please, ma'am" said the Marine, taking the documentation and entering the duty hut where another Marine was bent over a computer.

"Brubaker...your name is Brubaker?

"For this mission, my name is Brubaker" Diana replied.

'Okay, but someday you're going to have to explain where all this documentation came from, Williams" said Ernie. "I have the distinct feeling that it's *not* the U.S. Navy you're working for!"

"You know the new buzz phrase, Ernie...don't ask and don't tell."

"Somehow I don't think that buzz phrase was intended for nuclear larceny, Diana" said Ernie, shaking his head. "And also I thought we were doing maintenance on the SHKVAL torpedoes."

"If you must know, the MK 44's and the SHKVALs are very similar in appearance and structure. The Baseline G&C sections are different. For the book, we are here to upgrade the ADCAP G&C Sections."

"Can't these guys tell the difference?"

"It's doubtful. The SHKVALs were shipped as MK-44's. They look exactly the same but obviously that's as far as it goes. The big difference is the nose cones."

"Ah, the nose cones...better known in more colloquial circles as nuclear warheads."

"They're not armed. It's the uranium dioxide we need."

"I'm dying to know who we are!"

"I am so sorry, but it's *Top Secret*! Now put on your best torpedo man's mate face and let's get it done!"

"Aye, aye, ma'am" said Ernie with a sarcastic salute.

Meanwhile the Marine guard had entered the guard house.

"Corporal Luria, what do you know about some MK 44 torpedo heads needing maintenance?"

"What torpedoes?" he asked

"They're called MK 44 mod 5 ADCAP torpedoes, pogue" snapped the sergeant. "You're supposed to know about this shit! Here, take a look."

"Ah yes, MK 44 torpedoes...well, standard stuff... they must be the ones that came in two days ago. Where's the log book?"

"Right here" said the sergeant reaching for the blue note book on the shelf.

"Hmm, let's see here" said Luria opening the log and licking his fingers to turn the pages. "Here it is. They came in two days ago on a deuce. Yep, and they were designated MK-44 ADCAP. They had a SUFN designation and no further destination was assigned."

"What was their point of origin?" asked the sergeant.

"Sieverson Electronics, Stockholm Sweden via Rota Naval Base, Spain" Luria replied. "They were marked for Top Secret Clearance only. We put them in magazine number one."

"Well, it looks like the top secret clearances just showed up! Why don't we know about this?" asked Sergeant Suddington, obviously irritated.

"I don't know. Maybe something came over NAVMAC this morning."

"Well, check it now, something about an upgrade on them."

The other marine guard quickly logged onto the network. "Let me have a look see here. Okay...looks like we have some new emails here alright. Department of the Navy, HQ USMC, the Pentagon Washington D.C. ...let's open this attachment. I'll just click here, put in the password and bingo, here it is" said Luria as they waited for the attachment to open.

"It sure is slow" said the sergeant.

And as the attachment opened, Corporal Luria suddenly looked like he'd seen a ghost.

Holy shit! It's an FPCON CHARLIE!"

"Which means?" asked the sergeant.

"An FPCON CHARLIE means Force Protection Condition. It refers to the Defense Departments assessment of a terrorist threat. What it means is an attack on the base could be imminent."

"What!! Damn, I never figured that would be happening down here. What would terrorists want with this base? There's nothing here, just a lot of explosive systems, a couple of torpedoes, some fuel and some RPG's! That's hardly an arsenal."

"Well it says our orders are to initiate a full alert. We'll need everyone on the perimeter for armed fence line patrols. With the CO on leave, you're the man, sergeant. We'll need to issue weapons from the armory."

"But how do we know it's authentic?"

"It couldn't have been sent on this network if it wasn't."

"Who signed it?"

"It's signed Office of Homeland Security. Here, take a look."

Sergeant Suddington bent over and squinted to see the screen. "Wow, this is unbelievable. It sure looks authentic. What's Homeland Security?"

"From what I've heard, it's a new extension of the Defense Department."

"It doesn't matter, does it? We need to be on alert status. Confirm the email and I'll pass the word down. We need to ready ourselves for battle!"

"What about those two outside? We have nothing on an MK-44 upgrade."

"Their papers look authentic. We have to prioritize. Take them to the magazine and let them at their task. But don't forget to follow procedure. They must have the *key*. It should have been issued to them already. But get your ass back here ASAP! This is an emergency here. We need to prepare for an attack!"

"Aye, aye Gunny" Luria replied. Reaching for his piss cutter, he hustled out the door to the two Navy personnel who were waiting in the jeep.

"Here are your papers, Ensign Brubaker. You can come through" said Luria with a salute. "Just a couple of things, do you have the key, ma'am?"

"Right here, Marine" said Diana lifting the chain from her neck. "It's issued by METL Operations, Coronado."

"And the upgrades?" asked Suddington.

"Right here" said Ernie, pointing to the crate in the rear seat.

"Let's see here" said the corporal as he lifted the top of the crate and gazed quickly at its contents before slamming it shut again.

"Looks good, now quickly follow me" yelled the Marine as he hastily hopped into the Navy Jeep nearby.

"What's the rush, Marine?" asked Diana.

"We're under threat, ma'am. We just got an FPCON CHARLIE alert."

"*What*, when did this happen?" asked Diana, obviously very surprised at this new development.

"It happened just now, ma'am! Now follow me, please" he screamed as he cranked the engine and floored it.

"Well, Mr. SEAL, it looks like your torpedoes passed the test. It's a good thing he was in a hurry" said Diana as Ernie raced after the other jeep.

"Oh ye of little faith" said Ernie.

"But how did they find out about the assault, I wonder?" asked Diana as the two jeeps flew down the road to the magazine bunker.

"The *assault*...what *assault*?" asked Ernie in disbelief. "Now hold on here, Williams, you let me in on this right now or I'm bailing, understand?"

"Just keep driving, Ernie."

"Listen to me, Diana. Either you let me in on this or I'm turning around right now!"

"Alright, alright, let's just say I work for some very influential people and I made a few phone calls when you weren't looking. They have arranged for us to have an escort off this base in the form of some air support, that's all. No one is going to be hurt. Now, let's just hope the air support is ready to go."

"Air support, now what might that mean?"

"This is *Plan B*, remember? There was once a *Plan A*. We just combined plans a little. It should take about twenty minutes for it to get here from the border. Now all we have to do is switch the torpedoes by the time the escort gets here."

"And what escort would that be?" Ernie inquired.

"You'll find out. I'm going to text someone here" said Diana. Pulling out her Blackberry and punching the keys rapidly she wrote: *Graham - am on base launch air support now, Brubaker.*

"Aren't we the secretive one today?" said Ernie.

"Ernie, you're just going to have to trust me. We *have* to be sure the torpedoes get off this base safely, that's all."

"Listen, either you let me in on this or I'm pulling over right now!" Ernie shouted as he slowed the jeep and down shifted into second gear.

"Alright, alright" yelled Diana. "I'll tell you all I know but swear on your mother's grave you will never divulge any of it to anyone!"

"My mother is still alive."

"Okay, whatever then! Just swear to me you won't let it go any further" Diana replied.

"Done, I swear."

"Alright, there is a secret faction of the U.S. government which calls itself CFAF or the *Committee for American Freedom*. I'm not exactly what it's all about but I received orders from them via a man very high up in the government to retrieve the torpedoes located here in Ensenada. I don't know why they need them other than they need the uranium dioxide in the nose cones. All I know is that they are very important. Originally, there was to be an all-out assault on this base to capture them but when I met you and you said you had the key to the ammo facility, I contacted my superiors and we implemented a new plan."

"So you've been using me all along!" asked Ernie, obviously perturbed.

"Yes, it started that way, Ernie. But it's not that way anymore. How can I say this without sounding corny… you've grown on me, guy! Look, I am getting paid a great deal of money to complete this mission. You and I could have a really nice life together, sailor. And besides, there is no turning back now. You have to help me complete the mission. I need your help here, please Ernie."

"Shoot, all I wanted was one small torpedo or just some small arms fire to insure our escape from the harbor and now I'm up to my neck in trafficking nuclear weapons and probably treason. Well, you're right, there's no turning back now. Just remember you owe me big time, Diana Williams. By the way, is that your real name?"

"Actually no, it isn't" Diana replied.

"So what is it really then?"

"It's Edna."

"No, no, say it's not so, Edna what?"

"Fitzgruber, its Edna Fitzgruber."

"That is one *ugly* mother honkin' name."

"I'm just jerking you around, cowboy. It's Diana alright, but *not* necessarily Williams."

Well thank the Lord then" Ernie replied quite relieved as the two jeeps pulled up in front of the magazine entrance. "I just can't picture introducing you as my girlfriend Edna."

"Just girlfriend?" asked Diana.

"One step at a time, Ensign, we just met, remember? Now let's get the torpedoes and get out of here!" said Ernie, obviously avoiding the issue. Hopping out of the Jeep, the two followed Corporal Luria to the magazine hatch.

"Okay, now you have obviously been briefed already on the procedure here" said the corporal. "I insert my key and then you insert yours. I'll leave you to do what ever you need to do and we'll check you on the way out. Is that understood?"

"Yes, it's understood, Corporal" replied Diana as Luria took the flat key from around his neck and inserted it into the massive steel door of what appeared to be an underground billet.

"Now your turn, ma'am" said the corporal.

Diana took the flat silver key from around her neck and inserted it into the same slot. A huge clank could be heard and then a hissing sound as the pneumatic door opened into a windowless room of shelves which were packed halfway to the ceiling with various armaments.

"As you can see, ma'am, we don't exactly have a huge inventory yet. The maintenance room is at the rear. You should find anything you might need for your upgrade there. Now if you'll excuse me, I have to return to the armory. I suggest you hurry. We could be under attack at any time" said the corporal with a salute.

"We'll hurry, corporal" said Diana returning the salute. "This shouldn't take long."

And as the corporal returned to his Jeep and sped back to the armory, Ernie and Diana entered the building and approached the crates which lay on the floor.

"Well, it's now time to take out the giraffe and put in the elephant. This is easier than I thought it would be. I'll get the *melon torpedoes* out of the Jeep. Be right back."

And as Ernie went back to the Jeep to retrieve the customized faux torpedoes, Diana took her inventory list from her pocket. "That's odd" she thought. "This list from the CFAF shows a fully stocked fuel and munitions facility. There doesn't appear to be even half of this list here. I wonder why that is."

"Okay, Diana, here they are" said Ernie returning from the Jeep. "Now all we have to do is find the MK 44 torpedo crates and remove the... what are they again?"

"They are designated the baseline ADCAP G and C sections" Diana replied as she strolled up and down the aisles checking the inventory list with the armaments on the shelves. "This is really weird!"

"What's weird?"

"According to this inventory list I received from the CFAF, this ammo storage facility should be filled to the brim with claymores, hand grenades, M 16's, anti-tank grenades, 30mm M919's and so on and so forth."

"Well...it looks like some of its here."

"Take a look here. Over there on the first row are the MK44s, obviously the last shipment to be placed here. But look at all these other crates."

"What about them?"

"All of these others are marked Portable Self Contained Explosive Systems."

"Oh yeah, we used them in the SEALS all the time. The military uses them in the field to explode concrete or steel buildings. They're extremely powerful and can be used with minimal preparation. It's a system that's generally used if explosives need to be planted quickly within a limited time frame and they're also easily hidden and can all be activated at once with a simple timing device."

"But there must be hundreds of them here and they're all marked the same way. And look, they all have the same destination."

"Which is what?"

"They all have Port of Entry as New York City but no destination there."

"So?"

"Just seems strange to me…don't know why exactly."

"I've got a bad feeling about this, Williams. Let's get this job done and get out of here. I don't know why but something tells me you've been set up somehow. Where are the torpedoes?"

"Here they are. Let's get the lid off and get them back to the maintenance room where I can get the G & C sections off" said Diana as Ernie grabbed a crow bar and removed the crate cover. Placing the torpedoes onto a dolly specifically constructed to hold explosives devices, he wheeled the torpedoes into the maintenance room and placed them into the vice-like containers used for maintenance.

"There you go, Diana. Go do your thing. I'm going to stay out front and keep my eyes peeled for anything unusual. Don't blow us up here."

"I told you. These are not supposed to be armed. They have no nitroglycerin charges yet. The uranium dioxide is in the G sections. I'll just remove them and we'll replace them with your faux ones. By the time anyone notices, we'll be long gone."

"Okay Ensign, get to it. I'll be out front."

"I'm on it then!."

And as Ernie walked back to the front of the facility, a crate on one of the shelves to his left caught his eye. "Oh sweet, I haven't seen any of these since my SEAL days."

It was marked *RPG-7GLs* and after lowering the crate to the floor, he grabbed the crow bar again and pried off the top. "Oh yes, yes…rocket propelled grenades… I have a feeling we're going to need a couple of these babies" he thought to himself as he picked one up and held it on his shoulder and popped the optical sight. "I'll just hide a few of these in the torpedo crate. The guards won't even check on our way out."

And as Ernie hid the RPGs in the crate, Colonel Graham was on the phone to Ernst Lamply who was on his way to the Marina to join El Presidente Pero in observing the Carnival boat parade and Mexican Navy maneuvers.

"What is it, Graham? Lamply growled into the limousine phone. "You had better have found something out or you're dust."

"Yes sir, Mr. Vice President, I have something quite important to tell you."

"Well, what is it?"

"The agent Brubaker is inside the munitions facility. I just got a text message from her. She wants to implement the *Plan A* air support to assure safe transport back to the corvette boat."

"Who is with her?"

"It's unknown, sir."

"Is it that *Tomato* guy?"

"I don't think so, sir. D'Amato has also been in touch. He is also headed toward the Marina. He's following Schofield who is with another unknown person."

"Hmm" thought Lamply. "This could be a golden opportunity for me."

"Okay, so listen up, Graham… here is what I want you to do. Launch the air support from the FEMA installation near San Diego. It shouldn't take long for one of the gun ships to reach Ensenada. Once it's there, have it follow her down to the corvette boat. But as soon as those torpedoes are safely on board, I want you to take them out, you understand? Terminate all of them! I want Tomato, Schofield, the agent and whoever else she is with taken out! I don't care if you have to open fire with a machine gun or a Gattling gun or whatever. Just terminate them. That's an order! Do I make myself clear, Colonel?" he screamed into the receiver.

"Yes sir, Mr. Vice President, I'll get it done, sir" Graham replied in a quivering tone of voice.

"Well see that you do and keep me updated. Do you understand, Colonel?"

"Yes sir, I understand" Graham said sheepishly as Lamply slammed the phone down in anger, the veins in his forehead bulging out like road maps.

"Fools" said Lamply, "they're all fools!" And as the limousine sped down Costero Blvd to the Marina, he turned to his aid and barked "Reno, prepare me another shot."

"You just had one a little while ago, Ernst. You don't need another. Besides, y'all look a little tired. I can't quite put my finger on it but you look a little different, if you don't mind my sayin' so, sir."

"Shut up Reno and just do as I say."

"Well okay, sir, another *vitamin* shot comin' right up."

And as Reno prepared the shot, a sinister and evil looking jet black Russian built MI-24 Hind A Attack Gunship helicopter with two 12.7 mm 4 barrel rotating machine guns and twin 30 mm canons and no markings or badges of any kind lifted off from the FEMA installation near Joshua Tree. And as it rose into the sky like a giant cobra preparing to strike, the turbulence from the blades cleared the dust from its landing pod and on that pod a name was inscribed on the concrete. It said: *The Devil's Chariot.*

~

The Pot of Tequila and the Devil's Chariot

"Excuse me, lady and gentlemen" said Bob in his typically polite British manner. "We are looking for the *Three Mighty Messengers*. Can you tell us if that might be you?"

Tom, Linda and Emmet all looked up from their task of stringing the lights up the mast to see a short, bearded and bald monk dressed in a robe and wearing grandfather spectacles followed by an entourage of three beautiful women and two handsome men. "Wow, when is the fashion shoot?' thought Linda.

"Three mighty messengers?" asked Tom. The three looked at each other quizzically. "Ah...not sure what you mean, sir. I can't say I've ever heard of *The Three Mighty Messengers*. Em, Linda, have you?"

Linda and Emmet shook their heads. "Nope, we've never heard of them."

"What's this all about, may I ask?" said Tom.

"Certainly, sir, allow me to introduce myself. I am Brother Bob of the Franciscan Order. These lovely ladies and handsome men are my associates. They are Lynne, Stephanie, Meredith, Christian and Dustin. May I show you this?" he asked as he produced the passenger manifest Ernie had printed on the hotel computer. "It has this slip number on it. We picked it up from the airport tarmac."

Unfolding the paper, he handed it to Tom who perused the document. After a few moments, a smile came over his face. "Looks like Ernie's up to his antics again. This is the passenger manifest that needs to go to the Harbor Master. He's named us *The Three Mighty Messengers,* do you believe that?"

"Three… why three…what am I…chopped liver?" asked Linda.

"Don't take it personally, Linda" said Emmet. "Ernie's not exactly known for his attention to detail."

"Sorry Linda" said Tom. I guess we are the *Three Mighty Messengers* plus one. But how can we help you, Brother Bob?" asked Tom.

"I shall be brief and to the point here. May I call you Tom?" asked Bob.

"Sure, that's no problem."

"Well then, Tom, let's just say we have come from Spain where we have learned that your lives may now be in great danger. It is quite a complicated story. May we come aboard?"

"Sure, come on aboard. And while we're chatting, Emmet, why don't you run this manifest up to the Harbor Master's office and get the engine key. I almost forgot it was left there."

"I'm on it…should only take a few minutes."

"Oh, and call Ernie and tell him *you* are going to pick it up."

"Alright, will do" Emmet replied as he jumped over the stanchions and landed on the dock. "I'll be bock!" he said, imitating Ahnold.

And as the crew came aboard the Swan, Tom noticed the computer case that Dustin carried over his shoulder. "What's the computer for? You're not from the IRS are you?"

"If they are, join the crowd because everyone else in the world seems to be after us" Linda commented.

"No, not the IRS" said Bob. "But Meredith, Lynne, Christian and Stephanie are with some other agencies you may have heard of."

"Do I want to know?" asked Tom.

"Yes, but only because it reflects the extreme danger you may be in. Meredith is with the CIA, Christian is with the Stockholm police, Lynne is with the FBI and Stephanie is with Interpol."

"Oh my gawd" gasped Tom. "What the hell did Ernie do now?"

"I think I better just sit down here" said Linda.

"Would it be possible to speak below deck?" asked Bob. "That way we can fill you in on the details in privacy."

"Sure, let's go below" said Tom.

"Thank you…Dusty, stand watch, here's the ankh" said Bob removing the encircled cross from his robe and handing it to Dustin.

"I'll put on a pot of Tequila" said Linda as they all went below. And as they all sat down on the sofas surrounding the dining table, Bob turned around and closed the hatch to the galley.

"Now, Tom and Linda" he said. "Allow me tell you a story. It's all about some very ancient books called the *Emerald Tablets of Troth*, some entities called *The Three*

Mighty Messengers and a demon who wants to destroy both them and the entire world."

~

"Okay, we're done here. I closed the ammo facility door and here are the heads with the uranium dioxide so now let's get out of Dodge. I'll just put these SHKVAL torpedo sections away in the crate here" said Diana reaching to lift the lid off the container.

"Um…wait a second, there's something I wanted to tell you first" said Ernie with his hand on the cover.

Diana batted his arm away and flipped open the top. Looking down her eyes suddenly opened wide and placing her hand on her hip she exclaimed: "What the hell are these, Ernie?"

"Just a couple of RPG's for the road, Ensign."

"*What* are you thinking, Ernie? We'll never get off the base with these, you know that!"

"They won't even look. They're too busy going on alert."

"Be sure and tell that to the bulls at Leavenworth! God, I don't believe you!"

"I'm willing to bet they wave us right through, Williams."

"Okay, I'll bet you my ten years in prison that you lose the bet. Now put them back!"

"Okay, but I think there's a little problem with that."

"Just do it now" urged Diana.

"I think you're forgetting something."

"What am I forgetting?"

"You locked the facility door. We need two keys to get back in, remember?"

"Oh shoot, that's right" said Diana batting her hand against her forehead. "Well, just leave them here and we'll tell the gate guards on our way out."

"Tell the guards what? That we removed the weapons and then deserted them in the face of an imminent terrorist attack? A good Marine never deserts his rifle."

"You're not a Marine."

"Okay then, a good Navy Torpedo-man's Mate never deserts his rifle."

"You're a disaster waiting to happen! You do know that, don't you?"

"Hey, I'm just looking out for everyone, that's all. If we want to get out of the Harbor safely, we're going to need some insurance, that's all."

"There you go with that *WE* thing again. I'll be leaving on a U.S Navy ship, sailor. You're on your own."

"What happened to our *nice life together*, Williams?"

"Forget it! That was a weak moment. I can't imagine what came over me."

"Is this our first lover's quarrel?" said Ernie sarcastically.

"I can't believe this is happening. Okay, Mr. SEAL, here's what we're going to do" sighed Diana. "We are going to drive to the gate and tell them that you mistook the RPG crate for the MK-44 one and that you removed it from the building but then forgot about it. After which we mistakenly locked the door before we could return them, *GOT IT*?"

"Ah, that's good thinking, Ensign. We'll do that. Unless of course they don't check the crate in which case we will proceed through the gate with the RPGs *as* they are. Have you *GOT THAT*?"

"Just drive, Ernie!" said Diana totally exasperated. "You are impossible!"

"Semper fi, baby!" said Ernie as he floored the Jeep with a roar and slammed it into first. "We'll be out of here before you can say *midshipman*."

"How you ever became a SEAL I'll never know."

And as Ernie steered the stolen Jeep down the dirt road leading back to the main gate, a call came through to Sergeant Suddington.

"This is Suddington... What? ...yes sir, one came through here about a half hour ago...What are the numbers? Wait...let me check the log... Yeah, go ahead... yes sir, that's the one... What? Oh my God... yes sir, we'll get on it right away sir. No, they won't get off this base. We'll go arrest them immediately sir!" he said as he slammed the phone down urgently.

"I don't believe this" the sergeant thought. "Luria, get in here!"

"What is it Sarge?"

"That Jeep that came through earlier, it was stolen."

"What? Well, that means....."

"They're not who they claim to be. Get in the A2 and ready the 50 cal. They may be part of the attack. We're going to go get them and bring them in. I'll pass the word and then let's go!"

And as Suddington passed the word down to the Marines on perimeter fence patrol, Luria fed the machine gun belt into the machine gun, pulled back the bolt and clicked off the safety.

"Haven't manned one of these since *Desert Storm*." he said to himself. "This should be good fun."

"Let's roll, Luria" yelled the sergeant as he fired up the Humvee and took his Glock off safety.

"*Oohrah*!" they both yelled as the Humvee took off like a rocket down the road where Ernie and Diana were fast approaching.

"There they are, Luria. Fire when ready. Warning shots first and if they don't stop… then take 'em out!"

"I'm locked and cocked" he screamed.

And as the two vehicles approached each other at full speed and closed within five hundred yards, Luria opened fire. The live rounds hit the dirt twenty feet short of the target and created a dust cloud just long enough to obscure the vision of the soldiers in the Humvee.

"Holy shit, Ernie, they're firing at us!" screamed Diana hysterically.

"I think we better change plans here" Ernie yelled back as his SEAL survival instincts kicked in and he swerved the Jeep off of the main road and headed it into the open desert, desperately searching for another exit.

"Shit…why are they shooting at us?" Ernie grumbled.

"Oh, I can think of a few things just off hand" Diana yelled back cynically.

"This shouldn't be happening, Diana! I think you've been set up. That's what I think."

And as the dust cloud cleared enough for the two Marines to get their bearings and turn their vehicle to pursue the Jeep, Corporal Luria once again pulled the bolt back on the 50 cal.

"Okay, this time I'm not gonna' be so nice" he whispered as the Humvee began to close distance on the Jeep.

"Damnit, Ernie, they're gaining on us!" screamed Diana. "Let's pull it over…at least we'll live that way!"

"No way, Diana, I'm not giving up yet!" he yelled back as he swerved the jeep around rocks and over the dunes as the Humvee followed in pursuit to within fifty yards of the fleeing commandos.

Ernie slipped the Jeep into 4WD to better lose the A2 but the superior horsepower of the Humvee soon brought the smaller vehicle within easy firing range and as Suddington closed in, he gave the order.

"One shot above their heads, if they don't stop…give 'em hell!"

"Yes sir" yelled Luria as he fired a burst above Diana's and Ernie's heads.

"Ernie, pull over or we're gonna' die!" pleaded Diana.

"There's a big dune up ahead. I can lose them on the other side!" screamed Ernie as he swerved in and out of the rocks and cactuses.

"Okay, cowboy…now your ass is mine!" said the corporal. And as he aimed the machine gun directly at the back of the fugitive's heads, the little Jeep reached the peak of the dune and flew over the front side, momentarily disappearing from the view of the pursuing marines.

"When we get over this dune, just take 'em out, Luria!" yelled Suddington from the driver's seat.

"Aye, aye sir" the corporal replied lowering his eye to the gun site so his volleys would be dead - on accurate.

But just before the Humvee reached the peak, the two marines heard the roar of a gigantic engine that sounded like a colossal tornado. And just before the Humvee hit the ridge, a huge, massive, foreboding black helicopter with whooshing blades fifty feet in diameter rose slowly from behind the dune like a monster black scorpion about to strike its prey!

"Holy shit!" screamed the two marines in unison. And as Suddington slammed on the brakes and fishtailed to a stop, he looked up at the massive terrifying death machine and realized he was practically close enough to look the pilot in the eye. And as he sat there in the vehicle frozen in fear, he could see that the pilot was dressed all in black and wore a black helmet which had an emblem. It was a fist grasping lightning bolts and over it read the letters FEMA. The pilot casually winked at him and then waved as if he were saying goodbye.

"Luria, jump!" Suddington yelled at the top of his lungs.

And as the two marines jumped from the vehicle and rolled down the dune to the safety of the bottom, the pilot engaged two S-25 350 mm rockets and fired.

The blast which sounded like an explosion from hell immediately obliterated the Humvee and sent metal, glass and engine debris into orbit which then rained back down on the two soldiers like a hail storm of metal acorns.

Hearing the blasts, Ernie and Diana turned around to see a huge conflagration behind the dune where the Humvee was last seen.

"Oh my gawd, what the hell is happening here?" screamed Diana.

"When we flew over the dune and saw that baby hovering I thought we were dead for sure" Ernie replied breathing hard.

"Oh oh… Ernie, look, it's turning around. Oh shit, shit…now we're dead!" moaned Diana as the *Devil's Chariot* swung around and began to drift menacingly toward the two like a monster black mosquito to a source of blood.

"Oh shit Ernie…drive, drive now!" screamed Diana. But the craft was on them in a New York minute and as the pilot engaged the 350 mm rockets once more, the two looked up and could see the pilot smile an evil smile as he pushed the fire button located on the stick.

"Good bye, Ernie" said Diana sobbing. But as they heard the whoosh of the rockets sounding their death knoll, Ernie noticed that the rockets were not on the same trajectory as before. And as the two froze in fear, the rockets flew over their heads and zeroed in on the chain link fence surrounding the perimeter five hundred yards dead ahead.

"Oh my God" cried Diana, ducking down and holding her head.

But the rockets weren't meant for them.

"Diana, they missed us!" yelled Ernie. And as she peeked over the dash, a huge explosion ensued. And when the dust had settled, they could see that a monumental crater the size of Alaska appeared where the fence had been, leaving an opening right onto Highway 3.

"Cool!" said Ernie. "I think that's our cue, Diana. Let's move out."

Flooring the Jeep and heading for the new exit, the *Devil's Chariot* hovered over them like a guardian angel until they reached the gaping hole where Ernie steered the vehicle around the crater and back onto Highway 3. Pulling onto the highway, Ernie and Diana looked back to wave thanks but the black chopper had already engaged its two jet thrusters and had disappeared back into the stratosphere like a bat on crack out of hell.

"So was that the air support you called in, Ensign?" asked Ernie.

"I guess it was. Damn, that was close, wasn't it?

"Yes, that was close but all in a SEAL's day's work."

"Oh give me a break, Rambo."

"So where to now?" asked Ernie chuckling.

"Let's get our butts over to the Navy Pier to unload these torpedoes onto the corvette boat. The sooner we can do that, the quicker we can get on our way and out of this burg."

"Sounds like a plan. But let me park the RPG's back on the Swan first. They'll be safe there and I have a feeling we're going to need them later" Ernie replied.

"Gladly, all I need is more trouble from you. Let's get rid of them ASAP."

"Good, now hold on" said Ernie, punching the accelerator. And as the two made their way down Highway

3 to the Marina, two other men, shadowed by a third, were walking down to the Harbor Master's office to locate a slip with a certain boat. It was one that was soon to be officially registered as the property of *The Three Mighty Messengers*.

~

The Escape

"Answer your damn phone, Ernie!" said Emmet, annoyed. "Why don't you ever answer your damn cell phone?"

"Hello" said Ernie after the ninth ring.

"Nesto, where are you? It's Emmet."

"Oh, hey Emmet" said Ernie. "S'up dawg?"

"Where the hell are you?"

"Diana and I just left a little party at the ammo dump. We're on our way down to the Swan. But I have to drop off the passenger manifest at the Harbor Master's office first."

"I'm already there. We have some guests on the Swan that picked up your manifest at the airport today."

"Really?" asked Ernie reaching into his pockets and finding only one of the manifest copies he had made that afternoon.

"I guess one of them fell out of my pockets. Anyway, I'll meet you there. We're just pulling into the parking lot."

"Okay, I'll wait here" replied Emmet.

But as Ernie and Diana pulled into the parking lot, Chief Warrant Officer D'Amato, who was straggling behind Jeremy and Schofield, had spotted the two and ducked behind one of the Eucalyptus trees which lined the parking stalls. And just as Ernie pulled the Navy

Jeep into one of them, he spotted them and stealthily maneuvered over behind one of the nearby vehicles to eavesdrop on the two.

"I'm going to run these RPG's down to the Swan and then meet Emmet at the Harbor Master's office. Why don't you stay here and guard the torpedo heads?" asked Ernie.

"There is no way, Jose! Are you kidding? I'm not waiting here alone. These torpedo heads are too valuable. Besides, they'll be looking for this Jeep."

"I guess you're right, Williams" Ernie replied. "We'll take a cab back to the corvette boat so you can dump these babies. By the way, what did you ever do with that black sphere I gave you?"

"It's in the hotel safe. I've got the room key right here so we can get it any time we want."

"Good" said Ernie. "Now grab an end."

And as Diana and Ernie grabbed the crate, D'Amato was thinking fast.

"Alright...I may have missed my chance once before but I'm not going to miss it this time" he thought. "The two torpedoes are right here and the key to get the black sphere is in her pocket" he said to himself as he reached into his pocket and removed his 45 caliber 'Saturday Night Special' and clicked off the safety. "Therefore, I'm gonna' waste these two mo' fo's!"

And as Diana and Ernie lifted the crate out of the backseat of the Jeep, he snuck up behind them, cocked the trigger and aimed it right at Ernie's head.

"Put the crate slowly back and then don't move!" he yelled as he held the weapon with both hands. "I've waited a long time for this."

"D'Amato, what the hell do you think you're doing?" asked Diana, turning around.

"Shut up, Brubaker. You think you're such a smart little bitch. Well, your time is up. Now I'll I be the only one collecting commissions on the torpedoes and with your room key, I'll finally get the black sphere back."

"Brubaker?" said Ernie. "There's that name again."

"Shut up" yelled D'Amato.

"I should have broken you in half at the parking lot at Turtle's, you little twerp" shouted Ernie.

"Shut up, I told you if I ever saw you again you'd be dead meat! Well now that's exactly what you're going to be! Say your prayers, you two" said D'Amato as he prepared to fire.

But suddenly, D'Amato heard the click of a trigger being cocked and felt the cold hard steel of a muzzle being thrust into the back of his neck. "I wouldn't do that if I were you. Now, slowly drop the gun and kick it over to the side. *DO IT NOW!*" the voice yelled.

Stunned, D'Amato eased back the trigger and dropped the gun, kicking it to the side where Diana picked it up.

"Thank God you were here, Peter" said Diana as D'Amato turned his head to see who had foiled his plan.

"Schofield, what the hell are you doing?" he screamed.

"Shut up, D'Amato! I'm not Schofield, the name is Peter Harrison."

"You two know each other? Ernie asked Diana, pointing to Peter.

"We work together" Diana answered.

"What do you mean you're Peter Harrison? We kidnapped him and turned him over to Hizbollah." shouted D'Amato.

"You're such a fool, D'Amato" Peter responded. "When you and Schofield kidnapped me and then took me hostage in Beirut, we already had the whole thing planned."

"Who's we and what are you talking about?" screamed D'Amato angrily.

"I'm going to tell you only because then you are going to jail for the rest of your life. Diana and I work for an independent arm of the United States government called *Intelligence Oversight.* Long story short, we suspect that the Vice President of the United States and others who support his agenda are involved in a plot to create a disaster within the borders of the United States in order to initiate and justify a war in the Middle East."

"You're crazy!" screamed D'Amato.

"Are we now?" asked Peter. "I am the witness that is going to bring down the CFAF and your little smuggling cabal. I've been with you every step of the way, you fool! From the art heist to the Pakistan to Beirut *connection* to Cadiz to Ensenada, I've witnessed every step of your sinister scheme."

"You'll never prove anything! I didn't steal anything. These two are the thieves." screamed D'Amato, pointing to Diana and Ernie.

"You only stole three paintings from the Stockholm Museum for starters!" Peter replied. "And now, once again I'm a witness to your treachery. Let's see, what other charges do we have here? How about attempted armed robbery of a nuclear device with the intention to illegally smuggle it onto a U.S. Naval vessel across an international border with intention to inflict massive damage on the people of the United States? What do you think, D'Amato? I'd say we can put a fork in you!"

"If you're not Schofield, then where is he?" D'Amato asked.

"Ah, my misguided twin Mr. Schofield is in our custody. You see, D'Amato, I am what is known in my profession as a triple agent. I knew of my brother long before you two knew of me. My background is not just art and art history. No, that's just a front. You see, I am also a trained agent in all aspects of intelligence and subterfuge."

"What?" D'Amato asked incredulously.

"Shut up and listen!" yelled Peter. "My father was a Commander in the Royal Navy but he also was an MI-6 agent. As I grew up, he trained and educated me in their ways. By the time I was sixteen, I could have been one of them. I had been studying to be my brother long before you knew of my existence. It is most useful in my profession to have two educations so one can slip out of one role and into another easily. When I visited Lebanon to purchase art, it was a ruse. We knew you would kidnap me and turn me over to Hizbollah. So we contacted them ahead of time."

"What do you mean?" asked D'Amato. "How could you have known?"

"When you saw me for the first time, you told Schofield. And he, being the great businessman that he is, immediately contacted Hizbollah to find out how much an American hostage was worth to them."

"I don't believe you."

"Believe what you will, D'Amato. But you see, there are also double agents in Hizbollah. So they contacted us and we made a deal. They arranged to have Palestinian prisoners released by the Israelis in exchange for me after they took me as a hostage. The Israelis couldn't wait to talk with someone who had been posing as an ISI agent."

"Damn it, I was sure you were Schofield! You've been him all along?"

"No, you imbecile, but I will explain it to you! After the Palestinians had been released, our man in Hizbollah contacted us to let us know you and Schofield had flown to London. When you arrived in London to purchase land along the Euphrates and open bank accounts fraudulently in Peter Harrison's name, we were waiting and watching"

"What do you mean?"

"One night when you were both having a drink in the bar, Schofield, my twin brother, went to the restroom. We were waiting. While he was relieving himself at the urinal, we surprised him and injected a little shot into his bum. He passed out and we carried him outside to a waiting ambulance. We switched clothes and I took his place. You never even knew the difference, you idiot! I've been

Schofield to you ever since. It was quite a performance, wouldn't you say?"

"Damn it!" exclaimed D'Amato.

"By last year, we already knew that the CFAF had picked his estate Tierra Bell as the final destination of the uranium dioxide, thanks to the undercover work of Miss Brubaker here. They, as well as you, assumed I was Schofield masquerading as Peter Harrison and you never suspected I was really Peter Harrison all along."

"Damn it!" screamed D'Amato. "I should have suspected when you made that comment about Harrison not necessarily being murdered by Hizbollah."

"Coulda', shoulda', woulda', D'Amato" answered Peter. "Your little lark is now over."

"As long as we're unmasking here at the ball, just who the hell are you, Diana?" asked Ernie petulantly.

"I'm sorry, Ernie but I had to use you. You helped me to set up D'Amato here, don't you see?"

"Will our mystery guest please sign in?" said Ernie. "So what faction of government are *you* working for? Or are you some sort of rogue agent for the Klingons?"

"I'm also a double agent, Ernie. I was hired by Intelligence Oversight to infiltrate the CFAF" Diana replied.

"And your name is really?"

"Twyla, its Twyla Brubaker."

"Oh no, say it's not so!" screamed Ernie holding his head.

Diana laughed. "You can relax, sailor, it's really Diana Williams."

"Thank God, but how did you ever infiltrate the CFAF or whatever it is?" asked Ernie.

"Allow me to introduce myself. I am known to the CFAF as Twyla Brubaker, Texas Christian graduate, member of the Young Republicans, the Young Americans, the Moral Majority, the Christian Coalition and graduate of the Pat Robertson School of Law." said Diana.

"You're kidding" said Ernie, wrinkling his nose like someone had just passed gas.

"I needed credentials first, Ernie. Believe me, it wasn't easy being an associate of all those *flag waving, Bible thumping, Young American* type fanatics."

"Aren't very fond of that type, are you?" asked Ernie.

"Getting into the minds of those people was truly a scary experience. But it worked. I eventually passed for one of them and soon I was hired in Washington and managed to gain the confidence of Lamply and his minions."

"And now we have enough evidence to bring them all down, thanks to you D'Amato" said Peter.

"You'll never get Lamply, he'll kill you all first" said D'Amato.

"Don't be so sure, D'Amato. We have a signed document recovered by an Interpol agent implicating him in obtaining and smuggling nuclear materials. He is not aware of that fact and it is going to bring him and his fascist cadre down."

"You'll have a hard time convincing the American people of all this. They're too naive to ever believe this could happen in their great democracy."

"We'll see about that. Now let's go."

"Go where, Harrison? Everyone in this town is looking for these two. You are not going anywhere" said D'Amato.

"Good point…Ernie can we take him down to the boat temporarily?"

"Absolutely, I'll personally rig the keel hauling lines."

And as Peter cuffed D'Amato and began to walk toward the Marina with Ernie and Diana, two other men were approaching them from the direction of the Harbor Master's office. It was Jeremy and Emmet.

"What's taking you so long?" asked Emmet.

"Oh, we're just apprehending someone here, Emmet" said Ernie.

"Uh huh, so I see. And who are *we*?"

"Emmet, this is Peter Harrison. I believe you've met Diana" said Ernie.

"Yes I have…hello again, Diana."

"Peter, what's going on?" asked Jeremy.

"Oh, and Jeremy, this is Ernie and Diana" said Peter. "And this is Chief Warrant Officer Anthony D'Amato. Once we're back in the states, he'll never see the light of day again."

"Hello Diana" said Jeremy. "I was hoping to see you again."

"Yes, hello Jeremy, I see you and Emmet have met."

"Yes, we met in the Harbor Master's Office."

"It was quite a coincidence, wasn't it?" said Emmet.

"Yes, it was. And then when you didn't show up after you said you were headed to the restroom, we thought we'd come find you."

"Well, you found us alright."

"Peter, just what is going on here? Why is that man in handcuffs?" asked Jeremy, shocked to see Peter holding a gun.

"No time to explain, Jeremy… I'll tell you all about it later, right now I have to figure out a way to get this guy back to the U.S. so we can prosecute him."

"You'll never get out of Mexico, Harrison. There are too many people looking for this group. The police, the Mexican Navy, the Mayor…they're all looking for these clowns. The airport will be covered as well as the roads and the border. You'll never get me back to the states! Even with a private plane, they'll be waiting for you" said D'Amato contemptibly.

"We're sailing back today. You could come with us" said Emmet.

Peter paused to think for a moment. "Hmm… thank you, we may just have to do that. Let's head down to the boat" said Peter, shoving D'Amato ahead of the group.

And as the group commenced the walk to the Swan, a motorcade of black stretch limousines turned into the parking lot and came to a stop fifty feet short of the walkway leading to Marina 1. And after a battalion of secret service agents swarmed out of the limos like hornets, Vice President Ernst Lamply glanced out of the heavily tinted window. And what he saw was CFAF agent Twyla Brubaker being escorted down the walkway by a man who held a pistol to an enlisted Navy man's back along with some others who carried a crate.

"Now what the hell is going on here, I wonder?" thought Lamply. Then it hit him.

"They must have gotten Brubaker. And that other guy must be that 'Tomato' guy. And that guy with the utilities that are too short, that must be the head of the terrorists! I've got to get hold of Graham now!" he said, extremely agitated. "Reno, get me Graham!" he screamed.

"Sure thing, Ernst, right away" Reno replied, punching in Graham's number.

"Graham here" said a voice a moment later.

"I've got him, Ernst" said Reno.

"Give me it" barked Lamply, grabbing the cell phone from Reno.

"Graham, do you hear me?"

"Yes sir, loud and clear!"

"Good. Now we have a situation here that requires immediate action, do you understand?"

"Yes sir, I understand."

"Are you in touch with the gunship?"

"Yes sir, he's in a holding pattern above Ensenada, sir."

"Good, now I want you to call in an air strike. And it has to be done right now, is that possible?"

"Absolutely sir, the FEMA gun ship can be there in five minutes."

"Graham, do not *EVER* let me hear you refer to it as that! Not *EVER*, do you understand?"

"Sorry, sir, I understand."

Good, now listen carefully. There is a group of terrorists walking toward Marina 1. They are a few minutes away. As soon as they reach their destination which is the slip off the dock, I want them taken out! That is, as in terminated with extreme prejudice, do you understand?"

"Yes sir, perfectly sir" replied Graham. "Consider it done!"

"But just one thing, Graham" said Lamply.

"Yes sir, what is that?"

"Tell the pilot to only use the machine guns… no rockets or incendiaries, got it?"

"Yes sir, I got it!" said Graham.

"I don't want anything happening to my little torpedo heads. I'll just take them back in Air Force 2 with me." Lamply snidely chuckled to himself as he hung up the cell phone and pitched it into Reno's lap.

"This is going to be a show worth watching, Reno. It'll be just like watching the fireworks on the fourth of July."

"Whatever you say, Ernst" said Reno as he pulled out his pocket comb and began to rake it through his hair while checking his reflection in the glass. "You sure are a handsome stud" he thought to himself. "But I wonder what is the hell is happening to Lamply's face? It's changing somehow."

Leaning back into his seat and grinning, Lampley's eyes momentarily glowed with a yellow hue and he snorted like an animal.

"What's that, Ernst?" asked Reno.

"What's what, you little snit?" asked Lamply as the yellow glow diminished and disappeared again.

"I just thought I heard you say something, sir"

"Just shut up and prepare another shot. I want to feel really good for the show that's about to commence. Let's go join Mr. Pero, shall we? And bring my binoculars."

"Ah sir, don't you think you've had enough for today?"

"Did I ask for your opinion, you little worm? Just do it and do it *NOW*!" he screamed.

"Okay, whatever you say, Ernst" replied Reno. And as Reno prepared another *vitamin* shot and grabbed the binoculars for the show, the black MI-24 Hind A attack gunship which was circling two miles above had received its orders. And as the orders appeared on the death chopper's OAsys screen, the pilot smiled and engaged the jet thrusters. "This going to be fun!" he smirked. "But I think I'll play with them a little first before I terminate them."

As the group began its walk to the Swan, the gunship began to descend on the Marina like a hawk on a field mouse. And when the group reached the ship, Bob had just finished telling Tom and Linda the story of the *Emerald Tablets of Troth* and *The Three Mighty Messengers*.

"Wow, that's quite a tale" said Tom. "Can I see the Tablets?"

"Certainly, Dustin, would you do the honors?" asked Bob.

"Here they are, Tom" said Dustin as he removed them from the computer case.

"Amazing, they look ancient. Almost like they'd turn to dust in your hands. But they're strong like sheet metal only really light weight. Check these out, Linda."

And as the two held them in their hands, the Tablets began to vibrate and glow once again.

"Whoa, what's going on here?" asked Linda.

"They are attuning to your thought patterns" said Bob.

"Troth is trying to communicate again" said Lynne. "Let's put them down here on the table so we can see."

And as Tom and Linda placed the tablets on the table, once again some phrases of the ancient language on the text took on a brilliant radiance and jumped out at the group like a neon sign flashing off and on.

"This is incredible" said Tom. Vibrating with ethereal energy, two phrases popped out of the text of the Tablets and flashed off and on in an intense red hue. They said *D'neta N'elger D'sentsa N'ailier, D'neta N'elger Dsentsa N'ailier* over and over again as if the words were trying to convey a sense of extreme urgency.

"What does it mean, Bob?" Meredith asked.

"I'm not sure. Lynne, what do you think?"

"I have a feeling it is desperately trying to tell us something. Let's wait another moment."

And as the group looked on in amazement, another set of letters popped out of the previous ones as Lynne had predicted. They read: **D'**net**a N'**el**ger D'sents**a N'**ail**ier

"*Danger, set sail* " said Lynne. "It's saying *Danger set sail* !"

And as the group looked at each other in amazement, a commotion could be heard outside the cabin on the dock.

"Ahoy, can we come on board?" yelled someone with a British accent.

"Sounds like your pal Peter" said Linda as Tom opened the hatch and climbed into the cockpit of the forty-four foot sloop.

"Wow, this is quite a soiree we're having today. What's the occasion here? Well, well, look who's here, if it isn't the Chief Warrant Munchkin himself." Tom said looking at D'Amato.

"Screw you!" said D'Amato back.

"So what's happening here?" asked Tom.

"Who wants to start?" asked Ernie.

"Tom, Mr. D'Amato here is under arrest for grand larceny with the intent to smuggle nuclear materials into the United States" said Peter.

"What, but you're an art curator. How can you arrest him?"

"It's a long story" Peter replied.

"And who are all these people?" asked Ernie as most of the crew from the galley piled on deck.

"It's a Dostoyevsky novel, I'm afraid." said Tom. "Come on aboard. Um, everybody introduce yourselves. I'm not very good with names."

"Bob, the letters from the Tablets, they're flashing really quickly and intensely." shouted Dustin from below!

"Tom, we need to get underway NOW! The Tablets do not lie." urged Bob.

"Here's the engine key, Tom" said Emmet.

"I guess we better shove off then. Ernie, get the bow line."

As Tom started the engine and threw it into reverse, Ernie cast off as Diana, Jeremy, Emmet, and Peter scrambled on board with the crate and D'Amato in tow to join Linda, Lynne, Meredith, Christian, Bob and Dustin. And as the Swan departed the slip and headed out of the Marina to join the boat parade, a malevolent black helicopter gunship began it's descent onto the marina area.

While the pilot punched the coordinates into his GPS, two old Vietnam Vets were sitting on the deck of their fishing boat two fingers down and nursing a couple of tall cool ones.

"Keller, why are you always polishing and cleaning that weapon?" asked Captain Jason Leyton as he took a sip of his seventh Corona of the evening. "You know damn well, you're never going to get a chance to use it."

"Leyton, when I took this weapon off that dead gook in the 'Nam, I had a feeling that I'd need this for something one day but I didn't know what! I still got that feeling." Keller replied as he poured himself another shot of Patron.

Leyton shook his head. "Kells, it's a frigging K50M sub machine gun. When in this Mexican Mayberry do you think you'll ever find a time to use it? One blast from that baby and you'd wipe out half the population here."

"I don't know, but after shipping it back to the states piece by piece, I'm not about to turn it over to the Mexican Federales. Besides, we may need this for protection someday" Keller replied while he assembled the fire rate selector lever and slipped it into place just in front

411

of the trigger mechanism. "There, done!" he said placing the French-style sliding wire butt stock to his shoulder and aiming it into the air.

"Protection?" said Leyton. "You don't even have rounds for that thing!"

"How would you know?" asked Keller.

"Where could you ever find rounds for it? You just like playing Rambo, admit it."

"I have the ammo."

"Get 'outta town, Keller. This is the five hundredth time I've seen you mess with that weapon and you never mentioned having ammo."

"You never asked."

"Well, I don't believe you. Where are you going to find rounds for that thing? It's damn near forty years old."

"Be right back" said Captain Keller as he tossed back the shot and climbed the ladder to the pilot's cabin. Before we were guests at the *Hanoi Hilton*, I not only sent the K50M home piece by piece but had something else smuggled back in a buddy's sea bag."

"That old dude is losing it. Now he thinks he's got ammo on this boat somewhere. Alzheimer's is setting in" Leyton thought to himself. Then he heard the clank of metal falling on the deck of the pilot's cabin before Keller reappeared and climbed back down the ladder.

"Here it is, check it out" said Keller as he tossed Leyton a pouch which obviously contained some sort of ammunition.

"Well, I'll be darned" said Leyton, unzipping the ammo pouch.

"I hid it in the bulkhead. There are one hundred rounds of 7.62 39mm NATO live rounds on a non-disintegrating metallic belt."

"I'm impressed, you crusty old dude. But how do we know they'll fire? I'll bet its dead ammo."

"You got yourself a bet, GI. Let's just take this old scow out to open water and do a little shark hunting with it. That'll prove you're wrong again, Leyton." said Keller as he climbed the ladder and reentered the pilot cabin and started the engine.

"You're on" yelled Leyton up to the pilot cabin. "You're on, baby!"

"Man, he is getting to be a crusty old salt" he thought as Keller backed the fishing boat out of the slip and pulled in right behind the Swan which was making its way out of the marina into the twilight with its eclectic crew.

And as the two boats entered the harbor together, the *Devil's Chariot* had gone into a dive as the smirking pilot calibrated his 12.7mm 4 barrel rotating machine guns and twin 30mm canons and adjusted his night vision sensors. But as it flew within visual of the marina and the slip, the pilot could see that the Swan had already cast off and was heading towards the carnival boat parade where other vessels were converging into a circle past the cruise ships dock beyond the Navy Pier.

"Damnit, they're not docked anymore. Now what?" the pilot screamed into his headset as he punched in the communications code to hail Graham in Washington.

After a few moments came the answer. "This is Graham."

"Colonel Graham, this is Blackbird 18. The chicken has flown the coup. I repeat the chicken has flown the coup. It is moving into the harbor…request permission to terminate in open water, over."

"Hold, Blackbird" Graham said, punching the hold button. "How in the hell did that happen? Now I've got to contact that bastard Lamply again! Damn!" he yelled one more time before clicking again on the intercom.

"Blackbird 18, proceed to target but hold fire. I repeat, proceed to target but hold fire, over." Now let's see if I can get hold of Mr. Personality himself" he said as he dialed Lamply's cell.

But when Graham dialed the cell number, it rang into the voice mail of the phone which had been left inside the Vice Presidential limousine. And as the phone rang futilely, Ernst Lamply and Doc Reno were being seated next to Presidente Vicente Pero in the VIP viewing stands on Playa Hermosa beach just off Todos Santos Bay to observe the boat parade and the Mexican Navy practicing maneuvers for the following day.

"Damn it" screamed Graham. "I can't reach the son of a bitch. Alright, let's think here" he said to himself. "The boat is in the harbor waters and he wanted the group terminated. Why can't we do it in the harbor waters? What's the difference? We'll just do a tactical air strike and get out of there fast. No one will even know what happened it will be so fast. Yes, what difference could it make?"

And as Graham hailed the chopper, the pilot had already done one low pass over the Swan and the fishing boat as they proceeded to the boat parade and open water.

As the *Devil's Chariot* initiated its first pass, Captains Keller and Leyton suddenly heard a very familiar sound reminiscent of their times spent in Southeast Asia.

"Sounds like a Huey gunship" Keller yelled down to Leyton from the pilot's cabin. Looking up as it passed over, Leyton yelled "What the hell is he doing? He shouldn't be flying this low! Keller, I think we may be under attack here!"

And on the Swan, the crew also heard the malicious whoosh of the super chopper's blades as its engines shrieked not far above the mast. Looking up, Ernie saw the same sinister black chopper with the same pilot with the same wicked smirk that he saw at the munitions facility. "I got a bad feeling about this" he thought.

As the pilot finished his first pass over the two vessels, Presidente Pero and the Vice President noticed this unusual event occurring back toward the sport fishing pier.

"What's happening over there, President Pero" asked Lamply, fully realizing it was the chopper he had ordered to render the Swan crew's deaths.

"I am not sure, Mr. Vice President. It must be part of the practice for the mock terrorist attack tomorrow."

"Damn" Lamply whispered. "That chopper was supposed to take care of business within the marina by the docks. Now they're headed into open water, damn it!"

Finishing its first pass over the vessels, the pilot of the Devil's Chariot received his orders on the OAsys screen. They said to PROCEED WITH ORDERS. TERMINATE IN HARBOR WATERS WITH EXTREME PREJUDICE. USE CANONS AND GUNS ONLY. END

"Alright, that's what I wanted to see. This is going to be fun! But I think I'll play with them a little first." Swinging the chopper around and heading back toward the Swan, the pilot clicked the red button on the joy stick. "We'll do the machine guns first and then the canons for the finish. This is going to be so sweet!"

Drifting around for another pass, Keller and Leyton's battle instincts kicked in as the chopper loomed. "Leytie, take the helm" Keller screamed. "If that bastard messes with us, I want him to know who he's dealing with." And as Leyton took the wheel, Keller jumped down to the deck and grabbed the K50M sub machine gun and fed the 100 round 39 mm metallic belt into the magazine chamber and pulled the bolt back. "You screw with us and you're gonna' die, Charlie!"

And on the Swan, Ernie had the same reservations about the situation. "I don't trust that guy at all! Where's that crate?" Seeing it was still on the starboard cockpit bench, he pried the cover off and grabbed one of the RPG-7s, then quickly descended the gangway and placed the other one on the aft cabin berth before returning to the cockpit.

And as both vessels armed themselves, the *Devil's Chariot* closed on them and opened fire, strafing the air above each vessel by only a few feet. Looking up, Ernie could see that the pilot was laughing as he began to swing the tail around again for another pass, this time a pass with *extreme prejudice.*

But as it swung around and began its deadly assault from the starboard sides of both vessels, Keller and Ernie had raised their weapons and were locked and cocked and ready for it this time.

"Go for the rear rotary blade, Kells" yelled Leyton as he turned the boat to the starboard so Keller could lay the weapon on the roof of the pilot's cabin and steady his aim. And as the fishing boat turned head on toward the approaching chopper, the pilot clicked the blue button on the joy stick and engaged the cannons.

"Everyone below, tie D'Amato up and duct tape his mouth! And take the crate!" screamed Ernie as he grabbed the impact grenade and loaded it into the front end of the launcher, lining it up with the trigger mechanism.

"Ernie, be careful" screamed Diana as the crew scrambled below and started to tie up D'Amato.

"We're staying topside" said Tom and Emmet. "We're not leaving you alone up here.

"Alright, Tom, take the helm while I load the pipe here! Emmet, stay low. Diana, take these binoculars. I don't want anything to happen to them."

Then as the *Devil's Chariot* approached the Swan with its tail in the air, ready to obliterate the vessel with its twin 30mm canons, Keller lined his sights up with the tail rotary blade and pulled the trigger.

Firing a burst from his sub, a very loud and repetitious "*ping, ping, ping*" was heard many times over as the bullets found their mark and shattered the blade into a thousand pieces. And as the pilot began to lose control of the black chopper, it began to swing wildly around in a circular motion.

At the same time, Ernie carefully lined up the iron sight of the grenade launcher with the cockpit where the smirking pilot fecklessly attempted to bring the chopper back under control.

"Eat this, mother fo'! This'll take that smirk off your face!'" he yelled as the grenade broke loose from the booster which propelled it toward its target at 294 meters per second.

And almost as if preordained, the malevolent aircraft and its smirking pilot swung around to a perfect position facing the Swan just as the grenade impacted the cockpit. Ernie looked up just in time to see the look of horror on the pilot's face.

KAHBLAMMMMMM KAHBOOOM!!!

The explosive noise thundered throughout the marina and the harbor as the helicopter first exploded into a million pieces and then became an immense conflagration when its gas tank ignited. Floating slowly down toward the water, it looked like an enormous dying ember returning to earth.

Ernie turned toward the fishing boat and waved. "Thanks, whoever you are."

Keller and Leyton each gave him a 'thumbs up' and a grin from ear to ear.

But in the grandstand, Lamply was agitated. "Pero, what the hell is going on over there? That's no practice terrorist attack."

"I don't know, Mr. Vice President. But I will find out. Commandante, call the Vice Admiral and find out what is going on. Then alert the commando team leader and tell him to get an HSB boat over to the Marina and find out what has happened and do it quickly."

"Si, Senor Presidente, I will take care of it immediately."

"Damnit, what went wrong?" Lamply whispered to himself. "Graham is going to hang for this."

"Sir, we must get you out of here" said a voice from over Lamply's shoulder. It was the head secret service agent and he spoke in a very authoritative voice. "Sir, this could be a terrorist attack. We must leave now and get you back to safety on Air Force 2."

"Damn!" said Lamply, gritting his teeth and frustrated. "How am I going to get those frigging torpedoes?"

"Sir, I must insist." pleaded the agent. "We must leave now, sir!"

"Oh alright" Lamply replied. "But first I want to take a look through the binoculars and then we have to pick up something at the hotel. Reno, give me those binoculars now."

"Relax, Ernst, here they are" said Reno handing him the binoculars.

And as Lamply took them and lifted them to his eyes, he focused them on the Swan and could see Bob, Dustin, Meredith, Lynne, Christian and Stephanie surge out of the galley and spill over onto the deck. Then suddenly something began to stir deep inside him. He could feel himself becoming enraged. And as his eyes took on an intense yellow glow, he started to tremble in anger.

"Ernst, what's wrong" asked Reno, tucking in his shirt for the third time that hour.

"Mr. Vice President, are you alright? Pero asked.

Lamply slowly lowered the binoculars and turned toward Reno and Pero. His eyes had become beacons of intense yellow light, like those of a wild animal. And as he held his fist up in an intense rage, he screamed in a deep guttural and deafeningly scratchy voice "I am *Wegreog* and I see the *Disciples of Troth*!"

And as Reno and Pero and the other surrounding VIPs in the grandstand began backing away in horror, Lamply lifted his outstretched arms and hands to the sky and let out an incredibly horrific, strident and ghastly shriek that emptied the bleachers faster than a Chinese fire drill.

As the shriek continued, massive bolts of pure electricity began to explode from his finger- tips up into the sky where the energy transmuted into immense black cumulonimbus cloud formations which began to move and swirl into a giant black thunderstorm from Hell. And as the storm gained in strength and severity, sending hail and lightening in all directions, one final mammoth electric blast burst forth from Lamply's outstretched arms and filled the sky with the violence of a hurricane as his body collapsed in an exhausted heap on the grandstand bench.

"I'll be danged!" said Reno. "What all did I put in that last injection?"

As the winds from the storm continued to build, the secret service agents grabbed Lamply and began to carry him away.

"Sir, we have to get you out of here now!" screamed the head secret service agent as the storm raged above. "We have to get you back to the plane."

"Holding his heart and trying to catch his breath he replied; "I must go back to the hotel. There is something there I must retrieve, do you understand me?"

As they carried Lamply off amidst the rage of the brewing storm, Bob stood on the bow of the Swan and had seen the spectacle unfold from the area of the bleachers. Looking up into the heavens, he knew that the time had come and that this was to be the battle he had been forewarned of in the Tablets.

"Dustin, bring the Tablets on deck with the ankh!" he yelled.

"Good God, this is incredible!" said Meredith, gazing skyward at the gathering storm.

"Vad har hant?" asked Christian. "God Jul, I have never seen anything like this."

"Lynne, what are you getting here?" asked Bob.

"I think this is the battle of light and darkness here, Bob! I feel we are all in great danger."

"Dustin, what did the Tablets say again?" Bob asked urgently.

"Here they are, Brother Bob" said Dustin, bringing the Tablets on deck. Opening them to the marked pages he said: "these are the passages you had indicated were the most pertinent!"

"Read them now, Dustin and give me the Ankh" Bob said as the lightening, wind and swells became increasingly powerful and intense.

"Okay, first is: *seek ye within the circle.*"

"Tom, steer us into the boat parade formation" shouted Bob.

"Okay, all ahead full. Scottie, where are those dilithium crystals? I need more power!"

"Just do it, Tom" said Linda. "You can skip the Captain Kirk imitation."

"Just trying to add a little levity here" said Tom.

"What else, Dustin?" asked Bob, trying to raise his voice above the uproar of the elements.

"It says to *beware the dwellers in angles.*"

"That must be the Mexican navy boats, don't you think, Ernie?" Diana asked.

"No doubt" Ernie replied. "If they're really SEAL boats, they're probably the thirty-eight foot double hull Kevlar open ocean high speed boats or HSBs that we used. Yep, they're angular looking for sure. We called them *the pointy bees on the high seas.*"

"What next, Dusty?"

"Next the passage says: *seek ye to find the path through the barriers, away from the light giver.*"

"What are the barriers, I wonder?" Stephanie asked as the boat began to surf the swells like a ball bearing on a roller coaster.

"Lynne, any ideas?" asked Bob. "What are the barriers and what is the light giver?"

Lynne held up her arm and turned her head to block the spray that was now beginning to drench the boat deck and the crew. "I'm not sure, it's not clear yet. No wait, it has something to do with navigation. Yes, that's it, navigation."

"Where are the binoculars? Will someone get me the binoculars?" said Tom.

"Here they are" said Diana, removing them from around her neck and handing them to Tom.

Tom took the binoculars and put the Swan on auto pilot while he raised the binoculars to his eyes. "The barriers, what are the barriers" he asked as he scanned the horizon between the raging swells. "I don't see any barriers...wait....of course, there they are."

"Where are what, Tom?" they all asked in unison.

"Of course, you're right, Lynne. It's the buoys, of course. Troth is showing us the way through the buoys by way of the boat parade. Here, take a look" said Tom as he handed the binoculars to Lynne.

Raising them to her eyes, Lynne could see that the buoys looked like large tin cans. Some had red flashing lights on their tops and others had green ones. But they all had something written on them which appeared legible when the lightening flashed. The writing said in large letters:

ALL CLEAR
Brushable WATER BARRIER

"They're marked *water barriers* alright" said Lynne. "But what is the light giver?"

"Seek ye the *path through the barriers*" said Stephanie. "But what path are they marking?

"Is the *Light Giver* Lamply again?" asked Meredith.

"I don't think so" Lynne replied. "It means something else in this case, but what?"

'Let me have the binoculars again" said Tom. "I can see some other markers out there."

Looking through the glasses, Tom could see between the waves crashing across the bow some more yellow markers interspersed with some others marked *danger* and *explosives*. Turning back toward Estero Beach he could see that the beam of light from the lighthouse located there was illuminating the yellow markers lining the entrance to the harbor.

"Ernie, get on the sat-phone and find out what the hell is going on here" screamed Tom.

"Oh, I forgot to tell you" said Emmet.

"What was that, Emmet?" Tom asked.

"I forgot to tell you! The harbor has been mined for some mock terrorist attack tomorrow. The harbor master told me to not leave the harbor but if we do, we have to navigate through the barriers to safely exit the harbor area. The yellow markers are a military only zone!"

"Emmet, hello?" screamed Tom. "What were you waiting for, the second coming of Christ? When were you going to let us in on this trivial little piece of information?"

"Well, I meant to but it's been one thing after another here so…."

Tom rolled his eyes. "Okay, at least we have our answer. *Seek ye to find the path through the barriers.* It's our only way out. We have to weave our way through the buoys".

"I'm hitting the running lights and the parade lights" Ernie yelled as the rain started to come down in sheets. We don't want any other boats ramming us in this storm. And we're almost at the parade formation."

"There they are, Tom" said Lynne pointing to the various vessels that had gathered in a circular pattern.

"Let's motor in between that *Hunter and the Catalina*" yelled Ernie above the howl of the winds. And just as the Swan slipped into the boat parade formation, two Mexican Navy SEAL HSBs flew over the swells and past the Swan headed for the marina location where Ernie had fired the RPG and downed the black chopper of death.

"That was close. We got into the formation just in time" said Diana. "At least they can't seem to tell which boat was involved in that little escapade back there yet. Good thing we strung the lights."

"Unfortunately, the SEAL boats are only one of our problems right now" said Bob, holding his arm up to avert the spray. "I believe our bigger problem is up there" he said, pointing to the raging storm above.

And as everyone's attention focused on the gathering storm, a huge bolt of lightning flashed across the foredeck, barely missing the mast as the winds increased to gale force.

"The parade's breaking up" screamed Ernie. "All the boats are headed in. We'll have to make a run for it."

"Are you friggin' nuts, Ernie? We'll never get out of the harbor in this storm!" yelled Tom.

"You want to go back and spend the rest of your days in a Mexican jail, dude?"

"You have a point there" said Tom.

"I agree" said Bob. "We will do battle with Wegreog here and now. It is the time. Lynne, what do you think?"

"I have this feeling that if we can get out of the harbor, we'll be safe."

"Then let's do it" yelled Tom. "We'll motor through the barriers. Ernie, Emmet, let's heave to. I'm turning the Swan through the wind. Back the jib and ease the mainsail. Make sure it's reefed in case we need it. I'll keep it as close to the wind as I can. And Bob, Dustin, make sure everyone has a life jacket."

"Aye, aye sir" replied the two.

And as everyone went to work, a monstrously loud thunderclap suddenly cracked the air and another bolt of lightning lit up the harbor area like a flash bulb, exploding with a boom as it hit the sea. Looking upwards at the tempest, Dustin saw the horrifying visage of a head of a goat with two fiendishly yellow eyes blazing from within the center of the storm like two fiery coals in a barbeque.

"Look" Dustin yelled, pointing to the apparition. And as all eyes on deck looked upwards, another deafening thunderclap sounded and another bolt of lightening burst out of the tempest and struck the top of the mast where it traveled downward in a nano second to the halyard and then arced over to the control panel next to the helm where it immediately exploded the gear lever, bursting the wiring into flames just as the craft had reached the first of the barriers.

"Peter, pass up the extinguisher" yelled Ernie. "It's mounted on the bulkhead!"

"Shit, that was close!" Tom screamed as he checked for injuries while Ernie put out the fire. "Now what, Ernie, we have no running lights and no motor!"

"Well, we're supposed to be sailors here. We'll just tack through the barriers" Ernie replied as another mammoth wave crashed over the foredeck, drenching the crew in the companionway and the cockpit."

"In this wind…are you crazy, Ernie?"

"You have another suggestion?" Ernie yelled back.

"I guess you're right" Tom grumbled as the winds howled. "Well alright then, let's bring in the traveler and reef the main some more. Everyone on deck, tie in!"

"Ease off on the main" Ernie yelled over the bedlam while balancing on the pulpit and adjusting the halyard.

Tom popped the spin lock and eased the main out. "Now, if I can just remember the story on these markers. Let's see, there are green light markers and red ones. We're still in the northern hemisphere so it's 'red right returning,' so with red off port and green off starboard side we should make it through the barriers."

Then as Ernie checked the halyard, Tom barked out some orders.

"Emmet, man the winch. Ernie, you tail. Everyone else below. Ernie, you ready?"

"I'm ready, Teddy" Ernie screamed as he returned to the cockpit and tied in.

"Okay then, ready about" Tom screamed as he turned the Swan into the wind. And just as the leeward rail kissed the salt water, another huge swell exploded across the bow, leaving the crew in the cockpit in two feet of water.

"Navigate the waves at an angle, Tom" yelled Ernie. "We don't want to pitch pole this baby."

"No shit, Ernie" answered Tom. "You want the helm here, Captain Hornblower?"

"You're doing great, Tom" Ernie replied as another thunderclap sounded and another bolt of lightning zipped by the main sail, exploding in the trough of the wave.

"Wegreog is playing with us" screamed Bob, raising his arm in front of his face to avert the stinging rain away from his eyes.

"Well, if we keep zig-zagging, maybe his aim won't be so great" Emmet screamed back as the boat pitched and yawed between the gargantuan swells that now were close to fifteen feet.

"Emmet, how many markers are there? Use the binoculars" yelled Tom above the pandemonium.

"It looks like there are only ten or so" Emmet replied, peering through the glasses.

"Piece of cake" yelled Ernie. "We can tack our way through them."

"Steady as she goes" said Tom, as he gripped the wheel like a vice, surfing the waves at an angle, trying to keep the hull speed at a minimum.

And as the Swan began to tack and jibe through the barriers, it was assaulted by a torrential bombardment of rain and hail with a barrage of lightning bolts, each of which missed the vessel only by inches. And as each lightning bolt lit up the sky, the terrifying and grotesque image of a malicious laughing goat could be seen amidst the turmoil of the storm.

"Keep it through the wind on the last tack, Tom" Ernie yelled above the howling squall as he adjusted the traveler and the main sheet for the last tack before the final barrier. And as the Swan tacked by the last barrier and headed toward the open sea, the evil entity looming above the yacht was becoming enraged that his electric projectiles were missing their mark as the boat bobbed and weaved and rolled between the buoys.

Tacking past the last of the barriers, the malevolent one had now become infuriated that the boat was still afloat and its crew still alive. So with a deafening roar, it gathered together all the strength of the elements at its command and began to swirl and spin into another form even more dreadful and chilling than before.

"Holy shit!" yelled Ernie, looking upward as the storm became more furious and powerful than ever.

"We may be in some deep doo-doo here, guys" added Tom as the storm suddenly dropped a leg into the sea and began to coalesce into a cylindrical wall of water swirling and spiraling upward around the eye of a monstrous raging funnel of watery death propelled by 175 knot winds.

"It's a frickin' waterspout" screamed Tom "Everyone below and hang on!" he yelled as everyone except Ernie and Emmet scrambled down the companionway in the hopes that the cabin would provide some sort of shelter from the uberstorm.

"What do we do, Ernie?" screamed Tom, gripping the wheel like a vice.

"Hang friggin' on, that's what" Ernie yelled back as the swells increased to twenty-five feet and the rain began to feel like rubber bullets stinging their faces.

Then Tom's analytical mind kicked in. "Okay, think here. We're in the northern hemisphere, so its spinning in a clockwise direction. So we'll want to approach this baby on a starboard tack beating close to the wind."

"Check your harness, you two" Tom yelled. "We're going in!"

"Ohhhhh shit!" screamed Ernie.

"Oh my gawd, oh my gawd!" exclaimed Emmet.

And as the bow of the Swan hit the wall of the waterspout, the wind shifted from a gale force wind over the bow to a hurricane-force blast of green water dead abeam.

"Ease the main" screamed Tom as a few tons of seawater burst over the rail. Practically horizontal in the wind, Ernie made his way to the spin lock and eased out the main as the Swan headed into the eye of the maelstrom.

"Steer for the eye on a beam reach when we hit the wall" screamed Ernie. "Watch the helm when we hit the eye!"

"What the hell does that mean?" thought Tom as the screaming wind and crashing water continued to escalate in intensity.

Then it happened. As the Swan entered the eye of the spout, the winds suddenly diminished and the boat rocked back over to windward from the sudden loss of pressure on the sail. And as it rocked over, almost capsizing, the force of the shift put the mast almost horizontal to the waves, throwing the passengers to the starboard side of the cabin where the cover of the crate carrying the torpedoes pitched to the bulkhead, causing the torpedoes to also become air born and crash through the windows like bombs on a green house, where they proceeded to sink into the deep, briny still waters of the eye of the spout.

"MMMMMMMMMFFFFFF" screamed D'Amato, obviously protesting this turn of events from behind his duct taped mouth.

"Well, I guess there goes the nuclear option for the CFAF" said Peter.

"Believe me, they'll think of something else" said Diana.

And as the Swan righted itself again, it's passengers in the main cabin scraped themselves off the deck of the galley and the fore cabin.

"Is everyone alright?" asked Peter as the group checked themselves for injuries.

"I think we're okay" said Christian, helping Meredith, Stephanie, Lynne and Jeremy to their feet.

"I should have stayed at Tierra Bella" moaned Jeremy, lifting himself up on the galley sink.

"Wegreog wants to kill us all" said Bob, brushing the broken glass from the broken starboard window off his robe. "We will need to bring the Tablets on deck if we ever get out of this storm. We must send him back again. Dustin, make ready the tablets."

"They're ready, Bob" Dustin replied.

Then, like a bay leaf in a fish bowl, the Swan found itself floating on a sea of glass as an eerie calm and an ominous silence pervaded the air in the eye of the storm.

Suddenly Ernie yelled down through the companionway.

"Hold on tight, we're gonna' hit the wall on the other side!"

And as everyone grabbed something to hang onto, the far wall of the spout slammed into the port side of the Swan with the force of a small nuclear detonation. Tom, Ernie and Emmet may as well have been standing under a horizontal waterfall as the spray, wind and mist intensified and they all wished they had diving masks to see through the onslaught of water.

Battered heavily but still intact after sailing through the screaming wind, the crashing water and the flying debris, the Swan continued its sail away from the spout on a broad reach, popping out the far side and then finally clearing the edge of the storm. Realizing that they had escaped the tempest unharmed, the crew let out a loud cheer as the huge swell and heavy seas began to subside once again. But just as the crew thought they were free of any further danger, a high pitched shriek permeated the air and a foul and vile odor began to waft its way into everyone's nostrils.

"Oh my God, what is that awful smell?" asked Jeremy as the waterspout dwindled and faded upwards into the scattering black cumulus clouds of the subsiding tempest.

"Oh no, it's the same smell as on the plane" screamed Stephanie.

"Dustin, bring the Tablets on deck. We must act quickly." said Bob. "Meredith and Lynne, we will need your presence also."

As the group started their way up the companionway, Ernie, Tom and Emmet were in awe that the Swan had made it through the storm.

"I can't believe it" said Emmet. "Now it's clearing up. I guess that goat head finally gave up."

"Don't be so sure, Emmet" replied Bob as he took the Tablets and lay them on the cockpit bench. "Meredith, Lynne, join hands around the Tablets like you did before. Now, everyone be silent and on the alert."

"Alert for what, Bob?" Linda asked.

"I hope nothing" Bob replied as he scanned the ocean, as if he anticipated that something was about to happen.

And as Meredith and Lynne did as he directed, Bob removed the ankh from his robe and held it tightly at his side like a six gun ready to be drawn. And as the clouds dispersed and the swells slowly subsided, there was another eerie silence and a creepy sort of stillness that accompanied the malodorous air surrounding the vessel.

"See, there's nothing" said Emmet.

"Shhhh" said Bob. "He's here, alright."

"Who's here, that goat guy?" asked Ernie. "He's gone, look at the sky."

And just as Ernie said *sky*, a huge, green and scaly hand with claw-like fingernails burst out of the seas aft of the transom and grabbed the ladder which was secured behind the helm. In one swift and rapid movement, a prodigious eight foot monster with the head of a goat and a repulsive reptile-like body with dripping, slimy green scales leaped onto the transom. It had a tail like a T-Rex which moved like a snake and as it pulled itself up, it hissed and spit like an aggressive hooded cobra.

Boarding the transom, it grasped the rear stanchions behind the helm and with an ear piercing shriek, ripped them right out of their gunwales like toothpicks and pitched them off to the starboard side.

"Oh, shit" Ernie whispered to himself. 'Maybe I spoke a little too soon."

As the Hellish entity climbed aboard, a snake's tongue darted in and out of the drooling aperture which resembled a mouth. Lifting its head, the crew could see that its yellow eyes blazed pure evil. And as the crew backed up toward the bow, the creature breathed fiery hot air and then spoke in a vile and guttural monotone which was not of this world.

"I am *Wegreog* and now you all shall join me in *Hell*!"

"Wheeeuuw!" said Tom, holding his nose. "That guy could use some mouthwash."

"I'm not sure this is the time for jokes, Tom" said Linda, backing up onto the foredeck as the creature began to move forward.

Reaching the foredeck, Bob raised the ankh and screamed "*Chequetet, Arelich, Volmalites…Chequetet, Arelich, Volmalites, Chequetet…*"

But before he could finish the incantation the creature had leapt forward with lightning speed, and with the back of his scaly claw, knocked the ankh out of Bob's grasp where it fell to the deck. Picking up Bob by the neck, he held him aloft, choking the monk with its odious grip. Then he spoke.

"Your words were not fast enough, Disciples of Troth. The passing of centuries and your many lives have made you slow and forgetful of the speed of my wrath. But now, one by one, you shall all join me in *Hell*!"

As he opened his disgusting and repulsive drooling jaws of death to rip the monk apart piece by piece, suddenly another body shot out of the companionway toward the aft of the Swan and dove overboard.

"It's D'Amato" yelled Peter. "He must have gotten loose."

Hearing the commotion, the creature dropped Bob onto the deck and turned to see a splash and a person swimming away from the boat as fast as he could.

"None of you shall escape me this time" it shrieked. "I shall have my revenge on each of you, one by one!" it raged.

And as the group looked on incredulously, the creature's body started to transform again and grow very long and thin and then manifested into some sort of coiled sea serpent. Slithering off the deck into the water, the serpent glided through the water in pursuit and quickly overtook the swimmer.

Reaching D'Amato within moments, the crew of eleven watched in horror as the reptilian creature quickly coiled its body around the Chief Warrant Officer. And as D'Amato screamed in sheer terror, the creature opened its jaws of piercing razor-like teeth and engulfed the swimmer like a meat loaf sandwich, dragging him below the water, never to be seen again.

"Quickly Dustin" said Bob, still shaking from his close call with death. "Let's grab the Tablets and take them to the bow." And as the two retrieved the Tablets, the creature had turned and was already swimming its way back to the Swan.

"Gather around" said Bob. "If we all speak the *word*, perhaps our combined powers as Disciples can send him back from where he came."

As they all gathered around the Tablets, Bob spoke quickly.

"Now, everyone focus. We have to send it back."

"How do we do that, Bob" asked Christian.

"Just think the *word*" Bob answered impatiently.

And as they all gathered around the Tablets, Bob commanded Lynne and Meredith to once again speak the *word*."

And they did.

Nothing happened.

"Try it again" said Bob.

Still nothing happened.

Sweating bullets now, Bob thought for a moment.

"Dustin, we are missing something. What are we missing here?" he asked urgently as the creature came closer and closer back to the Swan.

Dustin grabbed the Tablets and quickly turned the pages of the twelfth volume.

"Here it is, Bob" Dustin said excitedly. "We forgot this part" he said, handing the Tablet to Bob.

"Of course, it says to use the *Key of the Nine*. It says *the Fair Lady holds the Key*."

Ernie and Diana instantly turned toward each other.

"Diana, that's you" yelled Ernie. "You still have the key?"

"It's right here" said Diana, removing the key on the chain around her neck and handing it to Bob.

"I hope this is it" said Bob. "Now, everyone concentrate. Lynne, Meredith, on the count of three, speak the *word* and I'll hold the key above the Tablets. Ready?"

"Ready Bob" the two answered.

"Okay then, one… two…three."

And as Meredith and Lynne spoke the *word* and Bob held the Key above the Tablets, the boat shuddered. Turning around, the group could see that the creature had once again boarded the transom and taken its original form. With the blood of D'Amato still dripping from its nauseatingly repellent mouth, it eased its way forward, its claws held high and its eyes now glaring red hot. And with its tongue darting in and out and its scaly tail undulating like a malicious Komodo dragon, the creature from Hell spoke.

"Now, *which* of you wants to be next?" it hissed.

"How about a beer, buddy?" said Ernie suddenly. "We can talk about this, you know."

"Silence, you fool!" it screamed as it moved forward toward the Tablets over which Bob still held the Key.

"Come on Troth, what are you waiting for?" whispered Bob.

Then suddenly, as the group stood on the foredeck by the Tablets, a burst of brilliant light suddenly exploded from the key and like a bolt of lightning, joined with the Tablets which then exploded like a super nova in a burst of ethereal light that momentarily blinded the crew.

And when the intense blast of light dispersed and their eyes could see once again, a prodigiously blissful and divine presence could be seen floating in the air off to the starboard side of the Swan. Its light was so overwhelming that it could not be looked at directly and it pulsated with an awesome energy that was pure, powerful and benevolent.

"Oh my goodness, oh my goodness!" said Lynne as Bob crossed himself and fell to his knees. The rest of the crew could not speak or move.

The creature from Hell had stopped dead in its tracks as the heavenly being hovered and drifted from the starboard side of the Swan to a spot over the boat by the mast. And as the light being moved, the creature grimaced and held its scaly claws up to shield itself from the penetrating light that emanated from its presence.

Then as the crew recovered from their shock, they all noticed that they seemed to exist in a different world, a different dimension perhaps. It was as if they were all in a still life painting. The waves on the ocean that were previously turbulent ceased to move and the wind became non- existent and the clouds had become stationary. In an instant all time had ceased.

And yet, they all could see a divine energy everywhere. They could see that the temporal nature of all things was little more than a thin overlaying gasket on the permanent omniscient energy comprising the foundation of the eternal. Then the crew heard the angelic presence speak. It spoke not through symbols or words, but through the pure essence of its intentions.

Pulsating with bright ethereal light, it imparted: "that is enough, Wegreog. As you have waited for centuries to return and reap revenge on the world and my disciples, I also have been waiting for you! As the *word* enabled you to return, the *word* shall also see you return to your dark and evil domain. You have done much damage in your short time in this realm, but your lies and arrogance will now see retribution. It is time for you to return. This *Key* has made it so."

Holding its scaly claw up to shield the light, the creature rebutted "you cannot make me go back! The *word* is not enough anymore. The souls of mankind are lost in a sea of blood, greed and war. Now I rule this realm, Troth. It is you who must return" it screeched in a high pitched whine. "If you wish to make me return, you shall have to force me!"

"Let it be done then!" said the heavenly entity. And in the blink of an eye, the incandescent light coalesced and took the striking and imposing form of an ancient Egyptian warrior in battle dress. It was neither man nor woman, but rather a combination of both. Its face exuded breathtaking feminine beauty but it was tall and sinewy and its shining golden hair was pulled back in a braided pony tail which extended halfway down its backside. On its head sat a brightly colored flaming head dress and its muscular upper body was covered with a shimmering gold breast plate. Around its neck was draped a jeweled and inlayed gold and silver brocaded apron.

The crew was speechless.

At its side a long curved sword with an emerald and ruby inlaid ivory handle was sheathed and in its strapping right hand it held a spear of gold ten feet long. The piercing light from its deep blue eyes shined like two stars in the heavens. And as its whole being radiated with pure light and energy, it raised the spear skyward and a burst of energy like a nuclear blast shot up into the ether and ripped a hole in the static painting-like panorama of the surreal sky like a hot knife through butter.

Cringing in horror at the opening of the portal, the creature suddenly transformed itself, this time into a horrifying giant winged griffin with the head of a gargoyle. And in an instant, it soared up into the still frozen sky, emitting a petrifying prehistoric screech as it called back the storm clouds of the tempest from Hell.

"Is this really happening?" said Lynne.

"I'm afraid so" said Bob.

As the storm gathered around the evil beast, the warrior had once again become a bonfire of pure pulsating ethereal light and then fragmented into a hundred smaller balls of light which shot up into the air like ping pong balls from a Super Soaker.

Chasing the griffin and its turbulent elements up into the firmament, the spheres of light circled the tumult like sheep dogs, herding the winged beast and its storm back through the portal which had been slashed open by the explosive light from the warrior's golden spear.

But the malevolent creature had its own ideas. Whipping up the previous violent elements of the storm once again, it began to bombard the portal with electric charges, causing the inter-dimensional gash in the stationary heavens to split into two parts like a dividing amoeba. And as the two entities divided, the crew could see two opposing universes develop within the voids of the apertures.

One was black as night with wisps of black feathery darkness enveloping the outer edges while the other held light which displayed an opulence of luminosity gushing out through a tunnel like the head light beam from a locomotive.

As the crew looked upward, astonished that this all was occurring, the griffin, like a shifty tailback, faked an entry into the black hole and then turned on a dime, dodging between the light spheres. Temporarily outmaneuvering the spheres, it zigged and zagged its way to another space in the heavens where it emitted a deafening roar which thundered from the skies.

"EEEEEEEEEVOOOOOOOOORRRRRR!" came the roar as the crew looked up, covering their ears.

And before everyone's eyes, a third hole in the ether momentarily opened up like a crack in a vase, into which the griffin quickly slipped and then disappeared.

The spheres, realizing they had been outmaneuvered, turned also and before the crack could close completely, followed the creature through the same crack and also disappeared, at which time the two other openings disintegrated into nothingness before their eyes.

As if waking from a dream, the crew looked at each other and then all around. The physical world had been restored. The wind was blowing again and the frigid swells were once again breaking over the foredeck. Some stars could be seen as the clouds dispersed. And although a great sense of relief and gratitude that they all were still alive settled over the group, they were also still speechless from what they had witnessed.

Finally Meredith spoke. "Someone pinch me. I can't believe what just happened."

"Did everyone else see what I just saw?" asked Lynne.

"I think we all saw the same thing" said Diana. "But does anyone believe it?"

"None of my concerts have ever had special effects like that" added Jeremy.

"Maybe I'm not so damned important after all" said Emmet.

"And so much for my 'no good and no evil' theories…. those are out the window. And you Tom… that was one ballsy ride and you didn't crack…good job…very courageous!!" said Ernie.

"What was that all about, Brother Bob?" Linda asked.

"I'm not sure" Bob replied. "It would appear Troth and Wegreog have entered a different dimension to continue their battle. Let us hope that Troth will be triumphant."

"Skitbra" said Christian. "I hope to never see another case like this ever again."

"You won't" said Stephanie. "We could write a book but no one would ever believe it."

"Even a paranormal psychiatrist would have a hard time buying what just happened" added Lynne.

"Tom, I think we better get the hell out of here while the getting is good. We still have to make it to American waters." said Ernie as the swells continued to crash over the rails.

"You're right, let's get moving" said Tom. "Ernie, tighten down the jib and bring in the traveler. We should be able to get six knots now. Everyone below, this storm isn't quite over yet. And someone make some tea! I'm freezing my butt off."

"I can't believe we're finally headed home" said Emmet.

"I can't believe we actually escaped from Ensenada" added Linda.

"Well, I don't know about you guys, but I've gotta pee" said Ernie as he slid down the companionway and entered the head.

"Let's take the Tablets below, Dustin" said Bob.

But then, just as Bob, Dustin, Lynne, Meredith, Christian, Stephanie, Diana, Linda, Jeremy and Peter all started to go below, the engine of a fast moving water craft could be heard in the distance beyond the swells.

"Oh shit" yelled Tom. "Just when I thought we might be in the clear!"

And as he said that, a staccato "brrrrrrrrrrrttttttttttttttt" could be heard and everyone hit the deck as a barrage of

7.62 mm mini machine gun bullets zinged over the bow of the Swan.

"*Parada gringos... parada ahora...estamos opportando!*" yelled a voice through a bull horn off to the starboard side.

"Damn it!" thought Tom. "It's one of the HSBs! Just when I thought we were in the clear! Now we're dead. How in the hell did I get into this to begin with? This is the last time I ever listen to Ernie."

Crashing through a behemoth wave, he could see off to the starboard side, one of the Mexican HSB gunboats was on course to either board the Swan or ram her. He had only moments to think of something before he and the crew were to become inmates in a Mexican prison or residents of Davy Jones' Locker.

And when the Mexican HSB flew over the crest of a wave and came around broadside to the Swan's starboard side, the Mexican sailors readied their grappling hooks and began to swing them in the air to hook the swan and bring her within boarding distance.

But just then, as Tom had given up all hope of an escape, below deck an RPG-7 warhead was stealthily poked out of the very same starboard window that the torpedoes had crashed through a short time earlier. And before the Mexicans on the HSB knew what had happened, a grenade had been fired out of its launcher and had blown a hole in the port side of the gunboat before lodging itself in the engine compartment where it exploded with a KABOOM, leaving the HSB on fire and floating aimlessly adrift with no power to navigate the turbulent swells.

"Holy shit!" yelled Tom.

"Duck!" yelled Emmet as debris from the explosion rained down on the deck.

And as the crew was again rendered speechless by this auspicious turn of events, Tom and Emmet suddenly saw a face with a shit eating grin pop up through the foredeck hatch like a jack-in-the box and yell "Don't *ever* mess with a U.S. Navy SEAL, Pancho!"

A loud and rowdy cheer could be heard from the galley below.

Floating helplessly between the swells, the Mexicans scampered to put out the fire on board the wounded vessel. And by the time, they had tended to the fire and plugged the hole in the free port, the HSB had drifted far out of range of the Swan. And as Tom tacked to windward, staying close to the wind doing six knots through the rolling swells, the HSB soon was no longer in sight.

"Well, it looks like our resident maniac has saved the day here" said Tom as Ernie and Diana climbed up the companionway hand in hand to the cockpit followed by the rest of the crew who were cheerful and ebullient, slapping Ernie on the back and congratulating him on his heroics.

"We need to celebrate" yelled Emmet. "I'll get some champagne from below."

"Better hold off" said Tom. "Those South of the border swabees have probably already radioed in that we attacked them. There could be more of them after us soon. And we're only making six knots here! We need more speed to make American waters before they overtake us!"

Just then, another engine could be heard racing through the heavy swells.

"Damn" yelled Ernie. "I'm out of ammo."

"Oh no" screamed Tom. "We were so close to escaping!"

"There must be something we can do!" cried Linda.

"Are there any suggestions?" Tom asked the disconcerted group. "Please, someone say they can do something here."

But the previously ecstatic group was suddenly befuddled, despondent and gloomy. And as the engine of the vessel grew louder and louder, closing on the Swan's position, they all seemed to become resigned to their fate.

"Well, I guess we all had one hell of an adventure anyway." said Tom.

"Maybe we'll all be in the same prison so we can have dinner together occasionally" said Stephanie.

"I'd hate prison" said Ernie. "It's so hard to get a tan through the bars."

"This isn't funny, Ernie" said Diana.

And as the engine grew louder and the vessel closer, sealing the fates of the crew, Dustin noticed something different as the vessel burst over a swell and came into view.

"Look" screamed Dustin. "It's not a gunboat, it's something else!"

The group could not believe their eyes. Pounding through the waves they could see a fishing boat. And on the bridge Captain Keller and Captain Leyton were waving frantically to them and signaling them to use the radio by holding a pretend receiver to their ears.

"Emmet, take over here. I'm going below."

Jumping down the companionway, Tom turned on the radio and turned to channel 16. "This is the Swan, can you hear me, over" and turning the squelch button, he received an answer.

"We read you, Swan. This is Keller. We're going to throw you a line and tow your ass to American waters. You'll never make it if we don't, over."

"Captain Keller, you don't know how good it is to see you. Thank you, over!"

"No problem mate, we're comrades in arms now! We have to look out for each other, out."

Returning to the cockpit, Tom could see that Captain Leyton had already tossed Ernie a line. After jury rigging a tow hitch between the bow cleats, Ernie gave the thumbs up sign and the fishing boat slowly began pulling the sail boat north through the subsiding swells at fifteen knots.

And as the full moon began to break through the storm clouds and the blustery winds gradually settled into a gentle breeze, Emmet had cracked open four bottles of Moet & Chandon Dom Perignon and began pouring all around as the crew gathered together on deck.

"Well, cheers" said Emmet, raising his glass to Meredith, Lynne, Christian, Stephanie, Linda, Ernie, Diana, Bob, Dustin and Tom. *"Let's toast to the escape from Ensenada!"*

All raised their glasses and said "to the *escape from Ensenada*!"

"But Peter…there is something you should know first" said Lynne.

"Yes… what is it?"

"The Rembrandt and the Renoir are forgeries."

"WHAT?" Peter screamed.

"They're forgeries, Peter."

"Perhaps someone can explain this to me please."

"Of course, Peter…you see…" Meredith started.

"But wait…first, Peter" said Jeremy interrupting, "there is something else you should know first before that."

"Yes, what is it, Jeremy?"

"It's about the *Black Piper.*"

"What about it?"

"We don't have it anymore?"

"*What… when* did this happen? Where is it?"

"It's in the Vice President's room at the Hotel Coral Marina. I hid it there."

"Oh my God!" said Peter, "Oh my *God!*"

~

EPILOGUE

"Reno, get me another cup of coffee" screamed Ernst Lamply as he lit the fireplace and settled into an easy chair before his early morning meeting with the President regarding his trip to Mexico.

"Sure thing Ernst, whatever you say" Reno replied as he tucked in his shirt and checked out his reflection in the Queen Anne mirror which hung in the Vice President's quarters at the White House.

"And bring me the morning paper" you sniveling worm.

"Yes sir, Mr. Vice President, right away, consider it done. By the way, sir, the President called and said there was a development from your trip that he needed to discuss with you. He said it was quite urgent and he didn't sound very happy."

"Screw the President" Lamply replied. "He can just fricking wait. I call the shots here in this administration. He can just go clear some more brush for all I care. Now bring me the paper, Reno."

"Yes sir, Ernst" Reno replied. And after exiting the room for a few minutes, he returned with a cup of black coffee and the morning Washington Post.

"Here you are, sir" said Reno, handing the coffee and the paper over.

"Good" said Lamply. "Now get the hell out of here. I need some time alone here."

"Whatever you say, Ernst" said Reno as he turned and exited the room.

Putting the coffee on the Sheraton Regency side table, Lamply started to open the paper to the front page.

"Let's see what kind of tree hugging, bleeding heart, liberal crap this paper is espousing today" he chuckled as he unfolded the paper to the front page.

"Holy shit!" he said to himself in utter disbelief. "What the hell is this?"

There on the front page was the headline and it read:

**U.S. Gunship and Mexican Naval Vessel
Attacked by Rogue U.S. Pirate Ship!
Presidente Pero Claims Attack
is a Declaration of War!**

"This must be a fricking joke! We're at war with Mexico? This is too damn funny" he said to himself. And as he laughed out loud, obviously greatly amused by this development, he hit the call button on the phone.

"Yes Ernst" answered Reno.

Chuckling still, he said: "Reno, prepare my morning shot and make it snappy. I want to be alert for my meeting with the President."

"Yes sir, Mr. Vice President, right away, sir" Reno replied.

"Oh, this is too good" he thought to himself. But as his head moved downward on the page he saw another headline which drew his interest. It was small and in the lower right corner and it said:

Bizarre Thunderstorms Rage Over Middle East.
Strange Creatures and Spheres of Light Seen.
Could they be UFOs?

"Good, I hope it continues. It will take the public's eye off of my oil plans for that part of the world." he said as he put his cup of coffee down on the side table and reached for a black sphere which he now kept near him at all times.

And as he picked it up and stroked it adoringly, it seemed to come to life and vibrated with an intense gripping energy.

"Yes" he said to himself. "I'm not sure what this is but I have a feeling that it is going to be most helpful with my plans."

There was a knock at the door.

"Come in" screamed Lamply.

It was Reno.

"Here it is, Ernst" said Reno as he filled the syringe with the potent preparation and inserted it into Lamply's vein.

"Ah, that's better" said Lamply as the concoction began to flow through his body to his brain. "That's much better. Now get the hell out of here."

"Yes sir, Mr. Vice President, whatever you say, sir" said Reno.

But as Reno exited the room and closed the door behind him, he knew that there was something that just wasn't quite right. He couldn't put his finger on it but the Vice President was changing. Something was happening to his face.

"I'm not quite sure what's happening there but his face….it's becoming long and thin and his eyes…they're sinking into his head. And his nose seems to be growing. It's almost as if he's beginning to look like…well, he's almost beginning to look like….nah… it couldn't be."

And after stopping to comb his hair in the Hepplewhite mirror in the hallway, he continued his walk back to the White House Infirmary in the East wing.

"Still" he thought, "still…"

To Be Continued…..